VALLEY 10/31/2013
506900109
W9-BWE-567
Adler-Olsen, Jussi.
A conspiracy of faith /

VALLEY COMMUNITY LIBRARY
739 RIVER STREET
PECKVILLE, PA 18452
(570) 489-1765
www.lclshome.org

A CONSPIRACY OF FAITH

ALSO BY JUSSI ADLER-OLSEN

The Keeper of Lost Causes

The Absent One

A CONSPIRACY OF FAITH

A Department Q Novel

Jussi Adler-Olsen

Translated by Martin Aitken

Valley Community Library
739 River Street
Peckville, PA 18452-2313

DUTTON
Published by the Penguin Group
Penguin Group (USA) Inc., 375 Hudson Street,
New York, New York 10014, USA

USA / Canada / UK / Ireland / Australia / New Zealand / India / South Africa / China
Penguin Books Ltd, Registered Offices: 80 Strand, London WC2R 0RL, England
For more information about the Penguin Group visit penguin.com.

Copyright © 2013 by Jussi Adler-Olsen

Translation copyright © 2013 by Martin Aitken

All rights reserved. No part of this book may be reproduced, scanned, or distributed in any printed or electronic form without permission. Please do not participate in or encourage piracy of copyrighted materials in violation of the author's rights. Purchase only authorized editions.

REGISTERED TRADEMARK—MARCA REGISTRADA
LIBRARY OF CONGRESS CATALOGING-IN-PUBLICATION DATA
has been applied for.

ISBN 978-0-525-95400-2
Printed in the United States of America
10 9 8 7 6 5 4 3 2 1

Set in Apollo MT Std
Designed by Alissa Amell

PUBLISHER'S NOTE
This book is a work of fiction. Names, characters, places, and incidents either are the product of the author's imagination or are used fictitiously, and any resemblance to actual persons, living or dead, business establishments, events, or locales is entirely coincidental.

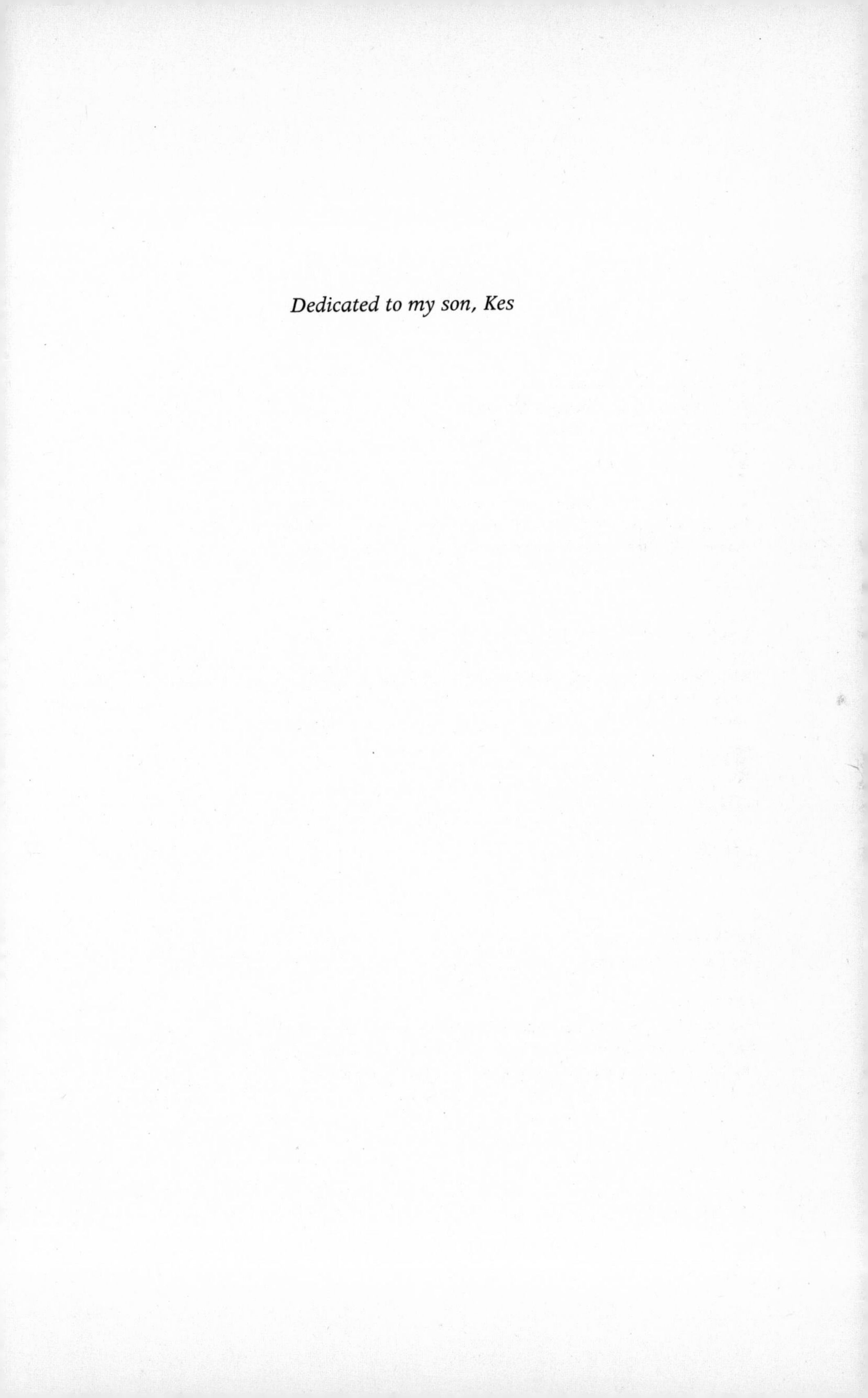

Dedicated to my son, Kes

PROLOGUE

It was the third morning, and the smell of tar and seaweed had got into his clothes. Under the boathouse floor, the mush of ice lapped soundlessly against the wooden stilts and awakened memories of days when everything had been all right.

He lifted his upper body from the bedding of wastepaper and pulled himself sufficiently upright to make out his younger brother's face, which even in sleep seemed tormented, chilled to the bone.

Soon, he would wake and glance around in panic. He would feel the leather straps tight on his wrists and waist and hear the jangle of the chain that constrained him. He would see the snowstorm and the light as it struggled to penetrate the tarred timber planks. And then he would start to pray.

Countless times he'd seen desperation in his brother's eyes. Through the gaffer tape that covered his mouth came the repeated sound of his muffled pleas that Jehovah have mercy upon them.

Yet both of them knew that Jehovah no longer paid heed, for blood had passed their lips. Blood that their jailer had let drip into their cups. The cups from which he had allowed them to drink before revealing to them what they had contained. They had drunk water, but in the water was blood, so forbidden, and now they were damned forever. And for that reason, shame pierced deeper even than thirst.

What do you think he'll do to us? his brother's frightened eyes seemed to ask. But how could he ever know the answer? All he knew, instinctively, was that it would all soon be over.

He leaned back and scanned the room once again in the dim light, allowing his gaze to pass across the collar beams and through the formations of cobwebs, noting each and every projection, each and every knot. The worn paddles and oars that hung from the apex of the ceiling. The rotten fishing nets that had long since made their last catch.

And then he discovered the bottle. A gleam of sunlight played momentarily on the blue-white glass to dazzle him.

So near, and yet so hard to reach. It was just behind him, wedged between the thick, rough-hewn planks of the floor.

He stuck his fingers through the gap and tried to prize the bottle upward by the neck, but the air froze upon his skin. When the thing came loose, he would smash it and use the shards to cut through the strap that kept his hands tied tight together behind his back. And when it succumbed, his numb fingers would find the buckle at his spine. He would loosen it, tear the tape from his mouth, remove the straps from around his waist and thighs, and as soon as the chain that was fastened to the leather strap at his waist no longer held him back, he would lunge forward and free his brother. He would draw him toward him and hold him tight until their bodies ceased to tremble.

Then, he imagined, he would use all his strength to gouge into the timber around the door with the broken glass. He would see if he could hollow out the planks to which the hinges were fixed. And if the worst should happen and the car came before he was finished, he would lie in wait for the man. He would stand poised behind the door with the broken glass in his hand. That was what he told himself he would do.

He leaned forward, folded his freezing fingers behind his back and prayed for forgiveness for his wicked thought.

Then he scraped again in the space between the planks to try to free the bottle. He scraped and scratched until the neck angled enough for him to grab hold of it.

He listened.

Was that an engine? Yes, it was. The powerful engine of a large car. But was it approaching or simply passing by in the distance out there?

For a moment, the low, deep sound seemed to get louder. He began to pull so desperately at the neck of the bottle that his knuckles cracked audibly. But then the sound died away. Had it been the wind turbines, rumbling and whirring? Maybe it was something else entirely. He had no idea.

He expelled warm breath from his nostrils. It steamed the air around his face. He wasn't so afraid anymore, not now. As long as he thought about the grace of Jehovah, he felt better.

He pressed his lips together and labored on. And when finally the bottle came free, he struck it so hard against the timber of the floor that his brother lifted his head with a startled jolt and looked around in terror.

Again and again he brought the bottle down against the floor. It was hard to get purchase with his hands behind his back. Too hard. Eventually, when his fingers were no longer able to maintain their grip, he let the bottle slide from his hand, turned himself around, and stared emptily at it as dust gently descended from the beams through the cramped space.

He couldn't break it. He simply wasn't able. A pathetic little bottle. Was it because they had drunk blood? Had Jehovah abandoned them?

He looked at his brother, who rolled himself slowly into his blanket and fell back onto his bedding. He was silent, not even attempting to mumble a word through the tape that sealed his lips.

It took a while to gather the things he needed. The hardest part was stretching himself, confined by his chain, to reach the tar between the roofing planks with the tips of his fingers. Everything else was at hand: the bottle, the sharp sliver of wood from the timbered floor, the paper on which he was sitting.

He pushed off one of his shoes and stabbed so sharply at his wrist with the wood that tears welled in his eyes. He let the blood drip onto his polished shoe for a minute, perhaps two. Then he tore a large shred of paper from his bedding, dipped the splinter in his blood, and twisted his body, pulling at his chain until he was able to see what he was writing behind his back. As best he could, and in the smallest handwriting, he put down in words what was happening to them. When he had finished, he signed the letter with his name, rolled up the paper, and stuffed it inside the bottle.

He allowed himself plenty of time to press the lump of tar down into the neck. He shifted his weight so as to see better, and checked and double-checked to make sure it was well done.

When finally there was no more to do, he heard the dull sound of a car engine. This time there was no mistake. He cast a pained glance at his little brother and stretched with all his might toward the light that seeped in through a broad crack in the timbered wall, the only opening through which the bottle would be able to pass.

Then the door was opened and a thick shadow entered amid a flurry of white snow.

Silence.

And then the plop.

The bottle was released.

1

Carl had woken up to better prospects.

The first thing he registered was the fountain of acid bubbling in his esophagus. Then, after opening his eyes to see if there was anything that might assuage his discomfort, the sight of a woman's wrecked and slightly drooling face on the pillow next to him.

Oh, shit, that's Sysser, he realized in horror, and tried to recall what mistakes he might have made the previous evening that could have led him to this. Sysser of all people. His chain-smoking neighbor. The chattering odd-job woman soon to be pensioned off from Allerød Town Hall.

A dreadful thought struck him. Gingerly, he lifted the duvet only to discover with a sigh of relief that he still had his boxer shorts on. That was something, at least.

"Christ," he groaned, removing Sysser's sinewy hand from his chest. He hadn't had a head on him like this since he'd been with Vigga.

"Please, spare me the details," he said, encountering Morten and Jesper in the kitchen. "Just tell me what the lady upstairs is doing on my pillow."

"She's heavier than she looks, the old bag," his stepson offered, raising a freshly opened carton of juice to his lips. The day Jesper would discover how to pour the stuff into a glass was something not even Nostradamus would hazard a guess at.

"Yeah, sorry, Carl," said Morten. "She couldn't find her key, you see, and you'd already crashed, so I reckoned . . ."

Definitely the last time anyone catches me at one of Morten's barbecues, Carl promised himself, and cast a glance into the front room where Hardy's bed was.

Since his former colleague had been moved in a fortnight ago, all semblance of domestic familiarity had gone down the drain. Not because the elevation bed occupied a quarter of the floor space and blocked the view of the garden. Not because IV bags dangling from stands or filled urine bags made Carl queasy in any way. And not even because Hardy's utterly paralyzed body emitted an unceasing flow of foul-smelling gases. What changed everything was the guilty conscience all this gave rise to. Because Carl himself possessed full control of his limbs and could chug around on them whenever it suited him. And moreover, he felt he had to compensate for it all the time. To be there for Hardy. To do good for this helpless man.

"No need to have a cow about it," Hardy had said a couple of months back, preempting Carl as they discussed the pros and cons of moving him away from the Clinic for Spinal Cord Injuries at Hornbæk. "A week can go by here without me seeing you. I reckon I can do without your tender loving care a few hours at a time if I move in with you, don't you?"

The thing was, though, that Hardy could be peacefully asleep, like now, and yet still be so present. In Carl's mind. In the planning of his day. In all the words that had to be weighed before being uttered. It was tiring, a bind. And a home wasn't meant to fatigue.

Then there was the practical side of things. Laundry, changing the sheets, manhandling Hardy's enormous frame, shopping, liasing with nurses and authorities, cooking. So what if Morten did take care of all that? What about the rest of it?

"Sleep well, old mate?" he ventured as he approached the bed.

His former colleague opened his eyes and forced a smile. "That's it then, eh, Carl? Leave of absence over and back to the treadmill. A fortnight gone in a flash. Didn't half go quick. Morten and I will do all right. Just say hello to the crew for me, eh?"

Carl nodded. Who would want to be Hardy? If only he could change places with someone for a day.

Apart from the usual lot at the duty desk, Carl didn't meet a soul on his way in. Police Headquarters felt like it had been wiped out, the colonnade winter gray and discouraging.

"What the hell's going on?" he called out as he entered the basement corridor.

He'd been expecting a raucous welcome, or at least the stench of Assad's peppermint goo or Rose's whistled versions of the great classics, but the place was dead. Had they abandoned ship during the fortnight's leave he'd taken to get Hardy moved in?

He stepped into Assad's cubbyhole and glanced around in bewilderment. No photos of aging aunts, no prayer mat, no boxes of sickly sweet cakes. Even the fluorescent tubes on the ceiling were switched off.

He crossed the corridor and turned on the light in his own office. The familiar surroundings in which he had solved three cases and given up on two. The place the smoking ban had yet to reach, and where all the old files that made up Department Q's domain had lain safe and sound on his desk in three neatly ordered piles, according to Carl's own infallible system.

He stopped dead at the sight of a wholly unrecognizable, gleaming desk. Not a speck of dust. Not a scrap of paper. Not a single closely written sheet of A4 on which he might rest his weary feet and thereafter dispatch into the wastepaper basket. No files. Everything was gone.

"ROSE!" he yelled at the top of his voice.

And his voice echoed through the corridors in vain.

He was little boy lost. Last man standing. A rooster with nowhere to roost. The king who would give his kingdom for a horse.

He reached for the phone and pressed the number for Lis on the third floor, Homicide Division.

Twenty-five seconds passed before anyone answered.

"Department A, secretary speaking," the voice said. It was Ms. Sørensen, the most indisputably hostile of all Carl's colleagues. Ilse the She-Wolf in person.

"Ms. Sørensen," he ventured, gentle as a purring cat. "This is Carl Mørck. I'm sitting here all forlorn in the basement. What's going on? Would you happen to know where Assad and Rose are?"

Less than a millisecond passed before she hung up. The cow.

He stood up and headed for Rose's domain a little farther down the corridor. Maybe the mystery of the missing files would be solved there. It was a perfectly reasonable thought, destroyed when he discovered to his horror that on the corridor wall between Assad's and Rose's offices someone had fixed at least ten pieces of chipboard and plastered them with the contents of the missing files.

A folding ladder of shiny yellow larch indicated where the last of the cases had been put up. It was one they'd had to shelve. Their second unsolved case in a row.

Carl took a step back to get the full picture of this paper pandemonium. What on earth were all his files doing on the wall? Had Rose and Assad become completely unhinged all of a sudden? Maybe that was why they'd vanished, bloody imbeciles.

They hadn't the guts to stick around.

Upstairs on the third floor it was the same story. The place was deserted. Even Ms. Sørensen's chair behind the counter yawned empty. He checked the offices of the homicide chief as well as his deputy. He wandered into the lunchroom, then the briefing room. It was like the place had been evacuated.

What the fuck was going on? Had there been a bomb scare? Or had the police reform finally got to the point where the staff had been kicked out into the street so all the buildings could be sold off? Had the new, so-called justice minister had a fit? When would the news channel be turning up?

He scratched the back of his neck, then picked up a phone and called the duty desk.

"Carl Mørck here. Where the hell is everyone?"

"Most of them are gathered in the Remembrance Yard."

The Remembrance Yard? What the hell for? September the nineteenth was six months away yet.

"In remembrance of what? As far as I'm aware, the anniversary of the internment of Danish police officers by the German occupying forces isn't even remotely around the corner. What are they doing?"

"The commissioner wanted to speak to a couple of departments about adjustments following the reform. Sorry about that, Carl. We thought you knew."

"But I just spoke to Ms. Sørensen."

"Most likely she's had all calls sent on to her mobile. I'm sure that'll be the explanation."

Carl shook his head. They were stark raving mad. All of them. By the time he reached the Remembrance Yard, the Justice Ministry would probably have changed everything around again.

He stared through the door at the chief's soft, enticing armchair. That was one place, at least, where a man could close his eyes without an audience.

Ten minutes later, he woke up with the deputy chief's paw on his shoulder and Assad's cheerful, round eyes peering point-blank into his face.

Peace over.

"Come on, Assad," he said, extracting himself from the chair. "You and I are going downstairs to pull all those sheets of paper off the wall sharpish, you understand? And where's Rose?"

Assad shook his head. "We cannot, Carl."

Carl stood up and tucked his shirt into his trousers. What the hell was the man on about? Of course they could. Wasn't he supposed to be the boss around here?

"Just come on, will you? And get hold of Rose. NOW!"

"The basement's closed off," homicide deputy Lars Bjørn butted in. "Asbestos sifting down from the pipe lagging. Health and Safety have been around and there's nothing we can do about it."

Assad nodded. "I'm afraid this is true, Carl. We had to bring all our stuff up here. There is not much room, but we did find a nice chair for you," he added, as though it could ever be a comfort. "We are only us two at the moment. Rose did not fancy it, so she is off on a long weekend. She'll be back later on today, though."

They might just as well have kicked him in the gonads.

2

She had sat staring into the candles until they burned out and darkness wrapped itself around her. It wasn't the first time he'd left her on her own, but he'd never done it on their anniversary before.

She inhaled deeply and got to her feet. Lately, she'd given up standing by the window to wait for him, had stopped writing his name with her finger on the pane as it steamed up from her breath.

It wasn't as if there had been no warning signs the time they first met. Her best friend had had her doubts, and her mother had told her straight out. He was too old for her. There was something shifty about him. A man you couldn't trust. A man you couldn't fathom.

So now she hadn't seen her friend or her mother for a very long time. And for that reason her desperation increased while her need for human contact was greater than ever. Who could she talk to? There was no one there.

She gazed into the empty, orderly rooms and pressed her lips together as the tears welled up in her eyes.

Then she heard the child stir and pulled herself together. Wiped the tip of her nose with her index finger and took two deep breaths.

If her husband was being unfaithful, then he would do well not to count on her.

There had to be more to life than this.

He came into the bedroom so silently only his shadow on the wall gave him away. Broad shoulders, arms wide open. He lay down and drew her in to him without a word. Warm and naked.

She had expected sweetness, but also well-considered apologies. Maybe she'd been afraid of the slight scent of some strange woman and guilt-ridden hesitation in all the wrong places, but instead he grabbed hold of her, turned her roughly onto her back, and began greedily to tear off her nightclothes. The moonlight was in his face. It turned her on. Now the waiting, the frustration, the worry, and the doubt were all gone.

It was six months since he'd last been like this.

Thank God, at last.

"I have to go away for a while, sweetheart," he said without warning over the breakfast table, stroking the child on the cheek. Distracted, as though his words didn't mean anything.

She frowned and pursed her lips to keep the inevitable question inside for a moment. Then she put her fork down on the plate and sat with her gaze fixed on the scrambled eggs and bacon. The night had been long. It was still with her, an ache around her pelvis, but also the kisses and cuddles when they had lain there spent, gazing warmly into each other's eyes. Until now, it had allowed her to forget all thought of time and place. Until now. For at this moment, the pale March sun forced its way into the room like an unwelcome guest to illuminate the facts. Her husband was going away. Again.

"Why can't you tell me what you do? I'm your wife. I won't tell anyone," she said.

He sat with his cutlery half-raised. His eyes grew dark then.

"Seriously," she went on. "How long am I supposed to wait this time for you to be like you were last night again? Are we back to where we were before? Me not knowing what you're up to, and you hardly being present, even when you're here?"

He looked at her with piercing eyes. "Haven't you known from the start that I can't talk about my work?"

"Yes, but . . ."

"Well, then. Let's leave it at that."

His knife and fork clattered against the plate, and he turned toward their son with something supposed to resemble a smile.

Her breathing was steady and calm, but despair surged inside her. It was true enough. Long before their wedding, he had explained to her that he was unable to speak about what he did. He might have hinted it was something to do with intelligence, she couldn't really remember anymore. But as far as she knew, people in the intelligence services still lived reasonably normal lives alongside their jobs. Their own life together was in no way normal. Unless intelligence work also involved being unfaithful, because as far as she could see, that was the only possible explanation for his behavior.

She gathered the plates and thought about giving him an ultimatum there and then. Risking the anger she feared but had yet to experience to its full extent.

"When will I see you again?" she asked.

He looked at her and smiled. "I'll be home next Wednesday, I imagine. This type of job usually takes a week, ten days at most."

"You'll be home just in time for your bowling tournament then," she said sarcastically.

He stood up and put his arms around her, drawing her in toward the bulk of his body, clasping his hands under her chest. The feeling of his head on her shoulder had always sent a tingle down her spine. But now she pulled away.

"True," he said. "I should be back in good time for that. So before you know it, it'll be last night all over again. OK?"

After he had gone and the sound of the car engine had died away, she stood for a long time with her arms folded and her gaze out of focus. It was one thing to be lonely in life. But it was quite another not to know what you were paying that price for. The chances of ever catching a man like hers cheating on her were minimal, she knew that, even though she had never tried. His territory was a vast expanse, and he was a careful man; everything in their life indicated that. Pensions, insurance, double-checking of windows and doors, suitcases and luggage, desk always tidy, no hastily jotted notes or receipts left behind in pockets or drawers. He was a man who left no trace. Not even the scent of him remained more than a few minutes after he had left the room. How would she ever uncover an affair unless she put a private investigator on him? And where was she supposed to get the means to do that?

She thrust out her lower lip and expelled warm breath slowly into her face. Like she always did prior to an important decision. On the riding ground before clearing the highest obstacle. Before choosing her confirmation dress. Even before saying her vows in the church. And before going outside to see if life might be any different there in that gentle light.

3

David Bell, a convivial hulk of a police sergeant, liked to take things easy, to sit and stare out at the waves as they smashed against the rocks. All the way up at John O'Groats, Scotland's very extremity, where the sun shone only half as long but twice as stunningly. This was David's birthplace, and it was where he intended to die when his time was up.

David Bell was made for the rugged sea. Why should he idle away his time sixteen miles farther south in the office of Bankhead Road Police Station in Wick, when this slumbering harbor meant so much to him? It was a fact he made no bones about.

It was also the reason why his boss always dispatched him to sort things out whenever there was trouble brewing in the communities up north. David would trundle up in his patrol car and threaten the local hotheads that he'd call in an officer from Inverness. It was generally enough to settle things down again. In these parts, no one wanted strangers from the city nosing about in their back gardens any more than they wanted horse piss in their Skull Splitter ale. It was more than enough having folk come through for the Orkney ferry.

Once things quieted down, only the waves remained, and if there was one thing Sergeant Bell had plenty of time for it was the waves.

Had it not been for Bell's characteristic sedateness, the man who found the bottle might have hurled it back whence it came. But since the sergeant happened to be sitting there in his neatly pressed uniform with the wind in his hair and his cap on the rock beside him, handing it to him seemed the obvious thing to do.

The bottle had been caught in a trawl and had glinted slightly, though time and the sea had dulled its sheen, and the youngest man on board the *Brew Dog* had seen right away there was something special about it.

"Chuck it over the side, Seamus," the skipper had shouted when he discovered the message inside. "Those things are bad luck. Wreckage in a bottle, we call them. The Devil's in the ink and waiting to be let loose. Don't you know the stories?" But young Seamus didn't, and he decided to take it ashore.

When Bell finally got back to the station in Wick, one of the local drunks had trashed two of the offices and the duty staff were rather weary of trying to keep the idiot pinned to the floor. That was how David Bell came to remove his jacket, whereupon Seamus's bottle fell out of its pocket. And it was how he came to pick the bottle up and put it down again on the windowsill so he could concentrate his attention on planting his full weight on the chest of this drunken oaf in order to squeeze some of the air out of him. But anyone treating a full-blooded Viking descendant in such a fashion is liable to get more than he bargained for. And so it was that the drunk delivered such a blow to David Bell's testicles that any recollection of the bottle was engulfed by the blaring sirens and flashing blue lights his nervous system frantically emitted as a consequence.

And so the bottle remained undisturbed in the sunny corner of the windowsill for a very long time indeed. No one paid it any heed, and no one worried that the paper it contained might be damaged by the sunlight and the condensation that with time appeared on the inside of the glass.

No one bothered to try to read the collection of semi-obliterated letters that appeared uppermost, and for that same reason no one gave a thought to what the word "HJÆLP" might mean.

The bottle did not come into human hands again until a young man who felt himself unreasonably treated on account of a measly parking fine swamped the intranet of Wick Police Station with a veritable tidal wave of viruses. In such a situation, the routine was to get in touch with a computer expert called Miranda McCulloch. When pedophiles encrypted their filth, when hackers covered up all traces of their online banking transactions, and when asset-strippers wiped their hard disks, it was Miranda McCulloch they kneeled before.

She was given an office. The staff were moved to tears and treated her like royalty, filling up her thermos with scalding coffee, throwing open the windows, and making sure the radio was tuned in to Radio Scotland. Miranda McCulloch was indeed a woman appreciated wherever she went.

Because of the open windows and the billowing curtains, she noticed the bottle on her first day.

What a fine little bottle, she thought to herself, and wondered at the shadow inside it as she dredged through cipher columns of malicious code. When on the third day she got to her feet feeling well satisfied, her job complete, and with a reasonable idea of what kind of virus might be anticipated next time around, she stepped across to the windowsill and picked the bottle up. It was a lot heavier than she had thought. And warm to the touch.

"What's that inside it?" she asked the secretary next door. "Is it a letter?"

"I've no idea," came the answer. "David Bell came in with it a long time ago. I think maybe it was just for fun."

Miranda held the bottle against the light. Was that writing on the paper? It was hard to tell because of the condensation on the inside.

She turned it in her hands. "Where is this David Bell? Is he on duty?"

The secretary shook her head. "No, I'm afraid he's not. David was killed not far out of town a couple of years back. They'd given chase to a hit-and-run driver and it all went wrong. It was a terrible thing. David was such a nice chap."

Miranda nodded. She wasn't really listening. She was certain now that there was writing on the paper, but that wasn't what had caught her attention. It was what was at the bottom of the bottle.

On close inspection through the sand-blown glass, the coagulated mass looked remarkably like blood.

"Do you think I could take this bottle with me? Is there anyone here I should ask?"

"Try Emerson. He drove with David for a couple of years. I'm sure it'll be all right." The secretary turned toward the corridor. "Hey, Emerson," she yelled, rattling the panes in their frames. "Come here a minute, will you?"

Miranda said hello. Emerson was a pleasant, stocky man with sad eyes.

"You want to take it with you? Be my guest. I'm certainly not wanting it myself."

"What do you mean?"

"It's probably just nonsense. But just before David died, he remembered the bottle and said he'd better get it opened and do something about it. Some lad off a fishing boat handed it in to him in John O'Groats, and then the boat went down with the lad and everyone else on it a couple of years after. David felt he owed it to the lad to see what was inside. But he died before he got around to it. Not exactly a good omen, is it?"

Emerson shook his head.

"Take it away, by all means. There's no good about that bottle."

That same evening, Miranda sat down in her terraced house in the Edinburgh suburb of Granton and stared at the bottle. It was some fifteen centimeters tall, blue-white in color, slightly flattened, and relatively long-necked. It could have been a scent bottle, though rather on the large side. More likely it had contained eau de cologne and was probably a good age, too. She tapped a knuckle against it. The glass was solid, that much was apparent.

She smiled. "And what secrets might you conceal, dear?" she mused, taking a sip of red wine from her glass before using the corkscrew to scrape out whatever it was that sealed the neck. The lump smelled of tar, but the bottle's time in the sea had made the exact nature of the material hard to determine.

She tried to fish out the paper inside, but it was clearly in a state of decomposition and damp to the touch. Turning the bottle in her hand, she tapped her fingers against the bottom, but the paper budged not a millimeter. This prompted her to take the bottle into the kitchen and strike it a couple of times with a meat tenderizer.

That helped. The bottle splintered into blue crystals that spilled out over the work surface like crushed ice.

She stared at the piece of paper that lay on the chopping board and frowned. Her gaze passed over the shattered glass and she took a deep breath.

Maybe it hadn't been the best of ideas after all.

"Yes," her colleague Douglas in Forensics confirmed. "It's blood all right. No doubt about it. Well done. The way the blood and the condensation have been absorbed into the paper is quite characteristic. Especially here, where the signature's completely obliterated. The color of it, and the pattern of absorption. Aye, it's all typical."

He unfolded the paper using tweezers and bathed it in blue light. Traces of blood all over, diffusely iridescent in every letter.

"It's written in blood?"

"Most certainly."

"And you agree with me that the heading is an appeal for help? It sounds like it, at least."

"Aye, I reckon so," Douglas replied. "But I doubt we'll be able to salvage much more than the heading. It's quite damaged, that letter. Besides, it might be very old. The thing to do now is to make sure it's properly treated and conserved, and then maybe we'll have a stab at dating it. And of course we'll need to have a linguistics expert take a look at it. Hopefully, they'll be able to tell us what language that is."

Miranda nodded. She had her own idea about that.

Icelandic.

4

"Health and Safety are here, Carl." Rose was standing in the doorway, looking like she wasn't going to budge. Maybe she was hoping to see a fight.

A small man in a well-pressed suit introduced himself as John Studsgaard. Small, and with an air of authority. Apart from the flat brown briefcase under his arm he seemed harmless enough. A pleasant smile and his hand outstretched. However, it was an impression that evaporated the moment he opened his mouth.

"There's a report of asbestos having been found in the corridor here and in the crawl space on the last inspection. We'll need to inspect the insulation so the area can be made safe for use."

Carl peered up at the ceiling. One bloody pipe. The only one in the entire basement. Bollocks.

"I see you've got offices here," the suit went on. "Would that be in accordance with official occupation and fire regulations for the building?" He was just about to unzip his briefcase, obviously in possession of a stack of documents that would provide him with the answer to his question.

"Offices? What offices?" said Carl. "You mean the archive briefing space here?"

"Archive briefing space?" The man looked lost for a second, but then the bureaucrat took charge. "I'm not entirely familiar with the term, but it seems clear to me that a lot of what I would call regular work-related activity is conducted here during the course of a day."

"You mean the coffeemaker? We can put it somewhere else if you want."

"No, it's not that. It's more the whole setup. Desks, bulletin boards, shelving, coat hooks, archives, office supplies, photocopiers."

"Oh, right, I'm with you now! Listen, do you know how many stairs there are up to the third floor from here?"

"No."

"OK, then you probably don't know either that we're short-staffed and that it'd take up most of the day if we had to shoot up and down those stairs every time we needed to photocopy something for the archive. Perhaps you'd prefer to have killers running around on the loose than for us to be able to do our jobs properly?"

Studsgaard was about to protest, but Carl raised a hand and stopped him. "Where is this asbestos, exactly?"

The man frowned. "This isn't about where or how. We have an incidence of asbestos contamination. Asbestos is a carcinogen. It's not something you wipe up with a floor cloth."

"Were you here when the inspection took place, Rose?" Carl inquired.

She pointed off down the corridor. "They found some dust along there somewhere."

"ASSAD!" Carl yelled, so loud the man took a step backward. "Come on, Rose, show me," he said as Assad popped into view.

"You too, Assad. Bring your bucket, a cloth, and those nice green gloves of yours. Job for you."

They walked the fifteen steps along the corridor and then Rose pointed to some white, powdery substance on the floor between her black boots. "There!" she exclaimed.

The man from Health and Safety protested and endeavored to explain that what they were clearly intending to do was quite inadequate. That the source would be left untouched, and that common sense and all the regulations dictated that contamination should be removed in accordance with existing precepts.

Carl ignored him. "Once you've wiped it up, Assad, I want you to get on the phone and call a joiner. We need a partition wall to separate Health and Safety's contaminated zone from our briefing space. Don't want to be breathing all that crap into our lungs, do we, now?"

Assad shook his head deliberately. "What space was that you said, Carl? Briefing space . . . ?"

"Just wipe the floor, Assad. The man's busy."

The official flashed Carl a hostile look. "You'll be hearing from us," was the last thing he said as he huffed off down the corridor, briefcase clutched tight against his rib cage.

Hearing from them! Carl didn't doubt it for a minute.

"Tell me now, Assad, what all my case files are doing up there on the wall," said Carl. "I hope for your sake they're copies."

"Copies? If you prefer copies, Carl, I can take them down again. I can get you all the copies you want, no problem."

Carl swallowed. "Are you telling me to my face that these are the original documents you've hung up to dry?"

"Look at my system, Carl. Tell me, by all means, if you do not find it so fantastic. That would be all right. I won't get mad."

Carl recoiled. "Mad?" he repeated. He'd been away a fortnight and his staff had gone off their heads from inhaling asbestos.

"Take a look, Carl." With an expression of glee, Assad held out two balls of string.

"Well done, Assad. You've pilfered some string. Blue string and red string. Excellent. In nine months you can gift wrap your Christmas presents."

Assad slapped him on the back. "Ha, ha, Carl. Very good. Now you are your old self again."

Carl shook his head. It irked him to think that his retirement depended on him reaching an age that was still so far off.

"But look." Assad drew off a length of blue string, then tore off a piece of adhesive tape, affixing one end of the string to a case dating back to the sixties. Then he pulled the string across a number of other cases, snipped it with a pair of scissors, and attached the other end to a case from the eighties. "Clever, don't you think?"

Carl put his hands behind his neck as if to keep his head in place. "A magnificent work of art, Assad. Andy Warhol would be proud."

"Andy who?"

"What is it exactly you're doing, Assad? Are you trying to suggest a connection between those two cases?"

"Just imagine if they actually were connected, then we would be able to see it." He indicated his blue string. "Right here! Blue string!" He snapped his fingers. "It means we think the cases might have something in common."

Carl inhaled deeply. "Aha! Let me guess what the red string's for."

"Yes, exactly! That is for when we know the cases really *are* connected. A good system, don't you think?"

Carl took in more air. "Yes, Assad. The only thing wrong with it is that none of the cases have anything at all in common. As such, it would be so much better for them to be in a pile on my desk so that we might peruse them at our leisure. Would that be OK with you?" It wasn't a question, but an answer came anyway.

"Well, all right, boss." Assad rocked back and forth in his worn-out Ecco shoes. "I will begin to photocopy in ten minutes. Originals for you, copies on the wall for me."

Marcus Jacobsen was looking older all of a sudden. A lot of work had passed over his desk of late. Not least the ongoing gang war and its attendant shootings in the Nørrebro district, but also a series of dreadful fires, all of them arson and resulting in enormous financial losses, as well as having cost human lives. Always at night. If Marcus had slept three hours a day this past week, he'd been doing well. Maybe it was worth being accommodating, whatever Marcus had on his mind.

"What's up, Chief? Dragging me all this way upstairs again?" Carl said.

Marcus fingered his empty cigarette packet. Poor sod, thought Carl, he'll never get past withdrawal. "Yes, I know there's not much room for you up here, Carl. But strictly speaking, I'm not allowed to have you in the basement. And now Health and Safety are on the phone telling me you're obstructing one of their officers."

"It's all sorted, Marcus. We're having a partition wall put up slap in the middle of the corridor with a door in it and everything. It'll all be shut off."

The bags under Marcus's eyes seemed to grow heavier. "That's exactly the kind of thing I don't want to hear, Carl," he said. "Which is why you and Rose and Assad are going to have to camp out up here. I can't be taking flak from Health and Safety. There's enough bother as it is. You know how much I've got on my plate at the moment. See for yourself." He indicated the neat new flatscreen on the wall. TV2 News was running a feature on the impact of the gang war. Calls for a funeral procession through the streets of Copenhagen to honor one of the victims merely inflamed matters further. People were braying about how come the police didn't just take the troublemakers by the scruff of the neck so the streets could be safe again.

Marcus Jacobsen was indeed a worried man.

"OK, if you move us up here, you can shut down Department Q right now, this very second."

"Don't tempt me, Carl."

"Meaning you lose eight million a year in funding. Wasn't that what we were allotted, eight million? Hell of a price for petrol for that old wreck we drive around in. Oh, yeah, and three salaries, of course, for me and Rose and Assad. Eight million. Not exactly plausible, is it?"

The homicide chief gave a sigh. Carl had him by the short and curlies. Without that funding, his own department would be short of at least five million a year. Creative redistribution. A bit like a government support scheme for outlying regions. Robbery made legal.

"Solutions, please," he said eventually.

"Where were you thinking of putting us up here, anyway?" Carl asked.

"In the bathroom? In the window alcove where Assad was yesterday? Or maybe here, in your office?"

"There's room in the corridor." Marcus Jacobsen winced noticeably as he spoke. "We'll find somewhere better soon. That's been the idea all along, Carl."

"OK, fine by me. We'll be needing three new desks, then." Carl stood and extended his hand as though it was a done deal.

The homicide chief backtracked slightly. "Just a minute," he said. "I sense something fishy going on here."

"Fishy? You get three extra desks, and when Health and Safety come back, I'll send Rose upstairs to pretty up the empty chairs."

"They'll never buy it, Carl." He paused a moment and looked like he might be taking the bait. "Then again . . . Sit down a minute, will you, Carl? There's something I want you to have a look at. Remember three or four years ago we assisted our colleagues in Scotland?"

Carl nodded hesitantly. Was Marcus now about to impose bagpipes and haggis on Department Q? It was bad enough with Norwegians once in a while, but Scots!

"We sent them some DNA from a Scot doing time in Vestre, I'm sure you remember. It was Bak's case. They solved a murder on that count, and now they've sent us something in return. A police expert in Edinburgh, Douglas Gilliam, has sent us this parcel. There's a letter inside. A message in a bottle, apparently. They've had a linguist take a look at it and discovered it must be from Denmark." He picked up a brown cardboard box. "They want to know the upshot, if we ever get a handle on it. It's all yours, Carl."

He handed him the box and gestured dismissively, plainly finished with him.

"What do you expect me to do with it?" Carl inquired. "How about passing it on to the post office instead?"

Jacobsen smiled. "Very funny, Carl. Sadly, Post Danmark aren't exactly specialists in solving mysteries, more in creating them, I'd say."

"We're busy enough as it is," Carl countered.

"I don't doubt it, Carl. But see what you can do. It's probably nothing. Besides, it meets all the criteria for Department Q. It's old, it's unsolved, and no one else could be arsed."

Something else to stop me putting my feet up, Carl mused to himself, weighing the box in his hand as he descended the stairs.

But then again.

An hour's shut-eye was hardly going to be detrimental to Danish–Scottish relations.

"I'll be finished with it all by tomorrow. Rose is helping me," said Assad as he considered where the case he now stood with in his hand might originally have fitted into Carl's three-pile filing system.

Carl growled. The Scottish box was on the desk in front of him. Premonitions tended to stick, and he had a bad feeling about the cardboard box with the broken customs authority seal on it.

"This is a new case, perhaps?" Assad inquired with interest, his gaze fixed on the brown cube. "Who has opened the box?"

Carl jerked his thumb upward in the direction of the third floor.

"Rose, come here a minute, will you?" Carl yelled into the corridor.

Five minutes passed before she appeared: enough time in her view to signal just who was in charge. You got used to it.

"What would you say to being assigned your first proper case, Rose?" He nudged the cardboard box gently across the desk toward her.

He was unable to see her eyes beneath the jet-black fringe of her punk hairdo, but he felt sure they were hardly sparkling with enthusiasm.

"Let me guess," she said. "It's to do with child porn or trafficking, am I right? Something you couldn't be arsed with. In that case, the answer's no. If you don't fancy it yourself, you can give it to our little camel driver to amuse himself with. I've got other things to be doing."

Carl smiled. She hadn't really sworn, and she hadn't kicked the door frame. And describing Assad as a camel driver was almost a compliment, coming from her. Anyone would think she was in a good mood. He nudged at the box again. "It's a letter. A message in a bottle. I haven't seen it yet. We could unpack it together."

She wrinkled her nose. Distrust was her partner in life.

Carl pulled the flaps of the box apart, removed handfuls of polystyrene packing, and retrieved a folder that he placed on the desk. Then he rummaged around in more polystyrene and found a plastic bag.

"What's that inside?" Rose asked.

"Shards from the bottle, I suppose."

"You mean they broke it?"

"No, they took it apart. There's a set of instructions in the folder telling you how to put it together again. Should be a piece of cake for a handywoman like you."

She stuck her tongue out at him and weighed the bag in her hand. "It's not very heavy. How big was it?"

He shoved the case file toward her. "Read it yourself."

She left the box where it was and went off down the corridor. Peace at last. In an hour it would be time to go home. He would take the train back to Allerød, buy a bottle of whisky, anesthetize himself and Hardy with a glass each, one with a straw and one with ice. A quiet night in.

He closed his eyes and dozed for all of ten seconds until Assad suddenly made his presence felt in front of him.

"I have found something, Carl. Come and have a look on the wall."

Funny how being off in the land of nod for only a few seconds always impacted so forcefully on one's sense of balance, Carl thought to himself, clutching dizzily at the corridor wall as Assad proudly indicated one of the case documents that was affixed to the notice board.

Carl dragged himself back to the real world. "Say that again, Assad. My thoughts were somewhere else."

"I asked only if you thought the chief might not consider this case in light of all the fires in Copenhagen."

Carl tested the floor beneath his feet to make sure it was steady, then went up to the wall upon which Assad's index finger was now planted. The case was fourteen years old. A fire in which a body had been found.

Murder, perhaps, in the area close to the city lake called Damhussøen. A case concerning the discovery of a body so badly burned that neither time of death nor gender could be established. All genetic material had perished. No missing person matched the body. Eventually, the case had been shelved. Carl remembered it well. It had been one of Antonsen's.

"What makes you think it has anything to do with the arsons going on now, Assad?"

"Arsons?"

"The fire-raising."

"Because!" said Assad, pointing eagerly at a photograph detailing skeletal remains. "This round groove in the bone of his short finger. It says something about it here, too." He removed the plastic folder from the notice board and found the page from the report. "Here it is described. 'As though made by a signet ring over a period of many years,' it says here. A groove going all the way around."

"So what?"

"On the short finger, Carl."

"And?"

"I remember from Department A, there was a body in the first fire that was missing its short finger altogether."

"OK. The correct term is little finger, Assad. Not short."

"Exactly. And in the next fire was a groove in the short finger of the man who was found. Just like here."

Carl's eyebrows lifted demonstrably.

"I think you should go up to the third floor and tell the chief what you've just told me, Assad."

Assad beamed. "I would never have seen it if it wasn't for that photo being stuck to the wall in front of my nose all this time. Funny, don't you think?"

It was as though with her new assignment a chink had appeared in Rose's impenetrable armor. At any rate, she did not begin by waving the document in his face and shouting but instead removed his ashtray and placed the letter carefully, almost respectfully, on his desk.

"It's very hard to read," she said. "It seems it was written in blood, which gradually absorbed dampness from the condensation and drew it into the paper. Besides, the capitals are poorly done. The heading's quite clear, though. See how legible it is. It says 'HELP.'"

Carl leaned grudgingly forward and studied what remained of the capital letters. The paper may once have been white, but now it was brown. Its edges were in tatters in several places, with bits missing, presumably lost when the paper was unfolded after being in the water.

"What tests have been done on it, does it say? Where was it found? And when?"

"It was found off the Orkney Islands. Caught up in a fishing net. In 2002, apparently."

"In 2002! They weren't in a hurry to pass it on, then."

"The bottle had been left on a windowsill and forgotten. That's most likely the cause of the condensation. It'll have been in the sun."

"They're all pissheads in Scotland," muttered Carl.

"There's a pretty useless DNA profile here. And some ultraviolet photos. They've done their best to preserve the letter. And look, here's their reconstruction of the wording. Some of it can actually be read."

Carl looked at the photocopy and immediately regretted his hasty caricature of the Scottish population. Comparing the original letter with the attempt at reconstruction, the results were impressive indeed.

He skimmed through the reconstructed wording. People have always been fascinated by the idea of sending a message in a bottle that might end up on the other side of the world, perhaps leading to new and unexpected adventures.

But that wasn't the case here. This was deadly serious. Nothing to do with boyish pranks, or a project by Cub Scouts on some exciting field trip. No blue skies and harmony here. The letter was almost certainly what it seemed to be.

A desperate cry for help.

5

The moment he left her, he left behind his day-to-day life. He drove the twenty kilometers or so from Roskilde to the secluded farm-laborer's cottage that lay almost midway between their home and the house by the fjord. Reversed the van out of the barn and then parked the Mercedes inside. Locked the barn door, took a quick shower, and dyed his hair, changed his clothes and stood in front of the mirror for ten minutes getting ready. He found what he needed in the cupboards, then went outside with his bags to the light-blue Peugeot Partner he used on his trips. An undistinguished vehicle, neither too big nor too small, its mud-spattered number plates not noticeably obliterated at first sight and yet still almost illegible. It was anonymous, and registered in the name he'd used when purchasing the cottage. It suited his purpose.

By the time he reached this stage, he was always thoroughly prepared. Research on the Internet, and in the registers to which he had collected access codes over the years, had yielded the information he required on potential victims. He was flush with cash, using large-denomination notes to pay at petrol stations and toll bridges, always looking away from the cameras, always keeping his distance if anything untoward seemed to be in the air.

This time, his hunting ground was mid-Jutland, a region in which the concentration of religious sects was high. A couple of years had passed since he had last struck there. Whatever else one might say, he spread death with the utmost care and attention.

For some time he had conducted observations, though as a rule only for a couple of days at a time. On the first occasion, he had stayed with a woman in Haderslev, then with another in a small place called Lønne. The risk of being recognized in the Viborg area, so far away, was minuscule.

His choice was among five families. Two were Jehovah's Witnesses, one was Evangelist, one was with the Guardians of Morality, and the fifth with the Mother Church. As things stood, he inclined toward the latter.

He arrived in Viborg at about eight in the evening, too early by half for what he was intending, especially in a town of this size, but it was better to err on the side of caution.

His criteria for selecting the bars in which he found the women who would put him up were always the same. The place mustn't be too small. It mustn't lie in an area in which everyone knew one another. It mustn't have too many regulars. And it mustn't be such a dive that no single woman of a certain standard between the ages of thirty-five and fifty-five would go there.

The first place on his tour, Julle's Bar, was too cramped and gloomy, all wooden kitsch and one-armed bandits. The next place was better. There was a small dance floor, and the clientele were a decent mix, with the exception of a gay patron who immediately planted himself on the adjacent bar stool at a distance measurable only in millimeters. If he found a woman there, the guy would almost certainly remember him, despite his polite rejection.

He found what he was looking for at the fifth attempt. The signs above the bar counter seemed to confirm it: *The quiet ones are the wild ones, The Terminal—your home from home,* and perhaps in particular *Best boobs in town are here* all struck the right tone.

The Terminal, tucked away in the street called Gravene, closed early at eleven o'clock, but people were well in the mood on Hancock Høker ale and local rock music. He felt sure he'd get off with someone before closing.

He picked out a woman, not exactly young, sitting near the slot machines. She had been dancing on her own when he came in, her arms floating free at her sides on the tiny dance floor. She was quite pretty, certainly no easy prey. A serious fisher in these waters. A woman who wanted a man she could trust, someone worth waking up next to for the rest of her life, not someone she reckoned on finding here. She was obviously just out with some girlfriends from work after a hard day's slog.

Two of her giggly, well-proportioned colleagues stood swaying to the music in the smoking cabin; the rest had taken possession of a number of the establishment's mismatched tables. Most likely the girls had been partying for some time already. At any rate, he felt fairly certain none of the others would be able to describe him in any detail in a couple of hours' time.

He made eye contact with her, and after five minutes he asked her to dance. She was tipsy, not drunk. It was a good sign.

"You're not from round here," she said. "What are you doing in Viborg?"

Her scent was pleasant, her gaze steady and firm. It was easy to see what she wanted him to say. That he visited Viborg often. That he was fond of the place. That he was educated and single. So that's what he said. Casually, without making an issue of it. He would say anything as long as it worked.

Two hours later, they were lying in her bed. She was satisfied and he was safe in the knowledge that he could stay with her for a couple of weeks without the usual questions: Did he really like her? Was he serious?

He was careful not to build up her expectations. He played coy and mysterious, keeping her guessing as to what depths of personality his nonchalance concealed.

He awoke at half past five the next morning as planned. Got dressed, rummaged around discreetly in her drawers and cupboards, finding out about her before she began to stir. Divorced, as he already knew. No children. Probably a decent little office job in the local authority that just as likely sapped her of all her energy. She was fifty-two years old and at this point in her life more than ready for adventure.

Valley Community Library
739 River Street
Peckville, PA 18452-2313

Before placing the tray of coffee and toast on the bed beside her, he drew back the curtains a chink so that she could catch his smile and all his freshness.

Afterward, she cuddled up close to him. Tender and submissive, the dimples of her cheeks now deeper than before. She stroked his face and was about to kiss his scar when he lifted his chin and asked: "Should I check into the Hotel Palads, or would you like me to come back here tonight?"

The answer was a formality. She snuggled affectionately closer and told him where she kept the key. And then he sauntered out to the van and drove away from his newfound residential bliss.

The family he had selected would be able to pay the usual million-kroner ransom he demanded. They might need to sell off some stocks, though it was certainly not the best time to do so, but apart from that they were well consolidated financially. Obviously, the recession had made it harder to commit even reasonably lucrative crime, but as long as his victims were selected with prudence there would always be a way. He was certain this family possessed both the ability and the will to meet his demands, and to do so with discretion.

He had been observing them for some time. He had visited their church and had spoken in confidence with the parents after prayer meetings. He knew how long they had been members of their community, how they had made their money, how many children they had and what they were called, and in broad outline the patterns of their daily life.

The family lived outside Frederiks, twenty minutes southwest of Viborg. Five children aged between ten and eighteen. All still living at home, all active members of the Mother Church. The two eldest attended the gymnasium school in Viborg; their siblings were taught at home by their mother, a former teacher of the Tvind schools in her midforties, who for want of a better life had turned to God. It was she who wore the trousers at home. She who steered the troops and their religion. Her husband was twenty years her senior and one of the area's wealthiest businessmen. Though he donated half his income to the Mother Church, as all members were obliged to, there was plenty left over. A business such as his, hiring out agricultural machinery and equipment to local farmers, was never in jeopardy.

The corn kept growing even when the banks went down the plughole.

The only drawback about this particular family was that the second son, who seemed otherwise to be an excellent choice of victim, had begun attending karate lessons. Not that there was any reason to be nervous about any physical threat this slight young man might pose, but it might upset the timing.

And timing was everything, once things got ugly.

Apart from that, this second son and his middle sister, the fourth child of the family, had all the characteristics required for his mission to be successful. They were enterprising, the best-looking of the siblings, and also the most dominant. Almost certainly the apples of their mother's eye. Good churchgoers but also rather unruly. The kind who ended up either as high priests or expelled from the Church altogether. Believers, and yet indomitably self-possessed. It was the perfect combination.

A bit like he had once been himself, perhaps.

He parked the van between the trees of the windbreak and sat for a long time looking through the binoculars, observing the children running around in the garden beside the farmhouse during their breaks from home schooling. The girl he had selected seemed to be up to something in a corner beneath some trees. Something not intended to be seen by the others. For some time she remained occupied, kneeling in the tall grass. This confirmed to him what a good choice she was.

Whatever she was doing, her mother and the Church would not approve, he thought to himself with a nod of acknowledgment. God always puts the best of his flock to the test, and twelve-year-old Magdalena, this girl soon to become a young woman, was no exception.

He watched for another hour or two, reclining inside the van, keeping his eye on the farmhouse that nestled in the bend of the road at Stanghede. Through the binoculars he could clearly see a pattern emerging in the girl's behavior. Every time the children were given a break, she would seek her own company in her corner of the garden, and when her mother called them in for their next lesson, she would cover up whatever it was she had been occupied with.

All things considered, being an almost grown-up girl in a family that had devoted itself to the Mother Church entailed no small amount of deference. Dance, music, printed matter issuing from sources other than the Church, alcohol, social intercourse with individuals outside the community, pets, television, the Internet—all these things were forbidden, and punishment for consistent disobedience was harsh: ostracism from both the family and the Church.

He drove away before the boys came home, satisfied with his choice of family. Now he would examine the father's company accounts and personal tax returns one last time before resuming his observations the next morning.

Soon, there would be no turning back, and he was content at the thought.

Her name was Isabel, this woman who now housed him, though she was hardly as exotic as her name. Swedish crime novels on the shelves and Anne Linnet on the CD player. This was the straight and narrow.

He looked at his watch. She could be home in half an hour, but there was plenty of time to check whether any unpleasant surprises might be in store. He sat down at her desk and switched on her laptop, growled audibly when it asked for a password. He tried six or seven combinations in vain before lifting the desk-protector to discover a comprehensive list of Internet passwords. It was always the same: women such as Isabel either used birthdays, the names of their children or dogs, phone numbers, or simply a straight sequence of digits, often in descending order, or they wrote down their passwords and concealed them no more than a couple of meters from the keyboard so they could read them without getting up.

He read her dating correspondence and noted to his satisfaction that in him she had found the man she had been seeking for some time. Perhaps he was a couple of years younger than she had imagined, but what woman would decline?

He went through her e-mail contacts on Outlook. One of them was a regular correspondent. His name was Karsten Jønsson. A brother, perhaps, or the ex-husband. It wasn't important. The significant thing was the suffix of his e-mail address: police.dk.

Not good, he thought to himself. When the time came, he would have to refrain from violence and instead make do with verbal abuse or simply leave his dirty laundry around the house, which according to her online dating profile was one of her major turn-offs.

He fished the little BlueTinum flash drive out of his pocket and stuck it into the USB port. Skype account and contacts, all at once. Then he typed his wife's mobile number.

She would be shopping at this time. Always the same routine. He would suggest she buy champagne and put it in the fridge, ready.

At the tenth ring, he frowned. She had never failed to answer before. If there was one thing his wife clung to, it was that mobile of hers.

He called again. No answer.

He leaned forward and stared down at the keyboard, feeling his cheeks flush.

She had better have a good explanation. Revealing unknown aspects of her personality now might force him to demonstrate some new aspects of his own.

And she wouldn't like that. She wouldn't like that at all.

6

"Well, I must say that Assad's observation has given us food for thought, Carl," said the chief, wriggling his shoulders into his leather jacket. In ten minutes he would be standing on a street corner in the Nordvest district, studying bloodstains from the night's shooting. Carl did not envy him.

He nodded. "You agree with Assad, then? That there might be a connection between the fires?"

"That same groove in the victims' finger bones in three out of four incidents. It certainly gives us something to think about. We'll just have to wait and see. The material's with the pathologists, so it's their shout now. But the nose, Carl . . ." He tapped an index finger against his distinctive protuberance. Not many noses had been poked into as many rotten cases as Jacobsen's had. Most likely Assad and Jacobsen were right. There was a connection. Carl sensed it himself.

He mustered a semblance of authority in his voice, no easy matter on the wrong side of ten o'clock. "You'll be taking over from here then, I assume."

"For the moment, yes."

Carl nodded. Now he could go back downstairs and mark the old arson case closed as far as Department Q was concerned.

It would look good in the statistics.

"Come and see, Carl. Rose has something to show you." The reverberating voice made it sound like a troop of howler monkeys from Borneo had appropriated the lower chambers. Assad certainly had no problems with his vocal cords, that much was plain.

He stood beaming, clutching a ream of photocopies. As far as Carl could make out, they weren't case documents. More like blowups of something fragmentary that at best could be described as blurred.

"Look what she did."

Assad pointed down the corridor at the partition wall the joiner had just put up in order to contain the asbestos contamination. Or rather, he pointed to where it ought to have been visible. For both the wall and the door in it were completely covered with photocopies that had been meticulously put together to form one single image. If anyone wanted to come through, they would need a pair of scissors.

Even at a distance of ten meters, it was clear that this was an enormous blowup of the message in the bottle.

HELP, it read, spanning the entire width of the corridor.

"Sixty-four sheets of A4, no less. Great, is it not, Carl? These are the last five in my hand here. Two hundred and forty centimeters high and one hundred and seventy wide. Big, yes? Is she not clever?"

Carl stepped a couple of meters closer. Rose was on her knees with her backside in the air, sticking Assad's copies into place in the bottom corner.

Carl considered first her backside, then the work the two of them had produced. The enormous blowup had its advantages and its drawbacks, that much was obvious straightaway. Areas where the letters had been absorbed into the paper were a blur, whereas others containing practically illegible, spidery handwriting that the Scottish forensics team had tried to reconstruct suddenly became meaningful.

The upshot of it all was that at a stroke they now had at least twenty more legible characters to add to the puzzle.

Rose turned toward him for a second, ignoring his little wave and dragging a stepladder out into the middle of the corridor.

"Get up there, Assad. I'll tell you where to put the dots, yeah?"

She shoved Carl aside and positioned herself in the exact spot where he had been standing.

"Not too hard, Assad. We need to be able to rub them out again."

Assad nodded from on high, pencil at the ready.

"Start underneath 'HELP' and in front of 'he.' My eye makes out three distinct blotches, one before 'he' and two after. Are you with me?"

Assad and Carl considered the mottled stains on the paper. They looked like gray cumulus clouds alongside the touched-up "h" and "e."

Then Assad nodded and placed a dot on each of the three blotches.

Carl took a step to one side. It seemed reasonable enough. Underneath the clearly legible heading *HELP*, the two characters that followed were flanked by visible blurs. Seawater and condensation had played their part. The three blood-written characters had long since dissolved and been absorbed into the pulp. If only they could figure out what they were.

He stood watching for a moment as Rose bossed Assad around. It was a meticulous business. And where would it lead, when it came down to it? To endless hours of guesswork, that was where. And what for? The message could go back decades. Besides, it was still quite possible that it might all have been just a practical joke. The hand seemed clumsy, as though it belonged to a child. A couple of Cub Scouts, a little nick in the finger, and there you have it. But then again . . .

"I'm not sure about this, Rose," he ventured. "Maybe we should just forget all about it. We've enough to be getting on with as it is."

He noted with bewilderment the effect of his words. Rose began to quiver, like jelly. If he didn't know better, he'd have thought she was about to burst into laughter. But Carl knew Rose all too well, and for that reason he retreated. Only a step, but enough to avoid the explosive splutter of invective that suddenly showered toward him.

It meant that Rose was dissatisfied with his meddling. He wasn't so gormless that he didn't get the gist.

He nodded. Like he said, there was plenty else to be getting on with. He knew of at least two folders of important case documents which, positioned correctly, would cover his face nicely while he caught up on his sleep. Rose and Assad could amuse themselves with their little puzzle while he took care of business.

Rose registered his cowardly retreat. She turned slowly and looked daggers at him.

"Ingenious idea, though, Rose. Very well done," he blurted out, but he was cutting no ice.

"I'll give you a choice, Carl," she hissed. Assad, at the top of the ladder, rolled his eyes. "Either you shut your gob, or else I'm off home. And for your information, I might just send my twin sister over instead, and do you know what'll happen then?"

Carl shook his head. He wasn't entirely sure he wanted to know. "Let me guess. She'll be over here with three kids and four cats, a pair of lodgers, and some shit of a husband. Am I right? Your office'll be a bit cramped, yeah?"

She planted her fists firmly on her hips and leaned menacingly toward him. "Whoever filled you with that crap doesn't know what they're talking about. Yrsa's living with me, and she's got neither cats nor lodgers." The word "MORON!" lit up in her black-painted eyes.

He held up his hands in front of him in capitulation.

The chair in his office beckoned.

"What's all that about her twin sister, Assad? Has Rose threatened to send her over before?"

Assad bounced jauntily up the steps of the rotunda alongside him, but Carl could already feel the lead accumulating in his legs.

"Don't take things so personal, Carl. Rose is like sand on a camel's back. Sometimes it makes the arse itch and sometimes it doesn't. It's all a question of how thick-skinned a person is." He turned his face to Carl and flashed two neat rows of pearly white enamel. If anyone's arsehole had been armored with hard skin through the years, it was probably his.

"She has told me about her sister, Yrsa. I remember her name because it sounds like Irma, the supermarket. I don't think they are very good friends together," Assad added.

Yrsa? Is anyone really called that anymore? Carl wondered as they reached the third floor, his heart valves dancing the fandango.

"All right, boys?" said a delightfully familiar voice on the other side of the counter. Lis was back! Lis, forty years of eminently well-preserved flesh and brain cells. A true gift to the senses, in stark contrast to Ms. Sørensen, who smiled benevolently at Assad while rearing her head toward Carl like a cobra poked with a stick.

"Tell the detective inspector what a lovely time you and Frank had together in the States, Lis." The heron smiled ominously.

"It'll have to wait, I'm afraid," Carl replied swiftly. "Marcus is waiting for us."

He pulled in vain at Assad's sleeve.

Thanks for fuck all, Assad, he thought to himself as Lis's glowing red lips gleefully related the events of a whole month spent in America in the company of a wilted husband who had suddenly turned into a bison in the double bed of their rented motor home. These were images Carl tried with all his might to erase from his mind's eye, along with thoughts of his own involuntary celibacy.

"Bloody old hag," he muttered under his breath. Assad wasn't much better, either. Not to mention the lucky bastard who had ensnared Lis. And then there was Médecins Sans Frontières or whatever they called themselves, who had enticed Mona, the focus of his desire, and dragged her away to darkest Africa.

"When does that psychologist of yours come home again, Carl?" Assad asked as they stood outside the door of the briefing room. "What was her name, now? Mona, is that right?"

Carl chose to ignore Assad's cheeky smile and opened the door. Most of Department A were there already, rubbing their eyes. They had spent a couple of exhausting days on the outside, up to their ears in society's quagmire, but now Assad's discovery had hauled them back to the surface again.

It took Marcus Jacobsen ten minutes to brief his team, and both he and

Lars Bjørn seemed more than a little excited. Assad's name was mentioned several times. His beaming smile was met by the narrowed eyes of his colleagues, clearly puzzled as to how this monkey of a cleaning assistant had suddenly appeared in their midst.

But no one had the energy to ask questions. Essentially, Assad had discovered a highly plausible link between old and new cases of arson. All the bodies found in the remains of the blazes shared the same groove in the bone of the little finger of the left hand, apart from the one body on which that finger was missing. It transpired that the pathologists had made a note of it in each case, though no one had made the connection.

The autopsies indicated that two of the deceased had worn a ring on their little finger. The cause of the groove in the bone had not been the heat of the blaze, the pathologists stated. A more likely conclusion was that the deceased had worn these rings since youth and that they had thus left their indelible mark on the osseous tissue. Such rings could have had cultural significance along the lines of the binding of feet in China, one pathologist had suggested, whereas another noted that some ritual might have been involved.

Marcus Jacobsen nodded. Something like that. Some kind of brotherhood could not be ruled out, either. Once the ring was on, it was never removed.

The fact that one of the bodies was missing a digit was another matter altogether. There could be any number of reasons for this, including someone having chopped it off.

"All we have to do now is tie up the whys and wherefores," the deputy chief, Lars Bjørn, concluded.

Almost everyone nodded, some with a sigh. What could be simpler?

"Department Q will notify us as to any similar cases they might turn up," added the chief, and Assad received a pat on the back from one of the detectives who most definitely wouldn't be doing any of the donkey work.

And then they were out in the corridor again.

"What was it now you were saying about this Mona Ibsen, Carl?" said

Assad, continuing terrier-like from where he'd left off. "Would you not like her to come home again before the bollocks weigh as heavy as cannonballs?"

Back in the basement, everything was pretty much as it had been when they left. Rose had dragged a stool in front of the blowup on the wall, and now she sat pondering so intensely one could almost see her frown from behind.

It seemed she was stuck.

Carl looked at the giant photocopy. It was certainly no easy puzzle to solve. To put it mildly.

She had now gone over all the characters with a felt-tip pen. It might not have been the wisest thing to do, but it did provide a better overview, that much he could see.

She dragged her fingers coquettishly through the bird's nest of her hair, her nails speckled with marker fluid as though to make everything match.

No doubt she would touch them up with black nail polish before long.

"Does it make any sense to you? Any sense at all?" she asked as Carl tried to read.

HELP

.he .. ..brary .... k...aped .. got .s .. the .us s.op on .. ut.op.... .. Bal.....—T.. man .. 18. t... .... hair ....— Hes got . ... hi. rit. ... .r.... . bl.e .an Mum ... .ow him— Fr..d.. .nd ...t.in. wit. . B— .. ..retn.d .. ..—... ..ing to .il us— .. .ressd . ... .ace ..rst .... .. .rother.—We drove .....y 1 hour ... ... .y wa.t.r .... win. .urb..s ....re—..... .. ..—.. ... . years

P... ....

A cry for help, as was obvious from the heading, and, besides that, reference to some man or other, a mother and driving. Signed with a "P," and that was it. No, it made no sense at all.

What had happened? Where, when, and why?

"I'm pretty sure this is the person who wrote it," said Rose, pointing her felt-tip at the "P" at the bottom. Who said she was thick?

"I'm also pretty sure that the person's name consists of two words each of four letters," she added, tapping Assad's penciled dots.

Carl's gaze slid from the felt-tip on her nails to the pencil marks on the photocopied message. Was it about time he had his eyes tested? How on earth could she be so certain there were two sets of four letters? Because Assad had put dots on some blotches? As far as he could see, there were umpteen possibilities.

"I've checked the original," she went on. "And I've spoken to that expert in Scotland. We're both in agreement. Two sets of four letters."

Carl nodded. That expert in Scotland, she had said. Well, that was it sorted, wasn't it? As far as he was concerned, she could consult a tartan-clad fortune-teller in Reykjavik, because his eyes were plainly telling him that most of what he saw was bollocks, no matter what Rose might have to say.

"It was definitely written by a male. I'm assuming no one in that situation would sign themselves using a nickname, and I've come up with no Danish girl's names of four letters beginning with 'P.' Looking at foreign names, I've found only the following that would fit: Paca, Pala, Papa, Pele, Peta, Piia, Pili, Pina, Ping, Piri, Posy, Pris, and Prue."

She listed them in a heartbeat, not even glancing at her notes. Was she right in the head, this Rose girl?

"Papa. A very strange name for a girl," Assad grunted.

Rose shrugged. It was something of a turnup, Carl had to admit. Were there really no Danish girl's names of four letters beginning with a "P"? That was what she said, anyway. Impossible, surely?

Carl glanced at Assad, who looked like he had question marks drawn all over his face. No one could ponder in as spellbound a fashion as his stocky assistant.

"It is not a Muslim name, either," he said from within his frown. "I can think only of Pari, which is Iranian."

Carl grimaced. "And Iranians don't live in Denmark, or what? Never mind, let's just say this bloke's called Poul or Paul; that makes things a lot easier, doesn't it? We'll have him found in a jiffy."

At this point, Assad's frown deepened. "Found in a what, did you say, Carl? Where is that?"

Carl sighed. Perhaps he ought to send his little helper over to see his ex soon. She could teach him idioms that would make his wide eyes roll in his head.

He glanced at his watch. "So his name's Poul, is that what we're saying? Well, I'm off on a break, then. Fifteen minutes, and when I get back, you've found him, OK?"

Rose did her best to ignore Carl's tone of voice, though her nostrils flared visibly. "I'm sure Poul's an excellent candidate. Or Piet, or Peer with two 'e's, Pehr with an 'h,' or Petr without an 'e.' Or it could be Pete, or Phil. The possibilities are endless, Carl. We're multiethnic now, as well, so there's all sorts of new names flying around. Paco, Pall, Page, Pasi, Pedr, Pepe, Pere, Pero, Peru . . ."

"All right, Rose, for Chrissake, that'll do. Anyone would think this was a register office. And who's Peru, anyway, when he's at home? I thought that was a country, not a bloody name . . ."

". . . and Peti, Ping, Pino, Pius . . ."

"Pius? Yeah, why not bring the popes in while we're at it? They're male, at least . . ."

"Pons, Pran, Ptah, Puck, Pyry."

"Are you finished?"

There was no answer.

Carl considered once again the signature on the wall. Whatever else he might think, it was hard to conclude otherwise than that the letter had been written by someone whose name began with "P." So who was this "P"? Piet Hein was hardly a candidate. Who, then?

"The first name may be a compound, Rose. Are you sure there's no hyphen in there?" He gestured toward the blur. "In which case it could be Poul-Erik, or Paco-Peti, or Pili-Ping." He tried to transfer his smile to Rose's face, but she was far away and impervious. Sod it, then.

"All right, should we let this magnified message look after itself for the moment, so we can get on with more important matters and Rose can get her poor nails painted black again?" Carl suggested. "We can hardly avoid coming back to it every now and then. Maybe some bright ideas will emerge. Like when you leave the crossword lying around in the bathroom for the next time you need to go."

Rose and Assad studied him with wrinkled brows. Crosswords on the toilet? Obviously neither of them spent as much time in there as he did.

"No, hang on a minute. I don't think we *can* leave it stuck to that wall. We need to get through the door. Part of our archive's behind it, in case you'd forgotten. All those old, unsolved cases. You've heard of them, I suppose?" He turned on his heels and headed for his office and the comfy chair that awaited him. Rose's ice pick of a voice halted him in his tracks after only two steps.

"You look at me, Carl."

He turned with caution and saw her pointing back toward her work of art.

"If you think my nails look like crap, I don't care. Get it? And besides that, do you see that word up there at the very top?"

"Yes, Rose, I do. In fact it's about the only thing I can say with any certainty that I do see. It very plainly says 'HELP.'"

With that, she waggled a blackened finger menacingly in his direction. "Good. Because that's the word you'll be wanting to scream if you remove so much as a single sheet of that paper. Do you get my drift?"

He released his eyes from her rebellious gaze and waved Assad to his side.

He would have to put his foot down before long.

7

Whenever she looked in the mirror, she always thought she deserved better from life. Nicknames such as Peach and Thyregod School's Sleeping Beauty were still part of the way she saw herself. When she took off her clothes, she could still be pleasantly surprised by her body. But what good was that if she was alone?

The distance between them had become too great. He never saw her anymore.

When he came home, she would say he wasn't to leave her again and that surely there had to be other job opportunities. She wanted to be close to him, to know about his work and to watch him wake up beside her in the mornings.

That's what she was going to say.

In former times, there had been a little rubbish tip at the bottom of Toftebakken, used by the old mental asylum. Now the tatty mattresses and rusty bed frames were long gone and in their place was an oasis of showcase residences, all of which enjoyed an unspoiled vista of the fjord.

She loved to stand here above the windbreak of trees, gazing out over the marina at the blue fjord in all its splendor, gradually allowing her eyes to drift out of focus.

In such a place, and in such a state of mind, it was no wonder that a person should feel defenseless when confronted by the randomness of life. Perhaps that was why she had not declined when the young man got off his bike and suggested they go somewhere for coffee. He lived in the same neighborhood as she did, and on several occasions they had acknowledged each other with a nod in the Føtex supermarket. Now they were standing here.

She glanced at her watch. There were still a couple of hours before her son had to be picked up. Surely there was no harm in a cup of coffee?

On that point, however, she was terribly wrong.

That evening, she sat like an old woman, rocking in her chair, clutching her belly as if that might relax the tension in her muscles. What she had done was unfathomable. Was she really that desperate? It was as though this handsome young man had hypnotized her. After ten minutes, she had switched off her mobile and had begun to tell him all there was to know. And he had listened.

"Mia, that's a nice name," he had said.

It was so long since she had heard anyone speak her name that it sounded almost foreign. Her husband never used it.

This man had been so easy to be with. He had shown interest in her life and told her about his own when she asked. He was in the army, and his name was Kenneth. His eyes were kind and it hadn't felt at all wrong when he had placed his hand on hers, even though the café was full of customers. And then he had drawn it toward him across the table and held it tightly.

And she had done nothing to stop him.

Afterward, she had dashed off to the day care, his presence lingering all around her.

Now, neither the darkness nor the hours that had passed since then could settle her breathing and make things normal again. She bit her lip. Her mobile lay accusingly on the coffee table in front of her, still switched off. She was stranded on an island and could see no escape. With no one to ask for advice. No one from whom to seek forgiveness.

Where could she go from here?

When morning came, she was still in her clothes, her thoughts still racing in bewilderment. The day before, while she had been with Kenneth, her husband had called her mobile. It had only just occurred to her. Three missed calls on the display would require explanation. He would call her and ask why she hadn't answered, and the story she would be forced to concoct would surely give her away, no matter how plausible it might seem to her. He was older and wiser and more experienced than she was. He would sense her deception, and the thought made her entire body tremble.

Usually, he would call just before eight, before she cycled with Benjamin to his day care. Today, she would try to leave a few minutes early. She wanted to speak to him, but she mustn't let him stress her out. If he did, things would go wrong.

The boy was already in her arms when the treacherous mobile began to rumble and spin on the table. Her little porthole to the outside world, always within reach.

"Hi, darling!" she said, trying to keep herself in check, her pulse pounding in her ears.

"I called you. Why didn't you call back?"

"I was just about to," she blurted. She knew it was a mistake as soon as the words left her mouth.

"You're on your way out with Benjamin, how could you be about to call? I know you."

She held her breath and put the boy down carefully on the floor. "He's a bit off color today. You know when they've got a runny nose the day care says to keep them at home. I think he's got a temperature." Cautiously, she allowed herself to breathe. Her whole body was screaming for air.

"I see."

The pause that followed worried her. Was he expecting her to say something? Was there something she had forgotten? She tried to focus. Stared out through the double glazing at the garden gate opposite. The bare branches. People on their way to work.

"I called more than once yesterday. Do you hear what I'm saying?" he asked.

"Yes, I'm sorry, darling. The phone just went dead on me. I think maybe it needs a new battery."

"I only charged it on Tuesday."

"Yes, I know you did. That's what I mean. Only two days and it was flat. Strange, don't you think?"

"So you charged it yourself, then? Could you work out how?"

"Yes." She forced herself to giggle in as carefree a manner as possible. "It was easy, I've watched you do it loads of times."

"I didn't think you knew where the charger was."

"Of course I do." Now her hands were shaking. He knew something wasn't right. Any second now he would ask where she had found that damned charger, and she had absolutely no idea where he kept it.

Think! Think fast! Her mind raced.

"Listen, I . . ." She raised her voice a notch. "Oh, Benjamin! Don't do that!" She gave the boy a little shove with her foot, provoking him to make a sound. Then she glared at him harshly and nudged him again.

When the question came—"Where did you find it, then?"—the child finally began to cry.

"We'll have to talk later," she said, sounding concerned. "Benjamin's hurt himself."

She snapped the mobile shut, crouched down, and pulled off the boy's romper, showering him with kisses and comforting noises. "There, there, Benjamin. Mummy's so sorry, so sorry. She didn't mean it. Would you like a piece of cake?"

The child sobbed and forgave her with a heavy nod, his big, sad eyes blinking. She thrust a picture book into his hands as the full extent of the catastrophe slowly manifested itself in her mind. The house they lived in was enormous, three hundred square meters, and the mobile charger could be in any place the size of a fist.

An hour later, not a single drawer, cupboard, or shelf on the ground floor was left unsearched.

And then it struck her: What if they only had the one charger? And what if he had taken it with him? Was his phone the same kind as hers? She didn't even know.

She fed the little boy, her brow furrowed with concern, and became convinced that that was indeed what had happened. He had taken the charger with him.

She shook her head and scraped the boy's lips clean with the spoon. But no, when you bought a mobile there was always a charger to go with it. Of course there was. Which meant there was a good chance that somewhere in the house there was a box that had come with the phone, containing a manual and most likely an unused charger. It just wasn't on the ground floor, that's all.

She glanced at the stairs leading to the first floor.

There were places in this house she almost never went. Not because he forbade her, but because that's how it was. Correspondingly, he hardly ever entered her sewing room. They had their own interests, their own oases, and their own time to spend alone, albeit his freedom was the greater.

She sat the child on her hip and went up the stairs, pausing at the door of his office. If she found the box with the charger in one of his drawers or cupboards, how would she then explain her presence in his domain?

She pushed open the door.

In contrast to her own room across the landing, his was devoid of all energy, lacking the zest of color and creative thought so characteristic of her own space. This was a place of gray and off-white surfaces, and very little else.

She opened the built-in cupboards one by one, staring in at what amounted to nothing. Had the cupboards been hers, she would have been overwhelmed by tearstained diaries and accumulated mementoes, collected and saved to remind her of happy days in the company of friends.

But on the shelves here were only a few books piled up in small stacks. Books to do with work. Books on firearms and policing, that sort of thing. And then a pile on religious sects. On the Jehovah's Witnesses, the Children of God, the Mormons, and others she had never heard of. Odd, she thought briefly, before standing on tiptoe to see whatever might be on the top shelves.

There was hardly a thing.

She opened the desk drawers one by one. Apart from a gray sharpening stone of the kind her father always used to hone his fishing knife, nothing caught her attention. The drawers contained paper, rubber stamps, and a couple of unopened boxes of floppy disks for the computer, the kind no one used anymore.

She closed the door behind her, all her emotions frozen. At this moment she knew neither her husband nor herself. It was frightening and unreal at the same time. Like nothing she had experienced before.

She felt the child's head loll on her shoulder, his breath steady against her neck.

"Oh, Mummy's little boy. Did you fall asleep?" she whispered as she laid him down in his cot. She had to be careful not to lose control now. Everything had to proceed as normal.

She picked up the phone and called the day care. "Benjamin has a cold; it wouldn't be fair to the others if I brought him in today. Sorry for leaving it so late," she said mechanically, forgetting to say thanks when the day-care assistant wished him a speedy recovery.

That done, she turned toward the landing and stared at the narrow door between her husband's office and their bedroom. She had helped him lug box upon box of stuff up the stairs into that little room. The main difference between the two of them had been one of ballast. She had come from her student accommodation with an absolute minimum of lightweight furniture from IKEA, whereas he came with everything he had amassed during the twenty years that made up the age gap between them. That was why their home was a jumble of furniture styles from different periods, and the room behind the door was filled with packing cases whose contents remained a mystery to her.

She almost lost heart as soon as she opened the door and peered inside. Though the room was less than a meter and a half in width, the space was still sufficient to contain packing cases stacked three wide and four high. She managed to peer over the top and could see the Velux skylight at the other end. In total, there were at least fifty boxes.

"Mainly stuff belonging to my parents and grandparents," he had said. A lot of it could be chucked out once they got sorted. He was an only child, so no one else would kick up a fuss.

She stood staring at the wall of boxes, feeling overwhelmed. It wouldn't make sense to keep a charger in there. This was a room for the past.

But then again . . . Her eyes settled on the overcoats that had been thrown into a heap on top of the rearmost boxes. Were they covering something? Might what she was looking for be hidden underneath?

She reached as far as she could but to no avail. Eventually, she pulled herself up onto the cardboard mountain, dug in with her knees, and managed to crawl forward a little. She tugged at the coats, only to discover with disappointment that they concealed nothing. And then her knee went through the lid of the packing case on which most of her weight was resting.

Shit, she thought to herself. Now he would know she had been up to something.

She wriggled backward, pulled the flap up, and noted that no damage had been done.

That was when she saw the newspaper cuttings inside. They weren't that old, hardly something her husband's parents had been saving. It was odd that he should have gathered together so many cuttings, but perhaps it was part of some hobby of his that had since been forgotten.

"Just as well," she muttered under her breath. But what possible interest could he have in articles about Jehovah's Witnesses?

She sifted through them. The material was by no means as homogeneous as she had first thought. Among articles on various sects, there were also cuttings about stock prices and market analyses, DNA tracking, even fifteen-year-old ads and prospectuses for holiday cabins and weekend homes for sale in Hornsherred. It was hard to imagine what use he could have for it all now. Maybe she ought to ask him if it wasn't about time they got this room sorted out. The space would make an excellent walk-in wardrobe, and who wouldn't like one of those?

She slid down from the packing cases with a sense of relief. Now she had a new idea in mind.

Just to make sure, she allowed her gaze to pass over the cardboard landscape one more time, finding no reason to be worried about the slight dent her knee had made in the box in the middle. He wouldn't notice anything.

And then she closed the door.

The idea was that she would buy a new charger. She would do it now, using some of the housekeeping money she had been putting aside unbeknown to her husband. She would cycle to the Sonofon store on Algade and buy a new one. And when she got home, she would make it look used by rubbing it in Benjamin's sandpit so that it became scuffed and scratched, and then she would put it in the basket in the hall with Benjamin's beanie hat and mittens, and produce it next time her husband asked.

Of course, he was going to wonder where it had come from, and she would naturally be perplexed that he should wonder so. And then she would suggest that perhaps it had been left behind by someone visiting, and that it might not be theirs at all.

She would recall the occasions other people had been in the house. It had been known to happen, though not for some considerable time now.

There was the meeting of the residents' association. Benjamin's health visitor. In theory, certainly, someone could quite conceivably have left a phone charger behind, even if it did seem a bit odd, because who on earth would have such a thing with them in someone else's house?

She could easily pop out and buy a new one while Benjamin was having his afternoon nap. She smiled quietly at the thought of her husband's astonishment when he asked to see the charger and she would pick it out from among the mittens in the basket. She repeated the sentence over and over in her mind so as to give it the right weight and emphasis.

"What do you mean it's not ours? What an odd thing to happen. Someone must have left it behind. One of the guests from the christening, perhaps?"

It was a straightforward explanation. Simple, and so unlikely as to be foolproof.

8

If Carl had ever been in doubt as to whether Rose could keep a promise, he certainly wasn't now. Hardly had he presumed to raise his weary voice in protest against her preposterous project of deciphering the message in the bottle than her eyes grew wide and she announced that in that case he could take his sodding bottle, regardless of it being in pieces, and shove it up his fucking arse.

Before he even had time to protest further, she had slung her scruffy bag over her shoulder and stormed off. Even Assad was in a state of shock, standing for a moment as though nailed to the floor, a hunk of grapefruit jammed between his teeth.

And thus they remained in silence for quite some time.

"I wonder if she really will send her sister," Assad finally ventured. His lips moved in slow motion, returning the grapefruit inelegantly to his hand.

"Where's your prayer mat, Assad?" Carl growled. "Be a sport and pray it doesn't happen."

"A sport?"

"A mate, a good bloke, Assad."

Carl gestured for him to step closer to the gigantic blowup that covered the partition wall. "Come on, we'll get this out of the way before she gets back."

"We?"

Carl nodded in acknowledgment. "You're right, Assad. Best you do it yourself. Move it all on to the other wall next to your string and all those cases you've been sorting out. Just make sure there's some space in between, OK?"

Carl sat for a while, considering the original message with a certain degree of attention. Though it had by now passed through a number of hands, and not all of them had treated the material as possible evidence in a criminal investigation, it never even occurred to him not to bother wearing his white cotton gloves.

The paper was so very fragile. Sitting alone with it now gave rise to a quite singular feeling. Marcus called it instinct. In Bak's terminology it was "nous." His soon-to-be ex-wife would say it was intuition, a word she could hardly pronounce. But whatever the fuck it was, this little handwritten letter set all his senses alight. Its authenticity was glaringly obvious. Penned in haste, most likely on a poor surface. Written in blood with the aid of some indeterminable instrument. A pen, dipped in blood? No, the strokes seemed too irregular for that. In some places it was as if the writer had pressed too hard, elsewhere not hard enough. He picked up a magnifying glass and tried to get a feeling for the paper's irregularities, but the document was simply in too poor a state. What once had been an indentation the damp had most likely turned into a blister, and vice versa.

He saw Rose's brooding face in his mind's eye and put the document aside. When she returned in the morning, he would give her the rest of the week to grapple with it. Then if nothing transpired, they would have to move on.

He thought about getting Assad to brew him a cup of that sickly sweet goo of his, only to deduce from the mutterings in the corridor that he hadn't yet finished cursing over having to run up and down the ladder and keep shifting it all the time. Carl wondered whether he should tell him that there was another ladder exactly the same in the storeroom next to the

Burial Club, but frankly he couldn't be arsed. The man would be finished in an hour anyway.

Carl stared at the old case file concerning the arson in Rødovre. Once he had read through it one last time, he would have to kick it upstairs to the chief so he could file it on top of the alp of cases that already towered on his desk.

An arson in Rødovre in 1995. The newly renovated tiled roof of a select whitewashed premises on Damhusdalen had suddenly collapsed in on itself and the blaze had consumed the entire upper floor in seconds. In the smoldering ruins a man's body had been found. The owner of the property had no idea whose corpse it was, though a couple of neighbors were able to confirm that lights had been on in the attic windows all night. Since the body remained unclaimed, it was assumed the victim had been some intruding derelict who had failed to exercise proper care with the gas appliance in the kitchenette. Only when the gas company informed police that the main line into the house had been shut off was the case turned over to the Rødovre Police's homicide section, where it languished in the filing cabinet until the day Department Q was brought into being. There, it might quite conceivably have led an equally anonymous existence had it not been for Assad latching on to that groove in the bone of the little finger on the victim's left hand.

Carl reached for his phone. He pressed the number of the homicide chief, only to wind up with the misery-inducing voice of Ms. Sørensen instead.

"Very briefly, Ms. Sørensen," he began, "how many cases—"

"Is that you, Mørck? Let me put you through to someone who doesn't cringe at the mention of your name."

One of these days he would make her a gift of some lethally poisonous animal.

"Hello, darling," came the sound of Lis's buoyant voice.

Thank Christ for that. Apparently, Ms. Sørensen was not entirely lacking in compassion.

"Can you tell me how many victims have actually been identified in these recent arsons? In fact, how many arsons have we got now, altogether?"

"The most recent, you mean? There are three, and we've barely established the identity of one of them."

"Barely?"

"Well, we've got the first name from a medallion he was wearing, but apart from that we don't actually know who he is. We might even be wrong on the first name."

"OK. Tell me again where the fires were."

"Haven't you read the files?"

"Only sort of." He exhaled sharply. "One of them was in Rødovre in 1995, I know that. And you've got, what . . . ?"

"One last Saturday on Stockholmsgade, one the day after in Emdrup, and the last one so far in the Nordvest district."

"Stockholmsgade? Sounds upmarket. Do you happen to know which of the buildings was most damaged?"

"Nordvest, I think. The address was Dortheavej."

"Has any link been established between these fires? What about the owners? Renovation work? Neighbors noticing lights on in the night? Terrorism?"

"None, as far as I know. There's loads of people on the case, though. You should ask one of them."

"Thanks, Lis. And I would, but it's not my case, is it?"

He added some resonance to his voice in the hope of making an impression, then dropped the folder back on the desk. Seems like they know what they're doing, he thought to himself. But now there were voices in the corridor outside. Most likely those fucking sticklers from Health and Safety had come back to have another go at them.

"Yes, his office is just there," he heard Assad's traitorous voice croak.

Carl fixed his eyes on a fly buzzing around the room. If he timed it right, he might be able to swat it in the face of that obsequious worm from Health and Safety.

He positioned himself behind the door with the Rødovre folder raised at the ready.

But the face that appeared was one he had never seen before.

"Hello," the visitor said, extending a hand. "Yding's the name. Inspector. Copenhagen West, Albertslund."

Carl nodded. "Yding? Would that be your first name or last?"

The man smiled. Maybe he wasn't sure himself.

"I'm here about these latest arsons. It was me who assisted Antonsen in the Rødovre investigation in 1995. Marcus Jacobsen said he wanted to be briefed in person. He told me to have a word with you so you could introduce me to your assistant."

Carl heaved a sigh of relief. "You just met him. He's the one climbing about on the ladder out there."

Yding narrowed his eyes. "The guy I just spoke to, you mean?"

"Yeah. Won't he do? He took his exams in New York, then all sorts of special training with Scotland Yard in DNA and image analysis."

Yding rose to the bait and nodded respectfully.

"Assad, come here a minute, will you?" Carl yelled, taking a sudden swat with the Rødovre folder at the fly.

He introduced Yding and Assad to each other.

"Are you finished putting those photocopies up?" he asked.

Assad's eyelids drooped. Enough said.

"Marcus Jacobsen tells me the original file on the Rødovre case is with you," said Yding as he shook Assad's hand. "He said you'd know where it was."

Assad pointed toward the folder in Carl's hand at the same instant that Carl was about to have another go at the fly. "That's it there," he said. "Was that all?" He was most certainly not on form today. All that carry-on with Rose had put a damper on him.

"The chief was just inquiring about a detail I couldn't quite recall. Do you mind if I have a quick look through the file?"

"Feel free," said Carl. "We're a bit busy here, so perhaps you'll excuse us while you're at it?"

He dragged Assad across the corridor and sat down at his desk beneath a poster showing some sandy ruin. It read *Rasafa,* whatever that was.

"Is that furnace of yours on the go, Assad?" he asked, pointing to the tea urn.

"You can have the last cup, Carl. I'll make fresh for myself." He smiled, his eyes lighting up in gratitude.

"As soon as What's-his-face has cleared off again, you and I are going out, Assad."

"Where to?"

"Nordvest. To see a building that's been all but burned to the ground."

"But that's not our case, Carl. The others will be angry with us."

"To begin with, maybe. But it'll blow over."

Assad looked anything but convinced. Then his expression changed. "I have found another letter in our message," he announced. "And now I have a very bad suspicion, too."

"You don't say. What is it, then?"

"Now I won't tell you. You will only laugh."

That sounded like the best news he'd had all day.

"Cheers, thanks," said Yding. He was poking his head around the door, his eyes fixed on the cup decorated with dancing elephants from which Carl was drinking. "I'll pop this up to Jacobsen, if that's all right with you?" He held up a couple of documents in his hand.

They both nodded.

"Oh, and by the way, I said I'd say hello from an acquaintance of mine. I bumped into him just now in the cafeteria. Laursen, from Forensics."

"Tomas Laursen?"

"That's him, yeah."

Carl frowned. "But he won ten million in the lottery and packed it all in. Sick and tired of dead bodies, that's what he used to say. What's he doing here? Back in the bunny suit, is he?"

"Sadly, no. Forensics could certainly do with him. The only funny garment he's got on now is an apron. He's working in the cafeteria."

"That's a joke, right?" Carl pictured the brick shithouse of a rugby player in his mind's eye. If the slogan on that apron didn't say something masculine along the lines of *BIG DADDY'S SWEAT RAG*, it would be a comical sight indeed. "What happened? I thought he'd invested in companies all over the shop."

Yding nodded. "He did. And got cleaned out. Bit of a downer, I'd say."

Carl shook his head incredulously. That's what you got for trying to be sensible. It was a good thing he didn't have a penny himself.

"How long's he been back?"

"About a month, so he said. Don't you ever eat in the cafeteria?"

"Do I look like a half-wit? There are ten million stairs to that soup kitchen from down here. I suppose you noticed the lift's out of order?"

The number of businesses and institutions that had not at some point been based somewhere along the six-hundred-meter stretch of tarmac that was Dortheavej could be counted on the fingers of one hand. At present, the street housed crisis support centers, a recording studio, a driving school, arts and cultural activity centers, ethnic associations, and lots more besides. A former industrial neighborhood, seemingly indomitable, unless razed to the ground as in the case of K. Frandsen Wholesalers.

The bulk of the clearance work had been completed in the yard, but the work of the investigation unit had barely begun. Several colleagues walked past without even a nod, but Carl wasn't surprised. He took this to be a sign of envy, knowing deep down that it probably wasn't. It didn't matter, because he didn't give a shit.

He stood in the middle of the courtyard in front of the entrance to the building and scanned the remains. It was hardly the kind of construction on which a preservation order would be slapped, but the galvanized fencing that surrounded the place was new. A glaring contrast.

"I have seen this kind of thing in Syria, Carl. The paraffin stove overheats, then *boom* . . ." Assad mimed an explosion with his hands in the air.

Carl gazed up at the first floor. It looked like the roof had lifted and then fallen into place again. Broad fingers of soot extended halfway up the fiber-cement roof cladding from beneath the eaves. The skylights had been blasted to smithereens.

"This didn't take long," he mused, then pondered on what might possess anyone to voluntarily spend even the briefest amount of time in such a charmless and godforsaken place as this. But maybe that was the operative word. Maybe it hadn't been voluntary at all.

"Carl Mørck, Department Q," he announced to a passing investigator of the younger generation. "Mind if we have a look? Are the SOCOs done?"

The lad gave a shrug. "I don't think anyone's going to be done here until the fucking place has been pulled down," he said. "But mind where you're going. We've put boards down to stop anyone going through the floor, but there's no guarantee."

"K. Frandsen Wholesalers? What did they import?" Assad inquired.

"All sorts of stuff for the printing business. All on the level," said the investigator. "They had no idea someone had occupied the attic, so everyone who works here was pretty shocked. They were lucky the whole place didn't go up in smoke."

Carl nodded. Firms of this kind ought always to be located within six hundred meters of a fire station, like this one. By some stroke of luck, the local fire services had survived the idiotic tendering exercise enforced on the public authority by the EU.

As expected, the entire first floor was wiped out. The sheets of plasterboard used to clad the sloping ceilings hung in tatters, and the partition walls that remained upright were jagged peaks reminiscent of the iron constructions of Ground Zero. It was a world laid waste, black with soot.

"Where was the body?" Carl asked an older man who introduced himself as a representative of the insurance company's own fire investigation team.

The insurance man indicated a stain on the floor, an obvious answer to the question.

"It was a violent explosion, staggered in two separate blasts with only the briefest interlude between," the man explained. "The first sparked off the blaze, the second drained the room of oxygen and put it out again."

"So we're not talking about the usual relatively slow-burning fire where the victim dies of carbon monoxide poisoning?" Carl said.

"No."

"Could the man have been rendered unconscious by the first explosion, do you think? And then simply have burned to death in the flames?"

"I can't say. The remains are so few I wouldn't like to hazard a guess. It's unlikely we'll find anything left of the respiratory passages in a case like this, so chances are we're going to be in the dark as to levels of soot concentration in the lungs and trachea." He shook his head. "It's hard to believe the body could be so badly damaged in such a short space of time in this particular fire. I mentioned it to your colleagues over in Emdrup the other day."

"What are you getting at?"

"Well, my take was that the fire had been arranged so as to hide the fact that the victim had died in a different blaze altogether."

"You mean the body was moved? What did they say to that?"

"They were in complete agreement, as far as I could tell."

"So we're dealing with a murder here? A man is murdered, incinerated, and then moved to another fire."

"Well, we don't actually know that he was murdered in the first instance at all. But otherwise, I'd consider it highly likely that the body had been moved here. I just can't see how such a short-lived blaze, albeit a very violent one, could do that kind of damage to a human body. I mean, we're talking skeleton here."

"Have you investigated all three fire scenes?" Assad asked.

"I could have done in principle, as I work for more than one insurance company, but Stockholmsgade was given to a colleague of mine."

"Were the other fire scenes similar to this one?" Carl asked. "I'm thinking about the actual spaces in which the fires were started."

"No, apart from them all being unused areas. Hence the suggestion that the victims were homeless."

"You think all the fires are the same? That all the dead bodies were put inside an empty room and then burned all over again?" Assad inquired.

The insurance man considered this unusual investigator with an unruffled stare. "I think we can proceed from that assumption, yes."

Carl lifted his gaze and looked up at the blackened collar beams. "I've got two questions for you, and then I won't take up any more of your time."

"Fire away."

"Why the two explosions, why not just let the whole place burn to the ground following the first? Any ideas?"

"The only thing I can think of is that the arsonist wanted to limit the extent of the damage."

"Thanks! My second question is, can we call you if we have any further questions?"

The man smiled and produced a business card. "Of course. My name's Torben Christensen."

Carl fumbled around in his pocket for a card of his own, fully aware that none existed. This would be another job for Rose when she came back.

"I do not understand." Assad stood slightly detached, drawing lines in the soot that covered the sloping wall. Apparently, he was the type who with just the smallest dab of paint on his finger could succeed in getting it all over his clothes as well as on just about every object in his immediate surroundings. At any rate, his face and clothing were now smeared in enough soot to cover a medium-size dining table. "I do not understand the significance of what you are talking about. It must all hang together. The ring on the finger, or the finger that is no longer, and then the bodies and the fires, and everything else as well." He turned abruptly to face the insurance investigator. "How much money does the company want from you for this place? It is a shitty, old place."

The insurance man wrinkled his brow. The idea of insurance swindle had now been duly presented, though he was by no means necessarily in agreement. "True, the building itself is somewhat lacking, but the company is certainly entitled to be compensated. We're talking about fire insurance here. As opposed to coverage for rot and fungus."

"How much?"

"Oh, somewhere in the region of seven, perhaps eight hundred thousand kroner, I'd say."

Assad whistled. "Will they rebuild on top of the damaged ground floor?"

"That would be entirely up to the policyholders."

"So they can pull it all down if that is what they want?"

"Certainly."

Carl looked at Assad. He was definitely on to something.

As they walked back to the car, Carl got the feeling that they were about to blindside their opponent on the very next bend, and that this time the opposition was not the usual villain but the Homicide Division of the Copenhagen Police.

What a triumph it would be to get an advantage over them.

Carl nodded aloofly to the investigators who were still assembled in the courtyard. Why should he even give them the time of day?

Whatever he and Assad needed to know, they could find out for themselves.

Assad stopped for a moment to decipher a row of graffiti: green, white, black, and red letters daubed across an otherwise neatly rendered wall.

Israel out of Gaza Strib. Palestine for the Palestinians, it read.

"They cannot spell," Assad commented as he got into the car.

Wonders never cease. I didn't think you could, either, Carl thought, but kept it to himself.

He started the car and glanced at his assistant, whose gaze was now firmly fixed on the dashboard. Assad was somewhere very far away.

"Hey, Assad, anyone home?"

His eyes didn't flinch. "Yes, I am right here, Carl," he said.

After that, not a word passed between them until they were back at Police HQ.

9

The windows of the little congregation hall were glowing like molten metal. So the cretins were well under way.

He pulled off his coat in the vestibule, greeted the so-called unclean menstruating women who stood listening to the exalted songs of praise from outside, and then entered as discreetly as he could through the double doors.

The meeting had reached the point where excitement mounted toward a climax. He had been there before, several times, and the ritual was always the same. The pastor was standing in his homemade vestments at the altar performing the Comfort, as they called the Eucharist. Shortly, everyone, children and adults alike, would rise on his command and shuffle together, converging in their lily-white robes, heads bowed.

This communion every Thursday evening was the highlight of the week. Here, the congregation received the bread and the wine from the Mother of God, personified in the pastor. Presently, those assembled here in the Mother's Hall would break into joyous dance and cascading words of praise for the Mother of God, who with the help of the Holy Spirit gave life to the Lord Jesus Christ. Their voices would overflow with the gift of tongues, they would pray for all the unborn children, embrace each other warmly, and recall the sensuality with which the Mother of God had abandoned herself to the Lord, and lots more in the same vein.

It was drivel, all of it, like everything else that went on in here.

He tiptoed quietly to the far end of the room and stood against the wall.

People smiled at him devoutly. The smiles told him everyone was welcome here. And in a few moments, when the congregation had gone into raptures, they would offer thanks for his coming to them in his yearning for the Mother of God.

In the meantime, he watched the family he had selected. Mother, father, and five children. Families were seldom smaller in these circles.

The father stood partly hidden behind the two boys, and in front of them the three girls swayed rhythmically from side to side, their long hair untied and flicking with their movement. Foremost among the women stood their mother, with lips parted, eyes closed, and hands loosely holding her breasts. All the women were standing like this. Lost to the world, pitching in the collective consciousness, trembling in the presence of the Mother of God.

The majority of the young women were pregnant. One, seemingly as close to giving birth as was possible, had lactated through her robes, which now were stained with her milk.

The men looked upon these fertile women in rapt submission. Apart from when she was menstruating, a woman's body was the most hallowed of objects for any disciple of the Mother Church.

In this assembly of fertility worshippers, the adult males stood with hands folded at their crotches, the smaller boys giggling and trying to imitate them, presumably possessing barely the slightest insight into what it was all about. They sang and did as their parents did. The thirty-five people in the congregation were as one. This was the togetherness so elaborately detailed in the Mother's Decree.

Togetherness in their faith, in their belief in the Mother of God, the very foundation of life itself. . . . He had heard it all until he was sick to the back teeth.

Each sect its own unassailable, unfathomable truth.

He watched Magdalena, the second of the family's three girls, as the pastor flung bread at the closest members of the congregation and jabbered in tongues.

The girl seemed far away, immersed in thought. Was she thinking of the Eucharist? Or of what she was hiding in the garden at home? Perhaps her mind was on the day they would initiate her as a servant of the Mother, when they would undress her and douse her in fresh sheep's blood? Or the day they would select a husband for her and sing praise to her womb that it might bear fruit? It was hard to tell. What goes on in the mind of a twelve-year-old girl, anyway? Only she would know. Perhaps she was frightened, and no wonder if she was.

Where he came from, it was the boys who had to pass through initiation rites, obliged to relinquish their free will, hopes, and dreams to the Church. They were the ones who bore the brunt. He remembered it all too well. All too well indeed.

Here, though, it was the girls.

He tried to catch Magdalena's eye. Perhaps her mind was on whatever it was she was hiding in the garden, after all? Perhaps the thought of this unmentionable secret niggled at forces within her that were stronger than her faith?

Most likely she would be harder to break than her brother. And for that reason, he was as yet uncertain which of them he would choose.

Which one he would kill.

He had waited an hour before breaking into the house, after the family had left for worship and the March sun had settled into the horizon. It had taken him only two minutes to unlatch a window in the main house and wriggle into the bedroom of one of the children.

The room he broke into belonged to the youngest of the girls. That much was immediately obvious to him. Not because it was pink, or because the sofa was strewn with small cushions embroidered with hearts. Quite the opposite. In this room there were no Barbie dolls, or pencils with teddy bears on the ends, or little shoes with ankle straps under the bed. In this room there was absolutely nothing that might be considered to reflect a normal ten-year-old girl's outlook on either herself or the world around her. The only thing to indicate that the room indeed belonged to the youngest sister was the christening gown on display on the wall. Such was the tradition of the Mother Church. The christening gown was the swaddling cloth of the Mother of God, to be treasured and passed down to the next-born girl, who was obliged to protect the gown with might and main. To brush it gently each Saturday before the hour of rest. To smooth its collar and lace when Easter came.

Fortune would smile upon the girl who treasured this holy cloth the longest. Indeed, not only would she find fortune in life, she would also be blessed with unusual happiness and joy. So it was said.

He went into the father's study and quickly found what he was looking for. Documents confirming the family's wealth, the annual appraisal specifying the Mother Church's assessment of each individual's place within it, and finally the contact lists that provided him with a new overview of the geographical distribution of the sect, both in Denmark and around the globe.

Since the last time he had struck within this particular movement, approximately one hundred new members had come to the fold in mid-Jutland alone.

It was not a pleasant thought.

Once he had checked all the rooms, he slid out of the window and pushed it back into place. He stared down the garden. Magdalena's little corner wasn't a bad spot at all in which to play. There she would be almost unseen from the main house and the rest of the garden.

He looked up at the blackening low-hanging cloud. It would soon be dark. He needed to get a move on.

He knew where to look, otherwise he would never have found it. Magdalena's hiding place was revealed only by a twig sticking up from the edge of a piece of turf. He smiled when he saw it, then carefully levered up the hand-size clod.

The hole was lined with a yellow plastic bag, and in it was a folded sheet of glossy paper.

He smiled when he unfolded it.

And then he put it in his pocket.

In the congregation hall, he stood for a long time watching this girl, with her long hair, and her brother Samuel, who was smirking defiantly. Here, they were safe among the congregation. Among people who would live on in ignorance, and those who very soon would be compelled to live with a knowledge that would be unbearable.

The terrible knowledge of what he was going to do.

When the singing was over, the worshippers surrounded him, caressing his head and face and upper body. This was how they expressed their delight in his seeking the Mother of God. This was how they repaid him for his trust, and all were enraptured, in transports of delight, for they had been blessed with the opportunity of showing him the way to eternal truth. Afterward, the flock stepped back and stretched its hands to the heavens. In a moment they would begin to caress one another with the palms of their hands. Their caresses would continue until one of them fell to the floor and allowed the Mother to enter her quivering body. He knew which of them it would be. The ecstasy of it all was already radiant in the woman's eyes. A slight, young woman whose greatest achievement in life was three fat children jumping up and down at her side.

Like all the others, he cried to the ceiling when it happened. The only difference was that he held back what everyone else with all their might now tried to release. The Devil within.

When the congregation eventually said their good-byes to one another on the steps outside, he moved imperceptibly forward and stuck out his foot, sending Samuel tumbling from the top step into empty space.

The crack that sounded as the boy's knee hit the ground was a release. Like the crack of a neck in a gallows.

Everything was right now.

From now on, he was in charge. From now on, it was all a foregone conclusion.

10

When he came home to Rønneholtparken on a night like this, with crap TV resounding through the concrete blocks and silhouettes of women in kitchen windows, he felt like a tone-deaf musician in a symphony orchestra unable to read music.

He still found it hard to grasp how things had come to this. Why he should feel so alone.

If a bookkeeper of ample waist and a computer nerd with upper arms like matchsticks could start families and make them work, why the hell couldn't he?

Reluctantly, he returned the wave of his neighbor Sysser, who was standing in the frigid light of her kitchen, frying something at the stove. Thank God she'd made her way back to her own place after that dodgy start on Monday morning. If she hadn't, he'd have been at his wits' end by now.

He stared dolefully at the nameplate on the door. There were new names on it now, besides Vigga's and his own. It wasn't that he felt a lack of company sharing these walls with Morten Holland, Jesper, and Hardy, and even as he stood there he could hear an inviting murmur of activity around the back. Perhaps they were a family of sorts, too.

Just not the kind he had dreamed about.

Normally, his sense of smell could inform him of the evening's menu the moment he stepped into the hallway. But what wafted into his nostrils now was not the aroma of Morten's culinary exertions. At least, he hoped not.

"All right?" he called into the front room, where Morten and Hardy were usually to be found. He put his head around the door. There wasn't a soul in sight. On the patio outside, however, it was all go. At the center, under the warmth of the patio heater, he could just see Hardy's bed with all his IV apparatus, and around it stood a crowd of neighbors in thermal jackets, stuffing themselves with grilled sausages and throwing bottled beer down their necks. By the gormless looks of them, they'd been at it for a couple of hours at least.

Carl tried to localize the foul odor that had assailed him as soon as he came in through the front door. His nostrils led him to a saucepan on the kitchen counter. The contents most of all reminded him of tinned food that had passed its sell-by date and been reduced to carbon on a glowing red hotplate. Most unpleasant. And a shame about the saucepan, whose future prospects were now decidedly dim.

"What's going on?" Carl inquired as he came out onto the patio, his eyes fixed on Hardy, who lay motionless under four duvets with a big grin on his face.

"Hardy's got some feeling back in a small area of his upper arm," Morten told him.

"So he says, yeah."

Morten looked like a boy who had just laid hands on his first dirty mag and was about to behold the contents. "So you know he's got a slight reflex in the index and middle fingers of one hand?"

Carl shook his head and glanced down at Hardy. "What is this, some kind of neurological guessing game? Just make sure it stops when we get to the nether regions, OK?"

Morten revealed wine-tinted teeth in a grin. "And two hours ago, he moved his wrist, Carl. Straight up. Made me forget I had dinner on the go!" He threw his arms wide with glee, revealing the full outline of his corpulent figure. He looked like he was about to leap into Carl's arms. Carl hoped he wouldn't.

"Go on then, Hardy, let's have a look," he said drily.

Morten pulled back the duvets to reveal Hardy's chalk-white skin.

"Come on, mate," Carl reiterated.

Hardy closed his eyes and clenched his teeth, his jaw muscles a clear indication of the extent of his exertion. It was as though he was commanding every impulse in his body along the nerves to this intensely monitored wrist. The muscles in his face began to quiver, and kept doing so for some time until eventually he was forced to exhale and capitulate.

A sigh ran through his audience, accompanied by various expressions of encouragement. But Hardy's wrist didn't move.

Carl gave him a comforting wink, then drew Morten toward the hedge.

"You've got some explaining to do, Morten. What's all this supposed to prove? You're responsible for him; it's your job, for Chrissake. Stop building the poor sod's hopes up. What is he, anyway, some kind of circus act? I'm going upstairs to slip into something more comfortable. In the meantime, you're sending everyone home and putting Hardy back where you found him, understand? We'll have a talk about this."

He wasn't in the mood for excuses. Morten could save them for the rest of the audience.

"Say that again," Carl said half an hour later.

Hardy's gaze was calm. He looked dignified, lying there. Two hundred and seven centimeters of life gone wrong.

"It's right enough, Carl. Morten didn't see it, but he was standing beside me. I moved my wrist. I've got a bit of pain, too. In my shoulder."

"How come you can't do it again, then?"

"I don't really know how I did it, but it was a controlled movement. Not just a spasm."

Carl put his hand on his crippled friend's brow. "From what I know, what you're saying is close to impossible. But OK, I believe you. I just don't know what to do about it, that's all."

"I do," said Morten. "Hardy still has this little area of his shoulder where he's got some feeling. That's where the pain's coming from. I think it needs stimulating."

Carl shook his head. "Hardy, are you sure this is a good idea? Sounds like bullshit to me."

"So what?" Morten intervened. "I'm here with him, so what harm can it do?"

"We'll run out of saucepans, for a start."

Carl glanced toward the hallway. One jacket short on the coat hooks again. "Won't Jesper be here for dinner?"

"He's with Vigga in Brønshøj."

That didn't sound right. What would he be wanting in that freezing garden shed? Besides, Jesper didn't get on with Vigga's new boyfriend. Not because the guy wrote poetry and wore thick-rimmed specs, more because he insisted on reading it out loud and being the center of attention.

"What's he doing there? He's not skipping school again, is he?" Carl shook his head in despair. The lad only had a couple of months to go before his final exams. With that pathetic new grading system and the government's miserable reform of upper secondary education, he would have to hang in there and at least pretend to be learning something, otherwise he'd be fucked.

Hardy interrupted his train of thought. "Relax, Carl. Jesper and I go through his homework together every day when he gets home from school. I test him before he goes off to see Vigga. The lad's doing all right."

Jesper doing all right? It sounded almost surreal. "Then what's he doing with his mother?"

"She called him and asked if he'd go and see her," Hardy replied. "She's not happy, Carl. She's fed up with her life and wants to come home again."

"Home? You mean *this* home?"

Hardy nodded. Carl had never felt closer to shock-induced collapse.

Morten had to bring the whisky twice.

The night was sleepless, the morning weary and subdued.

Carl was a lot more tired by the time he eventually sat down behind his desk at the office than he had been when he went to bed the night before.

"Any word from Rose?" he inquired as Assad put down a plate in front of him, on which were assembled lumps of some indeterminate substance. Apparently, the man was trying to pep him up a bit.

"I called her last night, but she was out. That is what her sister told me."

"You don't say." Carl wafted away his trusty old friend the fly and then endeavored to pick up one of the syrupy objects from his plate, only to find it surprisingly resistant. "Did this sister of hers say if she would be in today?"

"The sister, Yrsa, will come, but not Rose. Rose has gone away."

"What? Where's she gone? Her sister's coming, you say? Are you winding me up, Assad?" He extracted his fingers from the sticky fly trap on his plate. It felt like he lost skin in the process.

"Yrsa said Rose sometimes goes away for a day or two, but that we should not worry. Rose will return like she always does. This is what Yrsa told me. And in the meantime, Yrsa will come and look after Rose's job. They cannot afford to lose the money. This is what she said."

Carl tossed his head back. "You're kidding? So full-time employees can just swan off whenever it takes their fancy, eh? Not bad, is it? Rose must have lost her marbles." He would make sure to tell her as much in no uncertain terms as soon as she got back. "And this Yrsa! She won't get past the desk upstairs, not if I can help it."

"Oh, but I have already sorted this with the duty officer and Lars Bjørn, Carl. It's no problem. Lars Bjørn is not arsed, as long as her wages are still paid out to Rose. Yrsa is the temp while Rose is off sick. Bjørn is very happy we were able to find someone so quickly."

"Not arsed, you say? And Rose is off sick?"

"This is what we call it, am I right?"

It was tantamount to mutiny.

Carl picked up the phone and pressed Lars Bjørn's number.

"Hello, gorgeous," said Lis's voice on the other end.

What now?

"Hi, Lis. I'm trying to get through to Bjørn."

"I know. I'm taking his calls. He's in a meeting with Jacobsen and the commissioner about the staffing situation."

"Can you put me through? I just need to speak to him for five seconds."

"About Rose's sister, you mean?"

The muscles in his face tensed up. "This wouldn't by any chance have anything to do with you, would it?"

"Carl, you know I'm in charge of the temp lists."

As a matter of fact, he didn't.

"Are you telling me Bjørn gave the go-ahead for a temp to fill in for Rose, without asking me first?"

"Hey, take it easy!" she exclaimed in English, and snapped her fingers at the other end as though to wake him up from a stupor. "We're short-staffed. Bjørn's approving everything at the moment. You should see who we've got working in some of the other departments."

Her laughter did nothing to alleviate his frustration.

K. Frandsen Wholesalers was a limited company with equity amounting to little more than two hundred and fifty thousand kroner but whose value was estimated to be in the region of sixteen million. In the last financial year, ending in September, its paper stocks alone were set at eight million, so at first blush the company hardly seemed to be in financial difficulties. The only problem was that the company's clients were primarily weeklies and free newspapers, a sector that had taken a hammering during the current financial crisis. Which, as far as Carl could see, might well have impacted rather suddenly and with considerable force on K. Frandsen's coffers.

This line of inquiry became all the more interesting when similar pictures emerged for the companies owning the premises that had burned down in Emdrup and on Stockholmsgade. The firm in Emdrup, JPP Fittings A/S, turned over some twenty-five million kroner a year supplying mainly DIY stores and major timber outlets. Most likely a thriving business last year, and a struggling one now. The same seemed to be true of the Østerbro company, Public Consult, which earned its money generating tendering projects for leading firms of architects, and which had probably also felt the effects of hitting that nasty concrete wall called recession.

Besides the obvious vulnerability of all three companies in the present financial climate, however, they seemed to have little else in common. Different owners, different clients.

Carl drummed his fingers on the desk. What about the Rødovre blaze in 1995? Would that fit the picture? A business suddenly finding itself struggling against a headwind? This was where he needed Rose. Fucking woman.

"Knock, knock," said a husky voice at the door.

That'll be Yrsa, Carl thought to himself, glancing at his watch. It was a quarter past nine. She was even on time.

"What time do you call this?" he said with his back turned. It was something he had learned once. The boss who addressed minions with his back turned reigned supreme.

"I didn't know we had an appointment," a rather nasal male voice replied.

Carl whirled around in his chair so fast he carried on half a turn too far.

It was Laursen. Good old Tomas Laursen, forensics officer and rugby player. The man who won a fortune in the lottery, only to lose it again and end up working in the cafeteria on the top floor.

"Tomas. Fucking hell! What are you doing here?"

"Your kind assistant asked me down to say hello."

Assad put his cheeky face around the door. What was he up to? Had he really been upstairs to the cafeteria? Weren't his spicy specialties and culinary colon busters enough for him anymore?

"I popped up to buy a banana, Carl," Assad said, waving the curviform fruit in front of him. Who was he kidding? All the way to the top floor for a banana?

Carl nodded. Assad was a monkey. He'd known all along.

He and Laursen greeted each other with a handshake and squeezed as hard as they could. The same excruciatingly painful joke as always.

"Funny you should turn up, Laursen. I've just been hearing about you from What's-his-face, Yding from Albertslund. I gather your return to the madhouse isn't entirely voluntary?"

Laursen shook his head deliberately. "Well, it was my own fault, I suppose. The bank put one over on me, told me it was a good idea to borrow with a view to investment. The capital was there, so all I had to do was sign. And now there's fuck all left."

"They should cover your losses, the bastards," said Carl. He had heard it said on the news.

Laursen nodded. There was no doubt that he agreed, but here he was back again. Last man in. Buttering *smørrebrød* and washing up. One of the finest forensics officers on the force. What a waste.

"Still, I'm happy enough," he said. "I see a lot of people I know from when I was out in the field, without having to get back out there with them again." He smiled awkwardly, just like in the old days. "I got sick of it, Carl. Picking at corpses at all hours of the day and night. Not a single day went by the last five years when I didn't think of jacking it all in. So the money got me out, even if I did lose it all again. That's how I choose to look at it, anyway. Nothing's ever so bad as not to be good for something."

Carl nodded. "You won't know Assad, of course, but I'm sure he didn't drag you down here to discuss the cafeteria menu with an old colleague over a cup of peppermint tea."

"He told me about the message in the bottle. I think I got the gist of it. Can I see the letter?"

The crafty little—!

Laursen sat down as Carl gingerly removed the document from the folder. Assad came waltzing in with a chased brass tray with three minuscule cups on it.

The smell of peppermint thickened the air. "You will most definitely like this tea," said Assad as he poured. "It will do wonders for all sorts of things." He grasped his crotch and winked. The message was abundantly clear.

Laursen switched on another Anglepoise lamp and drew the light up close to the document.

"Do we know who preserved this?"

"A lab in Scotland," Assad replied. He produced the investigation sheet before Carl had even remembered where he had put it.

"The analysis is here." Assad placed it in front of Laursen.

"OK," said Laursen after a few minutes. "I see it was Douglas Gilliam who took care of business there."

"You know him?"

Laursen gave Carl the kind of look a five-year-old girl would when asked if she knew who Britney Spears was. Hardly respectful, but certainly enough to kindle Carl's curiosity. Who was this Douglas Gilliam when he was at home, apart from some bloke on the wrong side of the border with England?

"You're not likely to get very far on this," said Laursen, picking up his cup of peppermint tea between a thick finger and thumb. "Our Scottish colleagues seem to have done everything in their power to preserve the paper and recover the text by means of various forms of light treatment and chemicals. They've found minute traces of printer's ink, but as far as I can see nothing's been done to determine the origins of the paper itself. In fact, most of the physical investigation seems to be down to us. Have you run this through the Center of Forensic Services out in Vanløse?"

"No, but then I had no idea the technical investigations were incomplete," said Carl reluctantly. The mistake was his.

"It says so here." Laursen indicated the bottom line of the lab report.

Why the hell hadn't he noticed that? Shit!

"Actually, Carl, Rose did tell me this. But she did not think we needed to know where the paper came from," Assad chipped in.

"Well, on that count she was most certainly wrong. Let me have another look." Laursen got up and squeezed his fingers into his pocket. It was no easy task. Rugby thighs in tight jeans.

The type of magnifying glass Laursen now produced was one Carl had seen on many occasions. A small square that could be folded out to stand on top of the object. It looked like the lower part of a little microscope. Standard issue for stamp collectors and similar loonies, but the professional version, equipped with the finest of Zeiss lenses, was most certainly a must for a forensics expert such as Laursen.

He placed it on the document, muttering to himself as he drew the lens across the lines of mostly obliterated writing. He worked systematically from side to side, one line at a time.

"Can you see more characters through that glass?" Assad inquired.

Laursen shook his head but said nothing.

By the time he was halfway through the document, Carl was dying for a smoke.

"Just nipping out for a sec, OK?"

His words were hardly noticed.

He sat down on one of the tables in the corridor and stared blankly at all the equipment they had standing around idle. Scanners, copy machines, and the like. The thought annoyed him. Another time, he would have to make sure Rose finished what she was doing before she dropped everything and split. Poor leadership on his part.

It was at this very moment of painful self-awareness that a series of dull thuds suddenly came from the stairs, making him think of a basketball bouncing down a flight of steps in slow motion, followed by a wheelbarrow with a flat tire. He gawped as a person came toward him looking like a housewife who had just stocked up on duty-frees from the ferries that used to ply the Øresund to Sweden. The high-heeled shoes, the pleated tartan skirt, and the garish shopping cart she dragged in her wake all screamed the fifties more than the fifties probably ever did themselves. And at the upper extremity of this gangling individual was a clone of Rose's head topped with the neatest peroxide perm imaginable. It was like suddenly being in a film with Doris Day and not knowing how to get out.

In a situation like this, a person smoking a filterless ciggie will invariably end up burning his fingers.

"Ow, fuck!" he spluttered, dropping the end on the floor in front of the colorful newcomer.

"Yrsa Knudsen," she announced, extending a pair of fingers toward him, her nails painted as red as blood.

Never for the life of him would he have believed that twins could be so similar and yet so different.

He had reckoned on taking control from the word go, and yet here he was fawningly answering her inquiry as to the whereabouts of her office: "Down the corridor past all those sheets of paper flapping on the wall there." He completely forgot what he had been intending to say: his name and rank, and then a reprimand that the situation she and her sister had contrived was entirely against regulations and must cease forthwith.

"I'm expecting a briefing once I've got settled in. Let's say in an hour, shall we?" And off she went.

"What was that, Carl?" Assad asked as Carl stepped back into his office.

Carl glared at him. "I'll tell you what it was, Assad. It was a problem. More specifically, it was *your* problem. In an hour from now, I want you to put Rose's sister in the picture as to what's on our desk. Are you with me?"

"So that was Yrsa, the lady who walked past?"

Carl closed his eyes in confirmation. "Are you with me? You're going to brief her, Assad."

And then he turned to Laursen, who had now almost finished examining the document. "Anything turning up there?"

Laursen, forensics expert turned purveyor of French fries, nodded and indicated something invisible to the human eye that he had apparently placed on a microscope slide.

Carl stuck his head up close. OK, there did seem to be what looked like the tip of a hair, and next to it something tiny, round, and flat, and otherwise almost transparent.

"That's a splinter of wood," Laursen said, pointing at the hairlike fragment. "My guess is it came from the point of the writing instrument used by whoever wrote the letter. It was lodged quite deeply and lay in the direction of the pen. The other thing's a fish scale."

He straightened up from his rather awkward position and rolled his shoulders. "Perhaps we'll get somewhere with this after all, Carl. But we need to get it off to Vanløse first, OK? They should be able to determine the wood type relatively quickly, but finding out what kind of fish that scale belongs to is more likely a job for a marine scientist."

"Highly interesting," said Assad. "This is a very well-endowed colleague we have here, Carl."

Well-endowed? Did he really say that?

Carl scratched his cheek. "What more can you say about this, Laursen? Was there anything else?"

"Well, I can't tell whether the person who wrote it is right- or left-handed, which is quite unusual in cases where the paper is as porous as this. Usually, you can pick out raised areas all going in a certain direction. For that reason we might assume that the letter was written under difficult circumstances. Perhaps against an uneven surface, or with hands that were tied. Maybe just by someone unpracticed in writing. Besides that, my bet is that the paper was used to wrap fish in. As far as I can see, it's got traces of slime all over it, most likely from a fish. We know the bottle was watertight, so it won't be from having been in the sea. As for those shadowy areas there, I'm not sure. It could be nothing. Mold, perhaps, or more probably just stains from being inside the bottle."

"Interesting! What about the message itself? Do you think it's worth pursuing, or is it simply some prank?"

"A prank?" Laursen retracted his upper lip to reveal two slightly crossed front teeth. It did not mean he was laughing, but simply that whoever was listening would do well to prick up his ears. "I can see indentations in the paper showing the handwriting to be rather unsteady. The splinter we've got here drew a narrow, rather deep scratch across the paper until it broke off. In places it's so sharply done you'd think it was a groove on a vinyl LP." He shook his head. "So no, definitely not a prank. It looks more like it was written by someone whose hand was shaking. Again due to the circumstances, perhaps, but conceivably because the person was scared to death. So my instinct says yes, this is serious. Of course, you can never tell for sure."

At this point, Assad interrupted. "When you look so close at the letters and the scratches, can you see more letters?"

"One or two, maybe. But only up to where the point breaks off the writing instrument."

Assad handed him a copy of the message he and Rose had blown up and stuck to the wall in the corridor.

"Will you not then write the ones you think are missing here?" he said.

Laursen nodded and placed the magnifying glass against the original letter once again. After studying the first couple of lines for another few minutes, he said: "Well, this is my take on it, without putting my head on the block."

And then he added figures and letters of the alphabet, so that the first lines of the message now ran:

HELP

.he .6 febrary 1996 w. .... k..naped .. got .s .t the .us sdop on .aut.opv... i. Bal... u.—T.. man .. 18. t.ll ...h ...r. hair

They stood for a moment and considered the result until Carl broke their silence.

"February 1996! That means the bottle was in the sea for six years before it got caught up in that net."

Laursen nodded. "Yeah, I'm pretty sure about the year, but the nines were back to front."

"That'd be why the Scots couldn't work it out."

Laursen shrugged. Maybe.

Beside them, Assad stood frowning.

"What's up, Assad?" Laursen asked.

"It is just as I thought. Very bad shit, indeed," he sighed, indicating three of the words.

Carl scrutinized the letter.

"If we cannot find more characters in the last part of the letter, then our job will be very, very difficult," Assad went on.

And now Carl saw what he meant. Of all people on earth, it had fallen to Assad to recognize the full extent of the problem. A man who had lived in the country for no more than a few years. No one would credit it.

Febrary, kidnaped and *bus sdop.*

Whoever wrote the letter couldn't spell.

11

They hardly heard a peep from Yrsa in Rose's office. It was a good sign indeed. If she carried on like that, they could send her off home again in a couple of days and Rose would have to come back.

They needed the money, Yrsa had said.

Since the archive contained no information about any kidnapping in February 1996, Carl went back to the arson file and called up Antonsen, the superintendent out in Rødovre. Rather go to an old hand than an office boy like Yding. Why on earth the useless oaf hadn't made a note in the report about the financial state of the arson-hit Rødovre company was beyond his comprehension. In Carl's opinion it was tantamount to dereliction of duty. Moreover, the gas company had told them they had turned off the mains, so how come the place went up like it did? As long as questions like these were left dangling, anyone with a brain could see they were dealing with a possible murder, and in that case *everything* had to be considered.

"Well, here's a turnup for the books," said Antonsen when Carl's call was put through. "To what do we owe the honor of speaking to Carl Mørck himself, expert in blowing dust off antique case files?" he chuckled. "Have you found out who did away with the Grauballe Man?"

"Yeah, and we've nailed Jack the Ripper, too," Carl rejoined. "What's more, we might have one of your own cases cleared up soon. Looks that way, at least."

Antonsen laughed. "I know what you're getting at, I spoke to Marcus

Jacobsen only yesterday," he replied. "You'll be wanting to know about that fire in 1995, I suppose. Haven't you read the report?"

Carl repressed the urge to splutter some invective, knowing too well that Antonsen would respond in kind, swiftly and quite as incisively. "I have, yeah. And that report reads like something the cat dragged in. Would one of your lads be responsible?"

"Come off it, Carl. Yding did some fine work on that case. What do you need to know?"

"Details on the company that owned the premises. Important details completely ignored in this fine work Yding's supposed to have done."

"All right, I thought it might be something along those lines. And as it happens, we do have something here. There was an audit done on that firm a couple of years later, resulting in a charge being preferred against them. It never amounted to anything, but it did give us some more insight into their affairs. Do you want me to fax it over, or would you prefer me to come crawling and place it before your feet at the throne?"

Carl laughed. Colleagues who could parry Carl's bollockings as disarmingly as Antonsen were few and far between.

"I'm on my way over now, Anton. Get the coffee on."

Antonsen hung up with a groan.

Carl sat for a moment and stared at the flatscreen on the wall showing another of the news channel's endless loops on the shooting of Mustafa Hsownay, another innocent victim who happened to get in the way of the continuing gang war. Now, it seemed, police had given the go-ahead for his coffin to be paraded through the city streets. Certain jingoist flag-wavers he could think of would be choking on their bacon.

Then came a grunt from the door opening. "I'm waiting for something to do."

Carl gave a start. It wasn't the custom in the basement for people to go sneaking about without a sound. And if gangly Yrsa Knudsen could move with such stealth one minute and then sound like a herd of stampeding gnu the next, he was going to end up a nervous wreck in no time.

She swatted at something in the air. "Ugh, a fly. I hate those things, they're disgusting."

Carl followed the insect with his eyes and wondered what it had been up to since last time they'd seen each other. He picked up a case folder from the desk. Splattering time.

"I'm settled in now. Do you want to come and have a look?" Yrsa asked in a voice that sounded uncannily like Rose's.

Would he like to come and have a look? Nothing could interest him less.

For a moment he forgot all about his winged adversary and turned to face her.

"Did you say you needed something to do? Just as well, because that's why you're here. You can start by calling the Business Authority. Get them to send us the last five annual reports for K. Frandsen Wholesalers, Public Consult, and JPP Fittings A/S. Then have a look at their credit facilities and short-term loans. OK?" He wrote the three company names down on a piece of notepaper.

Yrsa looked at him as though he'd suggested something indecent. "I'd rather not, if you don't mind," she said.

This did not bode well.

"Why not?"

"Because it's a lot easier to do it online. Who wants to hang around on the phone all day?"

Carl struggled to ignore his ego crying for help from beneath the heel of her shoe. Maybe he should give her the benefit of the doubt.

"Carl, look at this," said Assad, appearing in the doorway, then stepping aside to allow Yrsa to get past.

"I have been studying it for a long time now," he went on, placing the photocopied letter on the desk in front of Carl. "What do you think? I found myself unable to escape the thought that it said 'Ballerup' there in the second line, and then I looked in the street atlas and searched through all the road names in Ballerup. I discovered that the only one to fit the word just in front of the 'i' is called Lautrupvang. The writer of the letter has written 'Lautrop' with an 'o,' but we know now that his spelling was very poor."

For a brief moment Assad's gaze locked on to the fly buzzing around below the ceiling. Then he looked at Carl.

"What do you think, Carl? Could it be like this?" He indicated the relevant passage in the photocopy. It now ran:

HELP

The .6 febrary 1996 we were kidnaped he got us at the bus sdop on Lautropvang in Ballerup—The man is 18. tall ...h ...r. hair

Carl nodded. It all seemed rather likely, no question about that. In which case, they should get their noses into the archive without delay.

"You nod, Carl. You think this is right. Oh, that is good," Assad exclaimed and almost threw himself over the desk to plant a kiss on Carl's forehead.

Carl recoiled and looked daggers at him. Sticky cakes and sweet tea were acceptable. But emotional outbursts of this Middle Eastern dimension was taking things to extremes.

"Now, we know the date to be either the sixteenth or the twenty-sixth of February in 1996," Assad went on unabashed. "We also know the place, and that the kidnapper is a man who is more than one hundred and eighty centimeters tall. Now we need the last words in the line, which are having something to do with his hair."

"Indeed, Assad. Plus the small matter of sixty-five percent of the rest of the letter," said Carl.

Apart from that, Assad's theory seemed to be sound.

Carl grabbed the document, jumped to his feet, and went out into the corridor to look at the blowup on the wall. If he had imagined Yrsa at this moment to be busy plowing through the annual reports of the three firms that had been hit by arson, he could think again. Here she was, standing in the middle of the corridor absorbing the magnified message in front of her.

"It's OK, Yrsa, this is something we're taking care of," said Carl. Yrsa didn't budge.

Cognizant of behavioral likenesses among twins, Carl elected simply to shrug and leave well alone. Sooner or later she would presumably succumb to a stiff neck, the way she was standing.

Carl and Assad stood next to her. Looking at Assad's suggested text and comparing it with the version on the wall, Carl found that faint and yet plausible corroborations, hitherto unseen, somehow seemed to present themselves.

In fact, Assad's take on the first few lines appeared more than credible.

"Well, it looks right to me," he said, then sent Assad off to check once again whether any crime had been reported that could even remotely be linked to a case of kidnapping on Lautrupvang in Ballerup in 1996.

Most likely Assad would be able to report back by the time Carl returned from Rødovre.

Antonsen was sitting in the cramped space of his office. The place reeked of banned pipe tobacco and cigarillos. No one ever saw him smoke, though undeniably he did. Rumor had it he remained on the job until the office staff went home just so he could light up in peace. It was years since his wife had proclaimed that he had finally stopped for good. Apparently, she was oblivious.

"Here's the report on the company on Damhusdalen," said Antonsen, handing him a plastic folder. "Like it says on the first page, they're an import-export company whose partners were registered in the former Yugoslavia. So they were probably faced with a difficult transition when the war broke out in the Balkans and everything fell apart at the seams.

"These days, Amundsen and Mujagic A/S is a flourishing business, but when it burned down, they hit bottom financially. At the time, we had no reason to believe the company was anything less than aboveboard, and that basically would still be our standpoint today. But if you've got anything to add in that respect, you're more than welcome."

"Amundsen and Mujagic. Mujagic's a Yugoslavian name, right?" Carl ventured.

"Yugoslavian, Croatian, Serbian. Same difference if you ask me. I don't think there's an Amundsen or a Mujagic left in the company these days. You can check if you want."

Carl rocked gently in his chair and considered the man opposite him.

Antonsen was an all-right policeman. He was a few years older than Carl and had always ranked above him, yet still they'd shared a lot of laughs and professional tussles, all of which had demonstrated that they were two of a kind.

Woe betide anyone who blew his horn at their expense. Moreover, they were both immune to all forms of bullshit, backslapping, and corridor gossip. If anyone on the force, at least in the capital region, was utterly unsuited to diplomacy, political maneuvering, or siphoning public funds to meet their own professional ends, it was Carl Mørck and Antonsen. Which was why Antonsen had never risen to commissioner and Carl had amounted to sod all. Neither of them gave a shit.

But now there was something niggling Carl. That fucking fire. And then, as now, Antonsen had been in charge of the shop.

"My feeling on this," said Carl, "is that the key to clearing up these recent arsons in Copenhagen lies in this blaze of yours in Rødovre. A body was found in the remains, and the bone of the little finger clearly indicated that the victim had worn a ring for a good many years. Exactly the same thing turns up again with the victims of these latest fires. So I need to know—and I want you to be frank with me on this, Anton—if you consider that case to have been properly handled at the time. I'm asking you straight out, you can tell me your answer and we'll leave it at that. But I need to know, in view of the way you led the investigation at the time, and with the officers you had on the job. Did you have any personal dealings with that company? Is there anything at all at any point in time that links you to Amundsen and Mujagic A/S?"

"Are you accusing me of acting unlawfully, Carl Mørck?" Antonsen's eyes narrowed, and all the joviality of earlier fell away.

"Not at all. I just can't fathom how your boys never got around to establishing with one hundred percent certainty the cause of the blaze and the identity of the body that was found in the ruins."

"So you're accusing me of obstructing my own investigation, is that it?"

Carl looked Antonsen in the eye. "If you put it that way, I suppose I am. Am I right? Because if I am, it means I've got something to go on."

Antonsen handed Carl a bottle of Tuborg, which Carl kept in his hand until they were finished talking. Antonsen gulped down a mouthful of his own.

The old fox wiped his mouth and thrust out his lower lip. "We weren't alarmed by the case, Carl, if truth be told. A roof fire and an unlucky tramp, that's how we looked at it. And to be honest, I suppose I allowed it all to slide. Not the way you're thinking, though."

"How come, then?"

"Because at the time, Lola was shagging someone else at the station, and I was drinking my way through the crisis."

"Lola?"

"Believe it or not, yes. But listen, Carl. She and I pulled through. It's all in the past, and everything's fine now. But I will concede that I ought to have been more on the ball in that particular case."

"OK, Anton. That's good enough for me. We'll stop here."

Carl stood up and glanced at Antonsen's pipe, lying there on its side like a boat stranded in a desert. In a moment or two, it would be sailing again. Office hours or not.

"Oh, hang on a sec," Antonsen said as Carl was halfway through the door. "One more thing. Remember last summer, that murder in one of the high-rises here in Rødovre? I said to you then that if you lot at HQ weren't nice to Samir Ghazi, I'd personally make sure you wished you'd never heard of me. Now I hear Samir's applying to come back to us." He picked up his pipe and began to stroke it. "What's the story there? Any idea? He's not saying a word to me, but as far as I understand it Jacobsen's been well pleased with him."

"He was your sergeant, wasn't he? I'm afraid I haven't got a clue. Hardly even know him."

"Well, I can tell you Department A are at a loss to understand it, too. Word is, though, that it has something to do with one of your lot."

Carl searched his mind. Why should it have anything to do with Assad? On the other hand, he'd been keeping away from Samir since day one. Why would Assad want to do that?

Now it was Carl's turn to thrust out his lower lip.

"Well, I'll ask around, but right now I wouldn't know. Maybe Samir just misses working with his old boss?" He gave Antonsen a wink. "Say hello to Lola for me, eh?"

He found Yrsa exactly where he had left her, in the middle of the corridor in front of Rose's enormous blowup of the message in the bottle. Her face was pensive, and she was standing with one leg drawn up under her skirt like a flamingo, as if in a trance. Apart from the clothes, it was Rose all over. It was enough to put the wind up a bloke.

"Have you been through those annual reports from the Business Authority?" he asked.

She glanced at him absently, tapping her forehead with a pencil. He was by no means certain she had even registered his presence.

He filled his lungs with air and discharged the question into her face for the second time. The batty woman gave a slight start, her only discernible reaction.

Just as he was about to turn and go, shaking his head in total bewilderment as to what the blazes he was supposed to do with these decidedly original sisters, she began to speak, softly and yet with such clarity he could hear every word.

"I'm good at Scrabble and crosswords and IQ tests and Sudoku, and I'm not bad at writing verse and occasional songs for confirmations and birthdays and wedding anniversaries. But this isn't working for me at all." She turned to face Carl. "Is it OK if you just leave me alone for a bit so I can have a think about this terrible letter?"

Was it OK? She'd been standing there all the time he'd been to Rødovre and back again, and now she wanted him to leave her alone? Seriously, she could pack her gear back in that eyesore of a shopping cart of hers and wheel her tartan robes and bagpipes and all the rest of her junk back to Vanløse or wherever the hell it was she came from.

"Listen, Yrsa," he said, trying as best he could to be nice. "Either you get those reports back to me in the next twenty-seven minutes, annotated with notes for my guidance, or else I'll have no option but to ask Lis from the third floor to write out a check on the spot for four hours of your totally superfluous presence here. In which case, you would be wise not to be banking on any pension scheme. Am I making myself clear?"

"My goodness, what a shitload of words, if you'll excuse my French." She beamed a smile at him. "Have I told you, by the way, how well that shirt suits you? Brad Pitt's got one exactly the same."

Carl cast a glance down at his checked monstrosity from the Kvickly supermarket. All of a sudden, he felt strangely homeless in the basement.

He withdrew into Assad's so-called office to find the man with his feet up on the top drawer and the phone stuck to the blue-black stubble on his face. In front of him were ten pens, most likely now missing from Carl's own office, and underneath them reams of paper filled with scribbled names and figures and Arabic friezes. He was speaking slowly and with remarkable clarity. His whole being exuded authority and composure, and in his hand was a Lilliputian cup of aromatic coffee. If Carl didn't know better, he'd think he was in a travel agent's office in Ankara, and the manager was in the process of chartering a jumbo jet for thirty-five oil sheiks.

Assad turned to face him and sent him a crinkly smile.

Apparently, he wanted to be left alone as well.

It was like an epidemic.

Perhaps the best thing in the circumstances would be a restorative snooze in his office chair. He could run a film on the inside of his eyelids about a fire in Rødovre and cross his fingers that the case had been solved by the time he opened them again.

He had just settled into place with his feet on the desk when this alluring and life-prolonging plan was interrupted by the sound of Laursen's voice.

"Is there anything left of the bottle, Carl?" he asked.

Carl blinked with surprise. "Bottle, what bottle?" Laursen's food-stained apron gradually came into focus, and Carl returned his feet to the floor. "The bottle, yeah. Well, there's three thousand five hundred pieces of it each the size of an ant's dick in a plastic bag in the cupboard here, if that's what you mean."

He produced the transparent bag, holding it up in front of Laursen's face. "Would that be any good to you?"

Laursen nodded and indicated a shard rather larger than the rest at the bottom of the bag.

"I just spoke to Douglas Gilliam, the forensics man from Scotland. He advised me to take the biggest piece remaining of the bottle end and then have a DNA analysis done on the blood traces. That must be it there. The blood's even visible."

Carl was about to ask if he could borrow Laursen's magnifying glass, but found he could see without it. The blood was hardly there, and what little there was looked completely impoverished.

"Didn't they do that themselves?"

"No, he says they only took samples from the letter itself. But he says we shouldn't reckon on finding anything."

"Why not?"

"Because there's so little of it to test, and because it's likely to be too old. Besides, the climate inside the bottle and all that time in seawater would be highly detrimental to the genetic material. Heat and cold, and then maybe a drop or two of salt water. The changing light. It all points to the DNA having perished."

"Does DNA change as it's broken down?"

"No, it doesn't change. It just deteriorates. But with all the adverse factors here, that might not make any difference in this case."

Carl considered the smidgeon of blood on the shard. "What if they do get a result? What good would it do us? We can't identify a body because we haven't got one. And we can't compare the genetic material with that of relatives because we don't know who they are. We don't even know who wrote the letter, so I can't see how it would help, to be honest."

"If we're lucky, we can determine skin color, eye color, and hair color. Worth a go, wouldn't you say?"

Carl nodded. Laursen was right, no two ways about it. The people at the Department of Forensic Medicine's Section of Forensic Genetics were amazing, he knew that. He had once attended a lecture given by the deputy head of the section. If anyone could determine whether the victim was lame, spoke with a lisp, or was a redheaded Greenlander from Thule, it was those guys.

"Let's give it a go," said Carl. And then he gave Laursen a pat on the back. "I'll be upstairs for a filet steak soon."

Laursen smiled. "You'll have to bring it with you, then."

12

Her name was Lisa, but she called herself Rachel. For seven years she had lived her life with a man who failed to make her pregnant. Weeks and months of infertility in mud huts, first in Zimbabwe, then in Liberia. Schoolrooms filled with wide ivory smiles lighting up the brown faces of the children, but also endless hours in negotiation with the local representatives of the NDPL and then eventually Charles Taylor's guerrillas. Praying for peace was no help. This was not a place for which a young teacher out of the DNS International Teacher Training College had been able to prepare. There were too many pitfalls and evil intentions, but such was Africa.

When she was raped by a passing group of NPFL soldiers, her boyfriend had not intervened. His passivity had forced her into taking matters into her own hands.

For that reason it was over.

The same evening, she had gone down on her bruised knees on the veranda and clasped her bloodied hands, and for the first time in her ungodly life she felt the kingdom of heaven to be truly at hand.

"Forgive me, and please let there be no reprisals," she prayed beneath the black sky of night. "Let there be no reprisals, and let me find a new life. A life of peace with a good man and many children. Please, God, I beg you."

The next morning, she was bleeding down below. She packed her suitcase and knew that God had heard her prayer. Her sins were forgiven.

Her rescuers came from a small, recently established religious community in the town of Danané in neighboring Ivory Coast. There they were all of a sudden, benevolent faces on the A701 highway, offering her shelter after two weeks of following refugees along the highway to Baobli and farther on beyond the border. These were people who had seen great hardship and who knew that wounds need time to heal. From that moment, a new life unfolded. God had heard her prayer, and God had shown her the way.

A year later, she was back in Denmark. Cleansed of the Devil and all his work, ready to find the man who would make her fertile.

His name was Jens, later to be called Joshua. Her body was rich temptation to a man who had lived alone in the farmhouse he had inherited from his parents and from which he carried on the family business, hiring out agricultural machinery and equipment. Jens discovered the way of God in ecstasy between her thighs.

Soon, the church on the edge of Viborg was two disciples richer, and ten months later she gave birth to their first child.

Since then, the Mother of God had given her new life and been merciful to her. Josef, eighteen years old, Samuel, sixteen, Miriam, fourteen, Magdalena, twelve, and Sarah, ten, were the fruits. Exactly twenty-three months between each.

The Mother of God took care of her own.

Now she had seen the new man on several occasions in the Mother Church, and he had looked so kindly upon her and her children when they abandoned themselves in their songs of praise. Only blessed words had passed his lips. He seemed honest and kind, and to possess a depth of soul and character. A rather handsome man who would surely attract a fine, new woman into the Church.

These were good signs, everyone agreed. Joshua called him worthy.

When he came to the church that evening, for the fourth time, she felt certain he had come to stay. They offered him a room in the farmhouse, but he declined, explaining that he was staying elsewhere and was in the process of looking for a house in which to settle. However, he would be in the area for a few days and would find it a pleasure to look in on them if he should happen to pass by.

So he was looking for a house, and this was the subject of much chatter in the Church, especially among the women. His hands were strong, he owned a van, and would be useful to his brethren. He appeared to be rather successful in life, and moreover was courteous and well dressed. A future pastor, perhaps. Or a missionary.

They would be especially accommodating toward him.

Only one day passed before he stood at their door. Unfortunately, it was a bad time. She was premenstrual and unwell, her head throbbing. All she wanted at that moment was for the children to be in their rooms and Joshua to attend to his business.

But Joshua opened the door and ushered the man through to the oak table in the kitchen.

"It might be the only chance we get," he whispered, entreating her to rise from the sofa. "Fifteen minutes, that's all, Rachel. Then you can lie down again."

With her thoughts on the Church and how welcome new blood would be, she stood up with her hand pressed against her abdomen and went out into the kitchen, confident in the belief that the Mother of God had meticulously chosen this moment to put her to the test. To let her know that her achings were but the touch of God's hand. That her nausea was little else but the scorching sand of the desert. She was a disciple, and nothing physical could stand in the way of that.

That was the whole point.

And so she came out to greet him, her pale face wearing a smile, and asked him to sit down and accept the gifts of the Lord.

He had been to Levring and Elsborg looking at cottages, he said from behind the steam rising from his coffee cup, and the day after tomorrow or Monday he would drive to Ranstrup and Resen to see a couple more that seemed promising.

"Lord Jesus be praised!" Joshua exclaimed with an apologetic glance in her direction. She disliked him taking His name in vain.

"Resen, you say?" he went on. "That wouldn't be on the way out toward Sjørup Plantation, would it? Theodor Bondesen's place? If it is, I can make sure you pay a fair price. It's been empty for eight months, at least. Longer, even."

An odd look passed faintly over the man's face. Joshua, of course, didn't notice. But she did. It was out of place.

"Sjørup?" the man repeated, and his eyes darted about the room, looking for something to fix on. "I'm not sure. But I'll be able to tell you more on Monday, once I've had a look at the place." He was smiling now. "What have you done with the children? Doing homework, I suppose?"

She nodded. He seemed to be uncommunicative somehow. Had she misjudged him? "Where are you staying now?" She wanted a straight answer. "Have you got somewhere in Viborg?"

"Yeah, with a former colleague of mine in the town center. We were reps together a few years back. He's on a pension now because of ill health."

"I see. Worn out, like so many these days?" she asked, catching his attention.

His eyes were kind again. It took a while, but perhaps he was just reticent by nature. That wouldn't necessarily be a bad thing.

"Worn out? No, though it would have been preferable. Charles lost his arm in a road accident."

He indicated the point of severance with the edge of his hand. Painful memories. He assessed her expression, then lowered his gaze. "A dreadful business, but he does all right for himself."

Then suddenly he raised his head. "Oh, by the way! There's a karate tournament going on in Vinderup the day after tomorrow. I was thinking perhaps I might ask Samuel if he'd like to come along. Or would it be too soon with that knee of his? He didn't break anything when he fell off those steps, did he?"

She smiled and glanced across the table at her husband. This was just the kind of care and feeling on which their Church was founded. Take the hand of thy neighbor and caress it with love, as their pastor always said.

"No, nothing broken," her husband replied. "His knee's swollen as thick as his thigh, but he'll be right as rain again in a couple of weeks. Vinderup, you say? I didn't know there was anything going on there." He stroked his chin. She could see he would pursue the matter presently. "We could see what Samuel says. What do you think, Rachel?"

She nodded. As long as they were back before the hour of rest it was fine by her. Perhaps he could take the other children along, too, if they wanted?

His expression became suddenly apologetic. "Well, I'd like to, of course, but I'm afraid there's only room for three on the front seat of the van, and it's against the law to take passengers in the back. But I'd be more than happy to take two of them along. The others could have their turn later, perhaps. What about Magdalena, would she like that, do you think? She seems like such an energetic young girl, and very attached to Samuel."

She smiled, her husband likewise. It was a fine observation, and so nice of him to ask. It felt almost like there was some special bond between them already. As though he knew how close to her heart the two of them had always been. Samuel and Magdalena. The two children who resembled her most.

"Well, I think that sounds marvelous, don't you, Joshua?"

"Indeed!" Joshua agreed. As long as no difficulty arose, he was easy enough to please.

She patted the hand of their guest that was placed flat against the table. And found it oddly cold to the touch.

"I'm sure Samuel and Magdalena would love to go," she said. "What time should they be ready?"

He pursed his lips and gauged the journey. "Well, the competition starts at eleven, so how about if I pick them up here at ten?"

After he had gone, the peace of God descended upon the house. He had drunk their coffee and afterward he had taken the cups from the table and rinsed them at the sink as though it were the most natural thing in the world. He had smiled and thanked them for their hospitality. And said how much he looked forward to seeing them again.

Her abdomen was aching still, but the nausea had gone.

Charity was such a wonderful thing. Perhaps the greatest of all God's gifts to man.

13

"It's not good at all, Carl," said Assad.

Carl had no idea what he was on about. One two-minute story on DR.'s Update channel about green bailouts to the tune of trillions and he was off in the land of nod.

"What's not good, Assad?" he heard himself say, from miles away.

"I have looked everywhere and now I am able to say with certainty that no incident of attempted kidnapping was reported at anytime in that place. Not for as long as any road called Lautrupvang has existed in Ballerup."

Carl rubbed his eyes. No, it wasn't good, Assad was right about that. Assuming the message in the bottle was on the level, that is.

Assad was standing in front of him with his trusty pocketknife stuck into a plastic tub covered with Arabic scribble and filled with some mystery foodstuff. He smiled in anticipation, dug out a dollop, and shoveled it into his mouth. Above his head, the faithful fly buzzed attentively.

Carl looked up. Maybe it was time he expended some energy on its extermination, he thought to himself.

He turned his head lazily in search of an appropriate murder weapon, finding it almost immediately on the desk in front of him. A battered bottle containing correction fluid, made of the kind of hard plastic flies most definitely did not survive collisions with.

It's all in the aim, he thought for a brief second before hurling the bottle toward the dratted insect and discovering the top hadn't been screwed on properly.

The splatter against the wall caused Assad to look up in perplexity at the white matter now slowly descending toward the floor.

The fly was nowhere to be seen.

"It's very odd," Assad muttered with his mouth still full. "All along I was thinking in my head that Lautrupvang was a place where people lived, but then I see that it is only offices and industry."

"So what?" said Carl, puzzling over what the smell of the mud-colored gunge in Assad's little tub reminded him of. Was it vanilla?

"Yes, offices and industry, you know," Assad went on. "What was he doing there, the person who claims he was kidnapped?"

"Presumably he worked there?" Carl suggested.

Assad's face contorted into an expression that could best be described as total skepticism. "Come on now, Carl. Think about it. He spelled so badly he could not even spell the name of the road."

"Maybe he just wasn't born into the language, Assad. Do you know the type?" Carl turned to his computer and entered the name of the road.

"Have a look here, Assad. There are all sorts of workplaces, schools, and colleges in that area. So there's bound to be any number of people of ethnic background around there during the daytime." He indicated one of the addresses on the screen. "Lautrupgård School, for instance. A school for kids with social and emotional difficulties. Maybe it was all just a sick joke, after all. Let's see once we've deciphered the rest of the message. It might turn out to be just a perverted way of nettling some poor sod of a teacher."

"Deciphering here and nettling there. Such words, Carl. But what if it is someone who worked for a firm there? The businesses are plenty."

"Yeah, but don't you think the firm would have reported it to the police if one of their employees went missing? I see where you're coming from, but we have to bear in mind that nothing even resembling the kind of crime mentioned in the message was ever reported. Are there any other streets of the same name anywhere else in the country?"

Assad shook his head. "You are saying perhaps that you do not think it to be the right kidnapping?"

"Something like that, yeah."

"I think you are mistaken, Carl."

"But listen, Assad. If there really was a kidnapping, what's to say whoever was kidnapped wasn't released again after a ransom was paid? It's conceivable, wouldn't you say? And then maybe it was all forgotten about. In which case, our investigations are going to lead us nowhere, right? Maybe only a very few individuals even knew about it."

Assad looked at him for a moment. "Yes, Carl. That is something we don't know. But we will never find out if you say we should not proceed with the case."

He turned and tramped off without another word, leaving his tub of goo and his pocketknife behind on Carl's desk. What the hell was the matter with him? Was it what he'd said about poor spelling and immigrants? He wasn't usually that sensitive. Or was he so wound up in the case he couldn't concentrate on anything else?

Carl cocked his head and listened to Assad's and Yrsa's combined voices in the corridor. Bellyaching, he shouldn't wonder.

Then he remembered Antonsen's question and got to his feet.

"Mind if I disturb you two turtle doves for a moment?" he quipped as he approached his two staff members, who were back in front of the blow-up on the wall. Yrsa had been standing there ever since she'd given him those annual reports he'd asked her for. Four or five hours that day, all in all, and not so much as an exclamation mark on the notepad she'd dumped on the floor in front of her feet.

"Turtle doves! You should let those thoughts of yours rotate a while inside your skull before opening your mouth and letting them out," said Yrsa, then turned once more toward the giant photocopy on the wall.

"Listen up a minute, would you, Assad? There's a superintendent over in Rødovre says he's received an application from Samir Ghazi. Apparently, Samir wants to go back there. Do you know anything about it?"

Assad looked at Carl as if he didn't know what he was talking about, but he was definitely on his guard. "Why should I know about that?"

"You've been avoiding Samir, haven't you? Maybe you're not the best of mates. Am I right?"

Was that an affronted look?

"I don't know this man, Carl. Not really. Perhaps he just wants to go back to his old job again." The smile that now appeared on his face was a tad too broad. "Maybe he can't take the pace and wants to get out of the kitchen?"

"Is that what I'm to tell Antonsen, then?"

Assad shrugged.

"I've got a couple more words here," Yrsa then announced.

She took hold of the stepladder and dragged it into place.

"I'll use a pencil so we can rub it out again," she said from the highest rung but one. "So now it looks like this. It's just a suggestion, mind, and I'm not entirely sure once we get past 'Hes got.' But the sequence fits and it makes sense, so why not? And whoever wrote it can't spell for toffee, but in places it's actually a help in a funny sort of way."

Assad and Carl exchanged glances. Hadn't they told her that?

"For example, I'm pretty certain that 'retnd' is 'thretned,' i.e., 'threatened.'"

She considered her work once again. "Oh, yeah, and I'm absolutely sure 'an' should be 'van,' there's just no trace of the 'v' anymore. But have a look and tell me what you think."

HELP

The .6 febrary 1996 we were kidnaped he got us at the bus sdop on Lautropvang in Ballerup—The man is 18. tall with short hair ....—Hes got a scar on his rite ... .r.... a blue van Mum and Dad know him—Fr.d.. .nd ...t.in. with a B— .. thretned us .. ..ve us ....—Hes going to kil us— .. .ressd . ... .ace ..rst .... .. brother.—We drove nearly 1 hour ... ... by warter .... win. .urb..s .... It smels here—..... .p ... .r .. .ry.gv.—.. ... . years

P... ....

"What do you reckon?" she asked, still without so much as a glance in their direction.

Carl read it through a couple of times. It appeared convincing enough, that much he had to concede. Hardly made up to slag off a teacher or anyone else who might have got the sender's back up.

Although there was definitely some authenticity about it, it was still by no means certain they were dealing with an actual cry for help. But if indeed it was genuine, a couple of sentences in particular gave rise to concern.

Mum and Dad know him, it read. Surely not the kind of thing a person would make up. And then: *Hes going to kil us.*

With no "might" or "perhaps" in sight.

"We don't know where he's got that scar of his, either, which pisses me off a bit," Yrsa continued, her fingers delving into her golden locks, then adding in English: "If you'll pardon my French."

"It's like there's too many body parts with three letters," she went on. "Especially if you can't spell. Leg, arm, toe, foot if you spell it with a 'u.' Would you agree that we can assume this scar to be on a limb or some other extremity? Is there any other part of the body with only three letters?"

"How about ear or eye?" Carl suggested. "Lip, or knee without the 'k'?" Apart from those I can't think of any more. But maybe we can rule out the legs. My guess is it's somewhere reasonably visible."

"What part of the body is visible in February in this refrigerator country?" Assad wanted to know.

"He may have taken his clothes off," said Yrsa, her face brightening momentarily. "He may have been a pervert. Maybe that's why he's a kidnapper."

Carl nodded. Unfortunately, it was a factor that couldn't be ruled out.

"In the cold, only the head is visible," said Assad. He stared at Carl's ear. "The ear can be seen if the hair is not too long, so the scar might be in that place. But what about the eye? Can a scar be on the eye?" Assad was obviously doing his utmost to visualize it. "No, not a scar," he concluded. "Not on the eye. That is not possible."

"Let's leave it for now," said Carl. "Hopefully, we'll get a better picture of our perp if and when the lab people over at Forensic Genetics manage to find some useful DNA on the bottle. These things take time, so we're going to have to wait. Any suggestions as to how to proceed in the meantime?"

Yrsa turned to face them. "Yeah, it's lunchtime!" she announced. "Anyone fancy a bread roll? I've brought my toaster with me."

When the gearbox begins to grumble, it's time for a change of oil, and right now Department Q was having considerable difficulty moving up the gears.

Time for an overhaul, Carl thought to himself.

"I think we'll try chucking the whole caboodle in the air and see how it all lands. Maybe it'll give us some new angles. What do you reckon?" he said.

They nodded. Assad rather reticently, perhaps taking the unfamiliar expression literally.

"Excellent. We'll swap around. You take a look at those company accounts, Assad. And Yrsa, you can ring around the colleges and other institutions in the area of Lautrupvang."

Carl nodded to himself. Of course. A cheerful female voice such as hers would have the desk jockeys running around the archives in no time.

"Get the administrative staff in those places to ask around and see if any of their older colleagues can recall anyone, a pupil or someone who worked there, who stopped turning up all of a sudden," he instructed her. "And Yrsa, give them something to go by. Landmark events in 1996. Remind them it was when the area had just been rebuilt."

At this point, Assad apparently felt he had heard enough and sloped off to his own office. It was obvious this new division of labor suited him badly. But Carl was in charge here, so he'd just have to put up with it.

Besides, the arson case was more substantial, and as such it was the one that gave them most leverage in relation to their colleagues in Department A, a point not to be taken lightly.

Assad would just have to put it behind him and roll up his sleeves. In the meantime, further musings about the message in the bottle could muddle along at Yrsa's plodding pace.

Carl waited until she was out of the door and then found the number of the spinal clinic in Hornbæk.

"I want to speak to the consultant. No one else," he said into the receiver, knowing full well he was hardly entitled to pressure anyone there.

Five minutes passed before the senior registrar finally came to the phone.

He didn't sound particularly happy. "Yes, I'm aware of who you are," he said wearily. "I assume this has something to do with Hardy Henningsen?"

Carl put him in the picture.

"I see," the doctor rattled. How come doctors' voices always turned more nasal with each rung they climbed up the salary scale?

"So you're asking me about the likelihood of nerve paths being restored in a case such as Hardy's?" he went on. "The problem is that Mr. Henningsen is no longer under our daily supervision, so we are unable to monitor his progress as we would otherwise wish. We did advise repeatedly against removing the patient from our care, as you well recall."

"If Hardy had stayed with you lot, he'd have been dead by now. Instead, he's found a modicum of spirit to go on living. I'd say that was a good thing, wouldn't you?"

There was silence at the other end.

"Couldn't one of you come out and take a look at him?" Carl continued. "Perhaps it might be a good time to assess the situation from scratch. For you, as well as for him."

More silence. Then, "You say he has some movement in his wrist? We already noted some spasms in a couple of finger joints. Perhaps he's mixing the two things up. It may be just some reflexive movement."

"Am I to understand that a spinal cord as damaged as Hardy's is never going to function any better than it does now?"

"Inspector, what we're talking about here is not whether your friend is ever going to walk again, because he isn't. Hardy Henningsen is paralyzed from the neck down and will be forever bound to his bed, and that's a certain fact. Whether he might regain some feeling in some part of the arm in question is another matter. I don't consider that we should expect anything more than such tiny contractions as those you have described, and probably not even that."

"So he won't ever be able to move his hand?"

"I can't imagine it."

"So you won't conduct an examination at home?"

"I didn't say that." There was a rummaging of paper at the other end. Probably a planner. "When did you have in mind?"

"As soon as possible."

"Leave it with me. I'll see what I can do."

When Carl checked Assad's office later, he found it empty.

On the desk was a note. *Here are the figures,* it read. Underneath was a formal signature: *Yours sincerely, Hafez el-Assad.*

Was he really so miffed?

"Yrsa!" he yelled into the corridor. "Where's Assad, do you know?"

No answer.

If Muhammad wouldn't go to the mountain, the mountain would have to go to Muhammad, he thought to himself, striding off to confront her.

Only to come to an abrupt halt as he put his head around her door. Anyone would have thought lightning had struck at his feet.

Rose's icily monochrome hi-tech landscape had been transformed into something not even the most aesthetically bewildered ten-year-old girl from Barbieland would be able to emulate. Everywhere he looked, he saw pink and bric-a-brac.

He gulped and turned to look at Yrsa herself. "Have you seen Assad?" he asked.

"Yeah, he left half an hour ago. He'll be back tomorrow."

"Where was he off to?"

She shrugged. "I've got an interim report for you on the Lautrupvang case, if you want?"

He nodded. "Anything turn up?"

There was a flutter of Hollywood-red lips. "Absolutely sweet fuck all. Did anyone ever tell you you've got the same smile as Gwyneth Paltrow?" she said.

"Gwyneth Paltrow? The actress?"

She nodded.

At that, he strode back to his office and called Rose's home number. Another day with Yrsa and things would go horribly wrong. If Department Q was to maintain its admittedly dubious standards, Rose would have to climb down and get back behind her desk at the double.

He got her answering machine.

"This is Rose and Yrsa's answering service informing you that the ladies are in audience with Her Majesty the Queen at the moment. As soon as ceremonials have been concluded, we'll call you back. Leave a message, if you must." And then came the tone.

Which of the two sisters had recorded the message, only God knew.

He slumped back into his chair and rummaged around for a smoke. Someone had mentioned the postal service was hiring again, and there might be some cushy jobs up for grabs.

It sounded like paradise.

Things were looking no better when he walked into his living room that evening and saw a doctor leaning over Hardy's bed, and Vigga, of all people, at his side.

He acknowledged the doctor's presence politely, then drew Vigga aside.

"What are you doing here, Vigga? You're supposed to call first if you want to see me. You know how much I hate these spur-of-the-moment visits."

"Carl, my love." She passed her hand across his cheek. It made a rasping sound.

This was indeed alarming.

"I think about you every day, and I've decided to come home again," she announced with conviction.

Carl felt his eyes widen. She wasn't joking, either, this garish almost-divorcée.

"You can't, Vigga. I'm afraid the idea just doesn't appeal."

Vigga blinked a couple of times. "Oh, but I can, dear, and I will. Half this house still belongs to me, in case you'd forgotten. Just you think on!"

And that was when he fell into a rage, making the doctor cower and causing Vigga to counter with tears. When at last a taxi finally took her away, he removed the top from the biggest marker pen he could lay his hands on and drew a thick black line through the name of Vigga Rasmussen on the front door. High fucking time.

And to hell with the consequences.

The inevitable upshot of this was that Carl sat up in bed for most of the night conducting endless one-way conversations with imaginary divorce lawyers, all of whom had their hands in his wallet.

This would be the ruination of him.

He found slight comfort in the fact that the doctor from the spinal clinic had come. And that he had actually registered a degree of activity, albeit small, in Hardy's arm.

Science was, in a positive sense, baffled.

He found himself passing the duty desk at Police HQ at half past five the next morning. There was no point lying in bed any longer.

"Pleasant surprise, seeing you here at this time of morning, Carl," said the duty officer in the cage. "I'm sure your little helper will be over the moon, too. Mind you don't give him a fright down there."

Carl needed to run through that again. "What? You mean Assad's here? Now?"

"Yeah. He's been coming in every day at this time. Usually just before six, but he was here around five today. Didn't you know?"

No, he certainly didn't.

It seemed Assad had already said his prayers in the corridor, because his prayer mat was still there, and this was the first time Carl had come so close to observing the ritual. It was something that usually went on behind Assad's closed door. He kept it to himself.

Carl heard the sound of Assad's voice coming loud and clear from his office, as though he were on the phone to someone hard of hearing. He was speaking Arabic, and his tone did not seem particularly friendly, though with that language you could never be sure.

He stepped toward the door and saw the steam from the boiling kettle rising to envelop Assad's neck. In front of him were notes in Arabic, and on the flatscreen was the flickering image of an elderly man with a mustache wearing a pair of enormous headphones. Now Carl realized that Assad was wearing his headset. Skyping with the man on the screen. Probably some relative in Syria.

"Morning, Assad," said Carl, failing to anticipate the reaction that came. He had expected Assad to be startled, of course, this being the first time Carl had ever been there so early, but the radical jolt that shook his assistant's body took him completely by surprise. Assad's arms and legs flailed in the air.

The old man he was talking to seemed alarmed and moved closer to the screen. Most likely he could see the outline of Carl appear behind Assad.

The man uttered a few hasty words and then disconnected. Meanwhile, Assad tried to collect himself on the edge of his chair.

His eyes were wide with bewilderment, as if to say: *What are you doing here?* He looked like a man who had been caught with both hands in the till.

"Sorry, Assad. I didn't mean to scare you like that. Are you OK?" He put his hand on Assad's shoulder. The fabric of his shirt was cold and clammy with sweat.

Assad clicked out of Skype, back to the document he had been working on before. Maybe he didn't want Carl to see who he had been connected to.

Carl raised his hands apologetically. "It's OK, I won't pry. Get on with whatever it was you were doing. Then come and see me when you've finished."

Assad had yet to say a word. That in itself was highly unusual.

A moment later, Carl plonked himself on his office chair, already feeling exhausted. Only a few weeks before, the basement underneath Police Headquarters had been his bolt-hole. Two reasonably amenable assistants and a general mood that on a good day might even be called pleasant. Now Rose was gone and had been replaced by someone equally odd, only in a different way, and Assad had gone funny on him. In such circumstances, keeping all the other hardships of this world at bay suddenly seemed like a tall order indeed. Not to mention what might happen if Vigga demanded a divorce and half his earthly possessions.

Bollocks to it.

Carl glanced up at a job opening he had lightheartedly pinned to the notice board a couple of months before: *National Commissioner of Police.* Just the ticket, he'd thought. What could be better than a job with minions bowing and touching their forelocks, an order of chivalry from the Queen, cheap travel, and a salary that would reduce even Vigga to silence? Seven hundred and two thousand, two hundred and seventy-seven kroner per annum, no less. Plus perks. Just uttering the figure took up half the morning.

Should have put in for it, he thought to himself. And then Assad was standing in front of him.

"Carl, do we need to talk about what happened just now?"

About what? That he'd been Skyping with someone? That he was on the job so early? That Carl's sudden appearance had scared the shit out of him?

The question was decidedly odd.

Carl shook his head and looked at the time. Still an hour until his shift officially began. "What you do here so early in the morning is your own business, Assad. I've no problem with you keeping in touch with people you don't see that often."

Assad looked almost relieved. Curiouser and curiouser.

"I have been studying the accounts of Amundsen and Mujagic A/S in Rødovre, K. Frandsen Wholesalers, JPP Fittings A/S, and Public Consult."

"OK. Find anything you want to tell me about?"

Assad scratched the barren patch in his black curls. "They seem to be rather solid companies most of the time."

"But?"

"In the months surrounding the fires they are not."

"How can you tell?"

"They borrow money. Their orders go down."

"You mean, first the orders go down, and then they borrow the money they've lost?"

Assad nodded. "Yes, that's it."

"OK, then what?"

"Well, we can see that only in the Rødovre case. The other fires are all so new."

"What happened there, then?"

"First there is the fire, then the company receives the insurance payout, and afterward the loan is gone."

Carl reached for his cigarettes and lit up. It sounded like copybook stuff. Insurance fraud. But where did the bodies with the finger rings come in?

"What kind of loans are we talking about?"

"Short term. One year at a time. In the case of Public Consult, the company that burned down on Stockholmsgade last Saturday, only six months."

"The loans fell due and they hadn't the funds to pay?"

"That is what it looks like."

Carl blew smoke into the room, prompting Assad to step back and flap his hands. Carl ignored him. This was his domain and his smoke. If Assad didn't like it, tough shit.

"Who lent them the money?" he asked.

Assad gave a shrug. "Various. Bankers in central Copenhagen."

Carl nodded. "Get me the names and tell me who's behind them."

Assad's shoulders sagged.

"All right, no need to get depressed about it. Do it when the offices open, Assad. That's a couple of hours away yet. Relax."

Carl's words did not appear to cheer him up at all. In fact, they almost seemed to make things worse.

The pair of them were getting on Carl's nerves with all their jabber and recalcitrance. It was like Assad and Yrsa were infecting each other. As if they were the ones who did the deciding around here. If they kept it up, he would give them each a pair of rubber gloves and have them scrubbing the basement floor on their hands and knees until they could see their faces in it.

Assad lifted his head and nodded silently. "Anyway, I will not keep you anymore, Carl. You can come to me when you're finished."

"What do you mean?"

Assad winked and flashed him a wry little smile. The transformation was utterly baffling. "Soon you will have both hands full," he added, winking again.

"Let me try that one more time. What the fuck are you going on about, Assad?"

"I am referring to Mona, of course. Do not try to tell me you had no idea she was back."

14

Like Assad had said, Mona Ibsen was back. Exuding tropical sunshine and an excess of experiences that had left unmistakable albeit graceful traces in the narrow creases around her eyes.

Carl had sat for a long time on his own in the basement that morning, trying to come up with gambits that might effectively counter any defensive steps on Mona's part. Words that might soften her gaze if she should happen to drop by.

It didn't happen. The only female presence in the basement that morning was Yrsa, heralded by the trundle of her shopping cart and her doubtless kindly intended but nonetheless earsplitting descant in the corridor five minutes after clocking in: "Bread rolls from Netto, ready for toasting, lads!"

It was one of those moments that brought home to him how far removed the basement was from the oblivious world above it, where people went about carefree and happy.

After that, it took him a couple of hours to realize that if he was planning on ever finding happiness himself he would have to get off his arse and go looking for it.

Having asked around, he eventually located Mona over by the Magistrates' Court in quiet discussion with the court clerk. Clad in a leather waistcoat and a pair of faded Levi's, she resembled anything but a woman who was done with taking on new challenges in life.

"Hello, Carl," she said, rather remotely. The look in her eyes was professional, making it abundantly clear that for the moment there was nothing more between them. All he could do was smile back at her, unable to muster a single word.

The rest of the day he could have spent in ever-decreasing circles, frustration mounting in the disintegrated ruin of his emotional life. But Yrsa had other plans.

"We might have something to go on in Ballerup," she announced with ill-concealed glee and a bit of Netto's bread roll stuck between her front teeth. "I'm an angel of good fortune this week. It says so in my horoscope."

Carl looked up at her with hope in his eyes. In that case, her wings could whisk her away into the stratosphere so he could be left to ponder his cruel fate in peace.

"I had such a job getting anything out of them," she went on. "First, I had to speak to the head teacher at Lautrupgård School, but he'd only been there since 2004. Then they sent me on to a teacher who'd been there since the school started, and she didn't know anything, either. Then I got hold of the caretaker, and he was just as blank, so then—"

"Yrsa! If there's a point to all this, then I'd like to hear it, please. I'm a busy man," Carl interrupted, trying to rub some life back into a sleeping arm.

"Well, as I was just about to say, afterward I called the College of Engineering, and that's where we got lucky."

The blood rushed back to his limb at once. "Excellent!" he exclaimed. "Go on."

"It was quite by chance, really. One of the teachers, a woman by the name of Laura Mann, was in the office when I called. She'd just started back this morning after being off sick. She's taught there since the place opened in 1995, and as far as she could remember there's only ever been one case that would fit."

Carl straightened up in his chair. "And what was that?"

Yrsa cocked her head and looked at him. "Oh, so you *are* interested, then?" She gave his hairy forearm a playful slap of her hand. "Bet you're dying to know now, aren't you?"

How in God's name had it come to this? He'd solved at least a hundred burdensome cases over the years, and here he was, reduced to playing guessing games with a temp in bright-green tights.

"Tell me about the case she recalled, Yrsa," Carl persisted, nodding briefly to Assad, who had put his head around the door. He looked pale.

"Well, Assad called the office yesterday asking the same questions. They'd been talking about it this morning over coffee, and the woman overheard," she continued.

Assad pricked up his ears and suddenly seemed to be back to his old self again.

"It all came back to her straightaway," said Yrsa. "They had this elite student once. A young lad with some kind of syndrome, she said, but absolutely brilliant at maths and physics."

"A syndrome?" Assad looked puzzled.

"Yeah, like very gifted at one thing and hopeless at everything else. Not autism, but something like it. What did she call it, now?" Yrsa wrinkled her brow. "Oh, I know. Asperger's syndrome, that was what he had."

Carl smiled. Most likely she had her own personal insights into what it was like.

"So what happened to this lad?" he went on.

"He took the first term and got flying marks in everything, and then he dropped out."

"Under what circumstances?"

"He was there the last day before the winter break with his younger brother, showing him around the place, and after that they never saw him again."

Both Assad and Carl narrowed their eyes at once. This was it. "What was his name?" Carl asked.

"His name was Poul."

Carl felt his insides turn to ice.

"Yes!" Assad exclaimed, and proceeded to wave his arms and legs about like a jumping jack.

"The teacher said she remembered him so vividly because Poul Holt was the closest thing to a Nobel candidate they would ever be likely to see anywhere near that college. And besides that, there had never been a single student there, before or after, who had that kind of Asperger's. He was all on his own in that respect."

"So that's why she remembered him?" Carl went on.

"Yeah, that's why. And because he was in the first year of students they ever had."

Half an hour later, Carl repeated the same questions in person at the College of Engineering and received exactly the same answers.

"It's not the kind of thing you forget," Laura Mann explained, flashing an ivory smile. "I imagine you remember your first arrest in much the same way?"

Carl nodded. A scrawny little alky who had lain down in the middle of Englandsvej. Carl could still see the glob of spit as it sailed through the air and stuck itself to his police badge while he tried to bundle the fool back to safety. So it was true: that first arrest remained indelible. With or without the spit.

He considered the woman sitting at the other side of the table. Sometimes she was on television when they needed an expert on alternative energy sources. *Laura Mann, PhD,* it read on her business card, and a lot more titles besides. Carl was glad he didn't have one of his own.

"He had some form of autism, is that right?"

"Well, sort of, but rather a mild form, I believe. People with AS are often highly gifted. Nerdish is how most people would think of them, I suppose. Einsteins. But Poul had practical talent as well. He was very special in all sorts of ways."

Assad smiled. He too had noted the horn-rimmed glasses and the hair gathered in a bun. She seemed to be just the right teacher for someone like Poul Holt. Nerdish minds think alike, as they said.

"Poul had his younger brother with him that day, the sixteenth of February 1996, you say, after which you never saw him again. How can you be so sure of the date?" Carl inquired.

"We kept a register of attendance in the first years. So we checked back to see when he'd been here last. He never came back after the holiday. Would you like to see the registers? They're all filed away in the office next door."

Carl glanced at Assad. He didn't seem that interested, either. "No, thanks, I think we can take your word for it. I understand you contacted the family when Poul failed to show up again, is that right?"

"Yes, but they were very standoffish. Especially when we suggested a meeting at home to talk things over with Poul."

"Did you speak to him on the phone?"

"No, the last time I spoke to Poul Holt was here at the college, and that would have been a week before the winter break. Later, when I called his home number, his father said Poul wouldn't come to the phone. And that was that. Poul had just turned eighteen, so of course he was free to decide for himself what he wanted to do with his life."

"Eighteen? Are you sure he wasn't older than that?"

"Yes, he was very young. He completed his upper secondary at seventeen and went straight on from there."

"Have you kept any data on him?"

She smiled. Naturally, she had come prepared.

Carl read aloud with Assad hovering at his shoulder.

"Poul Holt, born 13 November 1977. Maths and Physics major from Birkerød Gymnasium School. Final average 9.8."

And then came the address. Not far away, forty-five minutes by car at the most.

"Bearing in mind this would be the old grading system with thirteen as top of the scale, I'd say that wasn't a particularly impressive average for a genius," Carl mused.

"True, but that's how it pans out across the board with thirteen science and seven arts subjects," she replied.

"Are you saying, then, that he was poor in Danish?" Assad chipped in.

She smiled. "In written Danish, certainly. His reports left a lot to be desired in terms of his writing skills. But we often see that. Even in his spoken language he expressed himself rather primitively if the subject at hand failed to interest him."

"Is there a copy of this I could take with me?" Carl asked.

Laura Mann nodded. If it hadn't been for her tobacco-stained fingers and greasy skin, he would have given her a hug.

"Fantastic, Carl," Assad enthused as they approached the house. "We solved our problem within a week. We know who wrote the letter. This is the way to go! And now we are outside the family's home." He thumped the dashboard as if to underline their success.

"Yeah." Carl nodded. "Now we just have to hope it was all a joke."

"If so, then we must give this Poul a bollocking, Carl."

"And what if it wasn't, Assad?"

Assad nodded. If it wasn't, they would have a job on their hands.

They parked outside the garden gate and noted immediately that the name on the nameplate wasn't Holt.

When they rang the bell and the door was opened by a small, crumpled man in a wheelchair claiming to be the only person who had lived in the house since 1996, Carl clenched his teeth together on instinct and felt himself growing irritable.

"You'll have bought the place from the Holts, then?" he said.

"No, as a matter of fact it was from some Jehovah's Witnesses. The man of the house was a priest of some sort. The main room had been a kind of meeting place. You can come in and have a look, if you like."

Carl shook his head. "So you never met the family who lived here?"

"That's right, I never met them," the man replied.

Assad and Carl thanked him and went away.

"Do you get the feeling all of a sudden, Assad, that we're not dealing with boyish pranks here?" Carl said.

"Carl, just because people move house . . ." He stopped on the garden path. "OK, perhaps I know what you are thinking, Carl."

"Am I right, would you say? Would a lad like Poul be the sort to do something like that? And would it be the kind of thing a couple of young Jehovah's Witnesses would get up to? What do you reckon?"

"I don't know. All I know is that they are allowed to lie, only not to each other."

"You mean you know someone who's a member?"

"No, but that is how it is with these highly religious people. The members of the Church will shield each other against the world by whatever means. Also with lies."

"True. But the kidnapping thing can't have been a necessary lie. That'd be overstepping the boundaries. I'm sure all Jehovah's Witnesses would be able to see that."

Assad nodded. On that point they agreed.

So what now?

Yrsa was like an army of ants on the march back and forth between her own office and Carl's. For the moment, the kidnapping case was hers and she wanted to know everything, preferably in small installments. What did this Laura Mann look like? What did she have to say about Poul? What was the house like that they had lived in? What more did they know about the family, besides that they were Jehovah's Witnesses?

"Take it easy. Assad's checking the Civil Registration System. We'll find them before long."

"Come out here into the corridor with me for a minute, would you, Carl?" she said, dragging him with her to the blowup on the wall. Now she had added Poul's name at the bottom, as well as filling in a couple of the smaller words in the main body of the text.

HELP

The 16 febrary 1996 we were kidnaped he got us at the bus sdop on Lautropvang in Ballerup—The man is 18. tall with short hair ....—Hes got a scar on his rite ... .r.... a blue van Mum and Dad know him—Fr.d.. .nd ...t.in. with a B—He thretned us .. ..ve us ....—Hes going to kil us—.. .ressd . ... .ace ..rst .... .. brother.—We drove nearly 1 hour ... ... by warter .... win. .urb..s .... It smels here— ..... .p ... .r .. .ry.gv.—.. ... . years

POUL HOLT

"Right then! He was kidnapped along with his brother," Yrsa summed up. "His name is Poul Holt, and he says they drove nearly an hour, my guess being that they drove to some water." She planted her fists on her narrow hips. Now, clearly, she was going to present her own standpoint.

"If this lad had Asperger's or something like it, I don't think he would be making that kind of thing up, about them driving out to the water." She turned to face Carl. "Would he?"

"Maybe his younger brother's behind it. So far, we've no way of knowing, strictly speaking."

"No, but think about it, Carl. Laursen found a fish scale on the original message. If the younger brother had written it, would he go to the bother of sticking a fish scale on just to make his story more believable? Not to mention fish *slime*?"

"Maybe he's as bright as his brother. Only in another way?"

At this point, she stamped her foot, causing a resounding echo to clatter through the basement rotunda. "Carl, you're not listening. Put your thinking cap on. Where were they kidnapped?" She patted him on the shoulder as though to soften the harshness of her tone.

Carl noted how a few flakes of dandruff were sent whirling into the air in the process. "In Ballerup," he answered.

"Right, so what do you think if they were kidnapped in Ballerup and yet drive for nearly an hour to get to some water? It wouldn't take them an hour to Hundested, would it? How long does it take to Jyllinge from Ballerup? Half an hour at the most, I'd say."

"Stevns would be a possibility, yeah?" He growled slightly under his breath. No one liked to have their intellectual capacities dragged through the mud. And that included Carl Mørck.

"Exactly!" She stamped her foot again. If there had been rats in the crawl space beneath them, they were there no longer.

"But if the message is just a flight of fancy," she went on, "why make it all so difficult? Why not just write that they drove for half an hour to get to the water? Surely that's what any young lad making up a story would do? That's why I don't believe it's made up. We should be taking this letter very seriously, Carl."

He inhaled deeply. He hadn't the energy to share his take on the gravity of the situation. Maybe he would have done so with Rose, but not Yrsa.

"Yeah, OK, no need to get worked up," he said, trying to talk things down to a sensible level. "Let's see how things are looking once we've got hold of the family."

"What is going on?" Assad popped his head out of his pygmy-size office. It was obvious he was trying to weigh up the mood. Was this a proper argument, or what?

"I have the address, Carl," he announced, thrusting a piece of paper into Carl's hand. "Four times they have moved since 1996. Four addresses in thirteen years, all in Sweden."

Shit, Carl thought to himself. Sweden, the country with the world's largest mosquitoes and dullest cuisine.

"Let me guess," he said. "They moved up north to where even the reindeer get lost? Luleå or Kebnekaise, somewhere like that?"

"Hallabro. The place is called Hallabro, and it's in Blekinge. Approximately two hundred and fifty kilometers from here."

Two hundred and fifty kilometers. A jaunt, unfortunately. He saw the weekend disappear before his eyes.

He tried to wangle his way out. "OK, but they won't be in when we get there. And if we call them beforehand, they won't be in, either. And if by chance they're in, all they'll speak is Swedish, and how the hell's anyone from Jutland to understand a word? Am I right?"

Assad frowned, as if this were slightly too much information for him to process all at once. "But I already called. And they *were* in."

"You did what? Chances are they'll be out tomorrow, then."

"Not at all, Carl, because I did not tell them who I was. I slammed down the receiver at once."

A crabby pair, these two assistants of his. And such a flair for sound effects.

Carl shuffled back into his office and called home, giving brief instructions for Morten on what to do if Vigga turned up while he was away. Who knew what she was capable of next?

Then he instructed Assad on the continuing investigation into the arsons and told him to keep an eye on what Yrsa was up to. "Give her a good long list of religious sects to look into. And then go upstairs to Laursen and ask him to get on to Forensic Genetics, see if he can hurry them up a bit on those DNA tests, eh?"

After that, he stuffed his service pistol into his bag. You never knew with the Swedes.

At least not the ones from Denmark.

15

The next night, he made sure he brought his hostess and temporary lover to the brink of climax. In the seconds before she threw back her head and drew in breath to the very bottom of her lungs, he removed his fingers from her crotch and left her lying there, muscles quivering, eyes flickering.

He rose quickly, leaving Isabel Jønsson alone with the issue of how best to discharge her arousal. She looked bewildered, which was exactly his intention.

Above her little row house in Viborg, the moonlight contended with thick, downy clouds. He stood naked on the patio and looked up at them, exhaling cigarette smoke through his nostrils.

From now on, the hours would proceed according to a familiar pattern.

First the arguments. Then she would demand some explanation for why their relationship had to end, and so suddenly. She would plead and they would argue, and then she would plead again. He would spell it out to her and she would tell him to pack his things and go, after which he would be out of her life for good.

At ten o'clock the next morning he would be leaving the hills of Dollerup Bakker with the children next to him on the front seat, and when they asked why they had turned off the road too soon, he would chloroform them. He knew exactly where this could be done without fear of discovery. His research had been thorough. A dense copse of trees that would conceal the van and his activities during the few minutes it would take for him to neutralize them and transfer their sedated bodies into the back of the vehicle.

Four and a half hours after this took place, having crossed the Storebælt Bridge and stopped off for lunch at his sister's on Fyn, he would be back on Sjælland, at the boathouse by the woods of Nordskoven, north of Jægerspris. Just twenty paces through the thicket to the low-ceilinged space with the chains. Twenty paces, shoving two cowering figures on in front of him.

He knew the sound of urgent invocations from previous times crossing that little stretch of ground. He would hear it again.

Only then could negotiations with the parents begin.

He emptied his lungs of smoke and stubbed the cigarette out on the tiny lawn. He had a busy night and day ahead of him.

He was compelled to put aside his unpleasant suspicions that something was awry at home, something that threatened to turn everything on its head. If his wife was being unfaithful, it would be the worse for her.

He heard the patio door squeak behind him and turned toward Isabel's confused face. Her bathrobe barely concealed her trembling nakedness. In a moment, he would tell her it was over on account of her being too old, though she was nowhere near. Her body was exciting and piquant, her presence made him hungry for her. It was a shame, in more ways than one, that their relationship had to end, though the feeling was by no means new to him. It had happened so many times before.

"You'll catch your death out here with no clothes on. It's freezing cold." She tilted her head, not focusing on him. "What's happening between us?"

He stood in front of her and took hold of the collar of her robe. "You're too old for me," he said without feeling, drawing the garment around the bareness of her throat.

For a second, she seemed to be paralyzed. Ready to either lash out at him or scream her anger and frustration into his face. Invective surged, only to stall on her tongue. He knew she would say nothing. Respectable divorced public servants such as she would never make a scene with a naked man on their patio.

People would talk. They both knew that.

By the time he awoke early next morning, she had already gathered up his things from around the house and thrown them into his bag. There was no breakfast, not even coffee, just a barrage of rather pertinent accusations and questions indicating to him that she was still on her feet.

"You've been into my computer," she said, composed, though her face was bleached with anger. "You did a search on my brother. Fifty great big, elephant-size footprints in my data. Couldn't you have gone to the trouble of finding out what I actually do in the local authority while you were at it? Don't you think that was rather disrespectful of you? Rather stupid, perhaps?"

As she spoke, his mind was on the fact that he needed to use her shower, no matter what she said. The family out at Stanghede would surely not leave their children in the hands of an unshaven man smelling of sex.

What she said next, however, mobilized all his senses.

"I work in IT. I'm an expert. In charge of data security and IT solutions for Viborg Municipality. So I know what you've been up to. What the hell do you take me for? Don't you think I can read the log files on my own laptop?"

She looked him directly in the eye. She was quite calm now. The first crisis was over. She had aces up her sleeve, could rise above self-pity, tears, and hysteria.

"You found my passwords," she said. "But only because I put them there for you to find. I've been watching you. To see what you might get up to. There's always something not right about a man who tells so little about himself. Something not right at all. You see, what men love more than anything else is to talk about themselves. Obviously, you had no idea!" She smiled wryly, sensing his alertness. "How come he never says anything about himself, I wondered. And to be honest, it was rather intriguing."

He knitted his eyebrows in a frown. "So now you think you know me, because I'm silent about my own life and curious about yours?"

"Curious, that's an understatement. I can see why you might want to check my dating profile, but why would you want to know about my brother?"

"I thought he was your ex and that maybe I could figure out what went wrong."

She wasn't buying. She didn't care about his whys and wherefores. He had misjudged her, that was all there was to it.

"I will say to your credit, though, that at least you didn't empty my bank account," she said.

He forced an overbearing smile at her audacity. It was an expression he had been saving for their farewell after his shower, but these were new developments.

"But do you know what? We're as bad as each other when it comes to being inquisitive," she went on. "You see, I've been rummaging around in your things, too. And do you know what I found in your pockets and in your bag? Not a thing. No driver's license, no social security card, no credit cards, no wallet, no car keys. Nothing. But do you know what else, mister? Just like women always leave their passwords in the most obvious of places, men are always stupid enough to leave their car keys on top of the front wheel if they don't want to carry them around. And what a fine little bowling ball you have on your key ring. Does that mean you go bowling, then? You never said. And with a number one on it, too. Is that because you're so good at it?"

At this point he began to perspire. It had been a long time indeed since he had lost control. And nothing felt worse.

"It's all right, no need to worry. Your keys are back where I found them. And your driver's license. And the registration certificate for the van, and your credit cards, and all the rest of it, for that matter. It's all where I found it in the van. Tucked away underneath the mats."

He studied her neck. It was not the delicate kind, and his grip would need to be strong. It would take a couple of minutes, but he had plenty of time.

"It's true, I'm a very private person," he said, stepping forward and placing a hand cautiously on her shoulder. "Listen, Isabel. I'm very much in love with you, but I simply haven't been able to be honest with you. I'm married, you see. There are children involved, and this has been getting out of hand for me. That's why it has to stop now. Do you understand?"

She tossed her head in a proud swagger. Wounded, but not defeated. She had known married men before who had lied to her, he was certain of it. As certain as he was that he would now be compelled to make sure he was the last man ever in her life who could cheat on her.

She swept his hand away. "I don't know why you haven't told me your real name, and I don't know why everything else you told me was lies. You're trying to tell me it's because you're married, but do you know what? I don't believe that, either."

And with that she stepped away from him, as though having read his mind. As though preparing to grab a weapon that lay hidden and ready.

When you suddenly feel like you're adrift on an ice floe in the company of a slobbering polar bear, you do well to consider what avenues might be available. Right now, he had four.

Jump into the water and swim.

Leap onto another ice floe.

Wait and see whether the bear is hungry or not.

Kill the bear.

All four possibilities had their obvious advantages and drawbacks, but he was in no doubt that the fourth was the only real solution. The woman who had confronted him was injured and would defend herself by all means possible. Clearly because he had made her fall so deeply in love with him. He should have seen it coming. Experience had taught him that in situations such as this women easily became irrational. Often, the consequences would be fatal.

At this moment, he was unable to fully assess the scale of the damage she might inflict, and for that reason alone he would have to get rid of her. He would take the body with him in the van. Dump her somewhere, like the others before. Destroy her hard disk, make sure all traces of his presence in her home were removed.

He looked into her beautiful green eyes and wondered how long it would take before they ceased to sparkle.

"I've sent my brother an e-mail telling him all about you," she said. "So now he's got your car reg number, the number of your driver's license, your name, civil registration number, and the address on the vehicle registration certificate. It's not the sort of thing he normally deals with, but he's inquisitive by nature. So if it turns out you've stolen anything from me, he's going to find you. Get it?"

For a second, he was stunned. He wasn't stupid enough to drive around with any document or credit card that might reveal his true identity. His sudden paralysis now was because until this moment he had never been in a situation where he could be linked to anything at all, and certainly he had never had the police lurking in the background. He found himself momentarily unable to grasp how he had got himself into this. What had he missed, where had he gone wrong? Was it really down to something as simple as not asking her what exactly her job in the local authority involved? He supposed that had to be it.

And now he was in a squeeze.

"I'm sorry, Isabel," he said softly. "I've gone way over the mark here. Forgive me. I'm besotted with you, that's all. Don't think about what I said last night. I just didn't know what to do. Was I supposed to tell you I was married with kids, or tell you lies? I'd lose everything back home if I really fell for you in a big way, and I almost did. I've been so on the verge, I needed to know everything about you. I couldn't resist that, can't you see?"

She looked at him scornfully as he considered what to do on his ice floe. The bear would hardly pounce without reason. If he drove away and never again showed himself in these parts, she would be unlikely to draw on her brother for information about him. Why should she? But if he killed her or abducted her, the police would already have something to go on. Even his most meticulous efforts to erase all traces of himself here would not be sufficient to remove that one pubic hair, that tiny semen stain, a fingerprint. They would put together a profile, no matter that they would be unable to find him in their registers. Burning the place down was unfeasible. The fire services might quickly extinguish the blaze, and someone might have seen him drive away. It was too much of a risk. And now there was a police officer by the name of Karsten Jønsson who was in possession of the license plate number of his van. He would have a description of the vehicle. Maybe she had even given her brother a description of him.

He stared blankly into space while she took stock of his movements. Though he was expert at sloughing his skin, though he always operated under one or another assumed identity, her e-mail may have contained exact details of his height and build, the color of his eyes, and perhaps even of more intimate parts of his body. He had no way of knowing what she had put in that mail, and that was where the whole thing imploded.

He looked into the harshness of her gaze, and it struck him that she was not a polar bear at all. She was a basilisk. Serpent, cockerel, and dragon in one venomous reptile. And if a man looked into the eyes of the basilisk, he would turn to stone. Even crossing its path would be enough to cause death by its noxious influence. No being could crow out its version of truth to the world like the basilisk. And only its own image was powerful enough to kill it. This he knew.

Therefore he said: "No matter what you might say, Isabel, I shall think of you. You're so beautiful, such an amazing woman, I only wish I could have met you at some earlier time in my life. Now it's too late. I'm sorry, and I apologize. I never intended to hurt you. You're so lovely. I'm sorry."

And then he brushed his fingers gently against her cheek. It seemed to work. Her lips quivered slightly.

"I think you should go now. I don't want to see you again," was what she said, though without conviction.

She would mourn the loss for a long time to come. What they had together was the kind of thing that didn't come around so often at her age.

That was where he leaped from this ice floe to another. Neither the basilisk nor the polar bear would pursue him.

She let him go, and it wasn't even seven o'clock.

16

He called his wife as usual just before eight, still holding back on the contentious issue but relating experiences unlived and feelings for her which at present he did not possess. Leaving Viborg, he stopped at a Løvbjerg supermarket and freshened himself up as best he could in the customer toilets before heading toward Hald Ege and on to Stanghede, where Samuel and Magdalena were waiting for him.

Nothing was going to stop him now. The weather was OK. Looking ahead, he would be there just before dark.

The family received him with the smell of fresh-baked bread and lofty expectations. Samuel had been training all morning despite his injured knee, and Magdalena stood with eyes sparkling and her thick hair in long waves glossy from eager brushing.

They were so ready.

"Do you think we should stop by the hospital first and let them have a quick look at Samuel's knee, just to be on the safe side? I think we've time." He swallowed the last bit of his bread roll as he glanced at his watch. It was a quarter to ten, and he knew they would decline.

Disciples of the Mother Church did not frequent hospitals if it could be avoided.

"No, it's just a sprain, but thanks all the same." Rachel handed him a coffee cup and indicated the milk on the table. He could feel free to help himself.

"So where is this karate tournament?" said Joshua. "Maybe I can come along later in the day, if I've got time?"

"Oh, leave off, Joshua." Rachel swatted at him. "You know full well when you've got time and when you haven't."

Never, as far as he could make out.

"It's in the sports hall at Vinderup," he told the father. "The Bujutsu Club are organizing it. Perhaps there's some more information on the Internet."

There wasn't, but then there was almost certainly no Internet in the house. Another one of those ungodly inventions the Mother Church shunned.

He put his hand to his mouth. "Oh, I'm sorry. How stupid of me. I forgot, you won't have an Internet connection. It's nothing but a nuisance, anyway." He did his best to look repentant, noting that the coffee was decaf. It was all PC here. "But, yeah, it's all going on in the sports hall at Vinderup."

They waved. The whole family lined up in front of the farmhouse at the bend in the road, never again to rest in the peace and comfort of what once was. Smiling faces soon to contort in the pain of learning that the evils of this world cannot be kept at bay with weekly devotions and renunciation of the good things of modern life.

He did not feel sorry for them. They had chosen the pathway on which they would tread, and now it had crossed his own.

He looked at the two youngsters sitting on the seat next to him, waving back at their family.

"Have you got enough room, you two?" he asked as they drove through bare fields dashed with the dark stubble of maize. He stuck his hand into the side pocket of the door. His weapon lay at the ready. Not many would recognize it for what it was. It looked like the handle of an attaché case.

He beamed a smile when they nodded. They were sitting comfortably, and their minds were astray, unused to any departure from their quiet, restrictive lives. For them, this was a highlight.

There would be no difficulties here.

"I thought we might go by way of Finderup, just for the drive," he said, offering them miniature chocolate bars. Against the rules it may have been, but nonetheless a way of establishing community. Community was security. And security made his work that much easier.

"Oh, I'm forgetting, aren't I?" he said, noting their hesitation. "I've brought some fruit with us, too. Would you rather have a tangerine?"

"I think we'd like the chocolate best." Magdalena smiled irresistibly, revealing the braces on her teeth. It wasn't hard to imagine that this was a girl with secrets concealed in the garden.

He waxed lyrical on the beauty of the Jutland heath and told them how excited he was about moving to the area permanently. And by the time they reached the crossroads at Finderup, the mood was quite as he had hoped—relaxed, trustful, and chummy. That was where he turned off the road.

"Hey, not yet," said Samuel, leaning forward in his seat. "The Holstebro road's the next one."

"I know, but when I was driving around looking at houses the other day, I found this shortcut that leads up to Route 16."

He turned again, a few hundred meters from the memorial stone for the medieval king Erik Klipping.

Hesselborgvej.

"It's along here. A bit bumpy, I know, but a good little shortcut," he said.

"Are you sure?" Samuel read the sign as they passed: *Military vehicles strictly prohibited on bypaths.* "I thought this road just petered out," he said, and sat back in his seat.

"You'll see, it carries on beyond that yellow farmhouse there on the left, then on past another farm on the right that's all broken down, and then we turn left."

He nodded to himself a couple of hundred meters farther on. The unmade road turned into wheel tracks. Here was a landscape of stubble, undulating and dotted with woodland. One more bend and they were there.

"Hey, what did I tell you," Samuel exclaimed, pointing up ahead. "You can't get through here at all."

He was wrong, but there was no need for explanation now.

"Do you know what, I think you're right, Samuel," he said. "We'll just have to turn around again and go back. Sorry about that, kids. I was certain . . ."

He turned the wheel and brought the van to a halt at an angle across the track, then reversed in between the trees.

He pulled on the hand brake, swiftly drawing the stun gun from the side pocket. In one seamless movement, he released the safety catch, thrust the weapon against Magdalena's throat, and fired. It was a fiendish device that delivered 1.2 million volts into the body of the victim, resulting in momentary paralysis. Her scream, and not least the sudden, violent way her body jerked, at first threw Samuel completely. Like his sister, he was utterly unprepared. The look in his eyes was of terror, and yet of readiness to fight. In the brief second that elapsed from the moment his sister slumped toward him till he grasped the fact that the object about to be pressed against him was lethal, the full gamut of the youngster's adrenaline-driven mechanisms was activated at once.

And so, quick though he was, his sister's assailant was not quick enough to prevent the boy from shoving his sister aside, tearing at the door handle, and tumbling out before he could discharge his weapon again.

He gave the girl another shot and leaped out of the vehicle in pursuit of the boy, who had by now managed to limp some way along the lichen-green track, his bad knee buckling beneath him. It was only a matter of seconds before his turn came.

Reaching the fir trees, the boy turned suddenly. "What is it you want?" he yelled, invoking the assistance of his God, as though from out of the organized rows of fir some heavenly host would appear to defend him. He limped to one side and picked up a heavy stick spiked viciously with the sharp remnants of branches.

Shit. He should have dealt with the boy first. Why the fuck hadn't he listened to his instincts?

"Don't you come any closer," the boy screamed, waving his stick in the air. There was no doubt he would use it. The boy knew combat, and would fight as well as he could.

The thought flashed through his mind that he should have a Taser C2 instead. Armed with one of those, he would be able to incapacitate his victims from a distance of several meters. He knew there was not a second to be lost. They were only a few hundred meters from the farms and, although he had selected the location with care, there was no guarantee that some farmer or woodsman wouldn't suddenly materialize. And in a few moments, the boy's sister would recover sufficiently to be able to escape.

"That won't help you, Samuel," he said, and thrust forward to counter the boy's frantic blows. He felt the crack of the stick as it came down heavily against his shoulder at the same moment as the stun gun made contact with the boy's arm. The cries they emitted were simultaneous.

But this was not a battle between equals, and the boy fell to the ground.

He glanced at his shoulder where Samuel had struck him so cleanly. Shit, he thought again, as his blood spread like the points of a star in the fabric of his windbreaker.

Wishing again that he had a Taser, he dragged the boy into the back of the van, found the chloroform rag, and covered his face with it. For a moment the boy's eyes stared emptily, and then he was under.

He repeated the procedure with the sister.

Then he blindfolded them, bound their hands and feet with gaffer tape, gagged them in the same way, and put them in the recovery position on the thickly carpeted floor.

He changed his shirt and put on another jacket, standing for a few minutes, watching them to make sure they didn't react badly, throw up and choke on their own vomit.

When finally he was satisfied, he closed the doors and drove away.

His sister and brother-in-law had settled in a small cottage just outside Årup, with whitewashed walls and close to the road. It was only a few kilometers from the parish church where his father had spent his final incumbency.

It was the last place on earth he would think of settling.

"So where have you been this time?" his brother-in-law asked without interest, gesturing toward a pair of timeworn slippers that were always left in the hallway and which all visitors were obliged to shuffle about in. As if their floors had ever been worth shit.

He followed a sound into the front room and found his sister humming in a corner, a moth-eaten shawl draped across her shoulders.

Eva knew him by his step but said nothing. She had put on a considerable amount of weight since the last time he'd been here. Twenty kilos minimum. Her body had spread, and soon the image he retained of the sister with whom he had so gleefully frolicked in the garden of the pastor's residence would be gone forever.

There was no exchange of greetings between them. There never was. But then politeness had never been much cherished in their childhood home.

"I can't stay long," he said, squatting down beside her. "How are you doing?"

"Villy looks after me," she answered. "We'll be eating shortly. Perhaps you'd like something?"

"Just a spot of lunch. And then I'll be making tracks."

She nodded. Truth was she didn't care. Since the light had gone out in her eyes, the desire to be with other people and listen to what they had to say about themselves and the world around them had likewise waned. Perhaps it was necessary. Perhaps the faded images of childhood had suddenly taken up too much room inside her.

"I've got some money for you." He pulled an envelope out of his pocket and pressed it into her hand. "There's thirty thousand there. That should tide you both over until next time."

"Thanks. When will you be back?"

"In a couple of months."

She nodded and got to her feet. He offered his arm, but she declined.

The oilcloth that draped the table had seen happier days in decades long gone and was now adorned with supermarket liver pâté and indeterminate pieces of roast meat in foil trays. Villy knew all sorts of folk who shot more game than they could eat, so they were never short on calories.

His brother-in-law wheezed asthmatically as he bowed his head to his chest and said grace. Both he and his sister squeezed their eyes tight shut, though all their senses were directed toward the end of the table where he sat.

"Haven't you found God yet?" his sister asked after the prayer, her dead gaze fixed upon him.

"No, I'm afraid Father must have beaten Him out of me."

His brother-in-law raised his head deliberately and sent him a malicious glare. There was a time when he had been a handsome young man. Exuberant and full of ambitions about sailing the seven seas, exploring the corners of the world and the delights of all its luscious women. When then he found Eva, he fell in awe of her vulnerability and the beauty of her words. He had always known Jesus, though never as his best friend.

That was something Eva taught him.

"Speak respectfully of your father," Villy said now. "He was a reverent man."

He looked at his sister. Her face was without expression. If she had anything to say on the matter, now was the time. But she remained silent. Of course she did.

"You think our father's in heaven, don't you?"

His brother-in-law narrowed his eyes. That was his answer. One wrong word would suffice, it didn't matter whether he was Eva's brother or not.

He shook his head and returned his brother-in-law's stare. Ignorant, unenlightened individuals, he thought to himself. If the vision of a paradise housing that callous, small-minded, third-rate clergyman was so dear to Villy, then he would certainly have nothing against helping him get there as quickly as he liked.

"Don't look at me like that," he said. "There's thirty thousand kroner in an envelope for you and Eva. For that amount of money, you'd do well to keep a grip on yourself for the half hour I'm here."

He looked up at the crucifix on the wall above the disagreeable face of his brother-in-law. It was heavier than it looked.

He remembered. Its weight had been brought down against him.

He sensed them stirring in the back of the van as they crossed the great bridge that spanned the Storebælt. He pulled in for a moment at the toll area to give the two writhing bodies another whiff of chloroform.

As they settled again, he drove on, this time with the windows down and the annoying feeling that the second dose had been rather uncontrolled.

When eventually they reached the boathouse in Nordsjælland, it was still too light for him to lead the youngsters from the van. Out on the water, the last sailing boats of the day, the first of the season, were gliding back toward the marinas of Lynæs and Kignæs. One inquisitive soul with a pair of binoculars and all would be lost. The thing was, they were too quiet in the back of the van. It began now to concern him. Months of preparation would come to nothing if the chloroform had killed them.

"Come on, go down, for Chrissake," he muttered to himself, his gaze fixed firmly on the recalcitrant bloodred sphere in the sky that had wedged itself into the horizon amid flaming cloud.

Then he took out his mobile phone. The family at Stanghede would already be worried by his failure to return with their children. He had promised them he would be back before the hour of rest, and it was a promise he had not kept. He pictured them at this moment, waiting at the table with their candles and their robes, their folded hands. This would be the last time they placed their trust in him, the mother would be saying.

In a moment, she would feel the real pain of being right.

He called. There were no introductions, just his demand of one million kroner. Used notes in a small bag they were to throw from the train. He told them which departure to take, when and where to change, and on which stretch and which side they were to look for the strobe. He would be holding it in his hand and it would flash as bright as a camera. They should not delay, for this was their only chance. On delivery of the ransom, their children would be returned.

They should not consider cheating him. They had the rest of the weekend and Monday to raise the sum. And on Monday evening they were to take the train.

If the amount delivered fell short, the children would die. If they involved the police, the children would die. If they should try to trick him during delivery, the children would die.

"Remember," he said. "Money can be earned again, but the children will be gone forever." At this point, he always allowed the parents a moment to gasp for breath. To take in the shock. "Remember, too, that you cannot protect your other children forever. If I suspect anything to be amiss, be prepared to live in perpetual fear. That, and the fact that this phone cannot be traced, are the only two things on which you can rely."

And then he terminated the call. It was as simple as that. In ten seconds, he would hurl the phone into the fjord. He'd always had a good throwing arm.

The children were as pale as two corpses, but they were alive. He chained them inside the low-ceilinged boathouse, keeping them well apart. Then he removed their blindfolds and gags and made sure they did not regurgitate what he gave them to drink.

After the usual begging and pleading, the sobs and the fear, they accepted a small amount of food. His conscience was clear as he taped their mouths shut and then drove away.

He had owned the boathouse for fifteen years now, and no one besides himself had ever been near the place. The house to which it belonged was well hidden behind trees, and the stretch down to the water had always been overgrown. The only place from which this inconspicuous construction could on occasion be picked out was the water, but there were obstacles even there. Who would ever put in to that foul-smelling mush of seaweed and algae that extended across the net? The net he had drawn out between the fishing stakes after the time one of his victims had thrown something into the water.

The kids could whimper as much as they liked.

They would never be heard.

He looked at his watch again. He would not call his wife today before heading off toward Roskilde. Why should she know when to expect him home?

Now he would drive back to the cottage at Ferslev, put the van back in the barn, and then continue on in the Mercedes. In less than an hour, he would be home. And then he would see what to do with her.

The last few kilometers before he arrived, he found some kind of peace within himself. What had been the cause of this suspicion as regards his wife? Was it some failing of his own character? Did this unfounded doubt, these abominable thoughts, in fact find nourishment in the lies he thrived upon? Was it all not just a consequence of his own clandestine existence?

"The truth of the matter is we're happy together," he told himself out loud. It was his last thought before seeing the man's bike leaning against the willow in the driveway of their house.

Before seeing it, and before realizing that it was not his own.

17

There had been a time when their morning phone calls had given her a boost. Just the sound of his voice had been enough to see her through days without human contact. The thought of his embrace could see her through anything at all.

But it wasn't like that anymore. The magic was gone.

She had promised herself she would call her mother and patch things up with her. The day had passed, and morning came without her getting around to it.

What was she supposed to say? That she was sorry they had drifted apart? That perhaps she had been wrong? That she had met another man, and that he allowed her to see things in a new light? That he filled her with words that made her unable to hear anything else? She couldn't tell her mother any of this, that much was plain to her. But all of it was true.

The unending vacuum in which her husband had left her had now been filled.

Kenneth had been to the house more than once. He would be waiting there when Benjamin had been delivered to his day care. Always in a short-sleeved shirt and tight summer trousers, despite the vagaries of March. An eight-month tour of duty in Iraq, then ten months in Afghanistan had hardened him. The cold winter tamed a serviceman's hankerings for comfort, he explained.

It was quite irresistible. And quite terrifying.

Over the mobile, she had heard her husband ask after Benjamin and sensed his doubt that he could have fully recovered from his cold so quickly. She had also heard him say that he loved her and was looking forward to coming home. That he might be back sooner than expected. And she didn't believe the half of it. That was the difference now. Compared to when his words had dazzled her. Now she realized she had been blind.

She was frightened, too. Frightened of his rage, and of what he might do. If he threw her out, she would have nothing. He had made sure of that. There might be a little, but still nothing to speak of. Perhaps not even Benjamin.

There were so many words in him. Clever words. Who would ever believe her when she claimed Benjamin would be better off with her? Was she not the one leaving? Had her husband not devoted himself entirely to the family, made the sacrifice of long periods away from home in order to ensure their livelihood? She could hear them already. The local authority, the regional state administration to whom divorce applications were sent. The arbiters who would take note only of his responsible nature and her own misdeed.

She just knew.

She would call her mother later, she told herself. She would swallow all her pride, and the shame of it, and she would tell her everything. She's my mother, she said to herself. She will help me. I'm certain she will.

And then the hours passed, and her thoughts weighed down upon her. Why did she feel like this? Was it because in the space of only a few days she had come closer to a stranger than to the man to whom she was married? For this was a fact. The things she knew about her husband were the things they shared in the few hours they were together in the house. What more did she know than that? His work, his past, the packing cases upstairs, all of it remained closed to her.

But losing her feelings for him was one thing; justifying it was quite another. Had her husband not been good to her? Was her own fleeting infatuation preventing her from seeing things rationally?

These were the thoughts that preyed on her mind. And they were the reason she once again found herself drawn to the first floor of the house, to the door behind which his packing cases were stacked. She stood, considering it. Was this the time to seek out knowledge? Was this the time to transcend the boundary? Was this the point of no return?

Yes. It was.

She dragged out the packing cases one by one and arranged them in reverse order in the corridor. When she put them back, they had to be exactly as before, properly closed and with the pile of coats on top. It was the only way she could feel in control of the project.

That was her hope.

The first dozen boxes, from the rearmost row beneath the roof window, confirmed what her husband had told her. They contained old family items handed down. The same kind of clutter her own grandmother had left behind: a jumble of documents, porcelain, cigar cutters, lace tablecloths, watches and clocks, a twelve-piece set of cutlery, woolen blankets, bric-a-brac.

The picture of a family life long gone and consigned to memory. Just as he had described to her.

The next dozen added detail that seemed only to lay a confusing veil over this picture. Here were the gilded photo frames. Scrapbooks of cuttings. Albums prompting memories of events and occurrences. All of it from his childhood, and all with the strong undertone that lies and deceit are the silent attendants of reminiscence.

Because contrary to what he had always insisted, her husband was not an only child. There was absolutely no doubt that he had a sister.

One photo showed her husband in a sailor suit, his arms folded against his chest as he stared into the camera with eyes that were sad. No more than six or seven years old. His skin soft, the thick shock of hair parted at the side. Next to him was a little girl with long plaits and an innocent smile. It might have been the first time in her life she had been photographed.

It was a fine little portrait of two vastly different children.

She turned it over and considered the three printed letters. EVA. There had been more, but they had been crossed out with a pen.

She sifted through the other photographs, turning each one over. More words obliterated.

No names, no places.

Everything scribbled out.

Why would anyone do this? It was like willing people to disappear.

How often she had sat with her mother and peered blankly at old photos of people without names?

"That's your great-grandmother. Dagmar, she was called," she heard her mother say, though the name was nowhere to be seen. What would happen when her mother died? Where would all the names be then? Who would know who had given life to whom, and when?

But this little girl had a name. Eva.

She was definitely her husband's sister. The same eyes, the same mouth. In two of the photos in which they were pictured on their own together, she was gazing at her brother with admiration in her eyes. It was touching.

Eva looked like any other little girl. Fair and pure, and, with the exception of the very first photo, facing the world with a look that contained more trepidation than courage.

When brother and sister were pictured with their parents, they stood close together, as if to shield themselves from the world around them. Never touching, just standing close. Always the same tableau: children at the front, arms hanging limply at their sides; mother behind, her hands resting on the shoulders of the girl, and the father's hands on those of the boy.

It was as if those two pairs of hands were pressing down on the children, keeping them on the ground.

She tried to understand this boy with the weary eyes who would later become her husband. It was no easy task. There was a gulf of time between them, and she sensed this now more clearly than ever before.

Eventually, she returned the photos to their boxes and opened the scrapbooks, now with the certain conviction that everything would have been better if she and her husband had never met. That in fact she had been put into this world to share her destiny with a man such as the one she had now chanced upon and who lived only five streets away. Not the man she saw in these photos.

His father had been a pastor. He had never told her, but it was plain from the photographs.

He was an unsmiling man with eyes that exuded self-importance and authority.

The eyes of his wife were different. They were empty.

In these scrapbooks, she could see why. The father dictated everything. In the parish newsletters, he thundered against ungodliness, preached inequality, and renounced those who did not conform. There were pamphlets about holding the word of God in one's hand, releasing it only to hurl it into the face of the infidels. And all these outpourings made it clear to her that her husband's upbringing had been very different from her own.

Too different by far.

Throughout, this hateful torrent was infused with a nasty undercurrent of nationalist sentiment, malevolent opinion, intolerance, deep-rooted conservatism, and chauvinism. Though she acknowledged that this was the work of her husband's father and not of her husband himself, she nevertheless sensed, both now and, on reflection, in their daily life together, how the blight of the past had left within him a darkness that was assuaged only when he made love to her.

This was not what she wanted.

Something had been terribly wrong in that childhood. Whenever a name other than Eva's occurred, it was obliterated. And always it seemed with the same pen.

Next time she went to the library, she would Google Benjamin's grandfather. But first she needed to find out who he was. Something in these cuttings had to give her a name. And if she found a name, then she would surely be able to find some trace of this forceful and detestable man. Even in such a forgetful age as the present.

Perhaps she might even talk about it with her husband. Perhaps it might work something loose.

She moved on to a large number of shoeboxes stacked in one of the packing cases. Those at the bottom contained various items of limited interest: a Ronson lighter that worked, oddly enough, cufflinks, a letter opener and accumulated office articles, various indicators of different stages in a life.

The rest were a window on to what seemed to be a quite singular period. Cuttings, brochures, and political pamphlets. Each box revealed new fragments of her husband's life. Together they formed a picture of a disgraced and damaged individual becoming at once a mirror image and the diametrical opposite of his father. The boy moving instinctively away from the precepts laid down in his childhood. The youngster substituting reaction with action. The man taking to the barricades in support of everything totalitarian that was not concerned with religion. Seeking out the buzz of Vesterbrogade when the anarchists gathered. The sailor suit made way for hippie coat, combat jacket, Palestinian scarf, the latter pulled up in front of his face when circumstances dictated.

He was a chameleon in control of his colors. She saw that now.

She lingered for a moment, wondering if she should put everything back and forget about what she had seen. Collected in these boxes were things he clearly did not care to remember.

Was this not a sign that he was trying to put a lid on his past? Yes, it was. Otherwise he would surely have told her everything. Otherwise all these names would not be scribbled out.

But how was she to stop now?

If she did not immerse herself in his life, she would never be able to understand him. She would never know who the father of her child really was.

And so she turned to confront the rest of his life, put away so meticulously. Filing systems in shoeboxes, shoeboxes in packing cases. Everything labeled in chronological order.

She had been expecting to find periods in which he had ended up in trouble on account of his activism, but something prompted him to change direction. As though he had settled down for a while.

Each period of his life had been given its own plastic folder marked with the appropriate months and years. One year, he had apparently studied law. Another, philosophy. For a couple of years, he had backpacked in Central America, jobbing around hotels, vineyards, slaughterhouses.

Not until he returned home did he begin to emerge as the person she thought she knew. Again, these meticulous folders. Brochures from the armed forces. Jotted notes on the army sergeant school, the military police, the commando forces. After that, all personal records and the accumulation of cherished relics terminated.

There were no names, no specifics of places or personal relationships. Only outlines of the years that had passed.

The last indicator of where he might have been headed was a small collection of printed matter in a variety of languages. Trainee programs in shipping in Belgium. The Foreign Legion recruitment pamphlet with luscious photos of southern France. Copies of application forms for business education programs.

There was no suggestion what path he eventually would choose, only of the directions in which he was thinking at this time of his life.

Somehow, it all seemed quite chaotic.

And as she returned these boxes to their places, fear welled inside her. She knew his work was secret; he had told her so. Until now, the accepted truth had been that he served in a good cause. Intelligence services, undercover police work, something like that. But why had she been so certain that this was the case? Had she any proof?

The only thing she knew was that he had never led a normal life. He was an outsider; he existed on the edge.

Now she had pored through the first thirty years of his life, and still she knew nothing.

At last, she came to the packing cases that had been stacked uppermost. She had rummaged in a few already but by no means all. Now, opening them systematically one by one and sifting through their contents, the shocking question came to her: Why, of all his boxes, had these been left so accessible?

The question was shocking because she knew the answer.

The reason they were stored on top was that her prying in them had been deemed unthinkable. It was as simple as that. What could be more indicative of the power he exerted over his wife? She had accepted without question that this was his domain, and that her presence here was prohibited.

She realized just how completely he controlled her.

She opened these boxes with trepidation and dread, her lips pressed tightly together, breathing deeply and shakily through her nose.

They were full of files. A4 binders in all colors, though their contents were as black as the night.

The first bore witness to a period in his life when he had apparently sought to atone for his ungodliness. More printed matter, this time from all sorts of religious movements, meticulously filed away in plastic pockets. Flyers that spoke of the afterlife and the eternal light of God, and how it could be attained with guarantee. The pamphlets of new religious movements and sects, all absolutely certain that they alone possessed the definitive solutions to the tribulations of man. Names such as Sathya Sai Baba, Scientology, the Mother Church, Jehovah's Witnesses, God's Children, and the Community of the Eternal appeared alongside the Unification Church, the Fourth Way, the Divine Light Mission, and a host of others of which she had little or no knowledge. All of them claiming to be the only true path to salvation, harmony, and benevolence. The only true path, as sure as fate itself.

She shook her head. What had he been looking for, this man who had striven so hard to finally rid himself of the darkness and dogma of his childhood? As far as she was aware, none among this diversity of religious tenders had found favor in her husband's eyes.

No, the words "God" and "religion" did not easily find their way into their redbrick home in the mighty shadow of Roskilde Cathedral.

After she'd collected Benjamin from the day care and played with him for a time, she put him down in front of the television. As long as there were bright colors and the picture moved, he was happy.

She went upstairs and then wondered again if she ought to stop, put the remainder of the packing cases back without opening them, and leave her husband's tortured life alone.

Twenty minutes later, she was grateful not to have followed this impulse. Grateful, but scared. In fact, such was the extent of her distress that she now found herself seriously considering whether to pack a bag with some essentials, take the housekeeping money from the tin, and get on the first available train.

She had known that the last of the boxes might contain things that concerned the present period of his life, the one involving their marriage. But she was aghast to discover herself to be a project in her own right, the subject of one of his files.

He had told her that he had fallen head over heels in love with her the first time they had spoken. She had felt the same way. Now she knew that to be a deception.

How could their first encounter in that café have occurred by chance when here in his binder were cuttings from the show-jumping competition at Bernstorffsparken where she had won a place on the podium for the very first time? Months before they ever met. Where had he found these cuttings? Wouldn't he have shown them to her if he had got hold of them at some later date? Not only that, but he also had programs from competitions she had taken part in long before that one. He even had photos of her taken in places she knew they had never been together. He had been keeping her under surveillance right up to the time of their first meeting.

He had been waiting for the right moment at which to strike. She had been selected, and the fact was anything but flattering in view of how everything had panned out since.

The thought made her shudder.

She shuddered again when she opened a wooden filing box from the same packing case. At first glance, there was nothing special about it. Just a box containing lists of names and addresses unfamiliar to her. But on closer inspection of these papers she started to feel uneasy.

Why was this information so important to her husband? She was in the dark.

For each name on the list, a page of systematically ordered data was attached concerning the person in question as well as their family. First the religion they subscribed to. Then their status within their church community, followed by length of membership. More personal details followed, especially concerning children: names and ages and, most disturbingly, more intimate observations such as *Willers Schou, 15 yrs. Not his mother's favorite, but father extremely attached to him. Headstrong. Participation in church meetings erratic. Suffered colds most of the winter, twice confined to bed.*

What did her husband want with such information? And how did the listed incomes of these families concern him? Was he some sort of a spy working for the social authorities? Had he been selected to infiltrate religious sects in Denmark to uncover incest, violence, and other atrocities?

The uncertainty of it preyed horribly on her mind.

Seemingly, his work took him all over the country, so he would hardly be in the employment of any local authority. Yet neither did it seem likely that he was in the service of any government agency. Would data like this be kept in packing cases at home?

What, then? Private investigator? Was he on the payroll of some wealthy individual, charged with digging up dirt on religious communities?

Maybe.

Her uncertainty was compounded when she came to a document at the bottom, on which, beneath the details concerning the family, were printed the words: *1.2 million. No irregularities.*

She sat for a while with this piece of paper in her lap. As in the other cases, the information it contained concerned a family with a relatively large number of children and that was associated with a religious sect. This particular document was no different from the others apart from this last line and one additional detail: one of the children's names had been ticked. A sixteen-year-old boy about whom it was stated that he was loved by one and all.

Why had his name been ticked? Because he was loved?

She chewed on her lip and felt utterly lacking in ideas and initiative. All she knew was that everything inside her was screaming for her to get away. But was it the right thing to do?

Maybe this could give her leverage? Maybe it was how she could make sure Benjamin stayed with her. But as yet, she had no notion how.

She put the final two packing cases back inside the room. They contained nothing of consequence, only a few odd things of his they had found no use for.

Finally, she laid the coats carefully in place on top. The only sign of her indiscretion now was the indentation in the lid of one of the packing cases from when she had been looking for the phone charger, and even that was barely visible.

He won't notice, she told herself.

And then the doorbell rang.

Kenneth stood in the dwindling dusk with a gleam in his eye. As they had agreed, he held in his hand a crumpled edition of the day's paper, just as he had done the day before, ready to inquire as to whether their copy had arrived today. Prepared to deliver some spin about having found it in the road outside and how newspaper boys didn't seem to care less these days. All just in case her face signaled alarm when she opened the door, or if, against all expectations, her husband should answer.

This time she had no idea what expression to wear.

"Come in, but only for a minute," she said.

She glanced out across the road. It was getting dark now, and all was quiet.

"What's up? Is he on his way home?" Kenneth asked.

"No, I don't think so. He would have called."

"What, then? Are you not feeling well?"

"No." She chewed her lip again. What good would it do to involve him in all this? Wasn't it best to leave him out of her life for a while so that he wouldn't get mixed up in what was bound to come? Who would be able to prove any relationship between them if they broke off contact for a time?

She nodded to herself. "No, Kenneth, I'm not quite myself at the moment."

He remained silent, scrutinizing her. The keen eyes beneath his blond eyebrows were skilled in detecting danger. They had registered immediately that something was amiss. They had observed that whatever it was might impact on the feelings he no longer wished to keep in check. His defense instinct was awakened.

"Tell me what's wrong, Mia. Please tell me."

She pulled him away from the door of the living room where Benjamin sat happily in front of the television as only small children can. It was on little Benjamin she needed to concentrate her resources.

She would have turned to face him and told him there was nothing to worry about, but that she would have to go away for a while.

But at that same moment the headlights of her husband's Mercedes dissected the dusk in the driveway outside.

"You've got to go, Kenneth. Back door. Now!"

"Can't we—"

"NOW, Kenneth!"

"OK, but my bike's in the drive. What do you want me to do?"

Perspiration seeped from her armpits. Should she run away with him now? Just walk out through the door with Benjamin in her arms? No, she couldn't do it. She was too scared.

"I'll make something up. Just go! Through the kitchen, so Benjamin won't see!"

And then he was out, milliseconds before the key rasped in the lock and the front door opened.

She was sitting on the floor in front of the television with her legs out to the side, her arms around her son in a tight embrace.

"There you are, Benjamin," she said. "Daddy's here. Now we'll have lots of fun, won't we?"

18

On a foggy Friday in March, the primary route E22 traversing Skåne has little to recommend it. If you took out the houses and the road signs, you could just as easily be on your way from Ringsted to Slagelse, Carl thought to himself. It was flat, overcultivated, and devoid of anything that might be considered even remotely interesting.

And yet he could name at least fifty of his colleagues from HQ whose eyes lit up like fairy lights at the mere mention of Sweden. In their view, all human needs, without exception, could be satisfied as long as the blue and yellow flag happened to be fluttering over the landscape. Carl gazed out through the windscreen and shook his head. Apparently, he was missing something. That special gene that cast a person into raptures of delight at the utterance of even the smallest word of Swedish.

Only when he reached Blekinge did the landscape raise itself into something more becoming. It was said that when the gods distributed rocks across the earth, their hands were unsteady with fatigue by the time they reached Blekinge. While certainly more pleasing to the eye, there was little else to look at but trees and rocks. It was all still Sweden.

Not exactly deck chairs and Camparis, he mused as he drove into Hallabro, passing the usual combination of kiosk, petrol station, and auto repair shop with deals on refinishing jobs before continuing along Gamla Kongavägen.

In the dwindling light of day, the house seemed nicely situated up above the town. A drystone wall marked the boundary of the garden, and the light shining from three windows indicated that the Holt family had not been unduly alarmed by Assad's telephone call.

There was a knocker on the door. It was cracked, but he used it anyway. He waited, and heard no frenzied activity from within.

Then he realized it was Friday. Bollocks. Did Jehovah's Witnesses observe the Sabbath? If Jews observed the Sabbath on the Friday, then presumably it was in the Bible, and Jehovah's Witnesses followed the Bible to the letter.

He knocked again. Perhaps they weren't allowed to answer the door? Did the Sabbath prohibit all movement? What was he supposed to do then? Kick the door in? Probably not a good idea in these parts. Most likely everyone kept a hunting rifle under the mattress.

He stood there for a moment and glanced around. The town had tucked itself in for the evening. It was all feet up now, and fuck it, we'll do it tomorrow.

Carl wondered where the hell he was going to stay for the night in this far-flung outpost. And then suddenly a light went on behind the glass.

The door opened slightly, and the pale and solemn face of a boy aged about fifteen appeared in the crack and stared at him without a word.

"Hello, there," said Carl. "Are your mum and dad in?"

The boy closed the door just as cautiously as he had opened it, and locked it behind him. The face had been calm and without emotion. Apparently, he knew what to do in a situation like this, and letting uninvited visitors in seemed not to be an option.

A few minutes passed, during which Carl stood staring at the door. Sometimes it helped to be persistent.

A couple of local residents walked past beneath the streetlights, their eyes fixed on him as if to say: Who are you? Faithful watchdogs, every small town had them.

Then eventually the face of a man appeared at the pane in the door. Persistence paid off again.

The face stared at Carl without expression, though clearly perplexed, as though they had been expecting someone else.

And then he opened the door.

"Yes?" he said, delivering the initiative.

Carl produced his badge. "Carl Mørck, Department Q, Copenhagen," he said. "Are you Martin Holt?"

The man scrutinized Carl's ID uneasily and then nodded.

"May I come in?"

"What's it about?" the man replied softly and in perfect Danish.

"Perhaps we could talk about that inside?"

"I think not." He retreated and was about to close the door again when Carl grasped the handle.

"Martin Holt, may I have a word with your son Poul?"

The man hesitated. "No," he said after a moment. "He's not here, so I'm afraid that won't be possible."

"Then where would I be able to find him, if you don't mind me asking?"

"I don't know." He looked Carl directly in the eye. Rather too directly, given the nature of his utterance.

"You mean to say you have no idea of your son's whereabouts, no address?"

"That's correct. And now I should like you to leave us in peace. We're in the middle of Bible study."

Carl produced a document. "This is the Civil Registration System's list of persons occupying your home address in Græsted on the sixteenth of February, 1996, the day Poul gave up his studies at the College of Engineering. The names here are those of yourself and your wife, Laila, and your children Poul, Tryggve, Mikkeline, Ellen, and Henrik." He glanced down, the page. "The civil registration figures here tell me that the children are now thirty-one, twenty-six, twenty-four, sixteen, and fifteen years old. Is that correct?"

Martin Holt nodded and shooed away the boy who stood peering inquisitively over his shoulder. Most likely it was Henrik.

Carl studied the boy furtively. He had the same kind of passive, empty look in his eyes that people get when the only thing over which they have control is when to go to the toilet.

Carl looked back at the man in front of him, who seemed to keep such a tight rein on his family. "We know that Tryggve and Poul were together that day at the college when Poul was there for the last time," he said. "So if Poul has moved away from home, perhaps I might have a word with Tryggve instead? It won't take a moment."

"We no longer speak to Tryggve." The words were delivered in a voice that was cold and without modulation, but the light of the outside lamp revealed the gray pallor that characterizes people whose burdens at work weigh heavy. Too much to do, too many decisions to make, and too few positive experiences. Gray skin and dull eyes. The last things Carl noticed before the man slammed the door in his face.

Seconds passed, and the outside lamp was switched off. Then the light in the hallway. But Carl knew the man was still there, waiting for him to go.

And then he heard Martin Holt begin to pray.

"Bridle our tongue, dear Lord, so that we may speak not the cruel word that is untrue, the true word that is not the whole truth, the whole truth that is without pity. For the sake of Jesus Christ, our Lord," he pronounced in Swedish.

"Bridle our tongue, dear Lord" and "We no longer speak to Tryggve." What was that supposed to mean? Was all mention of Tryggve forbidden? Or Poul, for that matter? Had both been ostracized following whatever it was that had happened? Had they shown themselves to be unworthy of the kingdom of God? Was that what this was all about?

If it was, then it was no business of any officer of the law.

What to do, he wondered. Should he get in touch with the Karlshamn police and ask for assistance? But on what grounds? The family hadn't done anything they weren't supposed to. At least, not as far as he could make out.

He shook his head, walked silently away from the door, and got back in the car. He thrust the gear lever into reverse and backed slowly up the road, parking at a discreet distance from the house.

Removing the lid from his thermos, he found the contents to be stone cold. Brilliant. The last time he had done a stakeout at night had been ten years earlier, and he had been equally reluctant. Damp March nights in a car without a decent headrest, sipping stone-cold coffee from a plastic thermos lid wasn't exactly what he'd been dreaming of when he'd taken the chance and moved on to Copenhagen Police HQ. And now here he was. Without a clue, apart from this maddening, matter-of-fact instinct of his that told him how to read people's reactions and what they might lead to.

This man in the house on the hill had not reacted naturally. That much was clear to him. Martin Holt had been just a bit too dismissive, too gray in the face, too insensitive in speaking of his two eldest sons. And too uninterested in what a detective of the Copenhagen police might be doing in this rocky neck of the woods. It wasn't what people said but rather what they didn't say that gave the game away when they were hiding something. And that was definitely the case here.

He stared ahead toward the house on the bend, then wedged his coffee cup between his thighs. He would close his eyes now. Power napping, they called it.

Two minutes, that would be enough, he thought to himself, only to wake up twenty minutes later when he became aware that his genitals were being refrigerated by cold coffee.

"Bollocks!" he blurted out loud, flapping at the icy liquid seeping into his trousers. He repeated the utterance a moment later as the headlights of a car swept away from the house and down the road toward Ronneby.

He let the coffee soak into the seat cover and threw the car into gear. The night was dark. Once they were out of Hallabro, only the stars and the car ahead of him stuck out in the pitch black.

They drove ten, maybe fifteen kilometers until the beam of the headlights struck a hideously yellow house on the brow of a hill, built so close to the road that it seemed even a moderate breath of wind might be enough for the ramshackle construction to make a mess of the traffic.

The car turned in and remained in the driveway. After ten minutes, Carl left his Peugeot at the side of the road and cautiously approached the house, sideways like a crab.

Only now did he realize that there were passengers in the car. Motionless and barely visible. Four figures of various sizes.

He waited a few moments, taking note of the surroundings. Quite apart from its color, garish even in darkness, the house was hardly encouraging to look at.

Scrap metal, assorted junk, and machinery no longer in use lay everywhere. It looked like the owner had died years ago and the place had been left to fall apart.

A far cry from the family's elegant abode in Græsted, Carl thought to himself, his gaze following the headlights of a fast-moving car that swept up the hill from the direction of Ronneby, the beam illuminating the gable end of the house and the yard. For a brief second, a mother's face, swollen with tears, was made visible through the window of the parked car, and a young woman and two teenagers on the backseat. Everyone in the vehicle seemed to be affected by the situation. They were silent yet clearly upset, their faces filled with fright.

Carl moved forward to the side of the house and put his ear to the rotten wooden cladding. Close up, he could see that only the paint seemed to be keeping the place together.

Inside, words were being exchanged. Two men were arguing, and were obviously far from reaching agreement. The voices were harsh and irreconcilable. It was a shouting match.

When they stopped, Carl hardly had time to catch sight of the man as he slammed the door behind him and almost threw himself into the driver's seat of the waiting car.

There was a squeal of tires as the Holt family frenziedly reversed onto the road and tore off in a southerly direction. Carl had already made up his mind.

This ugly yellow house was whispering to him.

And he was all ears.

The nameplate read *Lillemor Bengtsen,* but the woman who opened the yellow door was nothing like the little housewife the name suggested. In her early twenties, with blond hair and slightly overlapping front teeth, she was quite simply adorable, as they used to say in another age.

Maybe Sweden wasn't that bad, after all.

"I think perhaps you might be expecting me." He produced his badge. "Would Poul Holt be here, by any chance?"

She shook her head but smiled. For all the ferocity of the disagreement that had just taken place, she had apparently kept herself well out of it.

"How about Tryggve, then?"

"You'd better come in!" she said briskly in Swedish, then indicated a closed door farther inside the house.

"He's here, Tryggve," she called into the living room. "I'm going to lie down, OK?"

She smiled at Carl as though they knew each other, then left him alone with her boyfriend.

He was tall and almost painfully thin, but then what had Carl been expecting? He extended his hand and received a firm handshake in response.

"Tryggve Holt," the young man said by way of introduction. "My father was here to warn me."

Carl nodded. "My impression was you two weren't on speaking terms?"

"We're not. I'm an outcast now. I haven't spoken to them for four years, but I've often seen them parked outside on the road."

His eyes were calm. They bore no trace of the altercation such a short time ago and seemed unconcerned by the present situation. So Carl went straight to the point.

"We found a message in a bottle," he said, noting an immediate flicker in the man's impassive face. "Actually, it turned up in a fishing net off the coast of Scotland some years back, though it only came into our hands at Police Headquarters in Copenhagen a week or so ago."

Now the reaction was more visible, if not to say undeniable, and what had triggered it were the four words: message in a bottle. As though all these years they had been at the back of his mind. Perhaps he had been waiting for someone to utter them. Perhaps they were the password to all the mysteries that remained inside him.

He bit his lip. "A message in a bottle, you say?"

"Yes, perhaps you'd like to see it." He handed the young man a copy of the letter.

In the space of two seconds, Tryggve shrank to three-quarters of his size, twisting around on his own axis and knocking everything within reach to the floor. Had it not been for Carl's quick reflexes, he would have been knocked over in the same way.

"What's going on?" It was the girlfriend, standing in the doorway with her hair untied, clad in a T-shirt that only just covered her naked thighs. Already on her way to bed.

Carl indicated the letter.

She picked it up, glanced through the contents, and handed it to her boyfriend.

Then no one spoke for several minutes.

When eventually he regained some composure, the young man glanced at the document as though it were a dangerous animal that might pounce at any moment and finish him off for good. As though his only defense was to read it again, word for word.

Lifting his gaze to Carl once more, he was visibly changed. His unruffled self-assurance seemed to have been absorbed by the message he held in his hands. The pulse in his neck throbbed conspicuously, his face was flushed, his lips trembled. There was little doubt that the letter had rekindled a very traumatic experience indeed.

"Oh, God," he said softly, closing his eyes and putting his hand to his mouth.

His girlfriend took his hand in hers. "It's all right, Tryggve. It had to come out sooner or later. Now it's over, and everything's going to be all right!"

He dried his eyes and turned to face Carl. "I never saw the letter, only watched it being written."

He picked it up and read it again, his trembling fingers continuously reaching to wipe the tears from the corners of his eyes.

"My brother was the cleverest, kindest person," he stuttered, his lips quivering still. "But it was so hard for him to express himself."

He placed the letter on the table in front of him, folded his arms, and leaned forward. "It really was."

Carl reached to put a hand on his shoulder, but Tryggve shied away and shook his head.

"Can we talk about it tomorrow?" he said. "I can't now. You can sleep here on the sofa, if you want. Lillemor will make a bed up for you. Would that be OK?"

Carl glanced at the sofa. It was on the short side, but thickly upholstered.

He awoke to the swish of passing cars on the wet road outside. He uncurled and stretched his body, turning in the same movement to face the windows. It was impossible to tell what time it was, though it was still quite dark. Across the room, the young couple sat holding hands in a pair of dilapidated armchairs from IKEA. They nodded. There was already a thermos on the table, and next to it the letter.

"You already know it was my elder brother Poul who wrote it," Tryggve began, once Carl had shown signs of life with the first aromatic wafts of coffee.

"His hands were tied behind his back." Tryggve's eyes flickered as he spoke.

Hands tied. Laursen had been right.

"I haven't a clue how he managed it," Tryggve went on. "But Poul was very thorough. He was good at drawing. He was good at a lot of things."

He smiled mournfully. "You've no idea how much it means to me that you've come here. To be sitting here with this letter in my hand. Poul's letter."

Carl cast his eye once more over the document. Tryggve Holt had added a couple more letters. If anyone could, then surely it was he.

Then Carl took a slurp of his coffee. Only his polite upbringing prevented him from immediately clutching his throat and spraying the hot liquid into the air with an explosion of guttural sound.

It was like drinking tar. Pitch-black caffeinated poison.

"Where is Poul now?" he asked, clenching lips and buttocks as hard as he could. "And why did he write that letter? We'd like to know so we can proceed with other investigations."

"You want to know where Poul is?" The young man fixed his mournful gaze on Carl. "If you'd asked me some years ago, I would have said he was in heaven with the one hundred and forty-four thousand. Now all I can say is that Poul is dead. This letter is the last thing he ever wrote. The last sign of life."

He swallowed with difficulty and paused for a moment.

"Poul was killed less than two minutes after he dropped the bottle into the water," he added, so quietly as to be barely audible.

Carl gathered himself on the sofa. This was information he would have felt better prepared to receive fully clothed.

"Are you saying he was murdered?"

Tryggve nodded.

Carl frowned. "You mean the kidnapper murdered Poul and let you go?"

Lillemor extended her slender fingers and caught the tears as they descended down Tryggve's cheek. He nodded again.

"Yes. The bastard let me go, and I've cursed him a thousand times ever since."

19

If he were to pick out one of his abilities that never failed him, it was being able to detect a false look.

When, in his childhood, the family gathered at the table and so disingenuously recited the Lord's Prayer, he could always tell when his father had beaten his mother. There were no visible marks, for he was clever enough never to hit anyone in the face. There was the congregation to think about. And his mother remained at heel, always with that inscrutable, sanctimonious look on her face, keeping an eye out to make sure the children remembered their manners and ate the apportioned number of potatoes with the apportioned amount of meat. But behind the calmness in her eyes were fear and hatred and utter despair.

He saw it clearly.

Sometimes, albeit more seldom, he would see the same false innocence in the eyes of his father, who nearly always wore the same expression. The routine meting out of corporal punishment was not in itself sufficient to dilate the icy, piercing pupils of the pastor.

So he knew all about falseness in a person's eye. And this was what he saw now.

At the very moment he walked into the room he detected a strangeness in the way his wife looked at him. She was smiling, certainly, yet this was a smile that trembled, and her gaze came to a halt in the empty space in front of his face.

Had she not clasped the child to her bosom as she sat there on the floor, he might have thought she was tired or had a headache, but there she was with the child in her arms and a distant look in her eye.

Something wasn't right.

"Hi," he said, inhaling the conglomerate of scents in the room. There was an aromatic undertone in the familiar smell of home, something that wasn't usually there. A faint odor of complication, and of boundaries that had been overstepped.

"Any chance of a cup of tea?" he asked, and stroked his hand across her cheek. It was warm, as if she were running a temperature.

"And how are you today, young man?" He took the child in his arms and looked into his eyes. They were clear and happy and tired. The smile came instantly. "He seems to be all right now," he said.

"Yes, he is. But he was full of cold yesterday, then suddenly this morning he was right as rain. You know how they are." She gave a hint of a smile, and it too seemed strange.

It was as if she had aged during the few days he had been away.

He kept his promise. Made love to her as intensely as the week before. But this time it took longer than usual. Longer for her to succumb and separate body from mind.

Afterward, he drew her into his arms and allowed her to rest against his frame. It was her habit to play absently with the hairs on his chest, stroke his neck with her slender, sensual fingers. But this time she did none of this. All she did was concentrate on keeping her breathing steady, and otherwise she was silent.

That was why he asked her so directly. "There's a man's bike in the driveway. Do you know where it came from?"

She pretended to be sleeping.

It wouldn't matter what she said.

A couple of hours later, he lay with his arms behind his head, watching the dawn of another March day, the lazy light seeping across the ceiling, meticulously enlarging the room surface by surface.

His mind was at rest now. There was a problem, but he would deal with it once and for all.

When she woke up, he would strip away her lies, layer by layer.

The interrogation proper did not begin until after she had put the child down in his playpen. It was just as she had expected.

For four years they had lived together without ever challenging the trust that existed between them, but now the time had come.

"The bike's locked, so it can't have been stolen," he said, sending her a look that was too neutral by far. "Someone left it there on purpose, wouldn't you say?"

She thrust out her lower lip and gave a shrug. How was she supposed to know? But her husband wasn't looking.

She felt the treachery of perspiration under her arms. In a moment, her forehead would begin to glisten.

"I'm sure we could find out who owns it, if we wanted," he said, and peered at her, his head lowered.

"Do you think so?" She tried to seem surprised rather than taken unawares. Then she put her hand to her forehead as though something were bothering her. Yes, it was damp now.

He stared at her intently. The kitchen was too small all of a sudden.

"How would we do that?" she went on.

"We could ask the neighbors. They might have seen someone leave it there."

She breathed in deeply. She knew with certainty he would stop short of that.

"Yes, I suppose we could," she replied. "But don't you think whoever left it there will come back for it at some point? We could put it out by the road."

He leaned back slightly. More relaxed now. She, however, was not. She drew her hand across her forehead again.

"You're sweating," he said. "Is something the matter?"

She pursed her lips and expelled air. Keep calm, she told herself. "I think I might be running a temperature. I must have caught something from Benjamin."

He nodded, then tilted his head. "By the way, where did you find the charger for your phone?"

She took another bread roll and split it in two. "In the basket in the hall, with all the hats and gloves in it." Now she felt herself to be on more solid ground. If only she could stay there.

"In the basket?"

"I didn't know where to put it after I finished, so I just put it back again."

He stood up without a word. In a moment, he would sit down again and ask what on earth a phone charger had been doing in the basket in the hall. And she would say that most likely it had been there for ages.

And then she realized her mistake.

The bike in the driveway outside ruined the story. He would link the two things together. That was the way he was.

She stared into the living room where Benjamin stood rattling the bars of his playpen as though he were an animal fighting to get out.

She felt the same way.

The charger looked small in her husband's hand. As if he could crush it with one squeeze. "Where's this from?" he demanded.

"I thought it was yours," she answered.

He said nothing. So he took his with him on his trips.

"You might as well tell me," he said. "I know you're lying."

She tried to look indignant. It wasn't difficult. "What do you mean? What are you talking about? If it's not yours, then someone must have left it behind. In which case it's probably been there since the christening."

But she was trapped.

"The christening? That was eighteen months ago. The christening!"

Clearly, he found the idea ridiculous. Only he wasn't laughing. "There were a dozen guests at most. Old biddies, mainly. None of them stayed the night, and not many were likely to own a mobile phone. And even if they did, why would they bring a charger with them to a christening? It doesn't make sense."

She felt an urge to protest, but he raised his hand to stop her.

"You're lying." He gestured toward the bike in the driveway. "It's his charger, isn't it? When was he here last?"

The reaction came promptly from the sweat glands of her armpits.

He gripped her arm, and his hand was clammy. She had been in two minds about the contents of the packing cases upstairs, but what decided her was this grip on her arm, as tight and forceful as a vise. And now he's going to hit me, she thought to herself. But he didn't. Instead, he turned away when she failed to answer, slamming the door shut behind him, and after that nothing more happened.

She stood up, hoping to catch a glimpse of his fleeting figure outside. As soon as she felt certain he was gone, she would take Benjamin with her and make her getaway. Down the garden to the hedge at the bottom, find the gap the previous owners' kids had made, and squeeze through. They would be at Kenneth's within five minutes. Her husband would never know where they had gone.

After that, she would have to take things from there.

But the fleeting figure outside never appeared. Instead came a heavy thud from upstairs.

"Oh, God," she breathed. "What's he doing?"

She glanced into the living room at her bouncing, laughing child. Could they make it to the hedge without her husband noticing? Were the upstairs windows still open? Was he standing at one of them, watching to see what she did next?

She chewed on her upper lip and looked up at the ceiling. What was he doing up there?

Then she picked up her bag and took all the housekeeping money from the tin. She was too afraid to go into the hallway to get Benjamin's romper and her jacket. They would just have to make do. And hope that Kenneth wasn't out.

"Come on, darling," she said, picking up her child. Once the patio door was open, it would take them less than ten seconds to get to the hedge. The question was whether the gap was still there. She had seen it last year.

It had been big enough then.

20

When he and Eva were children, they had inhabited another world. Their father closing the door of his study gave them peace. They could be in their rooms and let God take care of Himself.

But there were other times, too, in the obligatory Bible study lessons or during worship amid the outstretched hands, the cries of joy, the grown-ups in transports of ecstasy, when they turned their gaze inwards and retreated to their own reality.

They each had their own ways. Eva stole glances at the women's shoes and dresses and preened herself. Ran the pleats of her skirt between her fingers until they were crisp and neat. She was a princess inside. Free from strict looks and harsh words. Or else she was a fairy with gossamer wings that even the slightest breath of air could lift above the gray reality and imperatives of their home.

And there she hummed to herself. Hummed with glee in her eyes, her feet shuffling on the spot, their parents convinced that she was safely in the hands of God and that these fussy movements were her own form of praise.

But he knew better. Eva dreamed of shoes and dresses, and a world of adoring mirrors and loving words. He was her brother. He knew.

He himself dreamed of a world full of people who could laugh.

In the place where they were, no one ever laughed. Laughter lines in faces were something he saw in the town, and he found them displeasing. His life was without laughter. Without joy. Not since he was five years old, when his father had told them about a pastor of the Church of Denmark whom he had frightened away from his church amid curses and oaths, had he heard him laugh. And for that reason it took years for his soul to grasp that laughter could be something other than taking pleasure in hurting another person.

When finally he discovered that, he became deaf to his father's taunts and admonitions and learned to be on his guard.

He kept secrets that could make him happy, but they were also dangerous. Underneath his bed, in the farthest corner, underneath the mount board of a stuffed weasel, lay his treasures. Weekly magazines—*The Home* and *The Family Journal*—with the most marvelous illustrations and stories. Mail-order catalogs from Daells Varehus in Copenhagen, with photographs of women almost without clothes on, staring out at him from the page and smiling. And comic books, too, so insane they made him hoot with laughter: *Humor Half-hour, Daffy, Donald Duck*. Magazines that tickled and challenged the senses, but which demanded nothing in return. He found them in the dustbins of the neighbors when he crept out of his window after dark.

And he would lie beneath his duvet in the night and chuckle without a sound.

It was during this period of his life that he learned to pull the doors ajar, so he knew where everyone was inside the house. He learned to wait for an opening so that he might bring his trophies back home without risk of being caught.

He learned to listen like a bat on the hunt.

No more than two minutes passed from the moment he left his wife downstairs until he saw her sneak out through the patio door with the child in her arms. As he had expected.

She wasn't stupid. Young and naive and easy to read, perhaps, but not stupid. She knew he was on to something, and so she was scared. He saw it clearly in her face, heard it in the tone of her voice.

And now she was trying to escape.

As soon as she spotted an opening, she would react. It was only a matter of time, he had known that. That was why he stood now at the window upstairs, tramping his feet on the wooden floor so she'd know she could get away, stopping only when she was almost at the hedge.

It was so easy to make certain of her. He felt a wrench inside him, though he had long since grown accustomed to the faithlessness of others.

He looked down at the woman and the child. A life was about to close. In a moment, they would be gone.

The hedge had grown thick. He waited for a moment before descending the stairs in two bounds and following her out into the garden.

So conspicuous she was, this young, beautiful woman in her red dress with the child in her arms. It would be a simple matter to follow her from a distance, though she was already down the road by the time he squeezed through the hedge.

At the main road, she turned the corner, passed a single side street, then slipped back into the peaceful residential area once more.

It was a move he had not expected.

"Stupid woman," he muttered to himself. "Are you making a cuckold out of me on my own turf?"

The summer he turned eleven, his father's congregation erected a hired marquee on the town common when it was time for the annual fair. "If those godless socialists can do it," he declared, "the free churches can, too."

They labored all morning to make it ready. It was heavy work, but there were other children, too, bullied into lending a hand. And when they were finished putting down the floor, his father patted all the other children on the head.

His own children received no thanks and were instead deployed to put out the folding chairs.

There were a lot.

The fair opened. Four golden halos shone above the entrance of the marquee, and a guiding star swung from the center pole. *Embrace The Lord—Let Him In* implored a banner that ran along the side.

And they were there, in numbers, his father's flock, and they praised the good work that had been done. But despite all the colored leaflets he and Eva ran around handing out to people, not a single outsider came.

His father's anger and frustration was taken out on his mother when no one was around to see.

"You brats get out there again," he hissed. "And do things properly this time."

They lost each other by the stalls at the edge of the fair. Eva dallied over some rabbits that were on show, and he went on alone. It was the only way he could help their mother.

He held out his leaflets with beseeching eyes, ignored by everyone. If only they would take some, perhaps she might not be beaten when they got home. Then she might not cry all through the night.

He scouted around for a kind face, for someone who might share their fear of God. He listened out for a voice as mild and gentle as Jesus preaching.

That was when he heard children laughing. Not the way he had heard before, passing a playground, or on a television seen in the window of the electrical shop. These children were laughing as though their vocal cords would snap, and no one could resist their appeal. They laughed as he had never laughed at home beneath his duvet, and the sound of it drew him on.

The voice inside him could whisper for all its might about anger and repentance. He was simply unable to walk past and ignore the sounds he heard.

A small crowd had gathered in front of a stall, grown-ups and children together. On a banner of white linen, a child had written *GREAT VIDIO FILMS HALF PRIZE ONLY TODAY,* and on a makeshift table of planks was the smallest television set he had ever seen.

The children were laughing at the flickering monochrome images running across the tiny screen, and he soon found himself laughing with them. Laughing until it hurt inside, right down in the pit of his belly and in the part of his soul that was only now allowed to flourish.

"No one compares to Chaplin," one of the grown-ups said.

And everyone laughed at the little man as he boxed and danced his pirouettes on the screen. They howled when he twirled his cane and lifted his bowler hat, and when he pulled faces at the fat ladies and the men with blacking around their eyes. And he laughed, too, and the cramp in his belly and all that was delightful and unsuppressed and unexpected overwhelmed him, and no one slapped his neck or took the slightest notice of him because of it.

This experience would, in its own singular way, change his life, and that of a great many others besides.

His wife did not look back. In fact, she didn't see much at all, her legs propelling her and the child forward along the pavement as though invisible forces determined her route and speed.

And when someone becomes removed from reality in this way, the slightest little thing will often be enough to trigger catastrophe.

A nut loosening from the wing of an airplane. A drop of water short-circuiting the relay of a respirator.

He saw the pigeon settle in the tree above his wife and son as they were about to cross the road, and he noted its excrement splattering into ghostly fingers on the pavement. He saw his son point to it and his wife look down. And at the very moment they stepped out into the road, a car turned the corner and seemed almost to target them.

He could have shouted out. He could have yelled or whistled to warn them. But he did nothing. It wasn't the moment. Emotion didn't kick in.

The brakes of the car squealed, the driver behind the windscreen yanked at the steering wheel, and the world stood still.

He saw the frightened faces of his child and his wife turn in slow motion. The vehicle skidded and careered to the side, leaving tire marks on the road behind it like charcoal on drawing paper. And then it straightened out, the rear end found purchase again, and it was over.

His wife remained transfixed in the gutter as the car hurtled past, and he himself stood as though paralyzed, arms hanging limply at his side. Feelings of tenderness struggled against an odd rush of excitement inside him. He recognized it from the first time he had killed a person. It was a feeling he did not welcome.

He allowed the air compressed inside his lungs to escape and felt a warmth spread through his body. And he remained standing there just a moment too long, because Benjamin caught sight of him as he turned his head and clutched at his mother. He had clearly been given a fright by her reaction. But the sight of his father put him at ease again: he waved his arms and chuckled.

And then she turned around and saw him, and the look of terror from seconds before became fixed.

Five minutes later, she was sitting in front of him in the living room, her head turned away. "You're coming home now without a fight," he had said. "Because if you don't, you'll never see our son again."

And now her eyes were full of hatred and recalcitrance.

If he wanted to know where she had been going, he would have to force it out of her.

These were rare and joyful moments he and his sister spent together.

If he started in the right place in the bedroom, he could walk ten short paces before reaching the mirror. His feet splayed out, his head rocking from side to side, the cane twirling in his hand. Ten paces, and he was someone else in the world of the mirror. No longer the boy without a friend. No longer the son of the man the people of that small community held in such esteem. No longer the chosen one of the flock who was to carry the weight of the word of God and turn it like a thunderbolt upon the people. He was the little tramp who made everyone laugh, not least himself.

"I'm Chaplin, Charlie Chaplin," he said, and wriggled his lip beneath the imaginary mustache, and Eva almost fell off their parents' bed laughing. She had reacted in exactly the same way the other times he had put on his act, but this time would be the last.

After that, she never laughed again.

A second later, he felt the prod on his shoulder. The touch of an index finger was all it took for his breathing to cease and his mouth to turn dry. As he turned, his father's fist was already on its way toward his abdomen. His eyes were wild with anger beneath bushy eyebrows. There was no sound but the sound of the blow and the ones that followed.

He felt a burning sensation in his colon as gastric acid welled in his throat. He staggered backward, then stood still and looked his father defiantly in the eye.

"So the name's Chaplin, is it?" his father spat, glaring at him with the same look he employed on Good Friday when recounting the weary path of the Lord Jesus on his way to Calvary. All the grief and suffering of the world lay upon his willing shoulders. Of that there was no doubt, not even for a child.

And then he struck again. This time a lunging haymaker of a punch, for otherwise he would not have been able to reach, and no defiant child would ever have the pleasure of forcing him to step forward so that he might deliver his punishment.

"Who put such ungodliness into your head?"

He looked down at his father's feet. From now on, he would answer questions only when it suited him. His father could beat him as often as he wished, but he would not answer.

"Answer me, or I shall be forced to punish you!"

He was dragged by the ear back into his own room and hurled onto the bed. "You stay here until we come for you, do you understand?"

This question, too, he ignored. His father stood for a moment with a look of puzzlement in his eyes, his lips parted as though this child's defiance marked Judgment Day itself and the coming of the all-consuming Flood. And then he composed himself.

"Gather your things together and put them outside," he commanded.

At first he didn't grasp what his father meant, though his intention would soon become plain.

"Leave your clothes, your shoes, and your bedding. Put everything else outside."

He removed the child from his wife's gaze and left her sitting alone with the slats of pale light the Venetian blinds laid across her face.

Without the child, she would be going nowhere. He knew that.

"He's asleep now," he said when he returned from upstairs. "Now tell me, what's going on?"

"You want to know what's going on?" She turned her head deliberately. "Shouldn't I be the one asking that question?" she replied with darkness in her eyes. "What do you do for a living, exactly? Where do you get all that money from? Is it crime? Do you blackmail people?"

"Blackmail? What makes you think that?"

She turned away from him again. "It makes no difference. I want you to let me and Benjamin go. I don't want to stay here any longer."

He frowned. She was asking questions. She was making demands. Was there something he had overlooked in all this?

"I'm asking you, what makes you think that?"

She gave a shrug. "What doesn't? You're always away. You never tell me anything. You've got boxes piled up in a room like a shrine. You lie about your family. You . . ."

It wasn't because he interrupted her. She stopped of her own accord. Stared down at the floor, unable to retrieve the words that should never have passed her lips. Scuppered by her own overweening confidence.

"So you've been through my boxes?" he asked calmly, though the realization seared his flesh as though he were on fire.

She knew things about him, things she wasn't supposed to know.

If he didn't get rid of her now, he would be done for.

His father looked on as he gathered his belongings in a pile outside his room. Old toys, books by Ingvald Lieberkind with animal pictures in them, odds and ends he had collected. A good stick to scratch his back with, a jar full of crab's claws, fossilized sea urchins and belemnites. He put everything into the pile. And when he had finished, his father pulled his bed away from the wall and tipped it onto its side. And there lay all his secrets beneath the moth-eaten mounted weasel. The weeklies, the comic books, and all his hours of carefree pleasure.

His father surveyed them briefly. Then he gathered them together in a stack and began to count, wetting his finger occasionally to facilitate the process. Each magazine was a voice of dissent, each voice one lash of the belt.

"Twenty-four. I won't ask where you got them from, Chaplin, because I don't care. Now you will turn your back to me and I shall lash you twenty-four times. And when we're done, I wish never to see such filth in my house ever again, do you understand?"

He did not reply. He simply stared at the pile in front of him and bade farewell to each and every one of his magazines.

"Failure to reply. That doubles the punishment. Perhaps it might teach you a lesson."

It never did. Despite the weals all down his back and the bloom of bruises at his neck, he uttered not a word before his father again fastened his belt. Not a whimper.

The hardest part was not to burst into tears ten minutes later when he was ordered to set fire to his possessions in the yard outside the house.

That was what really hurt.

She cowered in front of the packing cases. Her husband had spoken as he dragged her up the stairs, an incessant flow of words, but she was saying nothing. Nothing at all.

"We need to get two things straight," he said. "Give me your phone."

She took it out of her pocket, safe in the knowledge that it would provide him with no answers. Kenneth had shown her how to delete calls.

He pressed some keys and studied the display, only to find nothing incriminating. She was glad that she had outwitted him. What would he do now with all his suspicions?

"You've learned to delete your calls, haven't you?"

She did not reply, but twisted the phone from his hand and returned it to her back pocket.

And then he gestured toward the small room in which his packing cases were stacked. "Very neatly done, I must say."

She breathed rather more easily now. He would find nothing here to give her away. Eventually, he would have to let her go.

"But not quite good enough, I'm afraid."

She blinked twice as she scanned the room. Weren't the coats put back in place? Was the dent in that one case really noticeable?

"Look at the marks here." He bent down and pointed. On the front edge of one of the cases a small notch had been made. And one exactly the same on another. Almost aligned, but not quite.

"When you remove boxes like these and then restack them, they'll settle in a different way." And then he indicated two more notches that weren't aligned. "You took the boxes out and put them back again. I can see that you did. And now you're going to tell me what you found inside them, do you understand?"

She shook her head. "You're insane. They're just cardboard boxes, why should they interest me? They've been there ever since we moved in. They've just settled some more, that's all."

It was a clever move, she thought to herself. A neat explanation.

But he shook his head. Not neat enough.

"OK, so let's check, shall we?" he said, pushing her back against the wall. Stay there or else, his frigid eyes told her.

She glanced about the landing as he began to remove the first of the boxes. There wasn't much for her to make use of in the narrow space: a stool by the door of their bedroom, a vase on the windowsill, the floor polisher against the sloping wall.

If she could deliver a clean blow to his neck with the stool, then perhaps . . .

She swallowed and clenched her fists. How hard was hard enough?

And as she stood there, her husband backed out of the doorway and dropped a packing case at her feet with a thud.

"Right, let's have a look, shall we? In a moment, we'll know for sure if you've been poking your nose in."

She stared as he opened the lid. It was one from the front, almost in the middle. Two cardboard flaps revealed the burial chamber of his innermost secrets. The cutting of her at the show-jumping competition in Bernstorffsparken. The wooden filing box with the many addresses and information on all those families and their children. He had known exactly where it was.

She closed her eyes and tried to breathe calmly. If there was a God, then He would have to help her now.

"I really don't see what all this is about. What have all those papers got to do with me?" she said.

He planted one knee on the floor, took out the first pile of cuttings, and put it to one side. He didn't want to risk her seeing the cutting about herself in case he was unable to prove her guilt.

She had worked him out.

Then, carefully, he took out the filing box. He didn't even need to open it. Just lowered his head and said in the softest of voices: "Why couldn't you leave my things alone?"

What had he seen? What had she overlooked?

She stared down at his spine, glanced at the stool and then again at his spine.

What was it about, the information in that wooden box? Why did he clench his fist so that his knuckles showed white?

She drew her hand to her throat and felt her jugular throbbing.

He turned toward her, his eyes narrowed to slits. A terrifying glare. His contempt so ferocious it almost prevented her from breathing.

The stool was three meters away.

"I haven't touched any of it," she said. "What makes you think I have?"

"I don't think. I *know*."

She moved slightly in the direction of the stool. He didn't react.

"Look!" He turned the front of the wooden box toward her. She didn't know what she was supposed to see.

"What?" she asked. "There's nothing there."

When snow falls as sleet, you can see its flakes evaporate in their descent toward the ground, their beauty absorbed back into the air whence it came, their magic gone.

She felt exactly like such a snowflake as he lunged at her legs and swept them from underneath her. Falling, she saw her life disintegrate and everything she had ever known turn to dust. She never felt the crack of her head against the floor, only that she was locked in his grip.

"Exactly! There's nothing there. But there should have been," he snarled.

She felt the blood trickle from her temple, but it didn't hurt. "I don't know what you're talking about," she heard herself say.

"There was a thread on the lid." He thrust his face into hers. "And now it's gone."

"Let go of me. Let me get up. Couldn't it have fallen off by itself? When did you last rummage around in those packing cases? Four years ago? All sorts of things can happen in four years!" And then she mustered all the air in her lungs and screamed as loud as she could: "LET GO OF ME!"

But he didn't.

She watched the distance between herself and the stool increase as he dragged her into the room with all the boxes. She saw the trail of blood she left behind on the floor. She heard his oaths and his grunts as he held her down with his foot against her spine.

She wanted to scream again, but she couldn't find the breath.

And then he raised his foot, took hold of her roughly, and threw her into the middle of the floor. And there she lay, helpless and bleeding in the valley of cardboard.

Maybe she could have reacted, but what happened next took her completely by surprise.

She registered only his legs stepping quickly to one side and the packing case as it was raised high above her.

And then he slammed it down hard against her rib cage.

For a moment, all air left her. But instinctively she twisted her body slightly onto her side and drew one leg up on top of the other. Then the second case descended, forcing her lower arm against her ribs and rendering all further movement impossible. And then, finally, a third on top.

Three full packing cases, weighing all too much.

She could see the landing beyond her feet, but then he closed off the space with another stack of boxes on top of her lower legs, and then another up against the door.

As he did so, he said nothing. Neither did he speak when he slammed the door shut, trapping her tight.

It was done so quickly that there had been no time to shout for help. But if she had shouted, who would have come to her aid?

She wondered if he would simply leave her there. Her chest felt immobile, and she was breathing from her abdomen now. All she could see in the remaining chinks of light from the skylight above her were brown surfaces of cardboard.

When finally darkness came, the phone in her back pocket rang.

Chimed until it stopped.

21

In the first twenty kilometers to Karlshamn, Carl smoked four full-strength Cecils just to settle his system again after ingesting Tryggve Holt's horrendous coffee.

If only they had finished the interview the night before, he could have driven home again and would at this moment be lying in his cozy bed with the newspaper spread across his chest and the enlivening aroma of Morten's rice porridge pancakes drifting into his nostrils.

He could taste his own malodorous breath.

Saturday morning. In three hours, he would be home. If he could keep his arse cheeks clenched.

Hardly had he tuned in to Radio Blekinge before his mobile chimed in the middle of a jig performed on Hardanger fiddles.

"Hey, Carlo, whassup? Where are you?" inquired the voice at the other end.

Carl glanced at the time on the instrument panel. It was nine o'clock, so this boded ill. When had his stepson ever been up this early on a Saturday morning?

"What's wrong, Jesper?"

The lad sounded peeved. "I don't want to stay with Vigga anymore. I'm going to move back in with you, if that's OK?"

Carl turned the volume down on the Swedish folkies. "With me? Hang on a minute, Jesper, just listen up for a second, will you? Vigga gave me an ultimatum. She wants to come back, too. And if that doesn't suit me, she wants to sell the house so she can run off with half the proceeds. So where are you going to live then?"

"She's joking, surely?"

Carl smiled. It never ceased to amaze him how little the lad knew his own mother. "Anyway, why do you want to come back all of a sudden? What's wrong? Fed up with the leaky roof in that garden shed of hers? Or was it your turn to do the washing up?"

He smiled to himself. A bit of sarcasm did his dodgy stomach no end of good.

"It's too fucking far from school! An hour each way, a total downer. And then there's Vigga's moaning all the time. Who wants that?"

"Moaning? What sort of moaning?" he heard himself say before he could stop himself. What a stupid question. "On second thought, Jesper, I think I'd prefer not to know."

"Nah, not *that* sort, Carlo! She moans whenever there *isn't* a bloke in the house, like now. It's getting on my nerves."

So Vigga was on her own at the moment? What about the poet in the horn-rimmed specs? Had he found himself another muse with more money in the bank? Someone able to keep their gob shut for five minutes at a time?

Carl gazed out at the rain-drenched landscape. The GPS told him to go via Rödby and Bräkne-Hoby. The route looked meandering and most likely muddy as hell. And how come there were so many trees in this country?

"That's why she wants to go back to Rønneholtparken," Jesper went on. "Then at least she'll have you for company."

Carl shook his head. What a compliment.

"OK, Jesper, I'll tell you what. There's no way I'm having Vigga back in the house. I'll give you a thousand kroner if you can talk her out of it. How does that sound?"

"Talk her out of it? How am I supposed to do that?"

"Easy. Find her a new bloke. Use your brains, lad. Two thousand if you can manage it this weekend. And then you can move back in with me. That's the deal."

Two birds with one stone. Carl was a happy man. Jesper, however, was stunned into silence on the other end of the phone.

"Oh, and one more thing. If you do come back, I want no more complaints about Hardy staying with us. If you don't like the setup, you can stay put in the little house on the prairie."

"On the what?"

"Are you with me? Two thousand if you get her sorted this weekend."

More silence as the proposition passed through the standard teenage filters of resentment and bone-idleness, together with a liberal spread of morning-after sloth.

"Two thousand, straight up?" came the response after a while. "OK, you're on. I'll run some flyers off."

"Deal." Carl had his doubts, though, as to Jesper's chosen method. He had imagined something more along the lines of him inviting a swarm of impoverished daubers to the allotment house where they could see with their own eyes the magnificent and, more important, gratis studio that might be part of the package when taking on a female hippie with mileage on the odometer.

"What are you going to put on those flyers, then?"

"Haven't a clue, Carlo." He mused for a moment.

"Maybe something like: Hey, my lush mum's looking for a lush bloke. Miserable bastards and down-and-outs needn't apply." He laughed at his own suggestion.

"OK, but have another think before you get started."

"No probs, Carlo!" Jesper laughed again, a hangover rasp. "Get your money ready!" And then he hung up.

Slightly bewildered, Carl peered out over the dashboard at red-painted houses and grazing cows in the pouring rain.

There was nothing like modern technology to muddle together life's elements.

It was a dejected, doleful smile Hardy mustered when Carl appeared in the front room.

"Where have you been?" he asked softly as Morten wiped mashed potato from the corner of his mouth.

"Oh, a little jaunt over to Sweden. Had to go to Blekinge and stayed the night. In actual fact, I stood outside a pretty sizable police station in Karlshamn this morning knocking on a locked door. It's even worse than here. Too bad if there's a crime on a weekend." He allowed himself an ironic chuckle. Hardy didn't think it was funny, either.

To be fair, Carl's story wasn't entirely true. The police station in Karlshamn had been equipped with an entry phone. The sign next to it read: *Press B and state business.* Carl had done so tentatively, only to find himself up against incomprehensible gobbledygook when the duty officer answered. The crackling voice had then spoken some Swedish variant of English that Carl likewise failed to decipher.

So then he'd buggered off.

He gave his corpulent lodger a pat on the back. "Thanks, Morten. I'll take over for a minute, if that's OK. Would you mind getting some coffee on the go in the meantime? Only not too strong."

His gaze followed Morten's waddling bulk as it disappeared into the kitchen. Had the man been living on a diet of cream cheese these past weeks? He looked like a pair of tractor tires.

Then he turned to Hardy. "You're looking a bit down in the dumps today. What's up?"

"Morten's killing me, bit by bit," Hardy whispered, catching his breath. "He force-feeds me all day long like there's nothing else to do. Fatty food that goes right through me. I don't know why he bothers. He's the one who has to wipe my arse. Can't you ask him to give it a rest? Just once in a while?" He shook his head as Carl raised the next spoonful to his mouth.

"And then there's his jabbering all day long. Driving me up the wall, he is. All sorts of shite about Paris Hilton and the Law of Succession and pension payouts. What do I care? One long blather, from one subject to the next."

"Why don't you tell him yourself?"

Hardy closed his eyes. OK, so he'd tried already. Morten wasn't the kind for making U-turns.

Carl nodded. "Of course. I'll have a word with him, Hardy. How are you doing, anyway, apart from that?" It was a cautiously posed question. Well inside the minefield.

"I've got phantom pain."

Carl saw Hardy's Adam's apple struggling to let him swallow.

"Do you want some water?" He took a bottle from the holder by the bed and put the straw to Hardy's lips. If Hardy and Morten were going to have a falling-out, who would be left to do all this?

"Phantom pain, you say? Where?" he asked.

"Behind my knees, I think. It's so hard to tell. All I know is it hurts, like someone hitting me with a wire brush."

"Do you want an injection?"

He nodded. Morten could take care of that shortly.

"What about the feeling in your finger and shoulder? Can you still move your wrist?"

Hardy's mouth drooped. Enough said.

"Talking of Karlshamn," Carl went on, "didn't you once work with them on some case or other?"

"Why do you want to know?"

"I need a police artist to do a likeness of a killer. I've got a witness in Blekinge who can give a description."

"So?"

"Well, I need to get it done pretty sharpish, and the Swedish plod seem to be just as good as we are at shutting up shop when it comes to local stations. Like I said, I stood outside this great big yellow building on Erik Dahlbergsvägen in Karlshamn at seven o'clock this morning, staring at a sign that said *Closed Saturday and Sunday. Open weekdays 9 A.M. to 3 P.M.* And that was that. On a Saturday!"

"So what do you want me to do about it?"

"You could ask your mate in Karlshamn if he could do Department Q in Copenhagen a favor."

"What's to say he's still in Karlshamn? It's been six years, at least."

"You're right, he's probably moved on by now. Still, if you give me his name, I'll do a search for him on the Internet. If we're lucky, he'll still be on the force. Bit of an apple-polisher, wasn't he, if I remember right? All you'd have to do is ask him to get on the blower and call a police artist. It won't be more trouble than that. Wouldn't you do the same for him if he were to ask?"

Hardy's eyelids were heavy, not a good sign. "It'll be expensive on a weekend," he said after a while. "Assuming there's a police artist anywhere near your witness, and that he or she might be interested."

Carl looked at the cup of coffee Morten put down for him on the bedside table. If he didn't know better, he would have thought it was residue from a can of motor oil concentrated into something blacker.

"It's a good thing you're back, Carl," said Morten. "So I can get going."

"Get going? Where to?"

"The funeral procession for Mustafa Hsownay. It starts at two o'clock from Nørreport Station."

Carl nodded. Mustafa Hsownay, another innocent victim of the war between the bikers and the immigrant gangs for control of the hash market.

Morten raised his arm and waved a little flag that looked like Iraq's. Wherever could he have got it from?

"I went to school with someone from the Mjølnerparken development where Mustafa was shot."

Others might perhaps have hesitated to share such a flimsy claim to solidarity.

But Morten was in a league of his own.

They lay almost side by side. Carl on the sofa with his feet on the coffee table, Hardy in his hospital bed with his long, lame body turned onto its side. His eyes had been closed since Carl switched on the television, and the bitter twist of his mouth seemed now to have smoothed.

They were like an elderly couple finally succumbing to the indispensable company of news programs and powdered presenters. Dozing off in front of the box on a Saturday evening. If they were only holding hands, the picture would be complete.

Carl forced open his eyelids and noted that the news program that suddenly flickered in front of him was the last of the day.

Time to get Hardy ready for the night and get some proper shut-eye.

He stared at the screen, at Mustafa Hsownay's funeral procession moving quietly along Nørrebrogade in a dignified and orderly manner. The cameras showed thousands of silent faces lining the street and pink tulips thrown to the hearse from windows above. Immigrants of all kinds, and just as many native Danes. Many clasping hands.

The cauldron that was Copenhagen had gone off the boil for a moment. The gang war was not the people's war.

Carl nodded to himself. It was commendable of Morten to have taken part. Not many people from Allerød would have been there. He wasn't, either, for that matter.

"Look, there's Assad," Hardy said quietly.

Carl turned his head. Had he been awake all this time?

"Where?" He glanced back at the screen just in time to see Assad's round face pop up amid the throng.

Unlike everyone else there, his eyes seemed to be fixed not on the hearse but on the mourners in the procession. His head moved almost imperceptibly from side to side like a predator following its prey through undergrowth. He was concentrating. And then the producer cut away.

"What the . . . ?" Carl muttered to himself.

"He looked like one of them from intelligence," Hardy snorted.

Carl woke up in his bed at about three o'clock, his heart pounding and his duvet weighing two hundred kilos. He wasn't feeling well. It was like a sudden fever. Like a horde of viruses had assaulted him and shut down his sympathetic nervous system.

He gasped for air and clutched at his chest. Why am I panicking? he asked himself, and felt in need of a hand to hold.

He opened his eyes in the darkness.

This has happened before, he thought, instantly recalling his previous collapse and feeling the sweat that made his T-shirt cling to his skin.

After he and Anker and Hardy got shot out in Amager, it had lain dormant inside him, ticking away like a time bomb.

Was it the same thing now?

"Think your way through what happened. It'll give you some distance," Mona had told him during his counseling.

He clenched his fists and recalled the impact that traveled through the floorboards when Hardy had been hit and he himself had felt the graze of the bullet against his temple. The feeling of body against body when Hardy pulled him down as he fell, covering him in blood. Anker's heroic attempt to stop the gunmen, despite being badly injured. And then the final, fatal shot that emptied Anker's blood so definitively onto the filthy wooden floor.

He went through it, over and over again. Recalling the shame of having done nothing and Hardy's bewilderment as to why it had all happened.

And his heart continued to pound.

"Bastards, bastards," he snarled, repeating himself as he reached for the light and a smoke. Tomorrow, he would call Mona and tell her he'd come unstuck again. He would be as charming as he could, though with a smidgeon of added despair. Then, maybe, she'd give him more than a consultation. He could always hope, anyway.

He smiled at the thought and inhaled the smoke deep into his lungs. Then he closed his eyes, only to feel his heart carrying on like a pneumatic drill again. Was he really ill this time?

He got out of bed with difficulty and edged his way down the stairs. If he was having a heart attack, he didn't want to be up there all on his own in bed.

And that was where he fell, to be woken up by Morten gently shaking him, a painted Iraqi flag fading on his forehead.

The raised eyebrows of the on-call doctor signaled that Carl had wasted his time. The verdict was short and to the point: overexertion.

Overexertion! An insult, followed by some standard wording about stress and a couple of tablets to take that hammered Carl into the land of nod until way past church time.

By the time he woke up on Sunday, it was half past one in the afternoon and his head was throbbing with all manner of unpleasant thoughts. His heart, though, was beating normally.

"Jesper wants you to call him," Hardy said from his bed when Carl finally tottered down the stairs. "Are you OK?"

Carl gave a shrug. "There's some stuff inside my head I can't control," he answered.

Hardy forced a smile, and Carl could have bitten off his own tongue. That was the thing about having Hardy around. You always had to think before opening your gob.

"I've been thinking about Assad, seeing him on telly last night," Hardy said. "What do you actually know about him, Carl? Don't you think you should meet that family of his? Maybe it's about time you paid him a visit."

"Why do you say that?"

"Isn't it normal to take an interest in your partner?"

Partner! Was Assad now his partner all of a sudden? "I know you, Hardy," he said. "You're on to something. What is it?"

Hardy drew back his lips in something resembling a smile. It was always gratifying to be properly understood.

"It's like I saw him in a different light. As if I didn't know him. Do *you* know Assad, do you think?"

"Ask me if I know *anyone*. Who really knows who, at the end of the day?"

"Where does he live?"

"Heimdalsgade, I think."

"You think?"

Where does he live? What's his family like? Was this some kind of interrogation? But Hardy was right. He knew fuck all about Assad.

"What did Jesper want?" he asked, changing the subject.

Hardy raised his eyebrows. He wasn't finished with Assad. For whatever reason.

"Hardy says you called," Carl said into his mobile a moment later.

"I did, yeah," said Jesper. "You can get your savings out of the bank now, Carlo."

Carl blinked uncontrollably. The lad sounded sure of himself.

"Carl! The name's Carl, Jesper. If you call me Carlo once more I shall be forced to momentarily go deaf at very decisive moments in your potentially short life, do you get my drift?"

"Got you, Carlo." He could almost see Jesper laughing at the other end of the connection. "Hope you can hear me now. I've found Vigga a bloke."

"You don't say. Is he worth two thousand kroner, or is she going to chuck him out with the bathwater tomorrow like she did with her man of letters? Because if she is, you can forget all about your dosh."

"He's forty years old. Owns an Opel Vectra and a convenience store. Nineteen-year-old daughter."

"Well, I never. And where did you dig him up?"

"I put a flyer up in his shop. It was the first one."

Easy money.

"And what makes you think this Grocer Jack can sweep Vigga off her feet? Does he look like Brad Pitt?"

"Try again, Carlo. Not unless Brad Pitt fell asleep in the sun for a week or two."

"You mean he's black?"

"Not black, exactly, but not fucking far off!"

Carl held his breath as the rest of the story was delivered in detail. The man was a widower, endowed with the kind of soulful brown eyes that Vigga was almost bound to find irresistible. Jesper had dragged him down to the house on the allotment, where the man had heaped praise on Vigga's paintings and exclaimed with obvious delight that her little place was the most charming he had seen in all his life. And that, apparently, had sealed it. At that very moment, they were having lunch together at some restaurant in the city.

Carl shook his head. He ought to be as pleased as punch, and instead all he felt was an ache in his stomach.

When Jesper was finished, he snapped his mobile shut in slow motion and turned his gaze on Morten and Hardy, who were gawping at him like a pair of stray dogs waiting for some leftovers.

"We're saved, so it seems. Let's cross our fingers, anyway. Seems Jesper's got Vigga paired off with the man of her dreams, so maybe we can stay on here for a while longer."

Whereupon Morten's jaw dropped and he clapped his hands with glee. "Oh, how sweet!" he exclaimed. "Who's the lucky white knight?"

"White?" Carl tried to force his mouth into a smile, but his muscles seemed to be stuck. "According to Jesper, Gurkamal Singh Pannu is the darkest thing north of the equator."

Did he hear them gasp?

The whole of the outer Nørrebro district was blue and white that day and populated by utterly miserable faces. Carl had never seen quite so many FC Copenhagen supporters looking so down in the dumps as they milled through the streets. Flags trailed along the ground, cans of beer seemed almost too heavy to be raised to the lips, and the chants had all but died away, only now and then to be superseded by roars of frustration that echoed through the city like the pained cries of gnu succumbing to lions.

Their heroes had gone down 2–0 to Esbjerg. Fourteen home victories on the trot, and then beaten by a team who hadn't won a single away match for a year.

The city was defeated.

He parked halfway along Heimdalsgade and glanced around. Since his patrolling days here, immigrant stores had sprouted all over the place. The area was alive, even on a Sunday.

He found Assad's name on a doorplate and pushed the buzzer. Better to be snubbed on the spot than turned down over the phone. If Assad wasn't in, he would drive out to Vigga's place and check out what new version of reality she was now operating in, just to make sure he knew what he was up against.

After twenty seconds, there was still no answer.

He stepped back and peered up at the balconies. It wasn't quite the ghetto he had been expecting. He saw no visible laundry and surprisingly few satellite dishes.

"Are you wanting in?" asked a chirpy voice behind him, and a young blond girl, the type whose eyes alone were enough to render a man speechless, stepped past him and unlocked the door.

"Thanks," he mumbled, following her into the stairwell of the concrete block.

He found the flat on the third floor, discovering that, unlike the densely populated nameplates of his two Arab neighbors, Assad's had only his own name on it.

Carl pressed the bell a couple of times, sensing already that he was out of luck. Then he bent down and flipped open the letter box.

The place looked empty. Apart from some junk mail and a couple of bills on the floor, he could see nothing but a pair of timeworn leather armchairs against the far wall.

"What the fuck do you think you're doing?"

Carl turned his head to see a pair of baggy white tracksuit bottoms with stripes down the leg.

He straightened up to face a powerhouse whose tanned upper arms looked like sides of beef. "I'm looking for Assad. Do you know if he's been home today?"

"The Shiite? No, he hasn't."

"What about his family?"

The man cocked his head slightly. "You sure you know him? Or maybe you're the fucker who's been doing the break-ins around here? What's with all the peering through people's letter boxes?"

He thrust his chest against Carl's.

"All right, hold on a minute, Rambo."

He put a hand against the man's complex of abdominal muscles and fumbled around in his own inside pocket.

"Assad's my friend, and so are you if you can answer some questions for me."

The man stared at the police badge Carl held up in front of his face.

"Who'd want to be friends with one of you lot?" he snarled, lips retracted.

He made to turn and go, but Carl grabbed his sleeve.

"Maybe you'll answer me anyway. It'd be a help . . ."

"Stick your questions up your arse, you fucking wanker."

Carl nodded. In about three and a half seconds, he would demonstrate to this overgrown, protein-powder monster who the real wanker was. The guy may have been built like a brick shithouse, but he wasn't so big he could ignore the firm grip of the law on his collar and the threat of arrest for insulting an officer on duty.

But then a voice came from behind him.

"Hey, Bilal, whassup? The man's got a badge."

Carl turned to see an even bigger individual, whose main occupation was clearly lifting weights. He was a window display of sports clothing. If his enormous T-shirt had been bought in a normal shop, then the place had certainly been well stocked.

"Sorry about my brother. He's on steroids," he said, extending a mitt the size of a provincial market town. "We don't have anything to do with Hafez el-Assad. In fact, I've only ever seen him twice. Funny-looking guy. Round face and big eyes, yeah?"

Carl nodded and let go of the giant's sleeve he was still clutching.

"Tell you the truth," the brother continued, "I don't think he even lives here. And if he does, it's not with any family, that's for sure." He smiled. "Just as well, it's only a one-room flat."

After calling Assad's number a couple of times with no answer, Carl got out of the car and took a deep breath before walking up the path to Vigga's little allotment garden house.

"Hello, angel," she sang in greeting.

Music of a kind he had never heard before poured from the tiny speakers in the front room. Was that a sitar, or some poor animal being tormented?

"What's this, then?" he asked, fighting the urge to put his hands to his ears and shut out the noise.

"Lovely, isn't it?" She danced a couple of steps that no Indian in his right mind could possibly consider well chosen. "Gurkamal gave me a CD. He says he's got lots more I can have, if I want."

"Is he here?" Stupid question in a dwelling with only two rooms.

Vigga smiled exuberantly. "He's at his shop. His daughter's got curling practice, so he had to take over."

"Curling! Age-old Indian sport, eh?"

She swatted at him playfully. "You say Indian, but I say Punjabi. That's where he's from."

"Oh, so he's Pakistani then?"

"No, he's Indian. But don't waste your brain cells on it."

Carl sat down heavily in a moth-eaten armchair. "Vigga, this whole situation's no good. Jesper flitting back and forth, and you putting the squeeze on us like that. I hardly know where I stand with the house."

"But that's life when you're still married to a woman who owns half."

"That's what I mean. Can't we come to some sort of fair arrangement so I can buy you out?"

"Fair?" She made the word sound almost odious.

"Yes, fair. If you and I were to draw up a deed in the amount of, say, two hundred thousand, then I could pay you back two thousand a month. How does that sound?"

Vigga's cogs began to whirr. When it came to smaller sums, she tended to be hopeless, but as soon as a figure contained enough zeros, she could be exacting indeed.

"Carl, my dear," she began, and he realized instantly that the initiative was lost. "This is neither the time nor the place. At some point, perhaps. Though we'd have to up the figure. Who knows what the future might bring?" And then she laughed out loud, without apparent reason, and he was back to his usual state of bewilderment.

He felt he should collect himself and tell her they should have a solicitor look things over, but his courage failed him.

"But I will say one thing, Carl. We're a family, and we need to support each other. I know how happy you and Hardy and Morten and Jesper are living at Rønneholtparken, and it would be a shame to disrupt things for you. I can see that."

Looking at her, he sensed that any second now she was going to table a proposal that would knock the wind out of him.

"So I've decided to leave you all in peace for the time being."

It was easy enough for her to say. But what would happen when this Gherkin, or whatever his name was, tired of her incessant jabber and knitted socks?

"But I want you to do me a favor in return," she added.

It was the kind of utterance that from the mouth of Vigga could entail no end of insurmountable problems.

"I think—" he managed to say before being interrupted.

"My mother would like you to visit her. She's always talking about you, Carl. She still thinks the sun shines out of your backside. So I've decided you should look in on her once a week. If that's all right with you. Starting tomorrow."

Carl swallowed. This was enough to turn any man's saliva to sandpaper. Vigga's mother! A completely deranged individual who hadn't even fathomed that Carl and Vigga were married until four years after the event. A woman who lived life in the firm conviction that God had created the world entirely for her own amusement.

"I know what you're thinking, Carl, but she's not nearly as bad as she used to be. Not since her Alzheimer's set in."

Carl took a deep breath. "I'm not sure I've time once a week, Vigga," he ventured, noting the immediate pursing of her lips. "But I'll see what I can do."

She extended a hand. It was odd, but they always seemed to be shaking hands on something that put him in shackles yet imposed on her only a bare minimum of inconvenience.

He parked the car in a side road by Utterslev Mose and felt very alone. There was life in his house, but it wasn't his. At work, he was mostly in a dream. He had no interests and didn't play any sport. He hated being with people he didn't know and wasn't thirsty enough to drown his sorrows in a local drinking establishment.

And now some bloke in a turban, straight out of the starting blocks, had swept his ex off her feet quicker than you could find Internet porn.

His so-called partner at work wasn't living at the address he had given, so hanging out with him was out of the question, too.

No wonder he was feeling downhearted.

He breathed in slowly, drawing in the marshy air, and felt goose bumps appear on his arms once more as sweat ran from all his glands. Was he about to hit bottom again? Twice in less than twenty-four hours?

Was he ill?

He picked up his mobile from the passenger seat and stared at the number he selected. *Mona Ibsen*, the display read. It had to be worth a go.

He sat there for twenty minutes, feeling the pounding of his heart increase, before eventually pressing the number and praying that counselors were willing to work on a Sunday evening.

"Hi, Mona," he said softly when he heard her voice at the other end. "It's Carl Mørck. I'm . . ." He was about to say that he wasn't feeling well. That he needed to talk. But he never got that far.

"Carl Mørck!" she exclaimed, though without sounding particularly pleased. "I've been waiting for you to call ever since I got home. It's about time."

Sitting on her sofa in a living room so fragrant with the scent of woman reminded him of that time behind some wooden pavilions on a school outing to Tolne Bakker with the hand of a tall and slender girl down the front of his trousers. It was all so madly exciting and off-limits, and yet he hadn't a clue what to do.

Mona wasn't just your average girl next door, so much was plain from the way his body was reacting. Hearing her moving around in the kitchen, he felt a treacherous pounding in the region of his breast pocket. Unpleasant as hell. It would be just his luck to pass out now.

They had exchanged pleasantries and broached his latest attack. They had enjoyed a Campari and soda and then a couple more, allowing themselves to be carried along by the moment. They had talked about her spell in Africa and had come very close to kissing.

Maybe it was the thought of what ought to happen now that was making the panic kick in.

She returned with some little triangles of bread, her stab at a midnight snack, but who cared, now that they were alone and her blouse clung so magnificently to the curves of her body?

Come on, Carl, he told himself. If a bloke called Gherkin with a braided beard can do it, you can, too.

22

He had shut his wife away in a prison, trapped under heavy boxes, and there she could stay until it was over. She knew too much.

He had heard her scraping against the floor upstairs for a couple of hours, and later, when he came home with Benjamin, he heard her muffled groans.

Only now, after he had packed the boy's things into the car, was she silent.

He inserted a CD of children's songs in the car stereo and smiled at his son in the rearview mirror. An hour on the road and the boy would be asleep. A trip across Sjælland always did the trick.

His sister sounded sleepy on the phone but livened up no end when he told her how much he would give them for looking after Benjamin.

"You heard right," he said. "Three thousand kroner a week. I'll come by once in a while and make sure you're doing it properly."

"We'll want a month in advance," she said.

"OK."

"As well as the usual on top."

He nodded to himself. It was a predictable demand. "Same as usual, no need to worry."

"How long will your wife be in the hospital?"

"I don't know. We'll just have to wait and see how it goes. She's very ill. It might take time."

No words of sympathy or regret were forthcoming.

Eva wasn't like that.

"Go to your father," his mother ordered him sharply. Her hair was tousled and her dress twisted up around her midriff. So his father had been rough with her again.

"What for?" he asked. "I'm supposed to finish reading Corinthians for the prayer meeting tomorrow. He told me to himself."

With childlike naivete, he had believed his mother would save him. That she would intervene, extricate him from his father's suffocating grip, and get him off the hook, just this once. His Chaplin impersonation was a game he liked to play. It was of no harm to anyone. Jesus must have played, too, when he was a child. They knew that.

"Get in there, now!" His mother's lips tightened, and she took him by the scruff of the neck. It was the same grasp that had marched him off so many times before to beatings and humiliation.

"I'll tell him you look at the neighbor when he takes his shirt off in the field," he said.

She gave a start. They both knew it wasn't true. That even the slightest glimpse toward liberty and a new life was a direct pathway to the inferno. They were reminded of it in church, in the prayers at table, and in each and every word read from the black volume residing close at hand in his father's pocket. In every glance exchanged between man and woman, Satan lurked. Satan was in every smile and in every touch. That was what the book said.

No, it wasn't true that his mother had eyes for the neighbor, but his father had never been known to give anyone the benefit of the doubt.

And then his mother said the words that divided them forever.

"You spawn of the Devil," she spat, cold as ice. "May Satan drag you down to where you belong. May the inferno sear through your skin and deliver you into pain from this day forth." She nodded emphatically. "Yes, you may well be frightened, but Satan has already taken you. You are no longer ours to care about."

She flung open the door and thrust him into the sherry fumes of his father's study.

"Come here," his father commanded, winding the belt around his hand.

The curtains were drawn, allowing only a sliver of light into the room. Behind the desk stood Eva, a pillar of salt in her white dress. Apparently, he had not beaten her, for his sleeves were still rolled down, and her sobs were restrained.

"Still playing Chaplin, are we?" his father barked.

Out of the corner of his eye, he saw Eva avert her gaze.

This would be violent.

"Here are Benjamin's documents. Best they're with you, in case he falls ill."

He handed his brother-in-law the boy's various certificates.

"Is that likely?" his sister asked anxiously.

"No, of course not. Benjamin's a healthy boy."

He saw it already in his brother-in-law's eyes. Villy wanted more money.

"A boy Benjamin's age eats a lot," he said. "That'll cost us a thousand a month on its own." If he didn't believe him, they could look it up on the Internet.

Villy rubbed his hands together like Ebenezer Scrooge. Five thousand extra, once and for all, was what they seemed to be asking.

But they wouldn't be getting a penny more. Most likely it would be passed on to some preacher of the kind who couldn't care less who was footing the bill or why.

"If you and Eva should cause me any difficulties, our arrangement may have to be reconsidered. Are you with me?" he said, and left it at that.

The brother-in-law agreed reluctantly, but his sister was already far away, her hands, unused to children, investigating the boy's soft skin.

"What color is his hair now?" she asked, her blind eyes turned upward in delight.

"The same as mine when I was a boy, if you remember," he said and noted how the lusterless eyes then dropped.

"And spare Benjamin the bloody prayers, understand?" he said finally, before handing them the money.

He saw them nod but didn't care for their silence.

The ransom would be paid in twenty-four hours. One million kroner in used notes. He was in no doubt.

Now he would drive up to the boathouse and make sure the kids were in a decent state. Tomorrow, when the payoff had been made, he would go there again and kill the girl. The boy would be chloroformed and dumped in a field near Frederiks on the Monday night.

He would give Samuel instructions as to what to say to his father and mother, so they would know what they had to contend with. He was to say that his sister's killer had his informants and would always know where the family were and what they were doing. That they had enough children for him to strike at them again, so they should never, ever feel safe. If he had the slightest suspicion that they had informed anyone of what had happened, it would cost them another child. This was what Samuel was to tell them. It was a threat with no expiration date. Moreover, they were to know that he operated only under an assumed identity. The man they thought they knew did not exist. He would appear again only in a new guise.

It had worked every time. The family had their faith to fall back on and would immerse themselves in it. The dead child would be mourned and the living would be shielded. The story of Job's faith under trial was their anchor.

And all around them, in the circles in which they moved, their explanation of the child's disappearance would be that she had been ostracized. In this case, it would be easy to believe. Magdalena stuck out, she shone, and in their community this was no advantage. Her parents would say that she had been sent away to family. And the community would concern itself no more with the issue. He would be safe.

He smiled to himself.

Soon there would be one fewer of those who put God before man to pollute the world.

The dissolution of the pastor's family occurred one day in winter, just weeks after his fifteenth birthday. In the months before, he had become aware that his body was changing, oddly and inexplicably. Sinful thoughts of the kind the community warned against had begun to pursue him. He saw a woman bend forward in a tight skirt, and that same evening he experienced his first, sudden ejaculation with her image on his retina.

He felt the sweat seeping from his armpits, and his voice trembled and lurched in all directions. The muscles of his neck became taut, and hair sprouted everywhere, dark and crinkly.

He felt like a molehill on a flat field.

When he made an effort, he could vaguely see himself in the boys of the congregation who had undergone the same transformation before him, but he had no idea what it was all about. The subject was never ever broached in the house his father referred to as "the home of God."

For three years, his mother and father had addressed him only when it could not be avoided. They never saw the efforts he made, never noticed him trying hard to make amends at prayer meetings. To them, he was Satan's image in the name of Chaplin. Nothing else. And whatever he might say or do could make no difference.

The congregation said he was strange and possessed, and they gathered in prayer so that no other child might become like him.

Only Eva stuck with him, and even she occasionally deserted him, and under pressure from their father would declare solemnly that he had spoken ill of his parents and wished not to obey them and heed the word of God.

Subsequently, his father had made it his second mission in life to break him down. Commands with no obvious point. A daily diet of ridicule and chastisement, with beatings and psychological terror for dessert.

To begin with, he had been able to seek comfort from one or two members of the congregation, but soon they too turned their backs on him. In such communities, the wrath of God towers tall above human compassion, and in its shadow the God-fearing individual looks only to the Lord and takes care of himself.

They chose sides and shied away. Eventually, all he could do was turn the other cheek.

Exactly as the Bible said.

And in this shadowy home in which nothing could breathe, the relationship between him and Eva slowly withered. How many times had she said she was sorry, and how many times had he turned a deaf ear?

Eventually, he no longer had even his sister, and on this day in winter everything broke.

"You sound like a squealing pig with that voice," his father told him as they sat down at the table in the kitchen. "You look like one, too. A swine. Look at yourself. See how repulsive and fat you are. Use that ugly snout to sniff in your foul odor. Go and wash, you disgusting creature!"

Such was the baseness, such were the snide commands, one after another. Matters of little consequence, like this order to wash his hands before dinner, accumulated, until finally he felt he could no longer cope. And when his father's outburst was over, he would no doubt have him scrubbing the walls of his room so that his smell might be purged.

So why not stand up to him?

"I suppose you want me to scrub my room with detergent before you're satisfied and finished with all your ridiculous orders? Well, you can do it yourself, you old fart," he spat.

And then his father began to perspire, and his mother to protest. Who was he to speak to his father like that?

His mother would try to drive him into a corner. He knew her. She would tell him to vanish from their lives, and when eventually he was exhausted by all their unreasonableness, he would slam the door behind him and stay away half the night. These were her tactics, and they had worked so often when things came to a head. But tonight they would fail.

He sensed his new body tighten, felt the blood pump in his veins, his muscles warming. If the clenched fist of his father should come too close, it would be met in kind.

"Leave me alone, you monster," he warned. "I hate your guts. I hope you die, you bastard. Stay away from me."

Seeing such a pious individual as their father disintegrate into a storm of invective only Satan could have delivered was too much for Eva. The retiring little girl who hid behind her apron and absorbed herself in her daily chores now leaped forward and pounded her fists against her brother's chest.

He would not be allowed to ruin their lives more than he had done already, she screamed at her brother as their mother intervened to pull them apart, their father suddenly darting to produce two bottles from the cupboard under the kitchen sink.

"Get thee to thy room, Chaplin-devil, and scour thy walls with lye!" he hissed, his face flushed with rage. "And if you don't, then mark my words I'll make sure you can't get out of bed for a week, do you understand me?"

And then his father spat in his face, pressing one of the bottles into his hand before standing back with a sneer to watch his saliva running down the boy's cheek.

His son unscrewed the lid of the bottle and began slowly to pour its corrosive contents onto the kitchen floor.

"What the hell do you think you're doing, boy?" his father bellowed, snatching the bottle from his hand. And an arc of caustic soda sloshed into the air and splashed to the floor.

His father's roar was deep and resonant. But it was nothing compared to the scream that came from Eva.

Her entire body shook, her hands flapping in front of her face as though she didn't dare to touch. In the few seconds that passed, the caustic soda ate into her eyes and removed her sight forever.

And as the room filled with their mother's cries and Eva's screams, and his own horror at what he had done, his father stood and stared at his hands as they blistered from the alkali, his face changing from red to blue.

Then suddenly his eyes widened and he clutched at his chest, doubling up and staggering forward, gasping for breath, lips twisted in surprise and disbelief. And when finally he fell to the floor, the life they had known was over.

"Lord Jesus Christ, Almighty Father, I rest in Thy hand," he rattled with the last of his breath, and then he was gone. Arms folded in a cross on his chest, a faint smile on his face.

He stood for a moment and stared at his father's frozen death mask while his mother begged for God's mercy and Eva howled.

The thirst for vengeance that had kept him going for so many months had lost its source of nourishment. His father was dead from a heart attack with a smile on his face and the word of God on his lips.

It wasn't what he had envisaged.

Five hours later, the family was split apart. Eva and his mother were in the hospital in Odense, and he was in a boys' home. The congregation had taken care of matters, and this was his reward for a life spent in the shadow of the Lord.

Now all he had to do was to pay them back.

23

It was a gorgeous evening. So still and dark.

Out on the fjord, the lights of a couple of sailing boats winked, and in the meadow south of the house, the grass whispered of spring. Soon the cattle would be out to pasture and summer would be near.

This was Vibegården at its best.

He loved the place. In time, he would render the redbrick walls, demolish the boathouse to get a clear view of the fjord.

This delightful little cottage was his. He would grow old here.

He opened the door of the outbuilding, flicked on the battery lamp that hung from a post, and emptied most of a ten-liter jerrican into the tank of the generator.

He always had the feeling of a job well done by the time he reached this stage in the proceedings, when he stood and pulled on the starter cord.

He switched on the electric light and turned off the lamp. In front of him, an old monument of an oil tank told of days gone by. Now it was to be put to use again.

He stretched up to remove the metal lid that had been cut out of the top, noting that the tank seemed to be dry and had thus been properly emptied the time before. Everything was right.

Reaching up to the shelf above the door, he brought down a duffel bag. Its contents had cost him more than fifteen thousand kroner, but to him the value of what was inside was priceless. Gen HPT 54 Night Vision turned night into day. Military-grade night-vision goggles, as used in combat.

He pulled the straps over his head, adjusted the goggles, and turned them on.

Then he went outside, following the garden path through the wet undergrowth and pulling the rubber hose that protruded from a hole in the wall of the outbuilding with him to the water's edge. With the goggles on, he could clearly see the boathouse there between the thicket and the reeds. In fact, he could see everything.

Gray-green buildings, and frogs leaping for their lives as he approached.

Apart from the gentle lapping of the fjord and the hum of the generator, all was quiet as he waded out into the water with the hose.

The generator was the weakest link. Previously, he had kept it running during the entire procedure, but after a couple of years, the axle had begun to screech after only a week in use, so now he was obliged to make this extra trip to the house in order to start it up. He was thinking of getting a new one altogether.

The water pump, on the other hand, was amazing. Before, he'd had to fill the oil tank with water by hand. He gave a nod of satisfaction as he listened to the efficient gulping of the hose above the undertone of the generator. Now it took only half an hour to fill the tank from the fjord, though still it was time spent waiting.

And then he heard the sounds from the boathouse.

Since he bought the Mercedes, those he held captive were easily surprised. It had been expensive, but comfort and a soundless engine cost. Now he could sneak up to the boathouse knowing that whoever was inside would be unaware of his presence.

And so it was now.

Samuel and Magdalena were special. Samuel, because he reminded him of himself at that age. Resilient, rebellious, and explosive. Magdalena was almost the opposite. The first time he watched her through the peephole in the boathouse wall he was astonished to discover how much she reminded him of a secret love he had once had, and of what it had led to. Events that changed his life forever. Looking at Magdalena, he remembered the girl only too well. The same eyes slanting down, the same pained expression, the same thin skin with its pattern of fine, blue veins.

Twice he had crept down to the wooden structure and peeled back the strip of tar that covered the hole.

And when he put his eye to the opening, he could see everything inside. The children a couple of meters apart. Samuel at the rear, Magdalena by the door.

Magdalena cried a lot, though quietly. When her frail shoulders began to tremble in the dim light, her brother tugged at his leather strap to catch her attention so that she might find comfort in the warmth of his gaze.

He was her big brother and would do everything in his power to release her from her chains, but he was powerless. And for that reason he too cried, though he wouldn't show it. His sister wasn't to see. He turned his head away for a moment, composed himself, and then looked at her again, clowning with his head and jerking his upper body.

Just like him and his sister when he imitated Chaplin.

He had heard the muffled sound of Magdalena laughing behind her tape. The smallest, briefest of laughs, after which reality and fear returned. This evening, as he came to quench their thirst one final time, he heard the girl humming ever so gently to herself even from a distance.

He put his ear to the planks of the boathouse wall. Even with the tape covering her mouth, her voice was clear and bright. He knew the words, for they had followed him throughout his own childhood, and he hated every one.

Nearer, my God, to thee,
Nearer to thee!
E'en though it be a cross
That raiseth me,
Still all my song shall be,

Nearer, my God, to thee,

Nearer, my God, to thee!

Cautiously, he removed the tar and put his goggles to the peephole.

Her head was bent forward, her shoulders drooping, making her seem smaller than she was. Her body swayed gently from side to side in time to the hymn.

And when she had finished, she sat back, drawing in air through her nostrils. Short, sharp inhalations. As with small, frightened animals, one could almost see how fast her heart had to pump in order to keep up with her thoughts, her thirst, her hunger, and the fear of what was to come. He turned his green gaze to Samuel and realized immediately that the boy had not succumbed in the same way as his sister.

He sat wriggling his upper body against the sloping wall. And this time he wasn't clowning around.

This was the sound he had heard, which at first he had taken to be simply more discord from the generator.

It was obvious what he was trying to do from the way he rubbed the strap against the planks of the wall behind him, struggling to wear down the leather.

Perhaps he had found some little projection in the wood, a knot rough enough to provide the necessary friction.

Now he saw the boy's face more clearly. Was he smiling? Had he made enough progress to make him smile?

The girl coughed. The damp nights had worn her down.

How frail the body is, he thought to himself as she cleared her throat behind the tape and began once again to hum.

He felt a shock. The hymn was a fixture of the funeral services his father had conducted.

Abide with me; fast falls the eventide;

The darkness deepens; Lord with me abide.

When other helpers fail and comforts flee,
Help of the helpless, O abide with me.

Swift to its close ebbs out life's little day;
Earth's joys grow dim; its glories pass away;
Change and decay in all around I see;
O Thou who changest not, abide with me.

He turned in disgust and went back to the outbuilding, where he pulled two heavy chains a meter and a half in length from a nail in the wall, then found two padlocks in the drawer underneath the workbench. The last time he had been here, he had noticed that the leather straps around the waists of the children had looked slightly worn, but then they had been used so often before. If Samuel carried on working as intensely as he was doing now, reinforcements would be needed.

The children looked up at him in bewilderment when he turned on the light and crawled inside. The boy in the corner struggled in his chains, but it was no use. He kicked out and protested vociferously behind the tape that covered his mouth as the new chain was placed around his waist and attached to the one that was already affixed to the wall. But he no longer had the strength to resist. Days of hunger and the awkward sitting position had taken their toll. He looked rather pathetic with his legs drawn up at an angle beneath him.

Like all the others before him.

The girl had stopped humming immediately. His presence drained what little energy she possessed. Perhaps she had believed her brother's efforts would be of use. Now she knew that nothing could be more futile.

He filled the cup with water and tore the tape from her mouth.

She gasped, then stretched her neck out and opened her mouth. The survival instinct, ever intact.

"Don't gulp like that, Magdalena," he said softly.

She lifted her head and looked fleetingly into his eyes. Confused and afraid.

"When are we going home?" she asked, her lips quivering. No violent outburst. Just this simple question, and then she stretched again for more water.

"A day or two yet," he said.

There were tears in her eyes. "I want to go home to my mum and dad," she wept.

He smiled at her and raised the cup to her lips.

Perhaps she sensed what he was thinking now. In any case, she paused and looked at him for a moment, her eyes moist, then turned her face toward her brother.

"He's going to kill us, Samuel," she said in a trembling voice. "I know he is."

He turned his head and looked straight at the boy.

"Your sister's confused, Samuel," he said in a low voice. "Of course I'm not going to kill you. Everything will be fine. Your parents are wealthy, and I am not a monster."

He turned again to Magdalena, whose head hung low now, as though she had given up. "I know so much about you, Magdalena." He passed the back of his hand over her hair. "I know how much you wish you could wear your hair short. How dearly you'd like to be able to decide things for yourself."

He put his hand in his pocket. "There's something I want to show you," he said, producing the sheet of glossy paper he had taken from her hiding place in the garden.

"Do you recognize it?" he asked.

He sensed her surprise, though she concealed it well.

"No," she replied.

"Oh, but I think you do, Magdalena. I've been watching you with your little secrets there in the garden."

She turned her face away. Her innocence had been violated. She was ashamed.

He held the paper up in front of her. It was a page torn from a magazine.

"Five female celebrities, all with short hair," he said, then read out their names: "Sharon Stone, Natalie Portman, Halle Berry, Winona Ryder, and Keira Knightley. I'm afraid not all of them are familiar to me, but I'm pretty sure they're all film stars, is that right?"

He took hold of her chin and turned her face toward him. "What could be so wrong about finding that interesting? It's their hair you like, isn't it? Because it's not allowed in the Mother Church?" He nodded. "I'm right, aren't I? You'd like to wear your hair like that, wouldn't you? You're shaking your head, but I think you would. But listen to me, Magdalena. Did I tell your parents about your little secret? I didn't, did I? So perhaps I'm not such a bad person, after all."

He withdrew slightly, taking a knife from his pocket and unfolding the blade. Always so clean and sharp.

"With this knife, I can cut your hair easily."

He grasped a tuft and sliced it from her scalp, startling the girl and prompting her brother to thrash at his tether, though to no avail.

"There we are!" he said.

She reacted almost as if he had cut into her flesh. What he had just done was obviously a deeply ingrained taboo for a girl who had lived all her life with this dogma of the sanctity of women's hair.

She sobbed as he taped her mouth. And then she wet herself.

He turned to her brother and repeated the procedure with the gaffer tape and water from the cup.

"And you, Samuel, have your own secrets, don't you? You look at girls from outside the congregation. I've watched you on your way home from school with your older brother. Is that allowed, Samuel?" he asked.

"I'll kill you as soon as I get the chance, so help me God," the boy replied, before he too was silenced by tape. It was the only reasonable thing to do.

His decision was right. The girl would be the one to go.

For all her daydreaming, her reverence was the greater, her faith the more entrenched. She would grow up to be a Rachel, or an Eva.

What more did he need to know?

Having reassured them that he would be back to set them free once their father paid the ransom, he returned to the outbuilding and saw that the tank was now quite full. He stopped the pump and rolled up the hose, then plugged in the heating element, which he immersed into the water before flicking the switch. He knew from experience that lye was much more effective once the water temperature rose above twenty Celsius, and at this time of year, the nights could still plunge below zero.

He picked up the container of lye from the pallet in the corner, noting that he would soon be needing more. And then he turned it upside down and poured the contents into the water.

Once the girl had been killed and her body dumped in the tank, the corpse would be dissolved within a couple of weeks.

Then all he had to do was to wade out some twenty meters or so with the hose in his hand and empty the whole lot into the fjord.

With a bit of wind it would wash away from the shore in no time.

He would rinse the tank twice, and all trace would be gone.

Chemistry.

24

They made an odd couple as they stood there in Carl's office, Yrsa with her bloodred lips and Assad, his face so belligerently stubbled that a hug from the man would be tantamount to attempted murder.

Assad was looking highly dissatisfied. Carl couldn't recall him ever radiating as much disapproval as now.

"It cannot be right what Yrsa is saying! Can we not bring this Tryggve to Copenhagen, Carl? What about the report?"

Carl blinked. He still had in his mind's eye the image of Mona opening the door into her bedroom, making him rather distracted to say the least. He hadn't been able to think of anything else all morning. Tryggve and the world's insanity would have to wait until he was ready.

"Sorry, what did you say?" Carl stretched in his chair. It had been ages since his body had felt this drained. "Tryggve? No, he's still in Blekinge. I asked him to come to Copenhagen, even offered him a lift, but he wasn't up to it, he said, and I couldn't force him. He lives in Sweden, Assad, remember? If he won't come of his own accord, we're not going to drag him here without the help of the Swedish police, and it's early days for that, wouldn't you say?"

He anticipated a nod from Assad, but it was not forthcoming. "I'll write a report to send up to Marcus, OK? Then we'll have to see. Apart from that, I don't really know how to proceed just at the moment. We're talking about a thirteen-year-old case that's never been investigated. It's up to Marcus whose desk he drops it on."

Assad frowned, Yrsa likewise. Was Department A going to run off with the honors, after all the work they'd put in? Was that really what he was saying?

Assad glanced at his watch. "We should go upstairs right away and get it sorted. Jacobsen comes in early on Mondays."

"OK, Assad." Carl straightened up. "But I want a word first."

He looked at Yrsa, bouncing on the balls of her feet, full of anticipation as to what might now be revealed.

"That's me and Assad alone, Yrsa. In private."

"Oh, I get it," she said, fluttering her eyelashes. "Men's talk." And then she turned on her heel and left them in a haze of her perfume.

He fixed his gaze on Assad, forcing his eyebrows almost to the bridge of his nose, hoping that this might be enough to make his assistant come clean. Instead, Assad peered at him solicitously, as though at any moment he might offer Carl a glass of something for heartburn.

"I was over at your place yesterday, Assad. Heimdalsgade, number sixty-two. You weren't there."

A tiny furrow appeared in Assad's cheek, only to miraculously transform into a cheerful dimple. "What a shame, Carl. You should have called me first."

"I did, Assad, but there was no answer."

"It would have been nice, Carl. Some other time, perhaps. Yes?"

"But that'd be somewhere else, wouldn't it?"

Assad nodded, then lit up. "You mean we should meet somewhere in town? Yes, that would be nice, too."

"I'd want you to bring your wife along, Assad. I've been looking forward to meeting her. And your daughters."

A pained expression passed fleetingly across Assad's face, as though his wife was the last person on earth he wanted to drag out in public.

"I had a little chat with some people there at Heimdalsgade, Assad."

The pained look returned, and Assad narrowed his eyes in puzzlement.

"You don't live there at all, do you? In fact, you haven't lived there for quite a while. And as for your family, they've never lived there, have they? So tell me, Assad, where *do* you live?"

Assad threw up his arms. "It's a very small flat, Carl. There was too little room for us."

"Shouldn't you have informed me of a change of address in that case? And given up the lease on the place?"

Assad looked pensive. "You are right, Carl. I will do so right away."

"So where *do* you live, exactly?"

"We have rented a house. Housing is cheap now, Carl. Many people have two places on their hands. The property market, you know."

"All right, Assad, I understand. But *where* are you living? I need an address."

Assad's head dropped. "OK, Carl. We are renting the place on a fiddle. Otherwise it would be too expensive. Can we not keep the other place on as a postal address?"

"*Where*, Assad?"

"In Holte, Carl. A small house only, on Kongevejen. But will you please call beforehand, Carl? My wife does not care for people turning up all of a sudden."

Carl nodded. He would return to all this another day. "One more thing. Why would your neighbors from Heimdalsgade say you were Shiite? Didn't you tell me you were from Syria?"

Assad thrust out his fleshy lower lip. "Yes, I did, Carl. And what about it?"

"Are there Shiites in Syria, Assad?"

The man's bushy eyebrows relocated halfway up his forehead. "You know, Carl," he smiled, "Shiites are everywhere."

Half an hour later, they stood in the briefing room in the company of fifteen Monday-morning miseries, with Lars Bjørn and homicide chief Marcus Jacobsen at the center.

No one was here for fun, that much was obvious.

Jacobsen related to the meeting what Carl had reported. This was procedure in Department A. Questions could be posed along the way.

"Tryggve Holt, brother of the murdered Poul Holt, has informed Carl Mørck that their kidnapper, Poul's killer, was a man known to the family," Jacobsen said, some way into his briefing. "For a time, our man had frequented prayer meetings held by the boys' father, Martin Holt, for local members of the Jehovah's Witnesses. It seems everyone had taken it for granted that he would enter the congregation."

"Have we got any photos of this man?" asked Bente Hansen, a chief inspector and formerly one of Carl's close colleagues.

Deputy Lars Bjørn shook his head. "I'm afraid not, but we do have both a description and a name: Freddy Brink. Presumably false. Department Q already checked it out and no match came up. Our Swedish colleagues in Karlshamn are sending a police artist over to Tryggve Holt, so we'll have to wait and see what they come up with."

Marcus Jacobsen stood at the whiteboard, scribbling keywords.

"So he kidnaps the two boys on the sixteenth of February 1996. That's a Friday, the same day Poul had taken his younger brother Tryggve with him to the College of Engineering in Ballerup where he studied. This Freddy Brink draws up alongside them in a light-blue van, laughing about what a coincidence it was for them to run into each other so far from Græsted. He offers them a lift home. Unfortunately, Tryggve is unable to provide a closer description of the vehicle, other than it being rounded at the front and square at the back.

"The boys climb into the front, and after a while he pulls in at a secluded lay-by and incapacitates them by means of electric shock. We don't know how, but presumably he'll have used some kind of stun gun. The boys are then thrown into the back and a cloth is pressed into their faces, most likely soaked in chloroform or ether."

"Can I just say at this point that Tryggve Holt wasn't entirely sure about how things actually proceeded here," Carl interrupted. "He was only half-conscious because of the electric shock, and subsequently his brother wasn't able to tell him much on account of the tape he was gagged with."

"Indeed," Jacobsen went on. "But I'm right in thinking, am I not, that Poul gave his younger brother the impression they had driven for approximately an hour, though of course we shouldn't rule out the possibility that this might be incorrect? Poul suffered from some kind of autism, and his grip on reality may not always have been firm, despite his rather exceptional intelligence."

"Asperger's syndrome, perhaps? I'm thinking of the wording of his message, and the fact that he made a point of noting the exact date, even in the terrible situation they were in. Isn't that kind of typical?" Bente Hansen asked, pen to paper.

"Maybe it is, yes." The homicide chief nodded. "Having reached their destination, the boys were left in a boathouse, which smelled strongly of tar and rotting seaweed. The space was rather confined, with only room enough for a man to stoop rather than stand upright. Probably intended for storing canoes or kayaks rather than rowing boats or sailing boats. And there they were held for four, perhaps five days until Poul was murdered. Exactly how much time elapsed is uncertain. We have to bear in mind that Tryggve was only thirteen at the time and very afraid. As such, he spent much of the time sleeping."

"Any landmarks to go on?" asked Peter Vestervig, one of the guys from Viggo's unit.

"None," Jacobsen replied. "The boys were blindfolded when they were led into the boathouse. However, while they saw nothing outside, Tryggve does say he heard a kind of deep rumbling sound that could have come from wind turbines. They heard it often, though not always as loud. Most likely that would have to do with the wind direction and other meteorological factors."

He fixed his gaze on his empty cigarette packet on the table. He'd got to the point now where it was all he needed to reenergize himself. Good for him.

"We know," he went on, "that this boathouse was situated in the shallows, presumably built on stilts, since Tryggve tells us that the water lapped beneath the planks of the floor. The entrance would seem to have been raised about half a meter or so off the ground, meaning that a person would have to literally crawl into the low-ceilinged space inside. Tryggve himself believed it to have been made for canoes or kayaks because of the paddles that were still kept there. And he thought the place might have been constructed from some other kind of wood than would normally be used in the Scandinavian tradition. He remembered it as being very pale in color and rather different in terms of grain, but we'll know more about that later. Laursen, our old friend from Forensics, discovered a splinter lodged in the paper on which Poul Holt wrote his message, apparently from a sliver of wood Poul used as a pen. That's with the experts at the moment, but it may be able to tell us what kind of wood the boathouse was made of."

"How was Poul killed?" one of the men at the back asked.

"Tryggve doesn't know. He had a canvas bag over his head when it took place. He heard some commotion, and when the bag was removed, his brother was gone."

"How does he know he was murdered, then?" the man persisted.

Marcus inhaled deeply. "The sound of it was more than enough for him to be sure."

"In what way?"

"Groans, thrashing about, a dull blow, and then nothing."

"A blunt instrument?"

"Possibly, yes. Would you like to take it from here, Carl?"

All eyes were on him now. This was a gesture on the part of the homicide chief, though hardly one that would be unanimously applauded. In the opinion of most of those present, Carl would do best to get his arse out of there and disappear into some far-off corner where he belonged, preferably on some other continent.

They'd had a bellyful of him over the years.

But Carl wasn't bothered. From the epicenter of his pituitary gland, hormonal aftershocks continued to ripple through his body following his ecstatic escapades of the night before. These sweet sensations, judging by the miserable faces now gawping in his direction, were his privilege alone.

He cleared his throat. "After his brother was killed, Tryggve was given instructions as to what he was to tell his parents: that Poul was dead, and that the man would not hesitate to kill again should they ever confide to anyone what had happened."

He caught Bente Hansen's gaze. She was the only person in the room who appeared to react in any way. He nodded to her. She'd always been all right, had Bente.

"This must have been a terribly traumatic experience for a thirteen-year-old boy," Carl went on, addressing her directly. "Later, when Tryggve came home again, he was told the killer had been in touch with the parents prior to Poul being killed and had demanded a million in ransom. Money that was actually paid out."

"You mean they paid?" Bente Hansen asked, astonished. "Would that be before or after the murder?"

"Before, as far as we know."

"I'm not getting this at all, Carl. Can you explain in a few words?" said Vestervig. It was rare in these parts for anyone to admit there was something they didn't grasp, so fair dues to him.

"OK. The family knew what the killer looked like, because he'd been at their meetings. Most likely they'd be able to identify him, as well as the vehicle and a whole lot more besides. He needed to make sure they wouldn't go to the police, and the method he chose was simple and gruesome."

One or two of those present leaned back against the wall, their thoughts probably darting back to other cases already piled up on their desks. The bikers and the immigrant gangs were using their balls for brains at the moment. The day before, there had been yet another shooting in Nørrebro, the third in a week, so the guys in the department had plenty to be getting on with as it was. Now it had got to the stage where even the ambulances preferred to stay away from the area. The threat was there all the time.

Several of the homicide officers had personally invested in lightweight bulletproof vests, and even here in the briefing room, one or two already had them on under their sweatshirts.

Up to a point, Carl could well understand their skepticism. Who cared about a message in a bottle from 1996 with so much else going on? But wasn't all that their own fault, in a way? More than half of those present had probably voted for the very parties who were now sending the country headlong into the shit with their police reform and failed integration policies. Yes, it was their own fucking fault. Carl wondered whether this thought ever occurred to them when they were out on duty in the middle of the night, while their wives lay dreaming of a man who could snuggle up and keep them warm.

"Our kidnapper selects a family with a large number of children," Carl went on, searching around the room for faces worth addressing. "A family who in many ways exists in isolation from the rest of society. A family whose habits are deeply entrenched and whose way of life is strictly constrained. In this case, a wealthy family of Jehovah's Witnesses. Not fabulously rich, by any means, but wealthy enough. Our man selects two of the children who in one way or another enjoy some particular status within the family. He kidnaps them both, and then when the ransom is paid he murders one of them. Now the family knows what he's capable of. He threatens them, says he'll kill another one without warning if he ever suspects they've gone to the police or their Church, or if they should try to track him down in any way. Then he returns the second child to the family. They're a million down, but the rest of the flock are still alive. And they keep their mouths shut, because they're afraid he'll come back, and because they want their lives to be as normal as possible again."

"But a child gone forever!" Bente Hansen exclaimed. "What about the people around them? Surely someone would notice that one of the children wasn't there anymore?"

"Correct. Someone must have noticed. But in such a strict community, not many would be likely to react if they were told the child had been sent away on religious grounds, even if that sort of decision is usually up to some kind of council. An explanation that the child had been ostracized would be highly plausible in many religious communities. In fact, a good many of them simply forbid contact of any kind with ostracized members, and for that reason alone no one would ever try. In that respect, the community displays complete solidarity. After his murder, the family declared Poul Holt ostracized. The story was, they sent him away to sort out his attitude. And that was that, no questions asked."

"But what about outside the community? Someone must have wondered, surely?"

"You'd think so, certainly. But often these people don't *have* contact with anyone outside the community. That's what's so fiendish about his choice of victims. In this case, Poul's tutor did get in touch with the family, but she ran into a brick wall. You can't force a student back on to a course if he's decided to leave, can you?"

The room was silent. They'd got the picture.

"All right, we know what you're all thinking, and so are we." Deputy Lars Bjørn looked around at the faces. As always, he tried to look more important than he was. "A never-reported crime of such a serious nature, in a community as insular as this, means it may well have happened more than once."

"It's sick," said one of the new guys.

"That's Police HQ for you," came the rejoinder from Vestervig, though clearly he was sorry he'd spoken when almost decapitated by a glare from Jacobsen.

"I should stress that we cannot draw any dramatic conclusions for the time being," said the homicide chief. "So we shan't be talking to the press until we've got a clearer picture. Understood?"

Everyone nodded, Assad in particular.

"What subsequently occurred within the family serves only to underline the kind of grip the killer had on them," Jacobsen continued. "Carl?"

"According to Tryggve Holt, the family relocated to Lund in Sweden only a week after his release. After that, members of the family were instructed never to mention Poul's name again."

"That can't have been easy for his younger brother," Bente Hansen commented.

Carl pictured Tryggve's face and could only agree.

"The family's paranoia about the killer's threat became plain whenever they heard anyone speak Danish. They moved on from Skåne to Blekinge, with two further relocations before settling at their present address in Hallabro. But everyone in the family received clear instructions never to let anyone speaking Danish into the house, and never to involve themselves with anyone outside their religious community."

"And Tryggve protested?" Bente Hansen asked.

"Indeed he did, and for two reasons. Firstly, he wouldn't stop talking about Poul. He loved his brother dearly and had got himself believing in some roundabout way that Poul had given up his life for him. And secondly, because he fell desperately in love with a girl who wasn't a Jehovah's Witness."

"So then he was ostracized," Lars Bjørn added, some seconds having elapsed since he had last heard the sound of his own exasperating voice.

"Exactly. Tryggve was ostracized." Carl picked up the thread again. "He's been on the outside for three years now. He moved a few kilometers down the road, absorbed himself in his relationship with the girl he had met, and took on a job as a service assistant at a timber outlet in Belganet. Neither his family nor other members of the local congregation ever spoke to him, even though his job was close to the family home. In fact, they've only spoken once, after I got in touch with the family. And on that occasion, the father did everything he could to impress upon Tryggve that he should keep his mouth shut. Which he did, until the moment I showed him the message his brother had sent in the bottle. That knocked him for six. Or rather, it sent him flying back into the real world, you might say."

"Did the family ever hear from the killer again after the kidnapping?" someone else asked.

Carl shook his head. "No, and I don't think they ever will, either."

"Why not?"

"Thirteen years have passed now. My guess is he's got other things to attend to."

Silence descended again. The only sound to be heard was Lis's relentless chatter out front. Someone had to man the phones.

"Is there anything at all to indicate there might be other cases similar to this one, Carl? Have you looked into that?"

Carl sent a grateful glance in the direction of Bente Hansen. She was the only one in the room he hadn't had any altercations with over the years and probably the only person in the department who never needed to assert herself. She was one of the lads, no two ways about it. "I've got Assad and Yrsa—that's Rose's temp—contacting support groups for apostates from all the various sects. If we're lucky, that might give us some information about kids who have been ostracized or who have simply left their congregations of their own accord. It's not much to go on, but the communities themselves are only going to stonewall us if we approach them directly."

A couple of the guys glanced at Assad, who looked like he had just got out of bed, even if he did have his day clothes on.

"Maybe this might be best left to professionals, people who know what they're doing?" one of them suggested.

Carl halted proceedings. "Who said that?"

One of the guys stepped forward. Pasgård, his name was, a hard case. Good at his job but the sort who shoved his way to the front to be interviewed whenever there was a TV camera around. Probably saw himself running the place in a few years. Someone should make sure he never got a look-in.

Carl narrowed his eyes. "OK, smart-arse, maybe you'd like to share with us your exceptional knowledge about religious sects and similar communities in Denmark who might be at particular risk of being targeted by a man such as the one who murdered Poul Holt? Would you care to pick out a couple for us now, while we're here? Let's say five, to be getting on with?"

Pasgård made noises, but Jacobsen's wry smile put him under pressure.

"Hmm!" He gazed around the room. "Jehovah's Witnesses. The Baptists aren't a sect, I suppose, but then there's the Moonies . . . Scientology . . . the Satanists and . . . the Father House." He gave Carl a triumphant look, then nodded smugly around the room.

Carl pretended to be impressed. "OK, Pasgård, you're right in saying that the Baptists aren't a sect, but then again neither are the Satanists, unless you're thinking specifically of the Church of Satan. So you're still one short. Any offers?"

The guy's mouth twisted pensively. The great world religions flashed through his mind, only to be dismissed. Carl could almost see the names forming on his silent lips. Then he finally came up with an answer, to sporadic applause: "The Children of God."

Carl, too, applauded, albeit briefly. "Well done, Pasgård, we'll bury the hatchet here. There are a lot more sects, religious movements, and free churches in this country than you'd think, and the majority of them aren't exactly household names." He turned to Assad: "Are they, Assad?"

The little man shook his head. "No, a person must do his homework first."

"Have you done yours?"

"Not quite finished yet, but I can mention a couple more if that would be relevant?" Assad glanced across at the homicide chief, who nodded.

"Well, in that case one could name the Quakers, the Martinus Society, the Pentecostalists, Sathya Sai Baba, the Mother Church, the Evangelists, the House of Christ, the UFO cosmologists, the Theosophists, Hare Krishna, Transcendental Meditation, the Shamanists, the Emin Foundation, the Guardians of Morality, Ananda Marga, the Jes Bertelsen movement, the disciples of Brahma Kumaris, the Fourth Way, the Word of Life, Osho, New Age, arguably the Church of the Transfiguration, the New Pagans, In the Master's Light, the Golden Circle, and perhaps also the Inner Mission." He took a deep breath, replenishing his empty lungs.

This time, there was no applause. The message that expertise was multifaceted had sunk in.

"Thank you, Assad." Carl gave a slight smile. "As I was saying, religious communities are many and varied. And a large number of them worship either a leader or a community in such a way that they automatically turn in on themselves after a while and become closed units. Given the right conditions, the pickings are rich indeed for a psychopath such as Poul Holt's killer."

The chief stepped forward. "You've now been filled in on this murder case. A case outside the jurisdiction of our own district, though close enough. We'll leave things at that for the time being and allow Carl and his assistants to proceed." He turned toward Carl. "Any further assistance you might need, you come to me."

Jacobsen turned to Pasgård, whose indifferent eyelids were already drooping over his frigid eyes. "And to you, Pasgård, I'd like to say that I find your enthusiasm exemplary. I'm glad you consider the department to be sufficiently well equipped to take on the case, but we on the third floor must keep a focus on those we are already investigating. Quite a job in itself, wouldn't you say?"

The idiot was forced to nod. Anything else would have made him look even more stupid.

"However, since you so strongly believe the case would be better off with us rather than Department Q, perhaps we should accord it some attention. I'd say we could release one man. And that, Pasgård, would be you, since you're so eager."

Carl felt his jaw drop, the air compress in his lungs. Were they really going to have to work with this moron?

A single look was sufficient for Marcus Jacobsen to catch on to the dilemma. "I understand a fish scale was found on the paper on which the message was written. So Pasgård, if you would make sure we know what kind of fish we're dealing with, as well as where the species might be found within a one-hour radius of Ballerup?"

He ignored Carl's startled expression. "And one more thing, Pasgård. Bear in mind the location may be in the vicinity of wind turbines or something that makes a similar kind of noise, and that whatever the source of that noise might be, it had to have been there in 1996. Understand?"

Carl heaved a sigh of relief. These were the kinds of jobs he gladly farmed out to the likes of Pasgård.

"Yeah, but I haven't got time," Pasgård protested. "Jørgen and I have got doorbells to ring out in Sundby."

Jacobsen glanced across at the hulk skulking at the opposite end of the room. Jørgen nodded. It was true.

"Well, Jørgen will just have to get by on his own for a couple of days," said Jacobsen. "Right, Jørgen?"

The big guy gave a shrug. He wasn't happy. The family waiting desperately for their son's attackers to be brought to justice probably wouldn't have been, either.

Jacobsen turned to Pasgård. "Two days, that ought to be enough, wouldn't you say?"

The homicide chief had made his point.

If you're going to piss on someone, make sure the wind's behind you.

25

The worst thing that could ever happen had happened, and Rachel was devastated.

Satan had materialized in their midst and punished them for their wantonness. How could she have allowed a total stranger to take her two darling children, and on this holy day? Yesterday, they should have been quietly absorbed in Bible study in preparation for the bliss of the Sabbath. They should have folded their hands together in the hour of rest and allowed the spirit of the Mother of God to descend upon them and bring them peace.

And now? God had thrust His arm out at them like a thunderbolt. They had succumbed to all the temptations resisted by the sacred Virgin Mary. Flattery, the disguises of the Devil, empty words.

Their punishment had come promptly. Magdalena and Samuel had fallen into the power of the sinner. A night and a day had passed, and they could do nothing.

And Rachel felt the shame. Exactly as she had done when she had been raped and no one came to her aid. Only then she had been able to do something. Now she was powerless.

"You must raise the money, Joshua," she implored her husband. "You must!"

He looked ill. The whites of his eyes merged with the pallor of his face. "But we haven't got it, Rachel. I made the voluntary tax payment the day before yesterday, you know that. One million at a good rate of interest, like we always do." He buried his face in his hands. "Like we always do, in the name of Jesus. Just like we always do!"

"Joshua, you heard what he said on the phone. If we don't raise the money, he'll kill them!"

"We must go to the congregation."

"NO!" Her scream was so loud their youngest daughter began to cry in the next room. "He took our children and now *you* will get them back, do you understand? If you tell anyone, we'll never see them again, ever. I'm certain."

He turned his head toward her. "How do you know, Rachel? Perhaps he's bluffing. Perhaps we should go to the police."

"What do you know about the police? The police may be in the pay of the Devil. And how can you be sure *he* won't find out? How can you be *sure*?"

"Our friends, then. People in the congregation would keep it secret. If we stand together in this, we can raise the money."

"What if he's there outside when you go to them? What if he has helpers among us? He was so close to us, and yet we failed to see his true self. How can you be certain there are no others like him? How, Joshua?"

She looked across at their youngest daughter, now standing in the doorway, clutching at the frame with tears running down her cheeks.

He had to find a way.

"Joshua, you must do something," she said again, getting up from the table. She kneeled in front of her little girl and held her head in her hands.

"You mustn't despair, Sarah. The Mother of Jesus will watch over Magdalena and Samuel. But you must pray so that they may be helped. And if this has happened because of something we did that we weren't supposed to, then we shall receive forgiveness when we pray. That's what you must do, my love."

She saw the girl react at the mention of forgiveness. How her eyes yearned for it. There was something she wanted to say, but her mouth would not open.

"What's wrong, Sarah? Is there something you want to tell Mummy?"

Sarah's mouth twisted, and her lips began to quiver. Something was the matter.

"Does it have to do with the man?"

The girl nodded, and now her tears began to flow.

Rachel held her breath instinctively. "What is it? *Tell me!*"

The girl was frightened by the sudden harshness of her mother's voice but began to speak regardless. "I did something you said I shouldn't."

"What was it, Sarah? Tell Mummy."

"I looked in the photo album during the hour of rest while you were all in the kitchen with your Bibles. I'm so sorry, Mummy. I know it was wrong of me."

"Oh, Sarah." Rachel's face dropped. "Is that all?"

Her daughter shook her head. "I saw the picture of the man who took Magdalena and Samuel. Is that why it happened? Is it because he's the Devil, and I looked at him?"

Rachel inhaled deeply. This was something she didn't know. "Are you saying there's a photograph of him?"

Sarah sniffled. "Yes, outside the congregation hall when we all had our picture taken at Johanna's and Dina's initiation ceremony."

Was he really on that photograph?

"Where is that picture, Sarah? I want you to show it to me, now!"

Obediently, the girl showed her the album and picked out the photograph.

Rachel's heart sank. It's useless, she said to herself. No help at all.

She considered the photo with disgust, removed it from its pocket, stroked her daughter's hair, comforting her, telling her she was forgiven. And then she turned back into the kitchen and slapped the photograph down on the table in front of the slumped figure of her husband.

"Here's our tormentor, Joshua." Her finger pointed to a barely visible head in the back row. He had managed to stand half concealed behind the man in front and was looking away from the camera. If she hadn't known it was him, it could have been anyone.

"You're going to the tax authorities first thing in the morning to tell them that that payment you made was a mistake. Tell them we need the money back right away, otherwise we'll go bankrupt. Do you understand me, Joshua? First thing in the morning."

Monday came and she gazed out of the window at the dawn as it broke over Dollerup Church. Long, dazzling rays of sunlight poked through the morning mist. The proffered hand of God in all His splendor. How could He enjoin her to bear such a cross? And how could she allow herself to even ask such a question? The Lord worked in mysterious ways. She knew that.

She tightened her lips to stave off tears, folded her hands, and closed her eyes.

All night she had prayed, the way she did so often within the comfort of the congregation, but this time peace was not forthcoming. This was the testing time, Job's hour of destiny, and the pain seemed endless.

By the time the sun lay nestled in the abundance of clouds and Joshua had driven off to the local authority to try to retrieve the business's voluntary tax payment, her strength was almost gone.

"Josef, you must stay home from school and look after your sisters," she had told her eldest. She needed Miriam and Sarah out of the way in order to get herself together.

When Joshua returned, he would, God willing, have the money with him. They had agreed he would pay the check into the Vestjysk Bank and instruct them to distribute the funds to their various accounts with Nordea, Danske Bank, Jyske Bank, Sparekassen Kronjylland, and Almindelig Brand Bank. All told, that would allow for cash payments of some one hundred and sixty-five thousand kroner from each bank, which ought not to provoke comment. Any new banknotes would have to be made grubby and creased and then mixed in with used notes from the other withdrawals so that the fiend who had taken their children would not suspect them of passing him marked notes.

She booked seats on the evening's InterCity connection arriving in

Odense at 7:29 P.M., then onward with the express to Copenhagen. And then she waited for her husband. She was expecting him some time between twelve and one o'clock, but he came back at half past ten.

"The money, Joshua. Did you get the money?" she asked, though she knew, just by looking at him, that he had failed.

"It wasn't that straightforward, Rachel. I knew it wouldn't be," he replied, his voice feeble. "The people at the local authority were helpful, but the account belongs to the tax authorities, so it would take some time. This is so terrible."

"You insisted, Joshua, didn't you? Tell me you insisted? We haven't got all day. The banks close at four." Now she was desperate. "What did you say to them? Tell me!"

"I said I had to get the money back. That the payment was a mistake. We were having problems with our IT system, I said, and had lost control of our payments. Money had been going into the wrong accounts and invoices were getting lost in the system. I told them we'd had suppliers on the phone this morning and that if we didn't pay what was outstanding we'd be losing them. I explained to them that the financial crisis has got suppliers feeling the squeeze and that they'd soon be reclaiming their harvesters and selling them off to others at a discount. I told them we'd be losing our leasing advantage, that it was going to end up costing us a packet, and that it was a critical time for us, too."

"Oh, Lord. Did you have to make it so complicated, Joshua? Why?"

"It was just all I could come up with." He sat down heavily on a chair and slapped the empty briefcase down on the table. "I'm under pressure too, Rachel. I can't think straight. I didn't sleep at all last night."

"Dear God, what are we to do?"

"We must go to the congregation. What else can we do?"

She tightened her lips and thought again of Magdalena and Samuel. Poor, innocent children. What on earth had they done to deserve such punishment?

They had made sure their pastor would be at home and were putting on their coats to go and see him when the doorbell rang.

Rachel wasn't going to answer, but her husband opened the door without thinking.

They didn't know the woman standing on the step with a folder in her hand, and neither did they wish to speak to her.

"Isabel Jønsson. I'm from the local authority," she announced, stepping into the hallway.

Rachel felt hope stirring. The woman had brought the necessary papers for them to sign. She had sorted everything out. Perhaps her husband hadn't been so stupid, after all.

"Come in. We can sit here in the kitchen," she said, relieved.

"I see you're on your way out. It needn't be now. I can come back tomorrow if that would be more convenient?"

Rachel sensed the clouds begin to gather as they sat down at the kitchen table. So the woman couldn't be here to help them get their money back at all. If she was, she would know how imperative it was. Why not just get to the point? She had said it needn't be now. What kind of a thing was that to say?

"I work in IT, as part of the business consultancy team. My colleagues informed me you were having some rather serious problems with your systems, so I've come to help." She smiled and handed them her card: *Isabel Jønsson, IT Consultant, Viborg Municipality.* This was the last thing they needed right now.

"I'm sorry," Rachel said after a moment, realizing that her husband was reluctant to take charge. "It's awfully nice of you, but I'm afraid it's a bad time for us. We're very busy."

She thought that would be enough and that the woman would make her apologies and leave, but instead she remained seated, staring at the table as though she were fastened to the chair. As though she would use whatever means necessary to enforce the right of the public authorities to poke their noses in.

Rachel stood up and flashed her husband a harsh look. "We need to be getting on, Joshua. We're in a hurry, remember?" She turned to the woman. "So, if you'll excuse us . . ."

But the woman didn't move. And that was when Rachel saw that what she was staring at was the photo Sarah had found in the album. The photo that had been lying on the table to remind them that in any flock there could be a Judas.

"Do you know this man?" the woman asked.

They looked at her in bewilderment. "What man?" Rachel asked in turn.

"This one here," the woman replied, placing her finger underneath the man's head.

Rachel sensed danger. The same way she had on that dreadful afternoon in the village near Baobli when the soldiers had asked her the way.

The tone of voice. The situation.

It was all wrong.

"You must go now," Rachel told her. "We're busy."

But the woman wasn't going anywhere. "Do you know him?" she repeated.

So now another devil had been sent to them. Another devil in an angel's guise.

Rachel stood in front of her, clenching her fists at her sides. "I know who you are and I want you to leave, now. Do you think I don't realize he sent you, that monster? Get out. You know how little time we've got."

And then she felt everything keeping her together inside fall to pieces. Suddenly she was unable to hold back the tears as rage and impotence took over and dragged her down. "GET OUT!" she screamed, her eyes closed and her hands clutching at her breast.

The woman rose, putting her hands on Rachel's shoulders and shaking her gently until she looked up. "I don't know what you're talking about, but believe me, if anyone has reason to hate this man, it's me."

Rachel opened her eyes wide and saw that it was true. Behind the woman's calm gaze, hostility smoldered, its embers glowing deep inside her.

"What has he done?" the woman asked. "Tell me what he did to you, and I'll tell you all I know about him."

The woman knew him, and her encounter with him had been anything but happy. That much was plain. The question was whether she could help them. Rachel doubted it. Only money could help, and soon it would be too late.

"Tell us. But hurry, or we'll go."

"His name's Mads Fog. Mads Christian Fog."

Rachel shook her head. "He told us his name was Lars. Lars Sørensen."

The woman nodded deliberately. "OK, it's possible both names are assumed. When I met him, he was calling himself Mikkel Laust. But I've seen documents, and I found an address, a house in the name of Mads Christian Fog. I think that's his real name."

Rachel gasped for air. Had the Mother of God heard her prayers? She looked again into the woman's eyes. Could they trust her?

"What address? Where?" Joshua's face had taken on a bluish-white tinge. This was obviously too much for him.

"A place in Nordsjælland, near Skibby. Ferslev, it's called. I've got the exact address at home."

"How do you know this?" Rachel's voice trembled. She wanted to believe it, but could she?

"He was staying with me until Saturday. I kicked him out on Saturday morning."

Rachel covered her mouth with her hand in order not to hyperventilate. This was all so terrible. He had come to them directly from this woman's home.

She looked up at the clock with a dreadful sense of fear, forcing herself to listen to the woman's account of how the man had exploited her, enthralled her with his charm, only to change in an instant.

Rachel recognized the man Isabel described, and when she had finished, Rachel looked across at her husband. For a moment, he seemed far away, as though trying to put everything into some perspective. Then finally he nodded. They should tell her, his eyes said. This woman was on their side.

So Rachel took Isabel's hand in hers. "What I'm about to tell you, you must not tell a single person in the entire world, do you understand? Not yet, at least. We're telling you because we think you can help us."

"If it's something criminal, I can't guarantee you anything."

"It is. But we're not the criminals. He is, the man you kicked out. And what he's done . . ." She took a deep breath, noticing for the first time that her voice was shaking. "What he's done is the worst thing anyone could do to a family. He's kidnapped two of our children. And if you tell anyone, he'll kill them. Do you understand?"

Twenty minutes had passed, and never in her life had Isabel been held in the grip of shock for so long. Now she saw everything as it was. The man who had been living with her, and whom for a brief, intense period she had taken to be a possible life partner, was a monster most likely capable of anything at all. She felt it now, as her senses recalled his hands on her body. Just a little too strong, too competent almost. She realized how fatal his entry into her life could have been. And her mouth went dry as she thought back to the moment when she had revealed to him that she had been gathering information on him. What if he had attacked her there and then, before she managed to tell him that she had passed on everything she knew to her brother on the force? What if he had discovered that she was bluffing? That she would never dream of involving her brother in her erotically derived catastrophes?

She hardly dared think about it.

She looked at these people and shared their pain. Oh, how she hated that man. And she vowed that regardless of what it might cost, he would not get away.

"Listen, I can help you. My brother's a policeman. He's in the traffic police, but we can get him to put out a description. That way we can spread the word, cover the whole country in no time at all. I've got the number of his van. I can describe everything in detail."

But the woman in front of her shook her head. She wanted to agree, but couldn't. "I told you, you're not to tell anyone. You promised," she said after a moment. "Now we've got four hours before the banks close, and we need to raise a million kroner. We can't sit here any longer."

"But listen to me. If we leave now, we can be at his address in less than four hours."

Again, Rachel shook her head. "What makes you think he took the children there? Surely that would be the stupidest thing he could do? My children might be anywhere at all. He may have taken them over the border. Anything can get through these days. Do you understand what I'm saying?"

Isabel nodded. "You're right." She looked at the husband. "Have you got a mobile phone?"

Joshua pulled his phone out of his pocket. "Here," he said.

"Is it fully charged?"

He nodded.

"Have you got one, too, Rachel?"

"Yes," was all she said.

"I think we should split into two teams. Joshua should try to raise the ransom, and we'll drive to Sjælland. We need to do it now!"

The couple looked at each other for a moment. This unlikely pair—Isabel understood them only too well. She had no children of her own, and that was cause for grief enough in itself. How must it feel to realize you were about to lose those you had, that you might fail to save them?

"We need a million kroner," said Joshua. "We're good for more, but we can't just go to the bank and ask them to give us the money, and certainly not in cash. A couple of years ago, maybe, when things were different. But not now. The only place we can go to is our congregation. It's a risk, but it's our only chance of getting the money." He looked at her urgently. His breathing was shaky, his lips a little blue. "Unless you can help us. I think you can, if you want to."

Here, for the first time, she saw the real person behind the name, so well known for the efficient running of his business. One of the best taxpayers in Viborg Municipality.

"Call your superiors," he said with sadness in his eyes. "Tell them to call the tax authorities. Tell them we've made a mistake with our voluntary payment and that they need to return the amount to our account immediately. Can you do that?"

And suddenly the ball was in her court.

When she had gone to work that morning, three hours ago, she had still been feeling stunned. Out of sorts and in a foul mood. Self-pity had been her only momentum. Now she could hardly recognize those emotions. At this moment, she was prepared to act, to do anything necessary. Even if it cost her her job.

Even if it cost her more.

"Let me go into another room," she said. "I'll be as quick as I can, but it may take some time."

26

"So, Laursen," Carl said to the former forensics officer, wrapping up his briefing. "Now we know who wrote the letter."

"Dreadful story." Laursen breathed deeply. "You say you've got hold of some of Poul Holt's possessions, so if there's any DNA on them, then we can establish beyond a doubt whether the blood used to write the letter was his. If it was, then alongside the brother's corroborating statement that he was killed, we should have enough to make a case. Assuming we find a suspect. But a murder case without a corpse is always going to be a dodgy business, you know that."

He stared at the transparent plastic bags Carl produced from his drawer.

"Tryggve Holt told me he still kept some personal items belonging to his brother. The two of them were close, and Tryggve took these with him when he left home. I persuaded him to hand them over to us."

Laursen wrapped a handkerchief around his large square mitt. "These are probably no good," he said, putting a pair of sandals and a shirt to one side. "This might be useful, though."

He examined the cap in detail. An ordinary white baseball cap with a blue peak proclaiming *JESUS RULES!*

"Poul wasn't allowed to wear it because of his parents. But he loved it, apparently. Kept it under his bed during the day and practically slept with it on at night."

"Anyone worn it other than Poul?"

"Seems not. I asked Tryggve the same question."

"OK, then we've got his DNA here." Laursen jabbed a thick finger at a couple of hairs adhering to the inside of the cap.

"Most excellent!" said Assad, appearing behind them with a ream of papers in his hand. His face was as bright as a fluorescent tube, which couldn't be attributable to Laursen's presence alone. What had he dug up now?

"Thanks, Laursen," said Carl. "I know you're up to your ears in fish-cakes upstairs, but things do get through the system a lot more smoothly if they come from you."

Carl shook him by the hand. It was about time he got his arse up to the cafeteria and let Laursen's mates up there know what kind of a guy they had in their midst.

"Hey," Laursen exclaimed, his eyes fixed somewhere in the air in front of him. And then he swiped a hand quickly and without warning at something invisible. He stood for a moment with his fist clenched, then made a movement a bit like hurling a tennis ball onto the floor. A split second later, he stamped his foot down and smiled. "I can't stand those things," he said by way of explanation, lifting his foot to reveal an enormous fly splayed out flat on the floor.

And then he was gone.

Assad rubbed his hands gleefully as Laursen's footsteps faded. "We are running just like a well-oiled machine now, Carl. Have a look at this."

He dropped his pile of papers onto the desk and indicated the sheet on top. "Here is the common I nominate in all the fires, Carl."

"You what?"

"The common I nominate."

"Common denominator, Assad. A compound noun. What common denominator?"

"Here. Suddenly it came to me as I was on my way through JPP's accounts. They borrowed money from a firm of bankers called RJ Invest, and this is very important."

Carl shook his head. The world had too many initialisms in it for his liking. What the fuck was JPP?

"JPP, was that the firm making fittings that burned down in Emdrup?"

Assad nodded and jabbed again at the document, then turned his head toward the corridor. "Hey, Yrsa, are you coming? I'm now showing Carl what we discovered."

Carl felt his brow wrinkle. Had Yrsa, that odd female beanstalk, been spending her time on things other than what she was supposed to?

He heard her feet tramping down the corridor loud enough to shame a regiment of U.S. Marines. How could she do that? She weighed maybe fifty-five kilos at the most.

She burst in through the door and had the documents in his face before she'd even come to a halt. "Have you told him about RJ Invest, Assad?"

Assad nodded.

"That's who made the loan to JPP shortly before the fire."

"This I have already told him, Yrsa," said Assad.

"OK. And RJ Invest are loaded," she continued. "At present, their loan portfolio stands at over five hundred million euros. Not bad for a firm that wasn't even registered until 2004, wouldn't you say?"

"Five hundred million euros," Carl mused. "Everyone's got that kind of money these days, haven't they?"

He thought of his own portfolio of pocket fluff.

"RJ Invest didn't in 2004. They were borrowing from AIJ Ltd. Who in turn borrowed their initial capital in 1995 from MJ AG, who in turn borrowed from TJ Holding. Do you see the link?"

What did she think he was, stupid or something?

"No, Yrsa, I don't. Unless it's the letter 'J.' And what do they all stand for, anyway?"

Carl smiled, knowing she'd have no answer.

"Jankovic," Assad and Yrsa replied in unison.

Assad spread the documents out on the desk in front of him. Annual accounts of the four companies they were investigating for the period 1992 to 2009. All had borrowed money, and the lenders were highlighted with a red marker.

All moneylenders with a "J."

"So what you're trying to tell me is that the same banking firm was behind all the short-term loans taken out by our four companies prior to their properties burning down?"

"Yes!" In unison again.

Carl studied the documents for a while. This was definitely a breakthrough.

"OK, Yrsa," he said eventually. "You gather all the information you can find on these four loan companies. Do we know what the other letters stand for?"

She smiled like a Hollywood actor with no other talent. "RJ: Radomir Jankovic. AIJ: Abram Ilija Jankovic. MJ: Milica Jankovic. TJ: Tomislav Jankovic. Siblings. Three brothers, and the sister, Milica."

"OK. Are they resident in Denmark?"

"No."

"Where, then?"

"Nowhere you could pronounce," she replied, her shoulders hovering somewhere in the region of her ears.

She and Assad looked like two schoolkids with a stash of something illegal in their backpacks.

"No, to put it to you straight up, Carl, all four of them are dead some years ago," said Assad.

Of course they were. What else had he expected?

"They made a name for themselves in Serbia when the war broke out," Yrsa explained. "Four siblings, arms dealers, and making a packet out of it. A very naughty bunch." She expelled a grunt that Carl supposed to be a laugh, and Assad picked up the thread.

"Indeed, this is an understatement of Yrsa, to promote understanding," he added.

Where would he be without Assad?

Carl searched Yrsa's chuckling face, then looked her up and down. Where the hell did this bizarre creature get her information? Did she speak Serbian?

"I'm guessing, then, that their highly dubious fortune got channeled into legal lending operations in Western Europe," Carl said. "But if that's the kind of case we're dealing with, then my view is that we should kick it upstairs to some of our colleagues who are a lot better equipped than us to deal with financial crime."

"You should have a look at this first, Carl." Yrsa rummaged through her documents. "We've got a picture here of the four of them together. It's quite old, but still useful."

She placed the photograph on the desk in front of him.

"OK," he said, digesting the image of four overfed specimens the size of Angus cattle. "A bit on the beefy side, then. Sumo wrestlers, perhaps?"

"Have a good look, Carl," Assad urged. "Then you will see what we mean."

He traced Assad's gaze to the bottom of the photo. The four siblings were sitting in an orderly line at a cloth-covered table. In front of each was a crystal goblet. All four had their hands neatly placed on the table in front of them, as though they had been instructed to do so by a strict mother standing just outside the picture. Four pairs of thickset hands—and each left hand displayed a ring on its little finger. A ring that had practically been engulfed by flesh.

Carl looked up at his assistants, two of the oddest individuals ever to have graced these forbidding corridors. Now they had lifted the case into a new dimension. A case that wasn't really even theirs.

It was like a surreal dream.

An hour later, Carl's carefully considered allocation of tasks was messed up again. Deputy Chief Lars Bjørn was on the phone. One of his men had been down in records and overheard an exchange between Assad and that new girl. What was going on? Had they found another link between those arson cases?

Carl outlined the situation, the stuffed shirt at the other end grunting at every second word to indicate that he was listening.

"I want you to send Hafez el-Assad over to Rødovre so Antonsen can be put in the picture. We'll proceed with the arsons here on our own patch, but you'll have to take care of the old case yourselves, now that you're under way," said Bjørn.

No peace for the wicked.

"I don't think Assad will want to, to be honest."

"Well, you'll have to do it yourself, then, won't you?"

Lars fucking Bjørn.

"You don't mean this, surely, Carl? You are pulling my leg, I think?" Great dimples appeared in Assad's stubble, only to vanish just as quickly.

"Take the car, Assad. And mind your speed once you hit Roskildevej. The traffic boys are out with their lollipops today."

"If I should think a thought now, it would be that this is very foolish, indeed. Either we must take all the arson cases or not any at all." He nodded emphatically.

Carl said nothing and handed him the car keys.

Once Assad's cloud of mother-tongue invective had faded with the echo of his footsteps on the stairs, Carl flopped down on his chair and contemplated the serenade emanating in an earsplitting key from Yrsa's vocal cords farther down the corridor. He realized how much he missed Rose's more than occasional muteness. And what the hell was she *doing*, anyway?

He jumped to his feet and went out into the corridor.

Of course. There she was, gawping at the blowup on the wall.

"There's no point in that now, Yrsa," he said. "Tryggve Holt's already given us his take on it, and I'd say he was the best judge, wouldn't you? What more's it got to tell us? Not much, if you ask me. So go on back to your office and do something useful, like we agreed."

She didn't stop singing until he had finished. "Come here, Carl," she said, tugging on his sleeve and dragging him with her into her little pink fairyland.

She planted him in front of Rose's desk, on which was a copy of Tryggve's version of the message from the bottle.

"Look at this. We're all in agreement as to the first few lines."

HELP

The 16 febrary 1996 we were kidnaped he got us at the bus sdop on Lautropvang in Ballerup—The man is 18. tall with short hair

"Right?"

Carl nodded.

"After that, Tryggve suggests the following."

dark eyes but blue—Hes got a scar on his rite . . .

"Yeah, and we still don't know where that scar is," Carl interjected. "Tryggve never saw it, and Poul never mentioned it to him. But it was exactly the kind of thing Poul would have taken note of, according to Tryggve. Maybe other people's little peculiarities offset his own. Anyway, go on."

Yrsa nodded.

drives a blue van Mum and Dad know him—Freddy and somthing with a B—He thretned us he gave us electric shocks—Hes going to kil us—

"All seems plausible to me." Carl peered up at the ceiling where another fly suddenly appeared to be laughing at him. He studied it more closely. Was that a spot of white on its wing? It was! This was the same fly he had attempted to obliterate with that bottle of correction fluid. Where the hell had it been hiding?

"So we agree that Tryggve was present when all this was going on, and that he was conscious," Yrsa went on, unperturbed. "This passage here is about the kidnapper's distinguishing marks, and if we put it together with Tryggve's description of him, we've got a pretty good idea of what he looks like. All we need now is the artist's impression from Sweden."

She pointed at the lines that followed. "I'm not that sure about the next sentences. The question is whether it really says what we think it does. Read it out loud, would you, Carl?"

"Read it out loud? What for, have you lost your tongue?" Who did she think he was, Mads Mikkelsen?

She slapped him playfully on the shoulder, then pinched his arm for good measure. "Come on, Carl. It'll give you the feel of it."

He shook his head in despair and cleared his throat. She was off her head. He read.

> **He pressd a rag in my face first then my brothers—We drove nearly 1 hour and now we are by warter There are some wind turbins close by It smels here—hurry up and come My brother is Tryggve—13 and I am Poul 18 years**
>
> **POUL HOLT**

She applauded his performance soundlessly with the tips of her fingers.

"Very nice, Carl. Now, I know Tryggve is pretty sure about most of it, but do you think the bit about the wind turbines is right? Some of the other words seem like they might be wrong, too. What if there's more hidden behind those dots than we're able to imagine?"

"Poul and Tryggve never spoke about sounds at all. They couldn't anyway, with gaffer tape over their mouths. But Tryggve does recall a deep rumbling sound every now and then," Carl said. "What's more, he said Poul would have been good at coupling sounds and machinery. But the fact of the matter is it could have been anything at all."

Carl pictured Tryggve reading the message from the bottle for the second time, eyes moist with tears in the growing light of a Swedish dawn.

"The message made an enormous impression on Tryggve. He said it was just like his brother not to bother with punctuation apart from a few dashes, and that Poul always wrote the way he spoke. He said that reading the letter was like hearing him say it out loud."

Carl released the image from his mind. Once Tryggve had had time to settle down again after the shock, they would have to get him over to Copenhagen.

Yrsa frowned. "Did you ask Tryggve whether there was any wind while they were there in that boathouse? Did you or Assad check with the Met Office?"

"You mean you want to know if it was windy in the middle of February? When isn't it? Anyway, turbines are on the go even in a breeze."

"Nevertheless, did you check?"

"Hand it on to Pasgård, Yrsa. He's the guy we've got checking up on the wind turbines. I've got another job for you now."

She sat down on the edge of the desk. "I know what you're going to say. You want me to talk to those support groups for people who used to be involved in religious sects, am I right?" She drew her handbag toward her and produced a packet of crisps. And even before Carl had formed his reply, she'd burst a hole in it and was busy devouring its contents.

He couldn't work her out.

As soon as he got back to his office, he checked the weather service's archive on the Internet and found that it only went back as far as 1997. He called them, explained his business, and put forward what he thought was a simple inquiry, expecting to receive an equally simple answer.

"Can you tell me what the weather was like during the days following the sixteenth of February 1996?" he asked.

The reply came after only a few seconds.

"There was a fierce snowstorm on the eighteenth of February that brought the country practically to a standstill for three or four days. Even the border to Germany was closed. It was that bad," said the woman at the other end.

"Really? That would include Nordsjælland, then?"

"The whole country, but worst in the south. In the north, roads were passable in widespread areas."

Why the hell hadn't they asked about the weather before now?

"So it would have been windy, then?"

"I'll say."

"What about wind turbines in weather like that?"

The woman paused for a moment. "Are you asking whether the wind was too strong to have them running?"

"Erm, I suppose so, yeah. Would they shut the turbines down in that kind of wind?"

"I'd certainly think so, though I'm not an expert on that. But yes, they'd have been shut down during the period, otherwise they'd have been wrecked."

Carl tapped a cigarette from the packet with his free hand as he offered his thanks. What on earth had the children heard, then, if it hadn't been wind turbines? Some of the noise would have been the storm itself, of course. They'd have been sitting there freezing inside the boathouse, unable to see out, so it was certainly possible that all they had heard was the wind. They might not even have known about the snow at all.

Carl found Pasgård's mobile number and called him.

"Yeah," came the reply. Unaccommodating even in a single syllable. Some people were like that.

"It's Carl Mørck. Did you check up on the weather during the days the children were being held?"

"Not yet, but I'll look into it."

"Save your energy. There was a snowstorm that lasted for three of the five days they were imprisoned."

"You don't say."

A typical Pasgård comment.

"Forget the wind turbines, Pasgård. It was blowing up a gale."

"What about the other two days?"

"Tryggve told me he heard the rumbling sound all the time. Maybe more subdued the last three days. That would be explained by the storm drowning it out."

"Maybe."

"Just thought you should know."

Carl chuckled silently. Pasgård was probably kicking himself.

"You'll need to be looking for another source of the noise than wind turbines," he continued. "Though still some kind of rumbling sound. What about that fish scale, anything turned up there?"

"One step at a time. It's with the Department of Biology for microscopy. Aquatic Biology Section."

"Microscopy?"

"Yeah, or whatever it is they do. I've already found out it's from a trout. The issue seems to be whether it's a sea trout or a fjord trout."

"Aren't they different altogether?"

"Apparently not. It seems a fjord trout is just a sea trout that can't be arsed to swim any farther, so it stays put."

Carl felt exasperated. Yrsa, Assad, Rose, and now Pasgård.

"One last thing, Pasgård. Call Tryggve Holt and ask him if he can tell us what the weather was like while they were in the boathouse."

The moment he ended the call, the phone rang.

"Antonsen," said the voice. The tone alone gave Carl cause for concern. "Your man Assad and Samir Ghazi have been knocking the snot out of each other here. If we weren't the police, we'd have had to call them. Propel yourself over here sharpish and take your little ruffian home with you."

27

Whenever Isabel Jønsson needed to describe her upbringing, she always said she grew up in Tupperwareland. She was raised by two sensible parents in a yellow-brick bungalow with a Volvo in the driveway. Ordinary people with ordinary educations and opinions broadly in line with the rest of the conservative masses. It was a neatly presented childhood, germ-free and vacuum-packed. Elbows off the table and playing cards back in the bureau after bridge. Table manners and polite handshakes. Isabel completed her schooling. And her brother even insisted on doing his military service despite having been exempted.

But she scattered these deeply entrenched standards to the four winds whenever she flung herself into the arms of a capable man. Or at times like this, slightly exceeding the specified top speed of her battered 2002 Ford Mondeo as she and Rachel raced along Route 13 and on to the E45.

The GPS gave them an ETA of 5:30 P.M., but she would beat that easily.

"I've got a suggestion," she said to Rachel, who sat clutching her mobile phone. "Promise not to get upset?"

"I'll try," came the quiet reply.

"If we don't find him or the children at this address in Ferslev, then I think we're going to have to do as he says."

"I know, we already talked about that."

"Unless, that is, we want to buy ourselves more time."

"What do you mean?"

Isabel ignored a succession of extended middle fingers as she tore along in the fast lane without reducing her speed, flashing her headlights to clear the way ahead.

"What I mean is . . . and this is where you mustn't freak out, Rachel. What I mean is that we don't actually know how safe the children are even if we give him the money. Do you understand me?"

"I think they'll be safe." Rachel spoke each word with emphasis. "If we give him the money, he'll let them go. We already know too much about him for him to run any more risks."

"Stop, Rachel. That's exactly my point. If you pay the ransom and get the kids back, what would stop you from going to the police afterward? Do you see what I'm getting at?"

"I'm certain he'll be out of the country as soon as he gets the money. He won't care what we do afterward."

"You think so? He's not stupid, Rachel. We both know that. Fleeing the country is no guarantee. Most of them get caught anyway."

"But what's the alternative?" Rachel shifted uneasily in her seat. "Please drive more slowly," she pleaded. "If we get stopped by the police, they'll take away your license."

"In that case, you'll have to drive. I take it you've passed your test?"

"Yes."

"Well, that's OK then," Isabel replied, sweeping past a pimped BMW full of young lads wearing precariously angled baseball caps.

"We haven't got time to hang about," she went on. "And here's my point: We don't know what he's going to do once he gets the money, and we've no way of knowing for sure what he'll do if the ransom isn't paid. That's why we need to be one step ahead. We need to take the initiative here. Do you understand?"

Rachel shook her head so vigorously that Isabel could see her reaction even though her eyes were fixed on the road.

"No, I don't understand at all."

Isabel moistened her lips. If this went wrong, it would be her fault. On the other hand, she had the feeling that what she was saying now was right and totally necessary.

"If it turns out this bastard really does have a house at the address we're headed for, it means we're much closer to him than he ever thought possible, even in his worst nightmares. He'll be racking his psychopathic brains to figure out where he went wrong. That will make him uncertain as hell about what you're going to do next, OK? He'll be vulnerable, and that's exactly what we need."

They passed fifteen vehicles before Rachel answered.

"Let's talk about it later. I need to be in peace for a while."

Isabel glanced at her as they crossed the bridge over the Lillebælt strait. Not a sound escaped Rachel's lips, but closer inspection revealed that they were in constant motion. Her eyes were closed, and her hands gripped her mobile phone, making her knuckles show white.

"You really believe in God, don't you?" said Isabel.

A brief moment elapsed while Rachel concluded her prayer before opening her eyes.

"Yes, I do. I believe in the Mother of God, and that She is here to look after unhappy women like me. That's why I pray to Her, and She will hear me, I'm certain."

Isabel frowned but nodded and remained silent.

Anything else would have been cruel.

Ferslev lay in a patchwork of agricultural land close to the Isefjord. A pastoral idyll, which couldn't be more different from the horror they were searching for, hidden away in a corner of the village.

Isabel felt her heart rate increase as they approached their destination. Close up, they realized that the house could hardly be seen from the road, tucked away as it was behind trees. Rachel took hold of Isabel's arm and asked her to pull in.

Rachel's face was white as a sheet, and she kept rubbing her cheeks as though trying to get her circulation going. Her brow was moist with perspiration, and her lips were pressed tightly together.

"Pull over here, Isabel," she said as they approached the windbreak.

She staggered out of the car and fell on her knees at the side of the road. Clearly, she was in a bad way, whimpering with each outpouring of vomit until her stomach was finally empty.

"Are you OK?" Isabel asked. A large Mercedes swept past.

Silly question. The woman was throwing her guts up, but convention dictated that Isabel ask.

"I feel better now," Rachel said, settling back in the passenger seat and wiping her mouth with the back of her hand. "What do we do now?"

"We drive up to the house. He thinks my brother in the police knows all about him. So if he's there, he'll let the children go as soon as he sees me. He won't dare do anything else. All he'll be able to think about is getting away."

"We should leave the car here so we're not blocking his way out, making him feel trapped," said Rachel. "Otherwise he might do something desperate."

"No, I think we should do just that. Block the track with the car. His only escape route then will be over the fields. If he's able to get away in the car, there's a risk he'll take the children with him."

Rachel looked like she might be sick again. She swallowed twice in quick succession and calmed herself.

"I know, Rachel. This is not something you're used to. Me neither, for that matter. I don't feel that great myself. But we're here now, and we're going to do it."

Rachel looked at her. Her eyes were filled with tears and yet devoid of emotion. "I've been through more in my life than you imagine," she said, her voice surprisingly harsh. "I'm scared, but not for myself. This mustn't go wrong."

Isabel parked the car diagonally across the track leading up to the house, and then they stood in the yard in the shadow of the trees and waited to see what would happen.

Pigeons cooed on the roof, and a gentle breeze whispered through the long grass at the sides of the house. Apart from that, the only sign of life was the sound of their own breathing.

The windows of the house were dark. Maybe they were just dirty, or maybe curtains had been drawn inside. They couldn't tell. Rusty garden tools, worn down by use, leaned up against the wall, and the painted woodwork was flaking everywhere. The place seemed dead, uninhabited. It wasn't what they had expected.

"Come on," Isabel said, and strode up to the main door. She knocked hard and fast. Then she stepped to one side and hammered her knuckles against the window of the porch. There was no response.

"Holy Mother of God. If they're inside, they might be trying to answer," said Rachel, suddenly breaking out of her trance. And then she snatched up a hoe with a broken shaft that lay on the cobbles at the base of the wall and swung it resolutely against the pane.

It was obvious to Isabel that being practical was an important part of Rachel's everyday life. She flipped the hoe onto her shoulder and unlatched the window. Everything about her now showed that she was ready to put the tool to use against the kidnapper if he should turn out to be inside with her children. Ready to demonstrate to him that he would be wise to give a great deal of consideration indeed to his next move.

Isabel kept close behind her as they moved through the house. Apart from four or five gas cylinders lined up in a row in the hall and a few pieces of furniture that seemed almost strategically positioned in front of the gaps in the curtains to make the place seem as if it might be inhabited, the ground floor contained absolutely nothing at all. A layer of dust on the floors and other horizontal surfaces, but otherwise there was nothing. No newspapers, no leaflets, no plates or utensils, bed linen, or empty packaging. Not even toilet paper.

No one lived here, and no one was meant to.

They found the stairs leading to the first floor and ascended with cautious, measured steps.

Upstairs, the walls were clad with plasterboard, papered in all sorts of patterns and colors, a confusion of incompatible styles and a distinct lack of financial means. Wafer-thin partition walls divided the space into three rooms containing only one piece of furniture: a flaking green wardrobe with its door half open.

The soft light of afternoon brightened the room as Isabel drew back the curtains. She looked in the wardrobe and gasped.

He had been here. She recognized the clothes on the hangers from when he had been staying with her. The suede jacket, the gray Wranglers, and the shirts from Esprit and Morgan. Certainly not the kind of clothing one would expect to see in a place like this.

Rachel gasped, and Isabel knew why. The smell of his aftershave alone was enough to make anyone feel sick.

She took out one of the shirts and examined it quickly. "This hasn't been washed, so now we've got his DNA," she said, pointing to a hair on the collar, the wrong length and color to be her own.

"Come on, we'll take some of this with us," she continued. "It's not likely, but there might be something in one of the pockets."

They gathered a handful of items together and Isabel looked out at the barn across the yard. She hadn't noticed the tire marks in the gravel before, but from up here they were clearly visible. Two compressed tracks in front of the barn, that looked very, very recent.

She drew the curtains.

They left the shards of glass where they were in the porch, closed the door behind them, and glanced around, finding nothing untoward in the garden, the field, or the trees. Then they turned their attention to the padlock that hung from the barn door.

Isabel gestured toward the hoe that Rachel still carried over her shoulder, and Rachel nodded. It took less than five seconds to break the lock.

Both of them gasped as they pulled open the door.

In the barn in front of them stood the van. A light-blue Peugeot Partner.

At Isabel's side, Rachel quietly began to pray. "Oh, please don't let my children be dead inside. Please, Mother of God. Don't let them be dead inside, please . . ."

Isabel was in no doubt. The predator had flown with his prey. She grasped the handle and opened the back doors. He hadn't even gone to the trouble of locking the van, so certain was he that he was safe here.

She put her hand on the hood. It was still warm. Very warm, in fact.

And then she went back out into the yard and stared through the trees toward the road where Rachel had been sick. Either he had gone that way, or else down to the fjord. In any case, he couldn't be far away.

But they were too late.

Rachel began to shake. The emotional turmoil she had struggled to keep inside on their long drive, the anguish that could not be expressed in words, the pain that had changed her expression and her posture, erupted now in one single scream that sent the pigeons aloft from the roof to seek refuge among the trees with a sudden beating of wings. And when finally the sound had been exhausted, snot ran from her nose, and the corners of her mouth were white with spit. She had realized that the only straw they had to clutch at had snapped.

The kidnapper wasn't here. Her children were gone. In spite of all her prayers.

Isabel nodded deliberately. This was terrible.

"Rachel, I'm sorry to have to say this, but I think I saw the car pass by while you were being sick," she said hesitantly. "It was a Mercedes. A black Mercedes. There are thousands of them."

They stood in silence for a while as the light of the sky dimmed.

What now?

"You mustn't pay," Isabel said finally. "You mustn't allow him to dictate what's going to happen next. We need to buy time."

Rachel looked at Isabel as though she had just committed apostasy and had spat upon everything Rachel believed in and stood for. "Buy time? I don't understand what you're talking about, and I'm not sure I want to know."

Rachel glanced at her watch. They were thinking the same thing.

In just a short time, Joshua would be getting on the train at Viborg with a duffel bag full of money, and that, as far as Rachel could see, was that. The ransom would be delivered and the children would be released.

A million kroner was a lot of money, but they would manage. Isabel would not be allowed to throw a wrench in the works. All of Rachel's body language made that abundantly clear.

Isabel gave a sigh. "Listen, Rachel. We've both met this man, and he's the most terrifying person we've ever had the misfortune to encounter. Think of how he deceived us. Everything he said and did was a lie." She reached out and took Rachel's hands.

"Your faith and my naive infatuation were his instruments. He tricked us when we were at our most vulnerable. He manipulated our feelings, and we *believed* him. Do you understand? We *believed* him, and he *lied* to us, OK? You can't deny that. Do you see what I'm getting at?"

She did, of course. She wasn't stupid. But the last thing Rachel needed now was to break down or abandon herself to blind faith. Isabel could see that. And for that reason Rachel had to search the depths, the place of all instinct. She needed to think freely and embark upon a dreadful voyage of comprehension. And Isabel felt for her.

When Rachel opened her eyes again, it was plain that she now knew how close to the edge she stood. Her children might no longer be alive. That was where she was.

And then she breathed in deeply and gave Isabel's hands a squeeze. She was prepared. "What do you think we should do?" she asked.

"We play along," Isabel replied. "As soon as we see that strobe, we throw the bag from the train as instructed, only without the money. And when he retrieves it and looks inside, he'll find items from the house here, proof that we've tracked him down."

She bent down and picked up the padlock and clasp, weighing them in her hand.

"We'll put these inside, and some of his clothes. And we'll write a note telling him we're on to him. That we know where he's hiding out, we know what name he's using, and that we're keeping the place under observation. We'll tell him we're closing in on him and that it's only a matter of time until we find him. He'll get his money, but he needs to come up with a way for us to know for sure that we'll get the children back. Until then, he gets nothing. We need to put the pressure on him, otherwise he'll dictate everything."

Rachel lowered her gaze. "Isabel," she said. "We're here in Nordsjælland, don't you realize? We can't get on the train from Viborg. We won't be on it to see the strobe between Odense and Roskilde." She looked up at Isabel and yelled her frustration into her face. "How can we throw him the bag? HOW?"

Isabel grasped her hand again. It was as cold as ice. "Rachel," she said calmly, "we'll get there. We'll drive to Odense now and meet Joshua on the platform. We've plenty of time."

At that moment, Isabel saw something in Rachel she hadn't seen before. She saw, standing in front of her, not a mother who had lost her children or a farm wife from Dollerup Bakker. All of a sudden, there was nothing rural or motherly about her at all. She was someone else. Someone Isabel had yet to fully encounter.

"Have you thought why he wants us to change trains at Odense?" Rachel asked. "There are so many other possibilities, aren't there? I'm sure it's because we're being watched. Someone will be at the station in Viborg and then again in Odense." Then she looked away and her thoughts turned inward. She could ask questions but was unable to supply any answers.

Isabel thought for a moment. "No, I don't think so. He just wants to hassle you. I'm certain he's on his own in all this."

"How can you be certain?" asked Rachel, without looking at her.

"Because that's the way he is. He's a control freak. He needs to know exactly what's happening and when. And he's calculating, too. He strolled into this local bar, picked me out as a victim straightaway, and was giving me perfectly timed orgasms only hours later. He could lay on breakfast and say things that would stay in my mind the rest of the day. Everything he did was part of the plan, and all of it performed by a virtuoso. He wouldn't be capable of working with anyone else, and besides, that ransom would be too small if there were accomplices involved. He's not the kind to share."

"What if you're wrong?"

"What if I am? Does it matter? We're the ones issuing the ultimatum tonight, not him. Putting these things in the ransom bag proves that we've been here at his hiding place."

Isabel looked around the dilapidated property. Who was this scheming individual? Why was he doing this? With his good looks, his intelligence, and his ability to manipulate others, the sky would seem to be his limit in any normal life.

It was hard to fathom.

"Let's get going," Isabel said. "You can call your husband on the way and put him in the picture. And then we can dictate to him what to write in the note."

Rachel shook her head. "I'm not sure. I'm scared. I mean, I'm with you up to a point, but aren't we putting the kidnapper under a lot of pressure here? Isn't he going to give it all up and get out?" Her lips were quivering now. "And what about my children, if he does? Won't they suffer? Perhaps he'll do them harm, something terrible. You hear about these things." Tears welled in her eyes. "And if he does, what do we do then, Isabel? What do we do then?"

28

"What the hell happened out there in Rødovre, Assad? I've never heard Antonsen sound off like that before."

Assad shifted uneasily in his chair. "Nothing to worry about, Carl. It was a misunderstanding, that's all."

A misunderstanding? Presumably the French Revolution had broken out over a misunderstanding, too.

"In that case, you need to explain to me how a so-called misunderstanding can lead to two grown men rolling around the floor of a Danish police station knocking the stuffing out of each other."

"Stuffing?"

"Yes, the stuffing. It's an idiom. For Chrissake, Assad, you know perfectly well there was a reason you laid into Samir Ghazi like that. And it's about time you came clean. I want a decent explanation. Where do you two know each other from?"

"We don't actually know each other at all."

"Oh, come on, Assad, don't give me that. People don't go around beating up strangers for no reason. If it's something to do with family reunification or forced marriage or someone's fucking honor, then I want to know—now! We need to get this into the open, otherwise I won't have you here, are you with me? Remember, Samir's the policeman, not you."

Assad turned his head toward Carl with a wounded look in his eye. "I can leave right now, if that is what you wish."

"I hope for your sake that my long-standing friendship with Antonsen will be enough for him not to make that decision on my behalf." Carl leaned across the desk. "Listen, Assad, when I ask you something, I expect you to answer. And if you don't, it tells me something's wrong. Maybe something serious enough to affect your residence here in this country, not just lose you this fucking fantastic job of yours."

"You will perhaps persecute me, then?" Hurt was too mild a word to describe the man's demeanor.

"Have you and Samir had any altercation with each other before? In Syria, for instance?"

"No, not in Syria. Samir is from Iraq."

"So you admit there's a grudge. But you still don't know each other?"

"Yes, Carl. Would you please not ask me any more about this?"

"I'll think about it. But if you don't want me to ask Samir Ghazi for a report on this fight of yours, you're going to have to give me something to go on and calm me down a bit. And you're definitely to stay away from Samir from now on, understood?"

Assad sat for a while staring into space before nodding. "I am to blame for one of Samir's relatives now being dead. It was never my intention, Carl, you must believe this. The truth is I did not even know."

Carl closed his eyes for a moment.

"Have you committed any crime in this country?"

"No, I swear at you, Carl."

"Swear *to* me, Assad. You swear *to* me."

"Yes, that is what I do."

"So this all happened some time ago?"

"Yes."

Carl nodded. Maybe Assad would open up another day.

"Have a look at this, you two." Yrsa barged in through the door without knocking. She had a serious look on her face, for once, and was holding a sheet of paper out in front of her. "It's a fax from the Swedish police in Ronneby. Just in two minutes ago. This is what he looked like."

She put the fax down on the desk. It wasn't a photofit, pieced together on a computer. This was the real thing. A proper drawing, with shading and all the rest of it, and in color to boot. A male face, pleasing at first blush, but which on closer inspection displayed a number of jarring elements.

"He looks just like my cousin," Yrsa commented drily. "A pig farmer from Randers."

"I had not imagined him to look like this exactly," said Assad.

Carl hadn't, either. Short sideburns, dark mustache neatly trimmed back above the lip. Hair slightly lighter, precisely parted. Thick eyebrows almost converging. Unremarkable, half-full lips.

"We need to bear in mind that this drawing may not reflect his true appearance. Remember, Tryggve was only thirteen at the time, and just as many years have passed since all this happened. Our man probably looks different now anyway. But how old would you say he was here?"

They were about to reply, but Carl stopped them. "Look closely. The mustache might make him look older than he is. Write down your guess here."

He tore off a couple of pages from a notepad and handed them to his two assistants.

"To think he's the one who killed Poul," Yrsa mused. "It's almost like he killed someone you knew."

Carl wrote down his own estimate and took Assad's and Yrsa's.

Two of them said twenty-seven. The other said thirty-two.

"Yrsa and I agree on twenty-seven, Assad. What makes you think he's older?"

"It is simply because of this." He pointed his finger to a diagonal line issuing from the eyebrow of the man's right eye. "This is not the wrinkle of a smile."

He indicated his own face, then lit up in a smile and pointed at the corners of his beaming eyes. "Look at these lines. They go out toward the cheek. And now look."

He turned his mouth down at the corners. Now he looked just like he had done when Carl had been giving him a bollocking a few minutes earlier. "Is there not a line just here?" He indicated a point next to his eyebrow.

"Maybe, but it's hard to tell," said Yrsa, then mimicked the expression herself and felt for a line with her fingertip.

"That is because I am a happy man. The killer is not happy. A wrinkle like this is something a person is born with, or else it appears because the person is not happy. And if it appears, it will do so only with time. My mother was not so happy, and hers did not come until she was fifty."

"Perhaps you're right, Assad. And perhaps you're not," said Carl. "But the fact is that all three of our guesses are in the same region, which fits in with Tryggve's assessment, too. So if he's still alive, he'll be somewhere between forty and forty-five now."

"Could we scan the picture into our system and add a few years onto him?" Yrsa inquired. "Computers can do that, can't they?"

"Of course, but the risk is you end up with something that may be even more inaccurate than the original. I reckon we should stick with what we've got. A decent-looking fellow, more attractive than average, and quite masculine. Otherwise a fairly subdued kind of appearance, a bit conservative, like an office worker."

"I'd say he looks more like a soldier or a policeman," Yrsa added.

Carl nodded. The man could have been anything at all. It was usually the way.

He glanced up at the ceiling. That bastard fly again. Maybe he should take the liberty, on behalf of the state, of investing in a can of flyspray. Most likely they'd prefer that to him expending a bullet on the bloody thing.

He forced his thoughts back to the matter at hand and looked at Yrsa. "Get this photocopied, and be sure to send it out to all districts. Do you know how?"

She gave a shrug.

"Oh, and Yrsa, let me see the wording before you put it out, yeah?"

"What wording?"

He sighed. In many ways, she was amazing, but she would never reach Rose's level. "You need to write a description of what the case is about, Yrsa. Something like: 'We suspect this person of having committed a murder, and we want to know if anyone has any knowledge of a man of this appearance having been in trouble with the police.'"

"Where does this get us, Carl? What's the connection? Any ideas?" Lars Bjørn frowned and shoved the photo of the four Jankovic siblings back across the table to the homicide chief.

"I'll tell you where it gets us. If you want to proceed with your arson cases, you need to look through the criminal registers for Serbs with exactly the same kind of finger ring as our four tubbies here. You might even find a match in the Danish archives, but if I were you, I'd get on to the police in Belgrade pretty sharpish."

"So you believe the bodies that were found at the scenes of the arsons are Serbs in some way connected to the Jankovic family, and that these rings signify that relationship?" Jacobsen ventured.

"Definitely. And what's more, my guess is that they were almost born with those rings on, judging by the extent of the deformation of the finger bone in each case."

"Some kind of crime syndicate?" Bjørn proffered.

Carl gave him a goofy smile. The man was on form for a miserable Monday morning.

Marcus Jacobsen eyed the flattened cigarette packet on the table in front of him as though he might devour it any minute. "Well, we certainly need to research the matter with our Serbian colleagues. If your assumptions are correct, then it would seem membership might even be hereditary. Do we know who's behind these banking firms now? The four founders are no longer with us, I understand."

"I've got Yrsa looking into that. It's a limited company, but the majority of the shares are still owned by people called Jankovic."

"A Serbian crime syndicate lending out money, then?"

"Looks like it. We do know that the companies hit by the arsons all owed money to the Jankovic family at one point or another. What we don't know is where the bodies come from and why. We'll gladly leave that one with you." Carl smiled and shoved another picture across the table.

"This is our presumed perp in the murder of Poul Holt and the kidnapping of his brother. Nice-looking bloke, yeah?"

Marcus Jacobsen considered the portrait in front of him as he would any other. He had seen murderers aplenty in his time.

"I understand Pasgård has made a couple of breakthroughs in the case today," Jacobsen stated drily. "Good thing he was able to assist you."

Carl frowned. What the fuck was he on about?

"Breakthroughs? What breakthroughs?"

"You mean he hasn't told you yet? He's probably writing his report as we speak."

Twenty seconds later, Carl was standing in Pasgård's office. A dingy room—the photo of the incumbent's family of three failed to cheer the place up, serving instead as a reminder of how immeasurably little the office of a public servant could resemble home.

"What's going on?" Carl demanded, as Pasgård's fingers danced across the keyboard of his computer.

"Two minutes, and you'll have your report. Then the case is all yours."

It all sounded too fucking efficient by half. Nevertheless, the man swiveled around on his chair what seemed like exactly two minutes later and announced: "You can read it off the screen before I print it out. Make any corrections yourself, if you feel the need."

Pasgård and Carl had started at HQ at about the same time, but though Carl could hardly be called biddable, the majority of decent jobs had fallen his way, much to the chagrin of an arse-licker like Pasgård.

So Pasgård's smug little smile now was a thinly veiled manifestation of the infinite pleasure that surged through him as Carl read his report.

When he had finished, Carl turned to face him.

"Nice work, Pasgård," was all he said.

"Are you off home, or can you put in a couple more hours tonight, Assad?" Carl asked. Hundred to one he didn't have the balls to say no.

Assad smiled. Most likely he thought of it as a pat on the back. Now they could get on with the job. Questions about Samir Ghazi and the issue of where Assad actually lived were on the back burner.

"Yrsa, you can come along, too. I'll drop you off at your place. It's on our way."

"You mean Stenløse? You must be joking, that's miles out. Thanks, but no thanks. I'll take the train. I love trains, me." She buttoned her coat and hung her nifty little fake-crocodile-skin bag over her shoulder. Like her thick-heeled brogues, this seemed to be inspired by old English films.

"You can give the train a miss today, Yrsa," he said. "I want to put you both in the picture on the way, if you don't mind."

Reluctantly, she climbed into the backseat, almost like a queen who'd been fobbed off with a taxi. Legs crossed and her bag on her lap. Soon, the cloud of her perfume settled beneath the nicotine-stained roof lining.

"Pasgård's had word back from the Section for Aquatic Biology. They've given us quite a bit to go on. First thing is they've now established that the scale comes from a species of trout most often found in fjords, where fresh-water and seawater converge."

"What about the slime?" Yrsa asked.

"Most likely from common mussels or fjord shrimps. That'll have to stay unresolved for the time being."

Assad nodded in the passenger seat next to him and flicked to the first page of Krak's map of Nordsjælland. After a moment, he placed his finger near the middle of the page. "OK, I see them here now. Roskilde Fjord and the Isefjord. Aha! I had no idea they joined together at Hundested."

"Oh, my God, don't tell me you're going to have to trawl around them both? What a job you'll have!"

"Right on both counts, Yrsa." Carl glanced at her in the rearview mirror. "Fortunately, we've got the help of a sailor with local knowledge. Lives in Stenløse, like you. You probably remember him from that double murder in Rørvig, Assad. Thomasen. The bloke who knew the father of the two who got murdered."

"Yes, indeed. His first name started with a 'K', and he had a fat belly."

"Exactly. His name's Klaes. Klaes Thomasen from the police station at Nykøbing. He's got a boat moored at Frederikssund and knows the fjords like the back of his hand. He's going to take us out. I reckon we've got a couple of hours before it gets dark."

"You mean we are going to sail on the water?" Assad asked in a quiet voice.

"We're going to have to if we want to find a boathouse projecting into the fjord."

"I am not so happy about this, Carl."

Carl chose to ignore him. "Besides being the stamping ground of the fjord trout, there's another indication that we ought to be looking for the boathouse in the vicinity of the mouths of the fjords. I'm loath to admit it, but Pasgård has done a very good job. After letting the marine biologists take their samples, he sent the paper on which the message was written to Forensics so that they could have a look at the shadowy areas Laursen picked out. It turns out to be printer's ink. Or at least the remnants of such."

"I thought they'd done all that in Scotland," said Yrsa.

"Their efforts were focused on the written characters rather than the paper itself. But when Forensics ran their tests this morning, it turned out there were remains of printer's ink all over it."

"Was it just ink, or did it say anything?" she asked.

Carl smiled to himself. Once, when he was a boy, he and one of the other lads had lain flat out on their stomachs at the fairground in Brønderslev staring at a footprint. Slightly obliterated by rain but still clearly distinct from the rest. They could make out the imprint of letters that seemed to have been scratched into the sole, but only after some time had elapsed did they realize that they were back to front. *PEDRO,* they read. And before long, they had put together a story that the shoe probably belonged to some machinist from Pedershaab Maskinfabrik who was afraid someone would nick his only pair of safety shoes. So after that, whenever the two lads stuffed away their own shoes in the lockers of the open-air baths at the other end of town, they always had this poor Pedro in mind.

It had been the beginning of Carl's interest in detective work, and now here he was, somehow back at the start again.

"Turns out the writing was back to front. There must have been a newspaper pressed against the paper for some time, and the lettering rubbed off."

"Get out!" Yrsa leaned as far forward as her crossed legs would allow. "What did it say, then?"

"Well, if the lettering hadn't been the size it was, we'd most likely never have known, but as far as I understand it they've figured out it says *Frederikssund Avis.* One of those free local papers that comes out once a week."

At this point, he had imagined Assad whooping with delight, but there was no reaction.

"Don't you see? This means we can narrow down the geography considerably, as long as we assume that the piece of paper the message was written on came from within the newspaper's circulation area. Otherwise, we'd have been looking at Nordsjælland's entire coastline. Have you any idea how many kilometers that would be?"

"No," came the curt reply from the backseat.

He hadn't, either, for that matter.

And then his mobile chimed. He glanced at the display and immediately felt a warm glow inside.

"Mona," he said in a completely different tone than before. "How nice of you to call."

He sensed Assad shift uneasily in his seat. Maybe he was no longer quite so confident that his boss was an also-ran in matters romantic.

Carl angled the conversation toward inviting her over that same evening, but that wasn't why she was calling. It was purely professional this time, she said with a laugh that made Carl's pulse race. Right now she had a colleague with her, and he would rather like to speak to Carl about his traumas.

Carl frowned. He would, would he? What did his traumas have to do with her male colleagues? His traumas were for her, and her alone. In fact, he'd been saving them up.

"I'm doing fine, Mona, so that won't be necessary," he said, picturing the gleam in her eyes.

She laughed again. "I'm sure you're fine after last night, Carl. It sounds like it, anyway. But before that you weren't doing too well, remember? And I can't always be there for you around the clock."

He swallowed, almost trembling at the thought. He was just about to ask her why not, but decided it would keep until later.

"OK, you win." He very nearly added "darling" but caught sight of Yrsa's gleefully attentive eyes in the rearview mirror and thought better of it.

"Tell your colleague he can come and see me tomorrow. We've got a lot on the go, though, so I can't give him much time, OK?"

He had forgotten to invite her over. Shit!

It would have to wait until tomorrow. Hopefully, she would still be interested.

He snapped his mobile shut and forced a smile in the direction of Assad. He had felt like Don Juan when he'd looked at himself in the mirror that morning. The feeling seemed to have gone now.

"Hey-aay, Mona! Tell you, Mona, what I'm gonna do. Get-a my house a-next door to you. Ooh, ooh, Mona!" Yrsa broke into song on the backseat.

Assad gave a start. If he thought he had heard her sing before, he certainly had now. Her voice was in a league of its own.

"I don't think I am familiar with this song," Assad said. He turned his head toward the backseat and nodded appreciatively. And then fell silent again.

Carl shook his head. Damn! Now Yrsa knew about Mona, which meant that soon everyone else would know, too. Maybe he shouldn't have answered the call.

"Just think," said Yrsa.

Carl glanced at her in the mirror. "Think what?" he replied, ready to launch a counterstrike.

"Frederikssund. Just think, he might have murdered Poul Holt here, near Frederikssund." Yrsa stared out ahead.

So the Carl and Mona thing had already been dismissed from her thoughts. And yes, he knew what she meant. Frederikssund wasn't far from where she was living now.

Depravity didn't discriminate between one town and another.

"So now you'll try to find a boathouse at the top of one of the fjords," she went on. "That's a scary thought, if it's right. But how come you're so sure it won't be further south? Don't people there read the local rag as well?"

"True. The paper could have been taken away from the Frederikssund area for whatever reason. But we have to start somewhere, and this seems to be the best bet, logically speaking. Am I right, Assad?"

His assistant in the passenger seat said nothing. Most likely he was already feeling seasick.

"This'll be fine," said Yrsa and pointed out at the pavement. "Just drop me off here."

Carl glanced at the GPS. A little farther along Byvej and then Ejnar Thygesens Vej, and they would be at Sandalparken, where she lived. Why did she want out here?

"We'll run you to the door, Yrsa. It's no bother."

He sensed she had excuses piled up at the ready. Something like she needed to get the shopping in. But if she did, she would have to do it later.

"I'll pop in with you for a second, Yrsa, if that's OK. I just want to say hello to Rose and have a quick word."

He noted the look of consternation that spread across her powdered face. "Won't take a second," he said again, relieving her of the initiative.

He pulled up outside number nineteen and jumped out of the car. "You stay here, Assad," he instructed, opening the back door for Yrsa.

"I don't think Rose is home," she said as they entered the stairwell. Her expression was one he hadn't seen before. More subdued than otherwise and rather resigned. It was the kind of look someone would have when leaving an exam room knowing that their performance had been mediocre at best.

"Just wait here for a moment, would you, Carl?" she said, putting the key in the door of her flat. "She may still be in bed, you see. She's been sleeping a lot of late."

Carl glanced at the name on the door as Yrsa called out for Rose inside. All it read was *Knudsen*.

Yrsa called again, then returned.

"She doesn't seem to be in, I'm afraid. Perhaps she's out shopping. Do you want me to give her a message?"

Carl wedged his foot inside the door. "Tell you what, I'll write her a note. Have you got a piece of paper?"

Years of practice and his inborn ingenuity got him farther into her domain. Like a snail propelling itself almost imperceptibly forward. You couldn't see his feet move, but after a while some distance had been covered, and all of a sudden he was impossible to get rid of.

"The place is a tip," Yrsa apologized, still with her coat on. "Rose can't keep things tidy when she's like this. Especially when she's on her own in the daytime."

She was right. The hall was a confusion of jackets and coats, empty boxes, and stacks of gossip magazines.

Carl glanced inside the living room. Rose's place was a far cry from how Carl imagined an emo girl with a punk hairdo and liquid spleen coursing through her veins would be living. It looked like it had been decorated by some vintage hippie who had just stepped down from a Nepalese mountaintop with a rucksack full of oriental knickknacks. Carl hadn't seen the like since the time he'd got lucky with a girl from Vrå. Here were incense-burners, great trays of brass and copper with elephants and all sorts of mystical little effigies on them. Tie-dyed tapestries hung from the walls and ox hides were draped over the chairs. If there had only been a defaced American flag as well, they could have been back in the midseventies. And all of it presented beneath a thick layer of dust. Apart from the gossip mags and other glossies, the room contained absolutely nothing to suggest even remotely that the two sisters, Yrsa and Rose, could be the architects of such an anachronistic mess.

"Oh, it's not *that* bad," he replied, his gaze passing over unwashed plates and empty pizza boxes. "How big is the flat?"

"Eighty-three square meters. Besides the living room we've got a bed-room each. But you're right, this isn't that bad at all. You should see our rooms."

She laughed, but underneath she would clearly rather plant an ax between his shoulder blades than allow him to move more than ten centimeters closer to the doors of their private bolt-holes. That was what she had just told him, in her own roundabout way. He wasn't that out of touch with women.

Carl scanned the room for something that stuck out. If you wanted to know people's secrets, it was always the things that stuck out that gave them away.

He found it almost immediately. A bare polystyrene head, the sort used to put wigs and hats on, and beside it a bowl full of pill bottles. He moved forward to get a closer look at the labels, only for Yrsa to step in front of him and hand him the piece of paper he had asked for.

"You can sit here to write," she said, motioning toward a dining chair with no laundry on it. "I'll pass it on to Rose as soon as she gets back."

"We haven't got much more than an hour and a half, Carl. Don't leave it so late another time, OK?"

Carl nodded his appreciation to Klaes Thomasen before turning to look at Assad, who sat in the boat's cockpit like a cornered mouse. In his bright-orange life jacket he looked completely forlorn, like a nervous child facing his first day at school. He had no confidence whatsoever that the overweight, elderly man at the rudder, who sat filling his pipe with tobacco, would be able to save him from the certain death he was about to meet in the five-centimeter-high waves.

Carl studied the chart beneath its covering of plastic.

"An hour and a half," said Klaes Thomasen. "And what is it exactly we're looking for?"

"We need to find a boathouse. One that juts out into the water but most probably rather secluded, away from any accessible road or path. We might not even be able to see it from the fjord at all. To begin with, I reckon we should sail from Crown Prince Frederik's Bridge and on up to Kulhuse. Do you think we'll get any farther than that?"

The retired policeman thrust out his lower lip and inserted his pipe. "She's no racer, just a leisurely old vessel," he muttered. "Seven knots is all she'll do. That should suit our hand down below. What do you reckon, Assad? Everything all right there?"

Assad's complexion, usually so dark, looked now like it had been peroxided. He was not having fun.

"Seven knots, you say. What's that, about thirteen kilometers per hour?" Carl asked. "We won't even make it to Kulhuse and back before it gets dark. I'd been hoping maybe we'd get over to the other side of Hornsherred. Over to Orø, then back again."

Thomasen shook his head. "I can get the wife to pick us up at Dalby Huse on the other side, but we won't get farther than that. Even then it'll be getting fairly dark the last part of the way."

"What about the boat?"

He shrugged. "If we don't find what we're looking for today, I can go back out on my own tomorrow and have a scout around. You know what they say: old coppers never rust in a headwind."

Obviously an idiom of the homemade variety.

"One more thing, Klaes. The two brothers who were held in this boathouse could hear a rumbling sound. Like a wind turbine, something like that. Anything ring a bell?"

He removed his pipe and peered at Carl with the eyes of a bloodhound. "There's been all sorts of fuss around here about what they call infrasound. They've been on about it for years, so it wouldn't surprise me if it went back to the nineties, too."

"What's infrasound when it's at home?"

"Sort of a hum in the background. Very resonant, infuriating noise. For a long time, they thought it came from the steelworks at Frederiksværk, but it seems that theory was disproved when the place shut down for a period and the noise still went on."

"The steelworks. Isn't that out of the way, on a peninsula?"

"You could say. But infrasound can be registered at quite some distance from the source. Some reckon you can hear it up to twenty kilometers away. There's been complaints from Frederiksværk and Frederikssund, even from Jægerspris on the other side of the fjord."

Carl gazed out over the water, its surface broken by raindrops. It all looked peaceful enough. Houses and cottages nestling among woodland, lush meadows, and fields. Sailing boats on gentle waters, gulls in flocks. And in this sodden idyll, the undertone of some inexplicable hum. Behind these pleasant facades people were going mad.

"As long as the source and the extent of the noise remain unknown, it's no use to us," Carl said. "I'd thought we might check the distribution of wind turbines in the area, but it's questionable whether they could be the source at all. It seems they were at a standstill all over the country during the days we're interested in. I think we've got a job on our hands here."

"Can we not go home, then?" came a quiet voice from below.

Carl glanced through the hatch at Assad. Was this really the man who had been in a fistfight with Samir Ghazi? The man who could break down a door with one kick and who once had saved Carl's life? If it was, then he had plainly gone downhill during the last five minutes.

"Are you going to throw up, Assad?" Thomasen inquired.

Assad shook his head. Which only went to show how little the man knew of the joys of seasickness.

"Here," said Carl, thrusting a spare pair of binoculars into Assad's hand. "Just breathe easily and go with the movement of the boat. Try to keep your eye on the coastline there."

"I cannot leave the bench, Carl," Assad replied.

"That's OK. You can see perfectly well through the window."

"You probably needn't bother with this stretch here," Thomasen said, steering directly toward the middle of the fjord. "It's mostly just sandy beach and fields going down to the water's edge. Our best bet's probably to go up toward Nordskoven. That's all woods down to the fjord, but then quite a few folk live there, so it's doubtful a boathouse could be kept hidden."

He gestured toward the road that ran north–south along the eastern side of the fjord. Flat agricultural land, dotted with tiny villages. Poul Holt's killer certainly couldn't have holed up on that side of the fjord.

Carl looked at his map. "If the theory about fjord trout is right, and if Roskilde Fjord here isn't the place to look, then that means we need to be over on the other side of Hornsherred, on the Isefjord. The question is, where? Judging by the map, there don't seem to be that many possibilities. It's mostly agricultural land, fields down to the water's edge. Where could anyone have a hidden boathouse there? And if we carry on to the Holbæk side or farther north toward Odsherred, we'll be too far, because that would take a lot longer than an hour from the site of the kidnapping in Ballerup." He suddenly became doubtful. "Or would it?"

Thomasen gave a shrug. "Not if you ask me. My guess would be an hour."

Carl took a deep breath. "In which case, we just have to hope our theory about that local paper is sound. Otherwise, this is going to be a tall order indeed."

He sat down on the bench next to the suffering Assad, who was by now a grayish shade of green and trembling. His double chin was in constant motion due to his involuntary regurgitation, and yet he still had the binoculars pressed against the sockets of his eyes.

"Give him some tea, Carl. The wife'll be upset if he throws up on her covers."

Carl pulled the basket toward him and poured a cup without asking.

"Get this down you, Assad."

Assad lowered his binoculars slightly, took one look at the tea, and shook his head. "I will not throw up, Carl. What comes up, I swallow again."

Carl stared at him, wide-eyed.

"This is how it is when riding camels in the desert. A person can become so weary in his stomach. But throwing up in the desert is to lose too much liquid. It is a very silly thing to do in a desert. That is why!"

Carl gave him a pat on the shoulder. "Well done, Assad. Just keep your eyes peeled for that boathouse, eh? I'll not bother you anymore."

"I am not looking for the boathouse, because then we will not find it."

"What do you mean?"

"I think it is very well concealed. Perhaps not between trees at all. It may be in a heap of earth or sand, or under a house, or in some thicket. It was not very tall, remember this."

Carl picked up the other pair of binoculars. His assistant was obviously not all there. He'd better do the job himself.

"If you're not looking for a boathouse, Assad, what *are* you looking for?"

"For the thing that rumbles. A wind turbine or some similar thing. Something that can rumble this rumbling sound."

"I'm afraid that's going to be difficult, Assad."

Assad looked at him for a moment as though he had tired of his company. Then he convulsed so violently that Carl drew back to be on the safe side. And when he had finished, he said in what was almost a whisper: "Did you know that the record for sitting against a wall as though in a chair is twelve hours and something, Carl?"

"You don't say?" He sensed that he probably looked all question mark.

"And did you know that the record for standing up is seventeen years and two months?"

"Get out!"

"Oh, but it is, Carl. An Indian guru. He slept standing up in the night."

"Really? I didn't know that, Assad. What are you trying to tell me?"

"Just that some things look more difficult than they are, and some things look easier."

"I see. And?"

"Let us find that rumbling sound, then we shall speak no more of this."

What kind of logic was that?

"All right. But I still don't believe that story about standing up for seventeen years," Carl rejoined.

"OK, but do you know what, Carl?" Assad looked at him intensely, then convulsed again.

"No, tell me."

Assad raised his binoculars. "That is up to you."

They listened and heard the hum of motorboats, the chugging of fishing vessels, motorbikes on the roads, single-engine planes photographing houses and farms so the tax authorities could make new appraisals on which basis to fleece the country's citizens of their savings. But no constant sound, nothing that might provoke the rage of the National Association of the Enemies of Infrasound.

Klaes Thomasen's wife picked them up at Hundested, and Thomasen promised to ask around if anyone knew of a boathouse like the one they were looking for. The forest officer at Nordskoven would be a good place to start, he said. The sailing clubs likewise. He assured Carl he would resume the search the following day. The forecast said dry and sunny.

Assad was still looking queasy after they were dropped off and continued south in their own car.

Carl felt a sudden affinity with Thomasen's wife. He didn't want Assad to puke on his covers, either.

"Give us a nudge if you're going to be sick, Assad, yeah?" he said.

His assistant nodded absently. Most likely it wouldn't be a matter of choice.

Carl repeated the appeal as they came into Ballerup.

"Perhaps we should have a little stop," said Assad after a pause.

"OK, can you wait two minutes? I've something to do first, it won't take long. It's on the way to Holte. I'll drive you home after."

Assad said nothing.

Carl gazed ahead. It was dark now. The question was, would they even let him in?

"I need to drop in on Vigga's mother, you see. Something I promised Vigga I'd do. You OK with that? She lives at a care center just around here."

Assad nodded. "I did not know Vigga had a mother. What is she like? Is she nice?"

It was a question that for all its simplicity was so hard to answer that Carl almost drove through a red light on Bagsværd Hovedgade.

"When you have been there, can you then drop me off at the station, Carl? You are going north, and there is a bus right to my door from there."

Assad certainly knew how to preserve his anonymity. His family's, too, for that matter.

"No, I'm afraid you can't visit Mrs. Alsing now. It's much too late for her. Come back tomorrow before two o'clock, preferably about elevenish. That's when she's most lucid," said one of the caregivers on evening duty.

Carl produced his police ID. "It's not a private matter. This is my assistant, Hafez el-Assad. It won't take a moment."

The woman stared in astonishment at the badge and then at the odd individual who stood rocking on the balls of his feet at Carl's side. This was not an everyday occurrence for the staff of Bakkegården.

"Well, I think she's asleep. She hasn't been doing too well of late."

Carl glanced at the clock on the wall. Ten past nine. What the hell was this woman on about? Normally, the day was only just starting for Vigga's mother about now. She hadn't been a waitress in Copenhagen's nightspots for more than fifty years for nothing. She couldn't be that senile, surely?

They were led, politely but reluctantly, to the area set aside for the center's dementia sufferers, coming to a halt outside the door of Karla Margrethe Alsing.

"Give us a shout when you want to get out again," said the caregiver, pointing farther down the corridor. "There's a staff room just down there."

They found Karla amid a clutter of chocolate boxes and hair clips. With her long, tousled gray hair and carelessly tied kimono she looked like a former Hollywood actress yet to come to terms with her career's demise. She recognized Carl immediately and leaned back in a pose, chirping his name and telling him how adorable he was standing there like that. It was plain to see how much Vigga took after her mother.

She didn't so much as glance at Assad.

"Coffee?" she asked, pouring a cup from a thermos without a lid. The cup looked like it had been used all day. Carl signaled that he was fine without but realized the futility of it. He turned instead to Assad and handed him the cup. If anyone needed a shot of cold coffee left over from this morning, it was Assad.

"Nice place," said Carl, glancing around at the furnished landscape. Gilded frames, ornate mahogany, brocade. Karla Margrethe Alsing had always taken pride in appearances.

"What keeps you busy, then?" he asked, expecting some lament about how hard it was to read and how bad the television programs had become.

"Busy?" A distant look appeared in her eyes. "Well, apart from this . . ."

She paused mid-sentence, reached behind the cushion at her back, and produced a luminous-orange dildo resplendent with all manner of nodulations and projections.

". . . there's bugger all to do."

Assad's coffee cup trembled on its saucer.

29

With each hour that passed, her strength diminished. She had screamed at the top of her voice when the sound of the car died away, but each time she emptied her lungs, it became more difficult to fill them again. The weight of the boxes was simply too great. Gradually her breathing became more shallow.

She wriggled her right hand forward and scratched at the box in front of her face. The sound of her fingernails against the cardboard was enough to raise her spirits. She was not entirely helpless.

After some hours, the strength to scream was unequivocally gone. Now all she could do was try to stay alive.

Perhaps he would show mercy.

She recalled the feeling of suffocation all too vividly. The sense of panic and impotence, and in a way also relief. The experience was familiar to her—she had been through it a dozen times at least. The times her thoughtless giant of a father had pinned her to the floor when she was small and squeezed the air from her lungs.

"Try getting away now!" he used to say, laughing. To him it was just a game, yet she was always so frightened.

But she loved her father, and so she said nothing.

Then one day, he was gone. The game was over, though she felt no sense of relief. "He's run off with some cow," her mother told her. Her wonderful father had found another woman. Now he would cavort and frolic with other children.

When she first met her husband, she told everyone he reminded her of her father.

"That's the last thing you want, Mia," her mother had replied.

That was what she had said.

Now she had been trapped under the packing cases for some twenty-four hours, and she knew she was going to die.

She had heard his footsteps outside the door. He had stood listening and then gone away again.

You should have groaned, she thought to herself. Perhaps he would have come in and put an end to her misery.

Her left shoulder had stopped hurting. All feeling had gone from it, her arm, too. But her hip, which absorbed much of the weight, pained her dreadfully. She had sweated profusely during the first hours in this claustrophobic embrace, but even that had stopped. The only secretion of which she was now aware was the occasional seep of urine against her thigh.

And there she lay, in her own pee, trying to turn her body just an inch or so in order that the pressure against her right knee, on which the weight of the boxes had settled, could be shared by her thigh. In this she failed, and the sensation remained, like the time she broke her arm and could only scratch against the outside of her cast when it itched.

She thought of the days and the weeks when she and her husband had been happy together. In the beginning, when he had fallen at her feet and treated her just the way she wanted.

And now he was killing her, without feeling or hesitation.

How many times had he done this before? She didn't know.

She knew nothing.

She *was* nothing.

Who will remember me when I am dead? she thought, and extended her fingers against her right arm, as though caressing her child. Benjamin won't. He's so small. My mother, of course. But in ten years, when she's no longer with us? Who will remember me then? Besides the man who took my life? No one but him and perhaps Kenneth.

That was the worst thing, apart from having to die. It was what made her try to swallow in spite of the dryness inside her mouth. And it was what made her abdomen convulse with grief, though no tears came to her eyes.

In a few years she would be forgotten.

Her mobile rang a few times. Its vibrations in her back pocket gave her hope.

After the ringtone died away, she would lie for an hour or two listening for sounds outside the house. What if Kenneth was there? Had he sensed something was wrong? He must have done, surely? He had seen with his own eyes the state she had been in the last time they saw each other.

She slept for a short while, only to wake with a start, unable to feel her body. Her face was all that remained. She was reduced to a face. Dry nostrils, a recurring itch around the eyes blinking in the dim light. This was all that was left.

Then she realized that something had woken her. Was it Kenneth or something in a dream? She closed her eyes and listened intently. There was someone there.

She held her breath and listened again. It *was* Kenneth. She opened her mouth in a gasp. He was standing below the window at the front door, calling her name so the whole neighborhood could hear it. She felt a smile spread across her face and mustered all her strength for the final cry that would now save her. The cry for help that would prompt the soldier at her door into action.

She opened her mouth and screamed as loud as she could.

So silently that not even she could hear it.

30

The soldiers came in a battered jeep late in the afternoon, one of them yelling that local Doe supporters had stashed away arms in the village school and that she was going to show them where.

Their skin glistened, and they were as cold as ice when she tried to tell them she had nothing to do with Samuel Doe's Krahn regime and that she knew nothing about any stash of arms.

Rachel—Lisa, as she was then—and her boyfriend had heard the shots ringing out all day. Rumor had it that Taylor's guerrillas were ruthless, and so they had been preparing to flee. Who wanted to hang around and see if the future regime's bloodlust could be held in check by the color of a person's skin?

Her boyfriend had gone upstairs to fetch the hunting rifle, and the soldiers had surprised her as she busied herself hiding the school's books away in the various outbuildings. So many houses had been razed to the ground that day that she wanted to spread the risk.

And there they were. The men who had been killing all through the day and who now needed to discharge the electricity crackling inside their bodies.

They exchanged words, words she did not understand, though their eyes spoke a language she knew. She was in the wrong place. Too young and all too available in the empty schoolroom.

She darted to one side and sprang up to the window opening, only for them to grab hold of her ankles. They pulled her to the ground and kicked her until she lay completely still.

Three faces blurred for a moment in front of her eyes, and then two bodies were upon her.

Superior strength and overconfidence prompted the third soldier to lean his Kalashnikov against the wall and help his comrades spread her legs apart. They covered her mouth and entered her one by one, whooping hysterically. She drew in air feverishly through sticky nostrils, then heard her boyfriend groan in the room next door. She was frightened for him. Frightened that the soldiers would hear him, too, and make short work of him.

But that groan was all that transpired. His only reaction.

Five minutes later, as she lay in the dust staring up at the blackboard on which only two hours before she had meticulously written the words "I can hop, I can run," her boyfriend had made his escape, taking his rifle with him. It would have been the easiest thing in the world for him to shoot and kill the perspiring soldiers who now lay spent at her side with their trousers around their ankles.

But he had not been there for her. And neither was he there when she jumped to her feet and grabbed the Kalashnikov to discharge a round of bullets that tore open the bodies of the three black men and turned the room into an echo of screams steeped in the smell of burned gunpowder and warm blood.

Her boyfriend had been there for her only for as long as everything had been all right. When life was easy and the day ahead bright. But he was absent when she dragged the carcasses onto the dung heap and covered them with palm leaves. And he was absent when she scoured the walls of the schoolroom, washing away the human flesh and the blood.

That was part of the reason why she had to get away.

It was the day before she gave herself up to God and repented her sins so fervently. But the vow she made that evening when she pulled off her dress and burned it, then washed and scrubbed her crotch until it hurt, was something she would never forget.

If the Devil should ever cross her path again, she would take matters into her own hands.

And if in so doing she broke the command of God, it would have to be a matter between her and Him.

As Isabel sped along the motorway, her gaze flitting between the road ahead, the GPS, and the rearview mirror, Rachel stopped sweating. Her lips ceased to quiver, from one second to the next. Her heart rate returned to normal. In an instant, she recalled how fear can be turned into anger.

The dreadful recollection of the NPFL soldiers, their satanic breath and the yellow eyes that showed no mercy, surged through her body, making her clench her jaw.

She had taken action before, and she could do so again.

She turned to her driver. "Once we've given Joshua what he needs, I'll do the driving, OK?"

Isabel shook her head. "You don't know the car, Rachel. It's temperamental. It oversteers, for one thing. The lights are dodgy, and the hand brake's loose."

She listed other things that were wrong with it, too, but Rachel didn't care. Maybe Isabel didn't believe that this pious woman in the passenger seat could match her behind the wheel. But she would soon know better.

They met Joshua on the platform at Odense. His face was like ash, and he was clearly ill at ease.

"I don't like what you're saying!"

"I know, Joshua, but Isabel's right. This is how we're going to do it. We have to make him know we're breathing down his neck. Did you bring the GPS like we said?"

He nodded and looked at her with red-rimmed eyes. "I don't give a damn about the money," he said.

She took a tight hold of his arm. "It's got nothing to do with the money. Not anymore. You just follow his instructions. As soon as you see the light flashing, throw the bag out of the window, but leave the money in the duffel bag. We'll be following the train as closely as we can. Don't do anything on your own, but make sure you can tell us exactly where the train is if we should ask. Do you understand?"

He nodded but with obvious reluctance.

"All right, give me the duffel bag with the money in it," she said. "I don't trust you."

He shook his head.

So she was right.

"Give me the money," she demanded, raising her voice now, but still he refused. And then she slapped him hard in the face, just under his right eye, and snatched the duffel bag from his hand. Before he realized what had happened, she had passed the money on to Isabel.

Rachel grabbed the empty bag and stuffed the kidnapper's clothes inside, apart from the shirt with the single hair inside the collar. On top she laid the padlock and the clasp and the letter Joshua had written.

"Here. And make sure you do what we've agreed. Otherwise we'll never see our children again. Believe me, I *know*."

Keeping pace with the train proved harder than she had imagined. Though they had a head start out of Odense, they were already behind before they reached Langeskov. Joshua's reports gave cause for concern, and Isabel's comments as she compared the GPS positions of the car and the train grew increasingly frantic.

"We need to swap places, Rachel," Isabel urged. "You haven't the nerve for this."

Rarely had words had such a forceful effect on Rachel. She put her foot to the floor, and for five minutes the roaring engine was pushed to the maximum. It was the only sound they could hear.

"I can see the train!" Isabel suddenly exclaimed as they approached Nyborg, where the E20 motorway bridged the railway. She pressed a key on the mobile, and a few seconds later she had Joshua on the other end.

"Look to your left, Joshua. We're just ahead of you," she instructed.

"The road veers away for the next few kilometers, so you won't see us in a minute. We'll try to catch up with you again on the Storebælt Bridge, but it won't be easy. We'll have to stop at the toll station on the other side. Has he called?" She listened for a moment to his reply, then snapped the phone shut.

"What did he say?" Rachel asked.

"Still no contact with the kidnapper. But Joshua didn't sound like he was bearing up at all. He refused to believe we could get there in time. He kept stuttering, saying maybe it didn't matter anyway. As long as the kidnapper understood the message in the letter."

Rachel pressed her lips together. He had said it didn't matter. But it did. They would be there when the kidnapper turned on his strobe. They would be there, and the bastard who had taken her children would find out exactly what she was capable of.

"You're not saying anything, Rachel," said Isabel. "But it's true what Joshua says. There's no way we can make it." Her eyes were glued to the speedometer. But the car couldn't go any faster.

"What are you going to do when we get to the bridge? There are cameras everywhere, and traffic. And what about the tollbooths at the other side?"

Rachel considered Isabel's questions for a moment as she swept along in the fast lane, flashing the headlights to clear the way ahead.

"Don't worry, Isabel," was all she said.

31

Isabel was terrified.

Terrified by Rachel's insane driving and her own inability to do even the slightest thing about it.

Only two or three hundred meters farther on, they would hit the toll booths of the Storebælt Bridge, and Rachel wasn't slowing down. In just a few seconds, the speed limit would be thirty kilometers an hour, and they were doing one hundred and fifty. Ahead of them, the train with Joshua on board tore through the landscape, and this madwoman was hell-bent on catching up with it.

"Slow down, Rachel!" Isabel screamed, as the toll station loomed up in front of them. "BRAKE!"

But Rachel gripped the wheel tighter. She was in a world of her own. She was going to save her children.

Whatever else might happen was of no consequence.

They saw toll officers by the lorry bays waving their arms, and a couple of cars in front of them veered sharply out of their way.

And then they smashed through the barrier with an enormous crash, and debris was slung out to the side and on to the windscreen.

Had her Mondeo been in better condition, they would now have been sharing its interior with a pair of exploding airbags. The mechanic had told her they were defective and needed replacing, but the cost had been prohibitive. She had wanted to have the work done for a long time, but now she was glad she hadn't. If the airbags had deployed into their faces as they hurtled through the toll station at this speed, things would have gone terribly wrong. But now the only signs of this willful destruction of government property were a huge dent in the hood and an ugly crack that spread across the windscreen.

Behind them, all hell was breaking loose. If the police had not yet been alerted about a car registered in her name having smashed through the toll barrier of the Storebælt Bridge, then someone must have been fast asleep.

Isabel exhaled sharply and pressed Joshua's number again. "We're over the bridge! Where are you?"

He gave the coordinates from his GPS and she compared them to her own. He couldn't be far ahead.

"I'm not happy with this," he said. "It's wrong. What we're doing is wrong."

She tried to calm him down as best she could, though with little success.

"Call when you see the strobe," she said and snapped the phone shut.

Approaching exit 41, they saw the train on their left. A sleek necklace of light sweeping through the darkened landscape. And there in the third carriage was a man whose heart was pounding.

When would the bastard make contact?

Isabel clutched the mobile in her hand as they pelted along the stretch between Halsskov and exit 40. There were no flashing blue lights in sight.

"The police will stop us at Slagelse, Rachel, you can be sure of it. Why did you have to demolish that tollgate?"

"You can see the train, can't you? It would have been gone if I'd slowed down and stopped even for twenty seconds. That's why!"

"But I've lost it. I can't see it anymore," Isabel replied frantically. She stared at the map on her knee. "Damn it, Rachel. The track veers off north here and passes through Slagelse. If he gives the signal to Joshua between Forlev and Slagelse we haven't a chance. Unless we get off the motorway, NOW!"

Exit 40 disappeared behind them as Isabel turned her head.

She bit down on her lip. "Rachel, if he does what I think he will, then Joshua's going to see that strobe any minute now. Three roads cross the railway before we get to Slagelse. Any one of them would be a perfect place to dump the ransom. But we can't get off the motorway now, because we just passed the exit."

Isabel saw right away that she had struck a chord. Rachel's eyes became desperate again. For the next couple of minutes, the mobile chiming was the last thing in the world she wanted to hear.

Suddenly she stepped hard on the brake and pulled onto the hard shoulder.

"I'm going to reverse," she explained.

Had she lost her mind? Isabel flicked on the hazard lights and tried to slow her pulse.

"Listen, Rachel," she said, as calmly as she could. "Joshua will do this just fine. We don't need to be there when he throws out the bag. Joshua's right. The kidnapper's going to get in touch with us anyway once he sees what's in the bag," Isabel said. But Rachel wasn't listening. She had a different agenda, and Isabel understood.

"I'm going to reverse along the hard shoulder," Rachel said again.

"Don't, Rachel."

But she did.

Isabel pulled off her safety belt and turned in her seat. Behind her were columns of traffic coming toward them. "You must be insane, Rachel! You'll get us killed. What good's that going to do Samuel and Magdalena?"

But Rachel said nothing. She sat there, the engine whining in reverse, as they tore back along the asphalt.

And then Isabel saw the blue lights come over the hill, some four or five hundred meters behind.

"STOP!" she screamed. It was enough for Rachel to lift her foot from the accelerator.

Rachel looked back at the blue lights, recognizing the problem at once. The gearbox protested audibly as she went straight from reverse into first. Within seconds, they were doing a hundred and fifty again.

"Just pray that Joshua doesn't call in the next couple of minutes to say he's dumped the bag. If he doesn't, we might still have a chance. But you need to turn off at exit 38, rather than 39," Isabel groaned. "The police will be waiting at 39. They may be there already. Get off at 38. We'll take the main road instead, it's closer to the railway. The train goes through farmland all the way to Ringsted, away from the motorway."

She put her belt on again and sat with her eyes fixed on the speedometer for the next ten kilometers. The blue lights behind were apparently taking no risks in the chase. Who could blame them? she thought.

As they passed exit 39, the road out of Slagelse was a ribbon of blue. The police cars would be there any moment.

Her fears were confirmed.

"They're closing in on us, Rachel. Faster, if you can," she urged, pressing Joshua's number on the mobile.

"Where are you now, Joshua?" she demanded.

But Joshua didn't answer. Did that mean he had already dumped the bag? Or had something worse happened? Was the monster on the train? The thought hadn't occurred to her until now. Could that be it? All that stuff about flashing strobes and throwing the bag out of the window, was it all just a smokescreen? Did he already have the bag in his possession and had found out there was no money in it?

She swiveled her head and glanced at the duffel bag with the ransom inside it on the backseat.

What would the bastard do to Joshua?

They reached exit 38 just as blue lights appeared up ahead on the opposite, westbound side, too. Rachel didn't touch the brakes as they hit Route 150 with a squeal of tires, as close to colliding with another car as they could possibly get. Had it not been for swift evasive action on the part of the other driver, they would all have been done for.

Isabel felt the sweat on her back. She was soaking wet. This woman at the wheel was not merely desperate, she was insane.

"There's no escape on this road, Rachel. Once the police get behind us here, all they need to do is follow our rear lights," she yelled.

Rachel shook her head and bore down so close on the still swerving car in front of them they almost locked bumpers.

"No, we won't let them," she said calmly, and turned off the lights. The automatic driving lights Isabel had been meaning to get fixed went out at the same time.

They saw the figures of an elderly couple through the rear window of the car in front. Terror seemed a mild interpretation of their frenzied gesticulations.

"We'll turn off first chance I get," Rachel said.

"You'll have to turn on the lights again."

"Leave that to me. You check the GPS. Where's the next side road that isn't a dead end? We need to get out of the way. I can see the police behind us."

Isabel glanced back over her shoulder. It was true enough. The lights were there now, flashing blue in the dark. Maybe only four or five hundred meters behind at the motorway exit.

"There!" she shouted. "Up ahead."

Rachel nodded. The headlights of the car in front had picked out a road sign. *Vedbysønder*, it read.

She stepped on the brake and veered away, lights out, into the darkness.

"OK," she said, slipping into neutral and rolling past a barn and some farm buildings. "We'll pull in behind the farm here. They won't see us. You call Joshua again, OK?"

Isabel looked back over the landscape as the blue lights loomed out of the dark, an ominous aura.

Then she pressed Joshua's number again, this time full of trepidation.

It rang a couple of times, and then he answered.

"Yes?" was all he said.

Isabel nodded to Rachel to say Joshua had taken the call.

"Have you delivered the bag?" she asked.

"No, not yet," came his reply. His voice sounded labored.

"Is something the matter, Joshua? Are there people around you?"

"There's one other man in the compartment besides me, but he's working at his computer and wearing earphones. So *that's* all right. But I'm not feeling good. I keep thinking about the children. It's so awful." He sounded short of breath and exhausted. Hardly surprising.

"Just calm down, Joshua." She knew it was easier said than done. "It'll all be over in a few minutes. Where's the train now? Give me the coordinates."

He read them out. "We're moving out of the town now," he said.

She was with him. It couldn't be that far behind now.

"Get your head down," Rachel commanded as police cars ripped along the main road and past the turning they had taken. As if anyone could see them here from that distance.

But in a moment, the elderly couple who had been in front of them would be waved in. They would tell the police about the lunatics they had encountered on the road, tailgating them with their headlights switched off, and how suddenly they had shot off down a side road. And then the police would turn back.

"Hey, I can see the train," Isabel suddenly exclaimed.

Rachel was alert. "Where?"

Isabel pointed south, away from the main road. It was perfect. "Down there! Come on, let's get going!"

Rachel switched on the lights, ran through the gears in five seconds, negotiating the two bends through the village in one maneuver, and within moments the chain of lights that was the train crossed the beam of the Mondeo's headlamps in the darkness ahead.

"Oh, God, I can see the strobe!" Joshua cried into the mobile. "Oh, dear Lord and Father, please protect us and have mercy on our souls!"

"Has he seen it?" Rachel said. She had heard the sound of his cry over the phone.

Isabel nodded, and Rachel bowed her head slightly. "Mother of God. Let Thy holy light shine down and show us the way to Thy splendor. Take us unto Thee as Thy children, and warm us at Thy heart." She exhaled sharply, then breathed in air to the bottom of her lungs as she pressed her foot down harder on the accelerator.

"I can see the strobe right ahead of me. I'm opening the window now," said Joshua over the mobile. "I'll need to put the phone down on the seat. Oh, God. Oh, God."

Joshua groaned in the background. He sounded like an old man with only a few steps remaining on the path of life. Too many things left to do, too many thoughts of which to keep track.

Isabel's eyes darted around in the darkness. She couldn't see the light flashing. So it had to be on the other side of the train.

"The road crosses the railway twice farther along here, Rachel. I'm sure he's on the same road as us," she shouted, as Joshua exerted himself audibly at the other end of the phone, trying to get the bag out of the window.

"I'm letting go of it now," said his voice in the background.

"Where is he? Can you see him, Joshua?" Isabel yelled urgently.

Now he had picked up the phone again. His voice came through loud and clear. "I can see his car. It's pulled in by some trees where the road cuts in toward the tracks."

"Look out of the window on the other side, Joshua. Rachel's flashing her headlights now."

She gave a sign to Rachel, who was hunched over the wheel, peering out of the windscreen in an effort to catch sight of something, anything at all, beyond the train in front of them.

"Can you see us, Joshua?"

"YES!" he cried back. "I can see you by the bridge. You're coming toward us. You'll be there any sec . . ."

Isabel heard him utter a groan. Then came a sound like the phone clattering to the floor.

"I can see it, the strobe!" Rachel exclaimed.

She drove on over the bridge and along the narrow road. A couple of hundred meters and they would be there.

"What's the man doing now, Joshua?" Isabel demanded, but there was no answer. Perhaps the phone had snapped shut when it fell.

"Holy Mother of God, forgive me for whatever evil I have done," Rachel chanted in the seat next to her as they swept past a couple of cottages and a farm at a bend, then another house on its own close to the tracks. And then the headlights picked out his car.

It was parked on a bend a couple of hundred meters ahead, perhaps fifty from the railway. And behind it there he stood, the bastard himself, peering into the bag. In a windbreaker and light-colored trousers. If they hadn't known better, they might have taken him for a tourist who had got lost.

As the full beam of their headlights illuminated him, he lifted his head. It was impossible to see his expression from their distance, but a thousand thoughts must have been racing through his mind. What were his clothes doing in the bag? Perhaps he had already seen that there was a note on top. Certainly he must have realized that there was no money inside. And now these headlights were coming toward him at breakneck speed.

"I'll run him down!" Rachel screamed at the same moment as the man threw the bag and himself into the car.

They were only meters away from him as his wheels found traction and pulled him out onto the road, his engine whining.

It was a dark Mercedes like the one Isabel had seen near the cottage at Ferslev. So it *was* him she had seen while Rachel was being sick.

The road ahead was lined by dense woodland, and the sound of their engine and the car ahead roared through the trees. The Mercedes was more powerful than the Ford. It wouldn't be easy to keep up, and what good would it do them anyway?

She looked at Rachel, deep in concentration behind the wheel. What on earth had she in mind?

"Keep your distance, Rachel," she yelled. "In a minute, we'll have the police behind us with reinforcements. They'll help us. We'll catch him, you'll see. They can set up a roadblock somewhere up ahead."

"Hello?" came the sound of a voice from the mobile in her hand. A stranger's voice. A man's.

"Yes?" Isabel's eyes were fixed on the rear lights of the car in front as they tore along the narrow road, but everything inside her focused now on this voice. Years of disappointment and defeat had taught her always to be on her guard, even in the most innocuous of situations. Where was Joshua?

"Who are you?" she demanded harshly. "Are you in on this, with that bastard? Are you?"

"I'm sorry, I don't know what you mean. Were you the person talking just now to the man who owns this phone?"

Isabel felt her brow turn to ice. "Yes, that was me."

She sensed Rachel shift uneasily in the driver's seat. Her entire being was a question mark as she tried to keep a straight course on the winding ribbon of asphalt, the distance between them and the car in front increasing all the time.

"I'm afraid he's been taken ill," said the voice on the phone.

"What are you saying? Who are you?"

"I was sitting here in the same compartment working when it happened. I'm so sorry to have to tell you this, but I'm quite certain he's dead."

"Hey!" Rachel yelled. "What's going on? Who are you talking to, Isabel?"

"Thank you," was all Isabel could muster in reply to the man at the other end. And then she snapped the mobile shut.

She looked at Rachel and then at the blur of trees as the car hurtled along. If a deer wandered out of the woods, or if they hit a patch of wet leaves at the wrong angle, they'd be done for. The slightest thing could mean disaster. How could she find the courage to tell Rachel what she had just heard? There was no telling how she might react. Her husband had died only seconds ago and she was tearing through this darkened landscape like a woman possessed.

Isabel had often felt depressed about her life. Loneliness was an ever-present shadow. In the long evenings of winter she had often succumbed to the darkest thoughts. But now, at this moment, her mind was quite differently engaged. Now, with vengeance spurring her on, with the responsibility for the lives of two children resting in her hands, and their kidnapper, Satan personified, speeding along in the car in front of them, Isabel knew that she wanted to live. She knew that no matter how awful the world might appear, she could find her own place in it.

The issue was whether Rachel could, too.

And then Rachel turned her head toward her. "Tell me, Isabel. Tell me now. What's happened?"

"I think your husband's had a heart attack, Rachel." That was as gently as she could put it.

But Rachel sensed that the sentence hung unresolved in the air. Isabel could tell.

"Is he dead?" Rachel demanded to know. "Oh, God! He is, isn't he? Tell me, Isabel!"

"I don't know."

"Tell me NOW! Or else . . ." Her eyes were wild. The car was already beginning to swerve.

Isabel reached out toward Rachel's arm to calm her down, but then she thought better of it. "Keep your eyes on the road, Rachel," she said. "This is all about your children for the moment, remember?"

Her words lodged inside Rachel's soul, and she began to tremble. "NO, NO, NO!" she screamed. "NO, tell me it isn't true. Oh, Mother of God, tell me it isn't true!"

She gripped the wheel, sobbing violently, saliva dribbling from her lips. For a moment, Isabel thought she was about to give up the chase and stop the car, but then she jerked her body upright again and put her foot down hard on the accelerator.

Lindebjerg—Lynge read a sign that appeared at the side of the road, but Rachel did not slow for a second. The road curved through a cluster of cottages, and then everything was trees again.

Now the bastard in front was clearly under pressure. His car snaked on a bend, and Rachel cried out for Mary, Mother of God, to forgive her for breaking the fifth commandment, for she was now about to kill.

"This is insane! We're doing almost two hundred kilometers an hour,

Rachel. You'll get us both killed!" Isabel screamed, thinking for a moment that she ought to pull the keys from the ignition.

But the thought of the steering wheel locking flashed through her mind, and instead she braced herself for the worst, her knuckles showing white as she gripped the sides of her seat.

The first time Rachel rammed the Mercedes in front, Isabel's head lurched forward and then jerked back sickeningly. But the Mercedes held the road.

"OK," Rachel yelled. "So *that* makes no impression on you, Satan?" And then she rammed his rear end once more, this time with such force that the hood of the Ford crumpled. Isabel braced herself again but was nevertheless surprised by the violent snap of her body against the safety belt.

"STOP THE CAR!" she commanded, feeling pain in her chest. But Rachel wasn't listening. She was somewhere else altogether.

In front of them, the Mercedes hit the verge, swerving out of control for a second before correcting again on a straight stretch where the road widened slightly and was dimly lit by yellow light from a large farm.

And then it happened.

At the same moment that Rachel was about to ram the back end of the Mercedes one more time, the driver veered suddenly to the left and jammed on his brakes amid a screeching of tires.

They flew past, and found themselves in front.

She sensed Rachel's panic. Now they were going far too fast, the Mercedes no longer there to absorb their speed in the repeated collisions. The front wheels skidded to one side. Rachel straightened up, braking slightly, though not enough, and then came the sound of crunching metal from the side, causing Rachel instinctively to brake again.

Isabel turned her head in shock toward the shattered side window and the rear door, now crumpled in against the backseat, and at the same instant the Mercedes came in from behind. The lower half of the monster's face was in shadow, but his eyes were clearly visible. It was as though the light of sudden clarity passed over his face. As though everything at once fell into place.

All that must never happen had now happened.

And then he rammed them one last time, causing Rachel to lose control of the vehicle. The rest was pain and glimpses of a world careering by in the darkness that surrounded them.

When everything was still again, Isabel found herself hanging upside down in her safety belt. At her side, Rachel lay lifeless, the steering wheel wedged beneath her bleeding body.

Isabel tried to turn, but her muscles would not respond. Then she coughed and felt the blood well in her throat and nostrils.

Odd, how nothing hurt, she thought briefly, and then her entire body exploded in pain. She wanted to scream but couldn't. I'm dying, she thought, and coughed up blood.

Outside, she saw a shadow approach. The footsteps on the shards of glass were measured and firm. They boded ill.

She tried to focus, but the blood from her mouth and nose ran into her eyes. When she blinked, it felt like her eyelids were sandpaper.

Only when he came close enough for her to hear what he said did she become aware of the heavy metal object in his hands.

"Isabel," he said. "You were the last person I'd expected to see today. Why did you have to get involved? Look what you've done."

He sat on his haunches and peered in through the side window. She presumed he was considering how best to deliver the final blow. She tried to turn her head to see him more clearly, but still she was unable to move.

"Other people know who you are," she groaned, feeling pain surge violently in her jaw.

He smiled. "No one knows me."

He walked around the car and stared at Rachel's body from the other side. "No need to worry about her anymore. Which is good. She could have been a threat."

Then suddenly he straightened up. Isabel heard the sirens. A flash of blue passed across his legs, making him reel a couple of steps backward.

And then her eyes closed.

32

The smell of burned rubber gradually grew stronger, forcing him to pull into a rest area just outside Roskilde. Once he had heaved the battered right wing away from the tire, he walked all the way around the car to inspect the extent of the damage. Obviously it had taken a beating, but he was still surprised at how little the results of the impacts showed.

As soon as things died down, he would have to get the car fixed. All traces would have to be removed. He would find a workshop in Kiel or Ystad, wherever happened to be convenient at the time.

He lit a cigarette and read the note he had found in the bag.

This was usually that special moment he'd been looking forward to. Standing somewhere in the dark with traffic zooming past, knowing that once again he had done what he needed to do. The money in the bag, and then back to the boathouse to finish the job.

But this time was different. He was still fazed by the experience of standing there on that little back road by the railway tracks, peering into the bag at the note and his own clothes.

They had cheated him. The money wasn't there. It was a bad situation.

He pictured the wreck of the Ford Mondeo and felt satisfaction at the thought of that God-bothering bumpkin having got what she deserved. But Isabel's involvement nagged at him.

He was to blame for the way things had turned out, right from the start. If only he had followed his instinct, Isabel would have been dead after confronting him like that in Viborg.

Who could have known there was a connection between Isabel and Rachel? From Frederiks to Isabel's little row house in Viborg was a long way. What had he overlooked?

He inhaled sharply through the cigarette and held the smoke inside his lungs for as long as he could. No ransom, and all because of stupid mistakes. Stupid mistakes, and coincidence that pointed in one direction: to Isabel. Right now, he had no idea if she was dead or alive. If he'd only had ten seconds more at that fucking car, he would have buried the jack in her skull.

He would have been safe then.

Now all he could do was hope nature took its course. The crash had been bad. The Mondeo had hit a tree and rolled over maybe a dozen times. The searing, scraping sound of mangling metal against the tarmac had hardly ceased before he got out of his Mercedes. How could she possibly survive that?

He rubbed his aching neck. Bastard women. Why hadn't they just done as they were told?

He flicked his cigarette end into the thicket, opened the door of the passenger side, and sat down on the seat, pulling the bag onto his lap to examine the contents once more.

The padlock and the clasp from the barn at Ferslev. Some of his clothes from the wardrobe, and this note. That was all.

He read it over and over again. He was in no doubt that he would have to react promptly. Whoever had written it knew too much.

But they had thought themselves safe, and that was their mistake. They had been certain the roles had been switched and that they had gained the upper hand. Now the women were most likely dead, but he would have to check and make sure.

Then only the husband, Joshua, and perhaps Isabel's brother in the police would be a threat.

Perhaps. A fateful word.

For a moment, he sat taking stock of the situation as the ribbon of lights from the motorway illuminated the rest area's toilet block in waves.

He had no fear that the police were after him. He was already several hundred meters from the scene by the time the patrol cars had arrived, and though he had encountered a couple more with sirens blaring before he reached the motorway, none would be especially interested in a lone Mercedes keeping to the speed limit.

Of course, the police would find traces of a collision when they examined Isabel's car, but the more exact circumstances of the crash could only remain a mystery. How would they ever find him?

No, Rachel's husband was his priority now. Joshua, and the money. And then he would have to be sure to erase any trace that might put anyone on to his tail. He would have to reboot his entire business from scratch.

He gave a sigh. It had been a miserable year.

His target had always been ten, and then he would pack it in. He was good at his work. The millions he had made in the first years had been invested wisely and provided a decent yield. But then came the financial crisis, and the bottom had fallen out of his portfolio.

Even a kidnapper and murderer was subject to the vagaries of the market, and now to all intents and purposes he had been forced to start again.

"Fuck," he muttered to himself, as a new angle suddenly occurred to him.

If his sister didn't get her money as usual, he would have another problem on his hands. She could bring up matters from his childhood. Names that weren't to be divulged.

That, too.

When he returned from the boys' home, his mother had a new husband, selected for her from among the eligible widowers by the elders of the congregation. The man owned a chimney-sweeping firm and was father to two girls of Eva's age. A pillar, as the new pastor had referred to him, with scant regard for truth.

To begin with, his stepfather refrained from beating him, but once his mother reduced the dose of her sleeping pills and began to indulge him in the marital bed, the man's conceit prevailed and his temper gradually found an outlet.

"May the Lord lift up His countenance upon you and give you peace." These were the words he used to conclude the thrashings he dealt out to his daughters. They were uttered frequently. If one of them had been deemed in any way to transgress the word of God, to whose interpretation their father believed himself to possess sole and exclusive rights, he would not hesitate to punish the fruits of his own loins. Generally, however, the girls did very little wrong, so his wrath was directed mainly at their stepbrother. He might forget the occasional amen, or perhaps smirk during grace. It was seldom more than that. Fortunately, awareness of his own physical limitations meant his mother's husband never dared lay a finger on her strapping young son.

Afterward came the pangs of guilty conscience, and this was almost invariably the worst of it. His own father had never bothered with anything like remorse, and so no one was ever in any doubt where they stood with him. But his stepfather would stroke the cheeks of his daughters and beg their forgiveness for his rage and for their evil stepbrother. And then he would retire to the study and put on the Robe of God, as his father had always referred to the vestment, and he would pray to the Lord that He might protect these vulnerable, innocent girls as if they were His own angels.

As for Eva, he never deigned to say a word to her. Her glazed, blind eyes repulsed him, and she sensed this.

None of the children understood him. Why should his own two girls be punished when it was the stepson he hated and the stepdaughter he held in contempt? And none of them could fathom why their mother did not intervene, or how God could manifest Himself in the hateful and conspicuously unjust deeds of this beastly man.

For a time, Eva would speak up in her stepfather's defense, but even her protests waned when the beatings meted out to her stepsisters became so violent that she almost believed she could feel the pain herself.

Her brother bided his time, saving himself for the final encounter. It would come when they were least expecting it.

Once, they had been four children, a husband, and a wife. Now only he and Eva were left.

He pulled the plastic pocket containing all the information about the family out of the glove compartment and quickly found Joshua's mobile number.

Now he would ring him up and confront him with the realities. That his wife and their accomplice no longer posed a danger, and that his children would be next unless the ransom was delivered to a new location within twenty-four hours. He would inform Joshua that he was a dead man if he had revealed anything about the kidnapping to anyone other than Isabel.

It was easy for him to picture the ruddy face of this good-natured man, who would almost certainly break down and do exactly as he was instructed.

He had seen it all before.

He dialed the number and waited for what seemed like an eternity before it was answered.

"Hello?" said a voice he immediately realized was unfamiliar.

"Hello, is Joshua there?" he asked as a pair of headlights swept past him.

"Who's this?" the voice replied.

"Is this Joshua's mobile?" he asked.

"No, you must have got a wrong number."

He glanced at the display. No, the number was right. What was going on?

Then it struck him. The name!

"Oh, I'm sorry. Joshua's what we all call him, but his proper name's Jens Krogh. I forget sometimes. May I speak to him?"

He stared through the silence into space. The man at the other end said nothing. This wasn't a good sign. Who the hell was he?

"I see," said the voice eventually. "And who am I speaking to?"

"His brother-in-law," he blurted out. "Is he there?"

"No, I'm afraid he isn't. You're speaking to Sergeant Leif Sindal of the Roskilde Police. You're his brother-in-law, you say. May I take your name?"

The police? Had the idiot gone to the police? Was he completely insane?

"Police? Has something happened to Joshua?"

"I'm afraid I can't tell you anything until you give me a name."

Something was definitely wrong. What now?

"It's Søren Gormsen," he said. That was his rule. Always give up an unusual name when dealing with the police. They'd believe it, because they knew they could check.

"I see," came the reply. "Can you describe your brother-in-law to us, Mr. Gormsen?"

"Yes, I can. He's a big man. Balding, in his late fifties, always wears an olive-green sleeveless jacket and—"

"Mr. Gormsen," the policeman interrupted. "We've been called because Jens Krogh was found apparently lifeless on board a train. The police doctor is with us as we speak, and I very much regret to inform you that your brother-in-law has been declared dead."

He allowed the word "dead" to resonate for a moment before responding. "Oh, no. That's dreadful. How did it happen?"

"We don't know yet. According to a fellow passenger, he collapsed."

He wondered whether he might be walking headlong into a trap.

"Where will you be taking him?" he asked.

He heard the police sergeant and the doctor confer in the background. "An ambulance will be coming to collect the body. There'll probably be an autopsy."

"So he'll be taken to the hospital in Roskilde?"

"We'll be getting off the train at Roskilde, yes."

He said his thanks and a few words of regret, then got out of the car to wipe the mobile, planning to hurl it into the windbreak of trees. They wouldn't be able to trace him on that account if it was all a setup.

"Hey," came a voice from behind him. He turned to see a couple of men climbing out of a car that had just pulled in to the rest area. Lithuanian plates and faded jogging suits. Gaunt, unfriendly faces.

They came straight toward him, their intentions clear. In a moment he would be sprawling on the ground with his pockets emptied. It was plainly their line of work.

He raised a hand in warning, indicating the mobile. "Here," he shouted, then hurled the phone hard against the forehead of the man in front, swiveling to one side and planting a back kick into the groin of his accomplice, causing his bony frame to crumple amid cries of pain, the switchblade he carried dropping to the ground.

He had the knife in his hand within a second, thrusting it into the abdomen of the first man, then into the side of the second.

And then he retrieved his phone and threw it and the knife as far into the bushes as he could.

Life had taught him always to strike first.

He left the two bleeding thugs to themselves and entered Roskilde Station into the GPS.

He would be there in eight minutes.

The ambulance had been waiting for some time before they came with the stretcher. He stepped into the array of inquisitive onlookers with their eyes fixed on Joshua's body underneath the blanket. As soon as he saw the uniformed officer with Joshua's coat and bag in his hands, everything was confirmed.

Joshua was dead. The money was lost.

"Fuck," he exclaimed under his breath, repeating it to himself as he pointed the Mercedes toward Ferslev and the cottage that had been his bolt-hole for years. His cover—his address, his name, his van, everything that made it safe to be him, was all tied up in the place. And now it was over. Isabel had the license plate number of the van and had passed it on to her brother, and the owner of the vehicle could be traced to the address. It was no longer safe.

By the time he reached the village and drove up the track between the trees to the cottage, peace had descended upon the landscape. The little community had long since succumbed to the torpor of the television screen. Only the main house of a farm across the fields displayed a pair of brightly lit windows. The alarm would probably be raised there.

He noted how Rachel and Isabel had broken into his garage and the house. He went through the premises, removing items that might withstand the flames. A small mirror, a tin of sewing equipment, the first-aid box.

Then he backed the van out of the barn, drove it around the side of the house, and reversed at full speed into the picture window that had afforded him such a good view over the fields.

The sound of shattering glass prompted a brief cacophony of crows, but that was all.

He walked around to the other side and went into the house, shining his torch in front of him. Perfect, he thought, seeing the van's rear tires punctured and its back end protruding onto the laminated floor. He stepped carefully between the shards of glass and opened the back doors, took out a jerrican, and emptied its contents in an even trail from the living room to the kitchen, out into the hall, and up the stairs.

Then he unscrewed the cap of the van's petrol tank, tore off a strip of moldering curtain, and inserted the end deep into the tank.

He stood for a moment in the yard and looked around before igniting the rag of curtain and throwing it into the petrol on the floor next to the line of gas cylinders in the hall.

He was already on the road, racing through the gears of the Mercedes, by the time the van's petrol tank exploded with a deafening boom. A minute later, the gas canisters went up. The explosion was so violent it almost raised the roof.

Not until he had passed the village grocery store and could see across the fields again did he pull in and look back.

The cottage was ablaze behind the trees, like a bonfire on Midsummer's Eve, spitting out sparks into the sky. Already it could be seen from miles away. And before long, the flames would lick the branches of the trees and everything would be razed to the ground.

There was no more to fear on that account.

The fire brigade would quickly see that nothing could be saved.

They would put it down to a boyish prank that had got out of hand.

It happened so often, out in the country.

He stood in front of the door of the room in which his wife lay trapped underneath the packing cases, noting once again with a strange blend of sadness and satisfaction that the place was as quiet as the grave. They had been good together, the two of them. She was kind and beautiful and a good mother to their child. It could all have been so very different. Once again, he had only himself to blame for things not having worked out. Before he lived with someone again, he would have to get rid of everything he had hidden away inside that room. The past had taken charge of his life until now, but he would not allow it to assume control of his future, too. He would do a couple more kidnappings, sell the house, and settle down somewhere far away. Perhaps he might even learn how to live a normal life.

He lay stretched out on the corner sofa for some time, thinking through the things he had to do. He could keep Vibegården and its boathouse, that much was clear. But he would need to find a replacement for the cottage at Ferslev. A little house far from the beaten track. A place where no one came, and best if the owner was some local outcast. An old soak who kept himself to himself and owed no one any favors. He might have to look farther south this time. He remembered a couple of places he'd considered at one time when driving around the Næstved area, but experience told him that making the final selection would be no easy matter.

The owner of the cottage at Ferslev had fitted the bill perfectly. No one had any interest in him, and he even less in others. He had spent most of his working life in Greenland and had apparently had some kind of old flame in Sweden, so they said in the village. *Apparently.* It was the very cloudiness of the word that gave him his lead. A man who kept his own company, living on money earned at a time when his life had been more successful, so the story went. The villagers called him "the odd bird," and thereby signed his death warrant.

More than ten years had now passed since he had taken the odd bird's life, after which he had meticulously made sure to pay the bills that on occasion dropped into the letter box of the cottage. After a couple of years he canceled the electricity and the refuse collection, and after that nobody ever came. He had a passport and driver's license made in the man's name, with new photos and a more plausible date of birth, by a photographer in Copenhagen's Vesterbro district. A decent, reliable man for whom forgery had become a skill comparable to that exhibited by Rembrandt's pupils at the behest of their master. A true artist.

The name Mads Christian Fog had accompanied him for a decade, but now it was over.

Now he was just Chaplin again.

At the age of sixteen and a half he had fallen in love with one of his stepsisters. She was vulnerable, ethereal, with a delicate, high brow and thin blue veins showing at her temples. In stark contrast to the crudity of his stepfather's genetic material and his own mother's stockiness.

He wanted to kiss her and hold her in his arms, vanish into her gaze, and descend into her inner being, and he knew it was forbidden. In the eyes of God, they were siblings, and in their house His eyes were everywhere.

Eventually, he found no other outlet but to enjoy what sinful pleasures he could derive alone under his duvet or from stolen glimpses in the evenings through the gaps in the ceiling boards of her bedroom.

And then he got caught in the act. He had been lying flat on his stomach, spying on her beauty below, which had been covered only by a flimsy nightdress, when all of a sudden she looked up and caught his eye. He was so flustered that he leaped to his feet and gashed his head on a nail jutting out from one of the roof beams, a deep wound just behind his right ear.

They heard his cries from the attic, and his pleasures were over.

Pious as ever, his sister Eva snitched to their mother and stepfather. What her blind eyes could not see was the hateful rage that consumed both parents at this act of debauchery.

They interrogated him under the threat of eternal damnation, but he refused to admit to anything. That he had spied upon his stepsister. That he had wanted to see the object of his desire naked. How could their curses make him admit to that? He had heard it all before and all too often.

"You've brought this upon yourself," his stepfather bellowed, grabbing hold of him from behind. He may not have been the stronger, but the full nelson he applied so unexpectedly was remarkably effective, his arms encircling the boy's torso, hands clasped and pressing down on his neck.

"Bring the crucifix!" he shouted to his wife. "Beat Satan from this infested body! Beat this boy until all his devils are banished!"

He saw the crucifix raised above his mother's frenzied eyes and felt her moldy breath against his face as the first blow was delivered.

"In the name of all glory!" she screamed, lifting the crucifix again. Beads of perspiration gathered on her top lip, and his stepfather tightened his hold, repeatedly grunting out his own exhortation: "In the name of the Almighty!"

After twenty blows against his shoulders and upper arms, his mother stepped back, exhausted and gasping for breath.

From that moment, there was no turning back.

His two stepsisters wept in the adjoining room. They had overheard everything and seemed genuinely shocked. Eva, on the other hand, appeared unmoved, though she, too, had most certainly been aware of all that had taken place. She went on reading her Braille, but was unable to conceal the embittered look on her face.

That same evening, he crushed sleeping pills and put them in his mother's and stepfather's coffee. And when night came, and they were sleeping heavily, he dissolved the rest of the bottle's contents in water. It took a while to turn them over onto their backs, and even longer for him to pour the thick mixture down their throats. But time was no longer an issue.

He wiped the empty pill bottle and pressed it into his stepfather's hand. Then he curled the fingers of both unconscious parents around a pair of drinking glasses, placing one on each bedside table, pouring some water into them before closing the bedroom door behind him.

"What are you doing in there?" said a voice.

He peered into the darkness. Eva's domain, and her advantage. The dark was her friend now, and her ears were keen as a dog's.

"Nothing, Eva. I just wanted to say sorry, but they're asleep. I think they took sleeping pills."

"Then I hope they sleep well," was all she said.

The bodies were collected the next day. The double suicide was a scandal in the little community, and Eva said nothing. Perhaps she already sensed, even then, that what had happened, and the fact that her brother was also to blame for her own blindness, which he grieved over in his own silent way, was to become her insurance against a life marked by poverty and powerlessness.

Their stepsisters had chosen eternity only a couple of years later. They walked hand in hand into the lake together, and the lake accepted them. Thus they were freed from the pain of recollection. He and Eva were not.

The deaths of their parents were now more than twenty-five years in the past, and still there were new fanatics who continued to misinterpret the word "benevolence."

To hell with them. He hated them more than anything else. To hell with all those who in the name of God believed themselves to be above all others.

They were to be removed from the earth.

He twisted the key of the van and the key to the cottage from his key ring and dumped them in his neighbor's dustbin underneath the top rubbish bag, glancing around to make sure he was unseen.

Then he went back into his own drive and emptied his letter box.

The mailshots went straight into the bin, and the rest he threw onto the table in the front room. A couple of bills, two newspapers, and a small, handwritten note with the logo of the bowling club on it.

It was too soon for there to be anything in the papers yet, but the regional radio station had something about a couple of Lithuanians who had apparently been at each other's throats and got themselves badly injured in the process, and then came the story about the car crash involving the two women. Details were sparse, but what they gave was enough: the scene of the accident, the women's ages, the fact that they had both suffered severe injuries after having raced across the country and smashed through the toll station barriers on the Storebælt Bridge. No names were revealed, but the possibility of a third party being involved was mentioned.

He searched for the accident on the Internet. The online version of one of the tabloids carried the additional information that the lives of both women remained in the balance after they had undergone surgery during the night, and that police were puzzled by their hazardous passage over the bridge. A doctor from the Trauma Center of the Rigshospital in Copenhagen was mentioned by name and seemed pessimistic as to their prospects.

Even so, he was worried.

He found a video presentation of the Trauma Center on the hospital's website, studied what they did and where, and then checked the map showing the locations of the hospital's various departments. He would know where to find them.

For the time being, however, he would simply monitor the two women's condition.

Next, he picked up the note with the bowling logo on it and read the handwritten message:

Stopped by today, but nobody in. Team tournament on Wed moved from 7:30 to 7 p.m. Remember winning ball afterward. Or maybe you've got balls enough as it is, ha ha? Maybe you'll both come? Ha ha, again! Cheers, The Pope.

He looked up at the ceiling, toward the room where his wife lay. If he waited a couple of days before taking the body up to the boathouse, he would be able to get rid of all three of them at once. A couple more days without water and the kids would be dead anyway. Who cared? They could thank their parents.

Pure idiocy. All that trouble for nothing.

33

He had heard some disturbance downstairs during the night, but hadn't realized that the doctor had been there again.

"Hardy's got some fluid on his lungs," said Morten. "He's having difficulty breathing." He looked concerned. His cheerful, chubby face seemed almost to have collapsed in on itself.

"Is it serious?" Carl asked. It'd be a tragedy, if it was.

"The doctor wants Hardy admitted to the Rigshospital for observation, so they can check his heart and stuff. He was worried about pneumonia, too. That could be fatal for a man in Hardy's condition."

Carl nodded. Clearly, they should be taking no chances.

He smoothed his hand over his friend's hair.

"Christ, Hardy, what are you playing at? You should have woken me up."

"I told Morten not to," Hardy whispered with a despondent look on his face. More despondent than usual. "You'll have me back, I hope? Once I'm discharged again?"

"Course we will, mate. The place wouldn't be the same without you."

Hardy smiled weakly. "I don't think Jesper would agree with you there. He'd love it if everything was back to normal when he got home this afternoon."

This afternoon? Carl had forgotten.

"Anyway, I won't be here when you get home from work, Carl. Morten's going with me to the hospital, so I'll be in good hands. Who knows, maybe

I'll be back in a few days . . ." He tried to smile as he gasped for breath. "Carl, something's been bothering me," he said.

"Like what?"

"Do you remember that case of Børge Bak's, a prostitute found dead underneath the Langebro Bridge? It looked like a drowning accident, maybe even a suicide. Only then it turned out not to be."

Carl nodded. He remembered it well. A black girl, not much more than eighteen years old. Naked, apart from a bracelet of twisted copper wire around her ankle. Nothing out of the ordinary, a lot of African women wore that kind of thing. More interesting were the needle marks on her arms. Typical for a junkie prostitute, but not for the African girls who worked the streets of Vesterbro.

"She'd been killed by her pimp, wasn't that it?" Carl said.

"More likely by those who sold her to her pimp."

Hardy was right, he remembered now.

"That case reminds me of the one you've got now. Those bodies in the fires."

"You mean the bracelet around her ankle?"

"Exactly," Hardy said. "The girl wanted out. Wanted to go home. But she hadn't earned enough, so they wouldn't let her."

"And that's why they killed her."

"Yeah. The African girls believe in voodoo. Only this one didn't. She was a threat to the system. They had to get rid of her."

"So they used the bracelet to remind the other girls of the repercussions of going against their masters or the voodoo."

"That's right. Someone had woven feathers and hair and all sorts of crap into the bracelet. None of the other African girls was in any doubt as to what it meant."

Carl stroked his chin. Hardy was definitely on to something.

Jacobsen stood with his back to Carl, looking out across the street. He did this often when he needed to focus. "Let me get this straight. You're saying

Hardy thinks the bodies in the fires were debt collectors entrusted with the collection of payments from the three firms involved, and that they hadn't been doing their jobs properly. The payments weren't forthcoming, and for that reason they were bumped off?"

"Right. The syndicate makes an example of them for everyone else on the payroll. And the firms use the insurance payout after the fires to settle their debts. Two birds with one stone."

"If the insurance money went to the Serbs, presumably one or more of the firms hit would then be lacking funds with which to reestablish their businesses," Jacobsen mused.

"Yeah."

The homicide chief nodded. Simple explanations often yielded simple solutions. These were vicious crimes indeed, but the Eastern European gangs and those from the Balkans were hardly known for their compassion.

"Do you know what, Carl? I think we'll go with that." He nodded. "I'll get on to Interpol straightaway. They can give us a hand getting some answers out of these Serbs. Do thank Hardy for me, won't you? How's he doing, anyway? Has he settled in all right at your place?"

Carl shook his head deliberately. Settled in would be stretching things somewhat.

"Oh, by the way. A tip-off for you." Marcus Jacobsen stopped him in his tracks in the doorway. "Health and Safety will be looking in on you sometime during the day."

"Yeah? How do you know? I thought that sort of thing was meant to be a surprise."

The homicide chief smiled. "We're not the police for nothing, you know. We *know* things."

"Yrsa, you're on the third floor today, OK?" Carl said.

But Yrsa wasn't listening. "Rose said to thank you for the note you left yesterday," she said.

"OK. What's her answer, then? Will she be back with us soon?"

"She didn't say."

Which was answer enough in itself.

He was stuck with Yrsa.

"Where's Assad?" he asked.

"In his office making phone calls to former sect members. I'm doing the support groups."

"Are there many?"

"Not really, no. I'll have to start ringing up ordinary ex-members soon, like Assad's doing."

"Good idea. Where are you finding them?"

"Old newspaper articles. There's plenty to be getting on with."

"When you go upstairs, take Assad with you. Health and Safety will be around in a while."

"Who?"

"Health and Safety. About the asbestos."

Obviously, it rang no bells. Yrsa stared vacantly into space.

"Hello, anyone there?" He snapped his fingers. "Wakey, wakey!"

"Hello, yourself. Let me say this like it is to your face, Carl. I haven't a clue what you're talking about. Don't you think you might be mixing me up with Rose?"

Had he really got her confused with her sister?

Jesus Christ, he couldn't even tell them apart anymore.

Tryggve Holt rang just as Carl was wondering if he should put a chair out ready in the middle of the room so he could clobber the fly next time it decided to settle in its favorite spot on the ceiling.

"Were you satisfied with the drawing?" Tryggve asked.

"Yes, were you?"

Tryggve said he was. "I'm calling you because there's a Danish policeman, Pasgård, who keeps ringing me up all the time. I've already told him everything I know. Can't you get him off my back? He's a real pain."

My pleasure, Carl thought to himself.

"Can I ask you a couple of questions first, Tryggve?" he said. "Then I'll make sure he leaves you alone, OK?"

Tryggve didn't sound entirely enthusiastic, but he wasn't protesting, either.

"We're having doubts about the wind turbines. Can you describe that sound for us again, in more detail perhaps?"

"What am I supposed to say?"

"How deep was it?"

"I couldn't say. I don't know how to describe it."

Carl hummed a tone. "Was it *that* deep?"

"Yeah, thereabouts, I'd say."

"Not very deep at all, then?"

"If you say so. I would have called it deep."

"Did it sound metallic in any way?"

"How do you mean?"

"Was it a soft tone, or was there more of an edge to it?"

"I can't remember. More of an edge, maybe."

"Like an engine?"

"Maybe. But all the time, for days on end."

"And it didn't go away in the storm?"

"A little bit, perhaps, not much. Anyway, I've been through all this with Pasgård. Most of it, at least. Can't you just ask him? I can hardly bear to think about it anymore."

Carl thought of suggesting therapy. "I understand, Tryggve."

"Anyway, there's another reason I'm calling. My dad's in Denmark today."

"Really?" Carl grabbed his notepad. "Where?"

"He's at a meeting of Jehovah's Witnesses, at their headquarters in Holbæk. Something about him wanting to be stationed somewhere else. I think maybe you put the wind up him. He doesn't want all this brought up again."

Like father, like son, Carl thought to himself. "I see. And what can the Jehovah's Witnesses in Denmark do about that?" he asked.

"They could send him to Greenland or the Faroe Islands, for a start."

Carl frowned. "How do you know this, Tryggve? Are you and your father on speaking terms again?"

"No, my younger brother, Henrik, told me. And you're not to tell anyone, otherwise he'll be in trouble."

After they had hung up, Carl sat for a moment and gazed at the clock. In an hour and twenty minutes Mona would be with him in the company of her super shrink, but why was she putting him through it? Maybe she thought he was going to leap to his feet all of a sudden like the first lamb of spring and declare: Hallelujah, I'm not traumatized anymore about my mate getting shot before my eyes while I did fuck all about it! Was that it?

He shook his head. If it wasn't for Mona, he would make short shrift of that quack of hers.

There was a gentle knock on the door. It was Laursen, with a little plastic bag in his hand.

"Cedar," he said, chucking the bag containing the splinter onto Carl's desk. "You're looking for a boathouse made of cedarwood. How many of them do you think were put up in Nordsjælland before the kidnapping? Not many, I can tell you. It was all pressure-treated timber back then. Before Silvan and all the other DIY chains convinced Mr. and Mrs. Denmark it wasn't good enough anymore."

Carl stared at the scrap in the bag. Cedarwood!

"Who says the boathouse is made of the same material as the splinter Poul Holt found to write with?" he asked.

"No one. But the possibility exists. If I were you, I'd ask around the timber merchants in the area."

"Excellent work, Tomas. But there's no telling how old that boathouse might be. The law only requires firms to keep copies of their accounts for five years in this country. No timber merchant or DIY store is going to be able to tell us anything about any amount of cedarwood they sold even ten years ago, not to mention twenty. That only works in films. Reality's a different thing altogether."

"Should have saved myself the bother, then." Laursen smiled. Shrewd as he was, he could doubtless already see the thoughts now bouncing around inside his former colleague's head. How to make use of the information? Where did it put them now?

"By the way, you might like to know Department A's in a frenzy upstairs," Laursen added.

"What for?"

"They've pulled in the owner of one of those firms that got hit by arson recently. Seems the bloke's cracked. He's in an interview room shitting himself. He thinks that lot he borrowed money from are going to bump him off."

Carl pondered the information. "I don't blame him. He's got every reason."

"Anyway, Carl. You won't be hearing from me for the next couple of days. I'm off on a course."

"You don't say. Cafeteria cuisine, is it?" He laughed, perhaps rather too heartily.

"As a matter of fact, yes. How did you guess?"

Now he caught the look in Laursen's eyes. It was a look he had seen before. Out there with the dead bodies, white SOC suits all over the place.

That pained look Laursen ought to have put behind him by now was back again.

"What's up, Tomas? Did they kick you out or something?"

Laursen nodded almost imperceptibly. "Yeah, but not the way you think. The cafeteria isn't paying its way. We've got eight hundred people working in this building and none of them are eating with us. So now they're packing it in."

Carl frowned. He had never been one of the privileged few who on account of their loyalty to the cafeteria had always been rewarded with an extra slice of lemon to go with their fish. But still, things were going totally down the plughole if they were closing the nosh house, the pig trough, the luncheonette, the greasy spoon, the staff restaurant, or whatever the hell else they chose to call the joint with the sloping walls its diners were always banging their heads against.

"You mean, they're actually closing down?" he said incredulously.

"Yeah. But the commissioner says there has to be a cafeteria, so now they're putting it out to tender. They've got us buttering bread until some twat or other kicks us out on to the dole queue in the name of the free market or else takes us on to chop lettuce all day."

"So you're sodding off now, before it happens?"

Laursen managed a crumpled smile that briefly lit up his weathered face. "Sodding off? You must be joking. I put in for this course so I'll be eligible to take over the place. That'll show the bastards."

They walked part of the way up the stairs together, before Carl found Yrsa on the third floor engaged in animated chat with Lis about who was the hotter, George Clooney or Johnny Depp. Whoever the fuck they were.

"Hard at work, then?" he commented tersely and caught sight of Pasgård darting from the coffee machine into his office.

"Thanks for your work, Pasgård," he said, catching up with him. "You're hereby off the case."

Pasgård gave him an uncertain look. He always assumed everyone else was just as full of shit as he was himself.

"Just one small job, Pasgård, then you and Jørgen can get back to knocking on doors in Sundby. Would you be good enough to make sure Poul Holt's father is brought to HQ for questioning? It seems Martin Holt is at this moment to be found at the national headquarters of Jehovah's Witnesses at Stenhusvej 28 in Holbæk, just in case you didn't know." He glanced at the clock on the wall. "It'd suit me to interview him in exactly two hours' time. He'll probably kick up a fuss, but this is a murder investigation and he's a Crown witness."

Carl turned on his heel. He could almost hear the howls of protest from the Holbæk Police. Marching into the Jehovah's Witnesses' most hallowed halls! Christ on a bike! But Martin Holt would come along of his own accord. Of the two evils, the greater would be having to admit to lying to his fellows in the community about his son being ostracized.

It was one thing to have lied to people outside the sect, quite another to have done so to the initiated.

He found Assad at his desk in the corridor outside Jacobsen's office. A computer of the kind that had been thrown into storage five years before whirred loudly. On the other hand, they had given him a relatively new mobile so he could retain contact with the outside world. No expense spared.

"Any luck, Assad?"

He raised his hand, a hold-on-a-second gesture while he finished the sentence he was in the middle of writing, committing his thoughts to paper before they disappeared. Carl was the same.

"It's odd, Carl. When I speak to people who have run away from a sect, they think I am trying to make them join a new one. Do you think it has to do with my accent?"

"What accent's that, Assad?"

Assad glanced up with a gleam in his eye and a grin on his face. "Ahh, you are making fun with me now. I understand, Carl." He waggled an admonishing index finger in the air. "But my piss cannot so easily be taken out of me."

"Yeah, right, Assad. So anyway, you mean there's nothing for us to go on?" Carl continued. It certainly wouldn't be Assad's fault if that were the case. "But Assad, maybe there just *is* nothing to go on. We can't be certain the kidnapper ever committed any crime other than this one. Do you get what I'm saying?"

Assad smiled. "There you take my piss again, Carl. Of course the kidnapper did this more than one time. I see in your eyes that you know this."

He had to be right. A million kroner was a lot of money, but it wasn't that much. Certainly not if kidnapping was your chosen profession.

Their man must have done it more than once. What reasons were there for assuming he hadn't?

"Keep at it, Assad. There's nothing else to do for the time being, anyway."

When he got back to the front desk, where Lis and Yrsa were still immersed in shockingly sexist drivel about what a proper man should look like, he tapped discreetly on the counter with his knuckles.

"I understand Assad's running the show on his own as regards the former sect members, so I've got something else for you to do, Yrsa. And if it's too much, Lis will help you out, won't you, Lis?"

"No, you won't, Lis," came the sound of Ms. Sørensen's caustic voice from the corner. "Detective Inspector Mørck here belongs to a different department. It's not in your job description to run errands for him."

"Well, I'd say that depends," said Lis, sending him one of those looks her husband seemed to have got her to specialize in during their libidinous road trip across the States. It was a look he wished Mona could have seen. Then maybe she would start fighting a bit harder to keep him on the hook.

In self-defense, he focused his gaze on Yrsa's red lips.

"Yrsa, I want you to check and see if you can find that boathouse on an aerial photo. Get hold of everything they've got in the property registration archives in Frederikssund, Halsnæs, Roskilde, and Lejre municipalities. You'll most likely find them via the official websites for each local authority, otherwise ask them to send us what they've got by e-mail. High-definition aerial photos showing the entire shoreline all the way around Hornsherred. And while you're at it, ask them to send us some maps detailing the position of every wind turbine in the area."

"I thought we agreed they were shut down during the storm?"

"We did, but it needs to be checked anyway."

"A poxy little job like that won't take her long," said Lis. "What have you got for me?" She fluttered her eyes directly at his crotch. What the fuck was he supposed to say to that in public? His double entendres were falling over each other in the rush.

"Erm. Maybe you could get on to the technical departments of those local authorities and ask if they gave planning permission for boathouses along the shoreline in the period prior to 1996, and if so, where."

She swayed her hips. "Is that all? I was hoping for a bit more." And then she turned her magnificently attractive, denim-clad backside toward him and strode off toward her phone.

Absolutely priceless.

34

The Helmand region had been Kenneth's personal hell, the desert dust his nightmare. One tour of Iraq, two of Afghanistan. It was more than enough.

His mates sent him e-mails every day. A lot of words about comradeship and great times together, but nothing about what was actually going on. Everyone just wanted to stay alive. That was all that mattered.

And for that reason he was done with it. He was clear about that. A pile of debris on a roadside. The wrong place in the dark. The wrong place in the daytime. The incendiaries were everywhere. An eye put to a telescopic sight. Luck wasn't the kind of companion on whom one could rely.

So here he was in his little house in Roskilde, trying to blunt his senses and forget. Trying to get on with his life.

He had killed a person and had never told anyone. It had happened very quickly, in a brief exchange of fire. Not even his comrades had noticed. A corpse, slightly apart from the others. His corpse. A direct hit in the windpipe. No more than a boy, the terrifying whiskers of the Taliban warrior little more than fluff on his chin.

He had told no one, not even Mia.

It wasn't the kind of thing to drop into a conversation when you were breathlessly in love.

The first time he saw Mia, he knew he would be hers unconditionally.

She had looked deeply into his eyes when he took her hand. Already then, it had happened. Total surrender. Pent-up longing and hope, suddenly liberated. And they had listened to each other with senses agape, knowing it was only the start.

She had trembled as she told him when her husband might be back. She, too, was ready for a new life.

The last time they saw each other had been Saturday. He had turned up on the spur of the moment, the newspaper in his hand as they had agreed.

She was alone but in a state. Let him in reluctantly but wouldn't say what was wrong. She clearly had no sense of what the day might bring.

If only they had had a few more seconds, he would have asked her to come with him. To pack some things, pick up Benjamin, and take off.

She would have said yes if her husband hadn't turned up, he was sure of it. And at his place, they would have had time together to unravel the knots of their ill-spent lives.

But instead he had to go. She'd been insistent. Out through the back door. Off into the dark like a timid dog. And without his bike.

He had thought about nothing else since. Not for a second.

Now three days had passed. It was Tuesday, and he had been to the house several times since Saturday's unwelcome surprise. So what if he ran into Mia's husband? So what if things came to a head? He no longer feared other people, only himself. What he might do to the man, if it turned out he had harmed Mia.

But when he returned the first time, he found the house empty, likewise when he came again. And still he felt compelled to come back. A suspicion, rooted in instinct, grew inside him. The same instinct that had taken hold of him the time one of his comrades had pointed down an Afghan side street where ten local citizens were later killed. He had just known they should stay away from that street, the same way he knew this house contained secrets that would never see the light of day without his help.

He stood at her front door and called out her name. If the family had been going on holiday, she would have told him. If she no longer wanted him, her radiant eyes would have avoided his gaze.

She *did* want him, but now she was gone. Even his calls to her mobile remained unanswered. For some hours he had reasoned that she was too frightened to answer, because her husband was there. Then he convinced himself her husband had taken the phone away from her, and that he knew everything.

If he did, he was welcome to come and confront him, he told himself. It would not be an equal fight.

And then on Monday, for the first time, he began to think that the answer might lie elsewhere.

His attention had been caught by a sound. It was an unexpected sound, of the kind a soldier was trained to hear: faint sounds that could mean death in a second if overlooked.

It was such a sound he heard as he stood outside the house and called her mobile.

The mobile that chimed so faintly inside the walls.

And then he'd snapped shut his own phone and listened. Nothing.

He had dialed Mia's number one more time and waited for a moment. There it was again. Her mobile was somewhere upstairs behind the closed, slanting window in the roof, responding to his call.

He'd stood there for a second, considering what to do.

She could have left it behind on purpose, but it was unlikely.

She called it her lifeline, and no one would give up a lifeline just like that.

That was something he knew.

He had come one more time since then and heard the mobile chime again inside the upstairs room above the front door. Nothing had changed. Why did he have this enduring suspicion that something was wrong?

Was it the hound in him, sniffing danger in the air? Was it the soldier? Or was it being in love that made him blind to the possibility that he had already become a parenthesis in her life?

And for all the questions, all the possible answers, this nagging suspicion remained.

Behind the curtains of the house across the way, an elderly couple sat watching him. As soon as he called out Mia's name they were there. Perhaps he should ask them if they had noticed anything untoward.

It took them a while to open the door, and they were hardly accommodating when they did.

Why couldn't he leave their nice neighbors alone, the woman asked.

He forced a smile and showed them how his hands were shaking. Showed them how frightened he was and how much he needed their help.

Reluctantly, they told him the husband had been home several times during the last couple of days. His Mercedes had been in the drive, but they had not seen his wife or their child for some time.

He thanked them and asked if they would be kind enough to keep an eye out, then gave them his phone number.

When they shut the door again, he knew they would not call. Mia wasn't his wife. That was the fact of the matter.

He called her number one last time, and one last time he heard her mobile chime inside the room upstairs.

Mia, where are you? he thought to himself with increasing anxiety.

Starting tomorrow, he would come back to the house at regular intervals during the daytime.

If he saw nothing to put his mind at rest, he would go to the police.

Not because there was anything tangible to go on.

But what else could he do?

35

A buoyant step. A face with manly furrows in all the right places. Obviously expensive clothes.

A superior combination of just about everything that could make Carl feel like something the cat dragged in.

"This is Kris," she said by way of introduction, responding only fleetingly to Carl's welcoming hug.

"Kris and I were together in Darfur. Kris specializes in war trauma and works more or less permanently for Médecins Sans Frontières. Isn't that right, Kris?"

She said *were* together in Darfur. As opposed to *worked* together in Darfur. You didn't have to be a psychologist to work that one out. He hated the poncey twat already.

"I'm fairly familiar with the details," said Kris, revealing a row of implausibly regular, implausibly white teeth. "Mona has confirmed with her superiors that she's allowed to put me in the picture."

Confirmed with her superiors. Bollocks, Carl thought to himself, and wondered why no one had confirmed with him.

"I take it we have your consent?"

A bit late in the day, wasn't it? He gave Mona a look, and she returned his gaze with the sweetest, most underplayed of smiles. Fucking hell.

"Of course," he answered. "Mona has my fullest confidence."

He smiled back at the guy, and Mona noticed. Nice timing.

"I've been allotted thirty hours to see if we can get you up and running again. I understand from your boss that you're quite indispensable." He let out a slight chuckle. Most likely it meant they were paying him more than he was worth.

"Did I hear you say thirty hours?" Was he supposed to keep this puffed-up windbag company for thirty hours? They were having him on, surely?

"Well, let's assess the extent of the damage first. But thirty hours tends to be more than sufficient in most cases."

"You don't say!" In this case, they might be in for a surprise.

They sat down in front of him. Mona smiling that smile of hers.

"When you think about Anker Høyer, Hardy Henningsen, and yourself in that allotment house out in Amager where you were shot, what's the first feeling you get?" the man asked.

Carl felt an icy shiver go down his spine. What was the first feeling he got?

Trance. Slow motion. Arms that were turned to stone.

"That it was a long time ago," he said.

The ridiculously named Kris nodded, demonstrating exactly how he had acquired his laughter lines. "Got your guard up, eh, Carl? But I've been warned, you see. Just testing."

Had he come here for a boxing match? It was an interesting prospect.

"Did you know that Hardy Henningsen's wife has applied for a legal separation?"

"No. Hardy never said a word."

"As I understand it, she has a certain weakness for you. But you rejected her advances. You paid her a visit to offer your support, I think she said. That tells me something about you, something that goes beyond the hard-boiled exterior. What would you say to that?"

Carl frowned. "What the hell's Minna Henningsen got to do with this? Have you been talking to people behind my back? If you have, then I'm not fucking happy about it, all right?"

The guy turned to Mona. "There you are, you see. Exactly as I predicted." They beamed at each other.

One more word out of place, and this twerp was going to get his tongue twisted around his throat. It would look nice alongside the gold chain dangling against his chest.

"And now you'd like to hit me, isn't that right, Carl? Work me over, punch my lights out. I can tell." He looked Carl straight in the eye, so the blue of his irises almost engulfed him.

And then he changed. Now he was serious. "Just calm down, Carl. I'm actually on your side, and you're feeling fucked, I know you are." He put up his hand to stop the protest. "No need to be on edge. And if what you're wondering right now is who in this room I'd most like to climb into bed with, the answer is you."

Carl's jaw dropped.

The guy had told him not to be on edge. It was a relief, of course, to know which side of the road he was on, but that alone didn't make everything all right.

They said their good-byes after agreeing how things would proceed from here. Mona nuzzled her head against his shoulder so that he nearly felt his legs give way underneath him.

"See you tonight at mine, OK? How about ten o'clock? Can you get away, or do you have to look after your boys at home?" she whispered in his ear.

In his mind's eye Carl weighed the image of Mona's naked body against that of Jesper's stroppy face.

Decisions, decisions.

"Yes, I thought we'd probably find people working down here," said the worm from Health and Safety, extending a clerkish, undersized hand. "John Studsgaard, Working Environment Authority."

Did the man think he was senile or something? It was only a week since he had been here last.

"Carl Mørck," he replied. "Detective Inspector, Department Q. To what do we owe the pleasure?"

"Well, for one thing, there's the asbestos problem along there." He pointed down the corridor toward the makeshift partition wall. "And for another, the spaces here in the basement haven't been approved as working areas for Police Headquarters staff, and yet here you are again."

"Listen, Studsgaard, let me be frank with you. Since you were here last, ten shooting incidents have occurred in this city. Two people have died as a result. The hash market has gone ballistic. The justice minister has ordered two hundred nonexistent police officers onto the streets. Two thousand jobs have gone down the drain, the government's tax reform has shafted the most economically vulnerable of this country's inhabitants, schoolteachers are getting their heads kicked in by the kids they're supposed to be teaching, young lads are getting blown up in Afghanistan, people's homes are being repossessed, pensions are worth fuck all anymore, and banks are collapsing all around us, unless they're busy screwing their customers for every penny. And in the midst of all this mayhem, our prime minister's running around trying to find himself a better job on the taxpayers' money. How, then, in fuck's name, can you be bothered about whether I'm sitting here or two hundred meters away in another basement room where everything imaginable is allowed? Is it not . . ." and at this point he inhaled deeply ". . . COMPLETELY FUCKING IMMATERIAL where I happen to sit, as long as I'm doing my job?"

Studsgaard had stood impassively listening to this bombast. When it was over, he reached into his briefcase and pulled out a sheet of paper. "May I sit down?" he asked, pointing to a chair on the other side of the desk. "Naturally, I shall have to make a report," he said drily. "It may well be that the rest of the country has gone off the rails, but fortunately some of us keep on going."

Carl sighed heavily. The man had a point.

"OK, Studsgaard. I'm sorry for shouting at you like that. Too much on my plate. You're right, of course."

The bureaucrat lifted his head.

"I'd very much like to cooperate with you. Perhaps you could tell me what we need to do to get this place approved?"

Studsgaard put down his pen. Now he'd probably be given a lecture, Carl thought, about how unfeasible it was and how much hospital capacity was taken up due to the effects of poor working environment.

"It's very simple. You ask your superior to put in an application. Then someone else will come, make an inspection, and issue instructions."

Carl thrust his head forward in astonishment.

"And would you be able to assist with that application?" Carl inquired, more humbly than he had intended.

"Well, let's see what else I have in my briefcase, shall we?" Studsgaard smiled and handed him a form.

"How did you get on with Health and Safety?" Assad asked.

Carl shrugged. "I gave the bloke a dressing down, then he went tame on me."

He could see that dressing down was an expression that failed to click with Assad. What did dressing gowns have to do with it, he was probably thinking.

"What about you, Assad. Any headway?"

He nodded. "Yrsa gave me a name who I then called. A man who used to belong to the House of Christ. Are you familiar with the House of Christ, Carl?"

Carl shook his head. Not exactly, no.

"They are very strange, I think. They believe that Jesus will come back to Earth in a spaceship with beings from other worlds that we humans are supposed to re-create with."

"Procreate. I think you mean procreate, Assad."

Assad shrugged. "This man said that many people had left the Church of their own accord this last year. There was a lot of fuss about it. No one he knew personally had been kicked out, but then he said he had heard of a couple who were still members and whose child had been expelled. He thought maybe it was five or six years ago."

"And what's so special about that information?"

"The boy was only fourteen years old."

Carl pictured his stepson, Jesper. He'd been headstrong at that age.

"OK, that's probably unusual. But I can tell you've got more you want to share with me, Assad."

"I don't know, Carl. This is just a gut feeling." He patted his paunch. "Did you know that ostracism is very uncommon in religious sects in Denmark, apart from Jehovah's Witnesses?"

Carl shrugged. Ostracized or merely shunned, what difference did it make? He knew quite a few people where he came from who were anything but welcome in their own evangelical homes. So what was Assad getting at?

"But it happens, one way or another," he said. "Officially or otherwise."

"Yes, unofficially." Assad raised an index finger into the air. "The House of Christ is very fanatical and threatens people with all sorts of things, but they never expel anyone officially. This is what I was told."

"And?"

"In this case it was the mother and father themselves who ostracized the child. The parents were criticized for it by the congregation, but they didn't care."

Their eyes met. Carl had his own gut feeling now.

"Did you get an address for these people, Assad?"

"I was given an old address where they no longer live. Lis is looking into it now."

At a quarter to two, Carl received a call from the duty desk. The Holbæk Police had brought in a man he wanted for questioning, and what were they supposed to do with him? It was Poul Holt's father.

"Send him downstairs to me, only make sure he doesn't do a bunk."

Five minutes later, two slightly bewildered young officers were standing in the corridor with the man in front of them.

"No easy job, finding this place," one of them said in a dialect that had West Jutland written all over it in capital letters.

Carl nodded to them both and waved Martin Holt in. "Please take a seat," he said.

He turned to the two young officers. "My assistant's office is just across the corridor there. He'll be happy to make you a cup of tea, though I wouldn't recommend his coffee. I'm assuming you'll be waiting here until we're finished. You can take Mr. Holt back with you once we're done."

Neither the prospect of tea nor of hanging around seemed to fill them with enthusiasm, he noted with Jutlandish understatement.

Martin Holt was not like he had been at his front door in Hallabro. There he had been obstinate, now he was different, rattled even.

"How did you know I was in Denmark?" was the first thing he said. "Am I under surveillance?"

"Mr. Holt, I can only imagine what you and your family have been through these last thirteen years. I'd like you to know that you, your wife, and your children have the full sympathy of all of us in this department. I don't wish to make this hard for you, because you have suffered enough as it is. However, it's important for you to know that we will spare no effort in our attempts to apprehend the man who killed Poul."

"Poul isn't dead. He's in America somewhere."

If this man had known how obvious it was that he was lying, he would undoubtedly have remained silent. The clenched hands, the head thrust backward, the pause just before he said *America*. That, and four or five other things of the kind Carl had learned to notice after years of experience with that segment of the population for whom telling the truth was not a natural choice.

"Has it ever crossed your mind that there might be others in the same situation as you?" Carl inquired. "That Poul's killer may still be at large? That he may have other murders on his conscience, before and after Poul's?"

"I told you. Poul is in America. If I had any contact with him, I would tell you where. Can I go now?"

"Listen to me, Martin. Let's forget all about the outside world for a moment, shall we? I know you people have your dogmas, your rules, and I'm perfectly aware that if you could get me off your back once and for all, you would. Am I right?"

"I'd like you to call those officers back now. This is all a misunderstanding. As indeed I tried to make you aware when we spoke in Hallabro."

Carl nodded. The man was still scared. Thirteen years of fear had hardened him against anything that threatened to burst the bubble with which he had surrounded himself and his family.

"We have spoken to Tryggve," Carl said, pushing the Swedish police artist's drawing across the desk. "As you can see, we already have a likeness of the perpetrator. For the purpose of our inquiries, I want you to give us your version of what happened. It might give us something more to go on. We realize that you feel threatened by this man." He planted his finger so demonstratively on the drawing that Martin Holt jumped.

"You have my assurance that no unauthorized person knows that we're on to him, so try to relax."

The man removed his gaze reluctantly from the drawing in front of him and looked Carl straight in the eye. His voice trembled as he spoke. "How easy do you think it will be for me to explain to the Jehovah's Witness circuit overseers why I was taken in by the police? And you're telling me no one else knows there's something afoot? You've hardly been discreet about it."

"All this could have been avoided if only you had let me into your home in Sweden. That trip was part of an effort to catch Poul's murderer."

Martin Holt's shoulders dropped. His eyes returned to the drawing on the desk. "It's a good likeness," he said. "But his eyes weren't so close together, and not quite as dark. That's all I can tell you."

Carl stood up. "I'm going to show you something you've never seen until now." He gestured for Martin Holt to follow him.

From Assad's office came the sound of laughter. The distinctive, booming laughter of West Jutland that most likely had evolved to drown out the engines of fishing boats in stormy weather. Assad certainly had the knack of entertaining. And with the young officers from Holbæk in his assistant's capable hands, Carl was in no hurry.

"Have a look at how many unsolved cases we've got here," he said, directing Martin Holt's gaze toward Assad's filing system on the wall. "Each of these cases involves some dreadful event, and in each case the grief that event has caused will hardly differ from your own."

He looked at the man next to him, whose eyes remained cold as ice. These cases were nothing to do with him, and the people involved in them were not his brethren. What happened outside the world of the Jehovah's Witnesses was seemingly of little concern to him.

"We could have picked out any one of these cases on which to focus our efforts. Do you understand? But we chose the one concerning your son. And now I'm going to show you why."

The man followed him the last few meters along the corridor. Like a dead man walking.

Then Carl pointed at Rose and Assad's blowup of the message in the bottle. "*That's* why," he said, and stepped back.

Martin Holt stood for a long time reading the message. So slowly did his eyes pass over the lines that Carl could follow how far he had read. And when he had finished, he started from the beginning again. He was a pillar, slowly crumbling. A human being for whom principles were more important than anything else. But also a man endeavoring to protect his remaining children by suppression and lies.

Now he stood here absorbing the words of his dead son. As halting as they were, they went straight into his heart. And suddenly he staggered backward, reaching his hands out behind him to support himself against the wall. Had it not been there, he would have fallen. Here were his son's pleas for help, as loud as the trumpets of Jericho. Help he had been unable to provide.

Carl allowed him to stand for a moment alone with his tears. Then Martin Holt stepped forward and placed a cautious hand against his son's letter. His hands trembled upon this contact, and gradually, slowly, his fingers traced backward from word to word, as high up the wall as he could reach.

Finally, his head dropped to one side. Thirteen years of pain released.

When they returned to Carl's office, he asked for a glass of water.

And then he told Carl everything he knew.

36

"The troops are gathered again," Yrsa hollered from the corridor, seconds before her head appeared around Carl's door. Judging from the state of her hair, she must have passed through the basement like a whirlwind.

"Tell me you love me," she twittered, dropping a stack of aerial photos onto the desk in front of Carl.

"Did you find the house, Yrsa?" Assad shouted back, dashing in from his cubbyhole.

"No such luck. But I did find some possibilities, though none with any boathouse visible. The photos are in the order that I'd check them out if I were you. I've put rings around the houses I think are interesting."

Carl picked up the stack and counted. Fifteen sheets and no boathouse. What the hell was she playing at?

He glanced at the dates. Most of the photos were from June 2005.

"Hey!" he exclaimed. "These were taken nine years after Poul Holt was murdered, Yrsa. That boathouse could have been pulled down and rebuilt a dozen times since then."

"A dozen times?" Assad intervened. "No, I do not think that can be correct, Carl."

"It's a figure of speech, Assad." Carl took a deep breath. "Haven't we got anything older than this?"

Yrsa winked at him. Was he putting her on?

"Do you know what, Mr. Detective?" she said. "If that boathouse was pulled down, it's hardly going to matter much now, is it?"

Carl shook his head. "Wrong, Yrsa. The killer may still own the house, in which case we might find him there, no? Get back upstairs to Lis and find some older photos."

"The same fifteen areas?" She indicated the stack on his desk.

"No, Yrsa. For the entire shoreline of the fjords prior to 1996. That can't be so hard to understand, surely?"

She stood and tugged for a moment at her curls, somewhat deflated, then turned and slunk off as best she could in her less-than-sensible shoes.

"I think it will be no easy task to make her glad again," Assad commented, fanning his hand in the air as if he had just burned his fingers. "Did you observe how annoyed she was with herself, because she did not think about the detail of the date?"

Carl heard a buzzing sound and saw the fly land on the ceiling. Back with bragging rights.

"Never mind, Assad. She'll get over it."

Assad shook his head. "Yes, Carl. But remember, no matter how hard you sit down on the fencepost, your arse will hurt when you stand up."

Carl frowned, wondering if he had understood him right.

"Do all your sayings involve arseholes, Assad?" he replied, dodging the issue.

Assad chuckled. "I know one or two without," he said. "But they are poor."

OK. If this was par for the course with Syrian humor, his laughter muscles could take things easy if he were ever so unfortunate as to get an invite to visit the place.

"What did Martin Holt tell you when you questioned him, Carl?"

Carl picked up his notepad. Not that he had written much down, but what he had noted certainly seemed useful.

"Contrary to what I expected, Martin Holt is not an entirely unlikable man," Carl said. "Your blowup out in the corridor put his feet back on the ground."

"So he told you about Poul?"

"He did. He spoke nonstop for half an hour. In a very shaky voice." Carl plucked a smoke from his breast pocket and turned it between his fingers. "Getting things off his chest, you could say. He hasn't spoken to anyone about his son for years. The pain of it was too much for him."

"What does it say on your notepad, Carl?"

Carl lit his cigarette, sparing a thought for Jacobsen's unsatisfied nicotine cravings. Sometimes a person could rise so far that he was no longer his own boss. It was a place Carl had no intention of going.

"Martin Holt said our drawing was a good likeness, but the kidnapper's eyes were too dark and too close together. The mustache was too big and the hair probably a bit longer over the ears."

"Should we have a new one done, Carl?" Assad asked, wafting away the smoke in front of him.

Carl shook his head. Tryggve's take could be just as good as his father's. The human eye interpreted differently depending on the beholder.

"The most important thing, though, was that Martin Holt could tell me exactly how and where the kidnapper took receipt of his ransom. A bag containing the money was simply thrown off a train. The man had a strobe light, and—"

"What is a strobe light?"

"A strobe light?" Carl took a good drag. "It's a kind of light they use in discos. They flash like a camera."

"Oh!" Assad beamed. "It makes people look like they are jumping, like in the old films. I know this very well."

Carl pondered his cigarette. Did it taste of syrup, or what?

"Holt was able to give us a fairly exact location for where the delivery took place," he said. "A stretch of road running alongside the railway between Sorø and Slagelse." Carl got out his map and pointed. "Here, between Vedbysønder and Lindebjerg."

"It looks like a good place," Assad commented. "Close to the railway and not so far from the motorway, allowing him to get away again quickly."

Carl traced the railway on the map. Assad was right. It was a perfect spot.

"How did the kidnapper get Poul's father to that place?" Assad asked.

Carl studied his cigarette packet. How the fuck did that syrup taste get there?

"He was instructed to get on a certain train from Copenhagen to Korsør, and then to keep an eye out for the strobe. He was to sit in a first-class compartment on the left-hand side of the train, and as soon as he saw the light he was to throw the bag with the money out of the window."

"When did he then find out that Poul was murdered?"

"When? He received further instructions over the phone as to where he could pick up the children. But when he and his wife arrived, they found only Tryggve lying in a field. He'd been given something to knock him out, probably chloroform. Tryggve was the one who told his parents that Poul had been murdered, and that they would lose more children if anything should get out about the kidnapping. Apart from the terrible news of Poul's death, Tryggve's shock over what had happened made an indelible impression on Martin Holt and his wife."

Assad drew his shoulders up to his ears as a shiver seemingly ran down his spine. "If it had been my children, then . . ." He passed his index finger across his throat and let his head flop to one side.

Carl didn't doubt his assistant meant what he said. He consulted his notepad again. "At the end of our interview, Martin Holt told me one final thing that may prove useful to us."

"What was that, Carl?"

"The key ring on which the kidnapper kept his car keys also had a miniature bowling ball with the number one on it."

The phone on Carl's desk rang. Probably Mona wanting to thank him for being so accommodating.

"Mørck?" boomed a voice at the other end, which turned out to belong to Klaes Thomasen. "Just to inform you that we took advantage of the good weather early this morning, and the wife and I have now sailed through the rest of the area we picked out. As far as we can see, there's nothing visible from the water, but there are several places in which the vegetation is very thick and runs right down to the shore, so we've marked them down for you."

Once again, a bit of plain old-fashioned good luck wouldn't have gone amiss.

"What area did you reckon might be the most promising?" Carl asked, stubbing out his syrupy smoke in the ashtray.

"Well . . ." Carl could almost see Thomasen with his pipe in his mouth. Probably still in his sailing togs on the jetty. "I'd say we should be focusing on Østskov near Sønderby, as well as Bognæs and Nordskoven. There were quite a few secluded spots, but like I said we couldn't see anything for sure. I'll have a word with the forest officer from Nordskoven later on today. Maybe he can help us out."

Carl made a note of the three locations and said thanks. He promised to say hello to some of Thomasen's old mates on the force. It had been years since any of them had worked at HQ, but Carl spared him that information for the sake of politeness, then hung up.

"Nothing," Carl said, as he turned toward Assad. "Nothing concrete to go on from Thomasen, though he did mention a couple of areas we might want to take a closer look at." He found them on the map. "Let's see if Yrsa can come up with something a bit better than before, then we can compare the data. In the meantime, just carry on with what you're doing."

He managed to get in half an hour's wholesome shut-eye with his feet up on the desk before a tickling sensation on the bridge of his nose dragged him back to consciousness. He shook his head vigorously, opened his eyes, and found himself to be the focus of a horde of shiny, blue-green flies in avid search of somewhere else to lay their eggs besides the gooey substance he found stuck to his cigarette packet.

"Bastards!" he spluttered, flailing his arms in the air and sending at least a couple of the pesky things hurtling backward onto the floor with all legs splayed.

This was the last straw.

He peered into his wastebasket. It had been weeks since he had thrown anything out, and there was his rubbish still, though organic matter of the kind that might tempt procreating flies was wholly absent.

Carl glanced out into the corridor. There was another one of the bastards. He found himself wondering whether one of Assad's exotic lunchtime treats had come back from the dead. Maybe his tahini had come alive, or perhaps his sickening Turkish delight was about to hatch out some imported pests?

"Do you know anything about these flies?" he demanded, even before walking into Assad's matchbox office.

There was a penetrating smell inside the room. Not the usual sugary scent. More like someone had been playing with a Zippo lighter.

Assad held him off for a moment with a hand in the air, absorbed in a phone call. "Yes," he repeated a few times into the receiver. "But we shall need to come and see for ourselves," he said eventually, his voice slightly deeper, his countenance slightly more authoritative than normal. He made an appointment and put down the phone.

"I asked if you knew anything about these flies," Carl said again, pointing to a couple that had settled on a kitschy poster depicting some camels traipsing through a large amount of sand.

"Carl, I think we have found a family now," Assad said, though with a rather skeptical look on his face. Like a man who had just studied his lottery ticket and discovered all the numbers fit the jackpot.

"A what?"

"A family who has been in the hands of our kidnapper. I think so."

"Would that be the people from the House of Christ, the ones you told us about before?"

Assad nodded. "Lis found them. New address and new names, but the same people. She checked with the Civil Registration System. Four children. The youngest, Flemming, was fourteen years old five years ago."

"Did you ask where the boy is today?"

"No, I did not think that to be so clever at this point."

"What was the bit about our having to come and see for ourselves?"

"Oh, I told the wife that we were from the tax authorities, and we found it odd that their youngest son, the only one of their children who seems not to have emigrated, did not send in his tax returns, despite him being over eighteen now."

"Assad, that's not right. We can't go around passing ourselves off as civil servants from other authorities. Anyway, how did you find out about him not submitting tax returns?"

"I didn't find out. I just made that up." He dabbed at his nose with a handkerchief.

Carl shook his head. All the same, Assad was definitely on to something. If people hadn't actually committed a crime, there was nothing like the taxman to put the wind up them.

"When's our appointment, and where?"

"A small place called Tølløse. The wife said her husband would be home at half past four."

Carl glanced at his watch. "OK, we'll go together. Nice work, Assad, very nice indeed."

Carl flashed him a smile that lasted a millisecond, then pointed at the fly convention gathering on Assad's poster. "Come on, Assad. Are you keeping something in here that might have caused these little bastards to start calling this place home?"

Assad threw up his arms. "I do not know where they are coming from." His face froze for a moment. "But I do know where that one is coming from," he added, pointing to a singular insect of smaller proportions than the flies. A frail, foolhardy creature that ended its days suddenly and at that very instant between the palms of Assad's brawny brown hands.

"Gotcha!" Assad exclaimed in triumph, wiping the remains of the little moth onto his notepad. "I have discovered many of these ones just there." He indicated his prayer mat, only to see with horror its death sentence pop up in Carl's eyes.

"But Carl, now there are not so many of these insects left in the prayer mat. This is a mat that belonged to my father, and I am so very attached to it. I beat it only this morning before you arrived. Behind the door by the asbestos."

Carl lifted a corner of the mat. Assad's rescue attempt was obviously a last-ditch effort. There was hardly anything left but the fringes.

For a brief moment, Carl pictured the police archives in asbestosland and wondered whether the reputations of one or two offenders might now be saved should these ravenous moths take a liking to yellowed parchment.

"Have you sprayed it with something?" he asked. "It stinks to high heaven in here."

Assad smiled. "Petroleum does the trick."

Apparently, the smell didn't bother him. Perhaps it was one of the incidental advantages of having grown up in a place where crude oil was bubbling out of the ground. If they actually had any oil in Syria.

Carl shook his head and fled the fumes. Tølløse in two hours. Still time to get to the bottom of that fly business.

He stood quite still for a moment in the corridor. A gentle hum seemed to emanate from somewhere above the pipes on the ceiling. He looked up and again caught a glimpse of his alpha fly, spotted with correction fluid. The bloody thing was everywhere.

"What are you doing, Carl?" Yrsa's voice rasped behind him. "Come with me a minute, will you?" she said, tugging at his sleeve.

The surface of her desk was hidden beneath a deluge of nail polish, cuticle remover, hairspray, and a lot more little bottles of the same kind containing strong solvents. All of which she now swept aside to make room.

"Have a look at this," she said. "These are your aerial photos, right? And I'm telling you now, it was all a waste of time." She raised her eyebrows, looking remarkably like his miserable aunt Adda. "Same thing all the way along the shoreline. Nothing new at all."

Carl's attention was diverted by a fly buzzing in through the open door to do a few laps beneath the ceiling.

"Same with the wind turbines." She pushed aside a coffee cup with crusty rings on the inside. "If you're saying low-frequency sound waves can be heard within a twenty-kilometer radius, then this is no use to us at all." She indicated a series of crosses on the map.

He knew what she was getting at. This was wind-turbine territory, and there were far too many of them to help narrow down the search.

A fly passed quickly before his eyes and settled on the edge of Yrsa's coffee cup. The same little bastard that had gone off with his correction fluid. It certainly got around.

"Shoo," said Yrsa. And casual as anything, she flicked the insect into her coffee with a long, bloodred nail. "Lis has been in touch with the local authorities," she went on as if nothing had happened, "and no one has given planning permission for any boathouse in the areas we're focusing on. Preservation orders, that sort of thing, you know?"

"How far back did she go?" Carl asked as he watched the fly doing the backstroke in caffeine purgatory. Yrsa could be amazingly efficient. There he was, getting more and more flustered, and all she did was . . .

"Back to the local authority reform in 1970."

1970! But that was eons ago. He could forget all about running around trying to find cedar suppliers, that was for sure.

Not without sadness, he observed the final death throes of the correction-fluid fly, and found closure.

Yrsa slapped her hand hard against one of the aerial photos on the desk. "If you ask me, this is where we should be looking!"

Carl looked down at the circle she had drawn around a house at Nordskoven. Vibegården, the place was called apparently. A nice little cottage, so it seemed, not far from the road leading through the woods, but no boathouse as far as he could tell. The location, though, was certainly perfect, tucked away among the trees and right at the shoreline of the fjord. But still, there was no boathouse.

"I know what you're thinking, but it could definitely be there," she said and tapped her finger insistently on the green area at the extremity of the property.

"What the blazes . . . ?" Carl spluttered. They were surrounded by flies. Yrsa must have disturbed them with all her tapping and slapping.

He thumped his fist hard against the desk, and the air around them came alive.

"Hey, what do you think you're doing?" Yrsa protested with annoyance, splatting a couple of flies on her mouse mat.

Carl bent down and peered underneath the desk. Seldom had he seen so much teeming life in such a small area. If these flies had decided on it, they could almost have lifted the wastebasket in which they were hatching.

"What the hell have you been putting in your bin?" he inquired, shocked.

"Nothing, I never use it. It must be something of Rose's."

Right, he thought. At least now he knew which of them *didn't* do the tidying up at home, if indeed either of them ever did.

He studied Yrsa, who now sat with a concentrated look on her face, squashing flies left, right, and center with the palms of her hands and with remarkable precision. Assad would have his work cut out cleaning this place up afterward.

Two minutes later, he was there, with his green rubber gloves on and a big, black bin liner in his hand to which the flies and other contents of the wastebasket were to be consigned.

"Disgusting!" exclaimed Yrsa, staring at the splatter of squashed flies on her hands. Carl was inclined to agree.

She pulled one of her bottles of cellulose thinner toward her, soaked a cotton wool ball in the stuff, and began to disinfect her hands. Instantly, the place smelled like a ship-varnish factory after a prolonged mortar attack. He only hoped this wasn't the day Health and Safety were thinking of paying them a visit.

It was then he noticed how the red nail polish on the index and middle fingers of Yrsa's right hand began to dissolve, and more specifically, what was revealed underneath.

He sat for a moment, mouth agape; then, as Assad emerged from the den of flies below the desk, he caught his gaze.

Now they both had eyes as big as saucers.

"Come with me," he said, pulling Assad out into the corridor as his assistant tied a secure knot in the bin liner.

"You noticed too, didn't you?"

Assad nodded, his mouth twisted up as if he were suffering from acute bowel trouble.

"Her nails were speckled with black felt marker underneath the red. Rose's felt marker from the other day. Did you see that?"

Assad nodded again.

How on earth had they missed it?

Unless some worldwide craze for flecking one's fingernails with black felt pen was sweeping the country, there was no doubt about it.

Yrsa and Rose were one and the same person.

37

"Look what I've got here for you lot," said Lis, handing Carl an enormous bunch of roses wrapped in cellophane.

Carl put down the phone. What the hell was this all about?

"Are you proposing to me, Lis? It's about time you began to appreciate my qualities."

She rolled her eyes at him. "They were sent to Department A, but Marcus thought you should have them."

Carl frowned. "What for?"

"Oh, come off it, Carl. You know what for."

He gave a shrug and shook his head.

"They found the last little finger bone with a groove in it. They went over the site of the blaze again and there it was in a pile of ashes."

"So we get roses?" Carl scratched his neck. Maybe they'd been found in the ashes, too?

"No, that's not the reason. Marcus'll tell you all about it. The flowers are from Torben Christensen, the investigator from the insurance company. Our work on the arson cases saved them a pile of money today."

She pinched his cheek like an aunt not knowing any more appropriate form of appreciation and waltzed back to where she'd come from.

Carl leaned sideways for a glimpse of her gorgeous backside.

"What is going on?" Assad inquired from the corridor. "We must leave in only a moment."

Carl nodded and dialed the number of the homicide chief.

"I'm to ask from Assad how come we get roses?" he said, straight to the point, when Jacobsen answered.

There was a brief noise that might have been mistaken for an expression of glee. "Carl, we've interviewed the three owners of the firms that burned down, and we're now in possession of three magnificent statements. You and your team were absolutely right. They were pressured into taking out high-interest loans and then, when they were unable to make the payments, the debt collectors turned nasty and demanded the entire sum. Intimidation, threats over the phone. Serious threats. The collectors became increasingly desperate, but what good was it going to do? There's nowhere else for firms with liquidity problems to go these days to borrow money."

"So what happened to the debt collectors?"

"We don't know for sure, but our theory is they were simply bumped off on orders from higher up. The Serbian police have seen it all before. Big bonuses for those who collect and deliver on time, and good night to those who can't."

"Surely they could just have burned the places down, without having to kill their own men?"

"Well, another angle is that they send their less successful collectors to Scandinavia, since the market here is supposed to be easier to handle. Then when that turns out not to be the case, they make an example of them and grab some attention in Belgrade. There's no bigger liability for a loan shark than a bad debt collector or someone who can't be managed or trusted. A few killings here and there can work wonders for discipline."

"Hmm. So they do away with their inefficient workers in Denmark. And if the perpetrators get caught, then at least they'll be tried in a country with lenient sentencing. Is that it?"

He could almost see Jacobsen's thumbs-up at the other end.

"Anyway, Carl," said the chief, "what we've achieved today ensures that the insurance companies won't have to make the full payout. We're talking about some considerable amounts of money here, hence the roses. And who deserves them more than Department Q?"

This was probably not an easy admission.

"OK, so now you've got some hands idle," said Carl. "Send them down here. I could use them."

Something like a chuckle came from the other end. So Jacobsen had other plans. "Nice try, Carl. We've still a lot more work to do on it. Now we need to find those responsible. But I see your point. There's the gang conflict still going on, so perhaps we should be diverting resources in that direction."

Assad appeared in the doorway as Carl put down the phone. For once, he looked like he was beginning to anticipate the Danish climate. His down jacket was the thickest garment Carl had ever seen worn in March.

"I'm ready now," said his assistant.

"Be with you in a sec," Carl replied, dialing Brandur Isaksen's number. Halmtorvet's Icicle, they called him, with reference to his extraordinarily thinly apportioned charm. Isaksen was the man in the know at Station City, the police station at which Rose had been employed before she was sent to Department Q.

"Yes?" Isaksen said curtly when he answered the call.

Carl explained his business, and before he had even finished, the man at the other end was in hysterics.

"Rose? Priceless, she was. Not that I'd want to hazard a guess at what's wrong with her. She was just odd, that's all. Too much boozing, jumping into bed with all the young cadets from the police college. A wildcat with an insatiable appetite, do you know what I'm saying? Anyway, why do you want to know?"

"No reason," said Carl, and hung up. Then he logged on to the Civil Registration System and typed an address into the search field: Sandalparken 19.

The result was unequivocal. *Rose Marie Yrsa Knudsen,* it read, along with a civil registration number.

Carl shook his head. All they needed now was for bloody Marie to turn up and they'd have the full house. Two versions of Rose was plenty to be getting on with.

"I can hardly believe this, Carl," Assad said, peering over his shoulder.

"Get her in here, would you, Assad?"

"You will not confront her straight in her face, will you, Carl?"

"What? You must be joking. I'd rather climb into a bathtub with a bagful of cobras," Carl replied. If they let on now that they knew Yrsa was Rose, there was no telling what might happen.

When Assad returned with Yrsa, she was already wrapped up in coat, mittens, scarf, and woolen hat. Standing before him now were two individuals who could each make a valiant challenge to the burka-clad in a competition to conceal the human body.

Carl glanced at the clock. End of the day. Yrsa was on her way home.

"You wouldn't believe . . . !" She stopped abruptly on seeing the flowers Carl was holding out in front of him. "Where did you get them from? They're lovely, they are!"

"They're for Rose, from Assad and me," Carl said, thrusting the whole bunch into her hands. "Tell her to get well, and that we hope she'll soon be back. Say they're roses for a rose. We've really thought about her a lot."

Yrsa stiffened and stood quite still for a moment, seeming almost humble, though she was probably just overwhelmed.

And then they shut up shop for the day.

"Is she really ill then, Carl?" Assad asked as the traffic piled up on the Holbæk motorway.

Carl gave a shrug. He had seen a lot of things in his time, but the only case of dissociative identity disorder he knew about was the ten-second transformation of his own stepson from an amiable young lad short of a hundred kroner into a stroppy teenager who refused to tidy up his room.

"We'll keep this to ourselves, Assad," was all he said.

They sat in silence for the rest of the way, immersed in their own thoughts, until the sign for Tølløse appeared. A place best known for its railway station, a cider factory, and the pro cyclist who was kicked out of the Tour de France while wearing the yellow jersey.

"Just a little way along here," said Assad, pointing down the main street, the absolute center of Tølløse and the vital artery of any small provincial town. Only here the blood seemed to have stopped pumping. Maybe the town's inhabitants were clogged up in the bottleneck of Netto's checkout line, or maybe they had all just moved away. At any rate, the place had seen livelier times.

"Opposite the factory site there," said Assad, pointing to a redbrick house that exuded about as much life as an earthworm suicide in a winter field.

A diminutive woman with eyes even bigger than Assad's opened the door. The instant she saw Assad's stubbly face, she jumped back into the hall with a start and called for her husband to come. No doubt she had read tabloid stories about robberies in the home and thought she was about to become a victim.

"What do you want?" said the man. Clearly, no hospitality was in the offing. Not even ordinary politeness.

Carl reckoned his best bet was to pursue the taxman line and stuck his police ID back in his pocket.

"You have a son, Flemming Emil Madsen. According to our records, he hasn't been paying his taxes. He's not registered with the social authorities, or the educational authorities for that matter, so we thought it best to come and see him in person."

Assad intervened. "You are a greengrocer, Mr. Madsen. Does Flemming work for you?"

Carl understood the tactics. Get the man into a corner from the start.

"Muslim, are you?" the man answered. It was a surprising utterance, an excellent counter. For once, Assad looked stumped.

"I think that would be a personal matter for my colleague," said Carl.

"Not in my house, it wouldn't," the man replied and made to slam the door in their faces.

Carl produced his badge.

"Mr. el-Assad and I are trying to clear up a number of unsolved murders. If you so much as look at me sideways, I'm going to arrest you on the spot for the murder of your son Flemming five years ago. Are you following me?"

The man said nothing, though he was obviously shaken. Not the way a man unjustly accused would be, but like one who was as guilty as hell.

They stepped inside and were directed to sit at a brown mahogany table that would have been every family's dream fifty years ago. There was no cloth on it, but an abundance of place mats.

"We've done nothing wrong," said the wife, fingering the crucifix that dangled from her neck.

Carl glanced around. At least three dozen framed photos of children of all ages were dotted about the place on various items of oak furniture. Children and grandchildren. Smiling individuals with big skies above their heads.

"These are your children, I take it?" Carl asked.

They nodded.

"And all of them emigrated?"

They nodded again. Words were seldom used here, Carl thought to himself.

"To Australia?" Assad inquired.

"Are you a Muslim?" the man asked again. He was sticking to his guns. Bloody cheek. Was he afraid that the sight of someone who subscribed to another faith might turn him into stone, or what?

"I am what God made me," Assad answered him. "What about you? Would that be true for you, too?"

The man's eyes narrowed. Perhaps he was more used to that kind of conversation taking place on other people's doorsteps than inside his own home.

"I asked if your children had emigrated to Australia?" Assad repeated.

The wife nodded. So her head was screwed on, after all.

"Here," said Carl, and placed the police artist's drawing of the kidnapper on the table in front of them.

"In the name of Jesus," the wife breathed, making the sign of the cross on her chest. Her husband pursed his lips.

"We've never said a word to anyone," he said curtly.

Carl fixed his gaze on him. "If you think we're in cahoots with this man in any way, you're mistaken. But we're on to him. And you can help us catch him."

The wife let out a gasp.

"I apologize if you find us insensitive," said Carl. "We needed you to be honest with us as quickly as possible." He jabbed at the drawing. "Are you able to confirm that this was the man who kidnapped two of your children, and that he killed Flemming after receiving a large ransom?"

The man paled visibly. All the strength he had drawn on over the years to keep himself afloat now seeped out of him. The strength to resist grief, to lie to his fellow believers, and to make a new life away from everything he knew. The strength to isolate himself, to say good-bye to the remaining children, and to carry on after taking the financial knock. And not least, the strength to live with the knowledge that the man who had murdered their beloved son remained at large and was watching them.

He let go of it all, in a house in Tølløse.

They sat quietly in the car for a while before Carl spoke.

"I don't think I've ever seen anyone quite as depleted as those two," he said.

"It was very hard for them when they took out the photograph of Flemming from the drawer, I think. Do you really believe they had never looked at it since they lost him, Carl?" Assad asked, wriggling out of his down jacket, having finally realized it wasn't that cold.

Carl shrugged. "Hard to tell, really. They certainly haven't been willing to risk someone getting a whiff of how much they still loved the boy. Their story was that they kicked him out themselves."

"A whiff? I am not sure of the meaning of this, Carl."

"Get a whiff of something. Like a hunting dog getting a whiff of its prey."

"Prey?"

"Never mind, Assad. These people kept their love for their son secret. No one else was to know. They could never tell who was a friend and who might be an enemy."

Assad gazed for a moment out toward brown fields that would soon sprout with life. "How many times do you think he has done this, Carl?"

How the fuck was he supposed to answer that? There *was* no answer.

Assad scratched his dark cheeks. "We have to catch him now, Carl. Yes? We simply must."

Carl clenched his teeth. Yes, they had to catch him now. The Tølløse couple had given them a new name. Birger Sloth was what he had called himself then. The police artist's likeness had stood up for the third time. Martin Holt had been right. The eyes of the man they were looking for had been rather farther apart. Everything else—the mustache, the hair, the look in his eyes—were things they had to disregard. What they were looking for was a man whose features were sharp and yet somewhat indistinct at the same time. The only thing they could be a hundred percent certain about was that he had collected a ransom in the same place on two different occasions. A short stretch of railway between Sorø and Slagelse, and they already knew the spot. Martin Holt had described it in detail.

They could be there in twenty minutes, only now it was too dark. Bollocks.

It would be their first priority in the morning.

"What shall we do about our Yrsa and Rose?" Assad asked.

"Nothing. We'll just try to live with it, that's all."

Assad nodded. "Most probably she is a camel with three humps," he mused.

"A what?"

"This is what we say where I come from. Rather apart. Hard to ride, but funny to look at."

"A three-humped camel. You might be on to something there, Assad. It sounds a lot better than schizophrenic, anyway."

"Schizophrenic? Where I come from, this is what we say about the man who praises another while shitting on him with his arse."

There he went again.

38

It was all so fuzzy and far away. Like the end of a dream that never reached its conclusion. Like a mother's voice barely recalled. "Isabel. Isabel Jønsson, wake up!" The words echoed, as though her skull were too vast to keep them together.

She tried to move and felt nothing but the heaviness of sleep bearing down on her. The drowsy sense of floating between then and now.

Someone was trying to rouse her, pulling at her shoulder. Gently. Repeatedly.

"Are you there, Isabel?" a voice said. "Just breathe deeply."

She heard sounds of fingers snapping in front of her face but was unable to make sense of them.

"You've been in an accident, Isabel," someone said.

Somehow she knew that.

Hadn't it just happened? A tumbling sensation, and then the monster approaching in the dark. Had that just happened?

She felt a jab in her arm. Was it real, or was she dreaming?

There was a sudden feeling of blood rushing inside her head, her mind collecting itself, bringing order to chaos. It was order she didn't want.

And then it came back to her, albeit hazy. Him. The man.

She gasped and felt once again the prickling sensation in her throat, her need to cough making her feel like she would be suffocated.

"Just relax now, Isabel," said the voice. Someone squeezed her hand.

"We've given you something to wake you up a bit, that's all." Another squeeze.

Everything inside her said yes, squeeze back, Isabel. Show them you're alive. Show them you're still here.

"You've been badly injured, Isabel. You're in the Intensive Care Unit of the Rigshospital in Copenhagen. Do you understand what I'm saying?"

She breathed in and mustered all her strength to nod. The slightest of movements. Just so she could feel it herself.

"Well done, Isabel. We saw that." Another squeeze of the hand.

"We've put you in traction, so you won't be able to move if you try. You've got multiple fractures, Isabel, but you're going to be all right. We're run off our feet at the moment, but as soon as there's a gap, there'll be a nurse along to get you ready so you can be moved over to another department. Do you understand, Isabel?"

She tensed the muscles in her neck again.

"Good. We know it's hard for you to communicate, but after a while, you'll be able to speak again. You've broken your jaw, so we've immobilized it just to be on the safe side."

Now she felt the clamps at her skull. The heavy bags wedged against her hips, like she was buried in sand. She tried to open her eyes, but they would not obey.

"I can tell from your eyebrows that you're trying to open your eyes, Isabel, but you're all bandaged up, I'm afraid. There were glass splinters in your eyeballs, but you'll see the sun shine again in a couple of weeks, just you wait and see."

A couple of weeks! Why was that bad? Why the twinges of protest darting through her body at the thought? Was time that precious?

Come on, Isabel, a voice inside her whispered. *What is it that mustn't happen? What has happened already? The man, and what else?*

She found herself thinking that reality could be many things. The lover who never came but who lived on in her dreams. The ropes hanging from the ceiling of the old gym at school, never quite scaled. Reality was also the things that were waiting to happen. It was the same pressure against her temples. The sensation was just as tangible.

And she breathed slowly and took stock of all these impressions that together made up her consciousness. First came discomfort, then disquiet, and finally an upheaval, ushering faces and sounds and words into her scrambled chains of thought.

Again, she felt the reflexive gasp that accompanied sudden realization.

The children.

The man, their kidnapper.

And Rachel.

"Hmnnnnn," she heard herself groan through immobilized teeth.

"Yes, Isabel?"

She felt the hand let go and warm breath pass over her face.

"What is it you're trying to say?" said the voice, up close now.

"Aaaaeehhh."

"Does anyone understand what she might be saying?" the voice said, directed elsewhere.

"Aaaarglll."

"Are you inquiring after your friend, Isabel?"

She managed a short sound.

"Yes, that was what you were asking, wasn't it? How is the woman you were admitted with?"

She made the same sound.

"She's alive, Isabel! She's here next to you," said a new voice at the foot of the bed. "She's rather worse off than you, I'm afraid. Much worse. We don't know whether she'll pull through yet. But she's alive and her body seems to be strong, so we're hoping for the best."

It could have been an hour or a minute, or even a whole day since they had looked in on her last. Time was elastic. All around her was the hum of quiet machines and the faint beep indicating the beat of her own heart.

The sheets underneath her felt clammy, and the room was warm. Perhaps it was something they had injected her with that made her feel things this way. Or maybe it was just her.

Outside in the corridor, trolleys rattled, and there were voices, as if in accompaniment. Was it dinnertime? Was it night? She had no idea.

She groaned, but nothing happened. She focused on the interval between her heartbeats and the throbbing in her middle finger, to which some little gadget was attached. Seconds or milliseconds, she couldn't tell.

But one thing was clear to her. The heartbeat she heard measured out in electronic beeps beside her bed belonged to someone else. She was sufficiently conscious as to be in no doubt. It didn't fit her own.

She held her breath for a moment. There was the sound of the monitor. Beep, beep. And then another machine, a faint sucking noise, abruptly terminated and followed by what sounded like the hydraulic air release of a bus door opening.

It was a sound she had heard before, during endless hours at her mother's bedside, before they finally switched off the respirator and gave her peace.

The patient with whom she shared her room was unable to breathe without help. And that patient was Rachel. Wasn't that what they had said?

She wanted to turn onto her side. To open her eyes and cut through the darkness. To see the person who was struggling for life next to her.

She wanted to speak her name: Rachel. To tell her they would pull through, though she didn't really believe it.

Maybe there was nothing left for Rachel to wake up for. She remembered all too vividly now.

Her husband was dead.

Two children were out there somewhere. And the kidnapper no longer had any reason to keep them alive.

It was terrible, and she could do nothing.

She felt moisture well in her eyes. Thicker than tears and yet so liquid.

The bandage wrapped around her head suddenly felt tighter against her eyelids.

Am I crying blood? she wondered, trying not to succumb to the grief and impotence. What good would it do to sob? It would bring only pain that no medicine they could administer would soften.

She heard the door open quietly and felt the air from the corridor seep into the silent room, registered the sounds.

Footsteps on the hard floor. Measured. Too careful.

A concerned doctor, now studying Rachel's heart rhythms? A nurse wondering how long before the respirator would no longer be of use?

"Are you awake, Isabel?" a voice whispered amid the dogged pumping of machines.

It made her start. She didn't know why.

Then she nodded, imperceptibly. Apparently it was enough.

She felt the hand take hold of her own. Like when she was a child feeling left out in the school playground. Like the time she had stood outside the dancing school without the courage to go inside.

The same hand had given her comfort then. A warm, loving, and unselfish hand. Her brother's. Her wonderful, protective older brother.

And at that moment, when she finally felt she was safe, the urge to scream mounted inside her.

"Yes, that's right, Isabel," her brother said. "Let it all out. Have a good cry. Everything's going to be all right. You're both going to make it. You and your friend."

We're going to make it? She repeated his words to herself as a question, struggling to regain control of her voice, her tongue, her breathing.

Help us, she wanted to say. Search my car. Find his address in the glove compartment. The GPS will tell you where we've been. It'll be the arrest of your life.

She was ready to kneel before Rachel's Lord in heaven, if only He would give her the power of speech for just a moment. Just for a single breath.

But she lay there mute and could only listen to the rattle of her throat.

To words that dissolved into consonants and vowels, consonants and vowels that dissolved into saliva bubbling between her teeth.

Why had she not called her brother when she had the chance? Why hadn't she done the right thing? Had she thought she was some kind of superhuman who could stop the Devil himself?

"You're lucky you weren't driving, Isabel. You'll be prosecuted, of course, though I don't think they'll get a conviction for incitement to dangerous driving. You'll have to get yourself a new car, though." He forced a chuckle.

But there was nothing to laugh about.

"What happened, Isabel?" he asked, though she hadn't yet shown herself able to speak.

She pursed her lips slightly. Perhaps he might understand. Just a part of it.

Then came the sound of a dark voice over by Rachel's bed.

"I'm sorry, but we shall have to send you out again, Mr. Jønsson. Isabel's going to be transferred now. Perhaps you might like to visit the cafeteria in the meantime. We'll be sure to let you know where Isabel's been moved to when you come back. Say, in about half an hour?"

She didn't recognize the voice as one of those from earlier in the day.

But when the voice spoke again, and her brother finally got to his feet, giving her hand a squeeze to say he would be back later, she knew it was no use.

For she knew the voice, now the only voice left in the room.

She knew it all too well.

For a brief time, she had thought it might give her something to live for.

Now she realized that nothing could be further from the truth.

39

Carl had spent the night with Mona and almost dislocated every joint in his body. This time, she had waited for neither sweet words nor assurances that she was the only woman in his life. She had simply heaved her blouse over her head and got rid of her knickers with unfathomable dexterity.

Afterward, it had taken him half an hour to realize where he was, and the other half to consider whether he would survive another bout.

She was a different woman since she had come back from Africa. So very much there, so very present all of a sudden. The fine lines around her eyes took his breath away. The slight upward curl of her painted lips would become, in a moment, a smile that could strip him of all his thoughts.

If ever there were a woman for him, she was the one, he thought to himself as she came to him again with her warm breath, clawing him softly with her nails.

The next morning, when she woke him up, she was already dressed and ready for the day. Sensual, smiling, soaring.

What more evidence did a man need, still pinned down by his duvet, legs heavy as lead?

This woman was superior to him in every way.

"What is the matter with you, Carl?" Assad asked as they climbed into the car.

Carl hadn't the energy to answer. How could he, when his body felt like he had been run over by a bus and his nuts were throbbing like a pair of gumboils?

"Vedbysønder coming up here," said Assad, after the best part of an hour watching the stripes in the middle of the road pass by.

Carl looked up from the GPS and gazed out at a small cluster of farms and cottages, a landscape of fields. Sparsely populated. Decent road surface. Trees and patches of dense vegetation. A good place to collect a ransom.

"Continue on past the building there." Assad pointed down the road. "We cross over a bridge, and there we must peel our eyes."

As soon as the first farmhouse appeared by the railway bridge, Carl recognized the place Martin Holt had described to him. Cottages on both sides of the road. The railway running behind the houses on the left. A little farther on a couple of buildings on their own, and then, at an angle, an unpaved byroad leading off toward the tracks. After that, a narrow band of trees and thicker vegetation on the bend. This was the place where at least two of the kidnapper's victims had dropped their money from the train.

They pulled in at the byroad, which dipped under a little viaduct, switching on the blue light so as to be clearly seen if another vehicle should happen by in the morning haze.

Carl got out of the car with difficulty and considered perking himself up with a smoke. Assad already had his eyes fixed on the earth at his feet.

"It is wet here," he said, mostly to himself. "Quite wet. It may have been raining recently but not so much. See for yourself."

He pointed to a set of wheel tracks, clearly visible in the dirt.

"Look. A car drew forward to this place here, very slowly," he said, getting down on his haunches. "And here he accelerated away, like he was in a hurry."

Carl nodded. "Either that, or the wheels just span with it being so wet."

Carl lit his cigarette and looked around. They knew two men had thrown bags containing ransom money out of a train window onto the field here, but neither of them had seen the car. All they had seen was the flashing strobe light.

In both cases, the train had come from the east, so the bags could have landed anywhere on the field right up to the cottage that stood on its own a couple of hundred meters away. The place looked like it had been done up only recently, so maybe the owners hadn't been here in 2004 when Flemming Emil Madsen's father made his drop. Even if they had, they were hardly likely to have seen anything that could give the police something to go on. It was usually the way.

Carl reached his hands behind his neck and stretched, exhaling smoke into the damp air that rose up from the earth with the burgeoning warmth of March. The scent of Mona was still in his nostrils. How the fuck was he expected to think straight now? How could he think about anything but seeing her again?

"Look, Carl. There is a car leaving the house up there." Assad pointed toward the cottage. "Should we stop it, do you think?"

Carl dropped his cigarette and ground it beneath the sole of his shoe.

The woman behind the wheel looked disconcerted as she pulled in behind the flashing blue light.

"What's wrong?" she asked. "Is there something the matter with my lights?"

Carl gave a shrug. How was he supposed to know? "We're interested in this piece of land here. Does it belong to you?"

She nodded. "Up to the trees over there. What about it?"

"Hi, I am Hafez el-Assad," said Assad, extending a hairy mitt through the car window. "Have you ever seen anyone throw anything from the train here?"

"No, I don't think so. When were you thinking of?" the woman asked. Her eyes were livelier now that she realized they weren't about to give her a ticket.

"More than once. Some years ago, perhaps. Have you ever seen a car waiting here?"

"Not years ago. We only moved in recently." She smiled, plainly relieved. "We've just finished rebuilding. You can see we've still got the scaffolding around the back." She pointed toward the house, then turned her gaze to Carl. Perhaps he looked more like a man who knew about scaffolding than Assad.

Carl was about to thank her. To step aside like a customs officer and wish her a safe onward journey. He was about to light up another smoke and think some more about Mona.

"But there *was* a car here the day before yesterday, the same time as that dreadful accident over near Lindebjerg," the woman went on.

Carl nodded. The wheel tracks in the dirt.

Her expression changed. "There was a car chase, apparently. Two women in one of the vehicles were very badly injured. My brother-in-law's cousin was one of the paramedics on the scene. He said it was touch and go."

Fits well enough, Carl thought. Driving could be a hazardous business in the country. What the fuck else was there to do but tear hell for leather around the landscape?

"What sort of car was it?" Assad asked.

The woman twisted her mouth. "We just saw the rear lights, that's all, and then they were switched off. We can just see the spot from the front room when we're watching TV. Me and my husband thought it was most likely some couple getting amorous."

She rocked her head from side to side. Presumably meaning there was no law against it and that she'd done it plenty of times herself.

"But then all of a sudden they weren't there anymore," she went on. "We saw another pair of lights, and then both vehicles were gone. My husband reckoned afterward it might have been the same cars that were in the accident." She smiled apologetically, as if to excuse him. "He's always one for drama."

"You say this was on Monday?" Carl glanced across at the wheel tracks. Whoever had pulled in here had chosen a strategic spot indeed. Good view. Close to the railway. And if anything unexpected should happen, you could be back on the road in seconds. "You mentioned an accident," he continued. "Where did it occur, exactly?"

"The other side of Lindebjerg. My sister used to live just a couple of hundred meters from the place." She gave a quick shake of her head. "Moved to Australia she has now, though."

And then she told them she was going that way herself as it happened, and that she would show them.

The woman drove at fifty kilometers an hour max through the woods, with Carl stuck to her back bumper.

"Should we not turn off the blue light now?" Assad asked a couple of kilometers farther down the road.

Carl rolled his eyes in exasperation. Of course, what was he thinking? Their little convoy must have looked ridiculous, crawling through the woods at a snail's pace.

"Look." Assad pointed to a patch of road where the sun was finally drying up the morning dew.

Carl saw it, too. Skid marks on the other side of the road, then ten meters farther along, a second set on their own side.

Assad leaned forward and peered through the windscreen. Probably a car chase was going on inside his head. He looked like he'd be wrenching an imaginary steering wheel any minute and stepping on pedals that weren't there.

"Over there as well!" he exclaimed, pointing to more marks on the road surface that seemed to show a vehicle had braked violently.

Then the woman in front pulled up and got out.

"This is where it happened," she said, gesturing toward a tree trunk all but stripped of bark.

They walked around a bit, finding a few remaining shards from shattered headlights and deep gouges in the road surface. Obviously, it had been a very serious accident, though why it had occurred seemed far less clear. They would have to get the details from their colleagues in the traffic department.

"OK, let's be getting back," said Carl.

"Would you like me to drive this time, Carl?"

Carl looked at his assistant. All this recent evidence of dangerous driving hardly made the prospect attractive. Definitely not. "We'll check with the traffic boys first," he said, and climbed in behind the wheel.

Carl didn't know the officer who had been in charge of the case and responsible for the on-scene investigations, but he certainly inspired confidence.

"We had the wreck transported to Kongstedsvej so we could carry out a thorough inspection," the man said over the phone. "We found traces of paint from the other vehicle at various collision points, though as yet we're not sure of its exact makeup. Dark in color, probably anthracite, but friction at the moment of collision may have affected the exact shade."

"What about the victims?" Carl asked. "Are they alive?"

He was given a couple of civil registration numbers so he could check for himself.

"So, as far as you can make out, there was a second vehicle involved?"

The officer at the other end laughed. "It's dead certain there was. We just haven't gone public with it yet. There are clear indications of a car chase over a stretch of road extending back at least two and a half kilometers before the scene of the accident. High-speed and completely reckless. So if the two ladies involved *are* still alive, it'll be a miracle."

"And there's no sign of the other driver?"

The traffic officer confirmed this.

"Ask him about the women, Carl," Assad whispered from the passenger seat.

He did so. Who were they? How did they know each other? That sort of thing.

"Well," the voice replied. "They're both from the Viborg area, which I suppose makes it all a bit odd, crashing on a country road in the middle of nowhere in southern Sjælland. We can see they were back and forth over the Storebælt Bridge a few times that day, but that's not the strangest part."

Carl sensed that the man had been keeping the best bit until last. Typical traffic department, letting the crime boys know they weren't the only ones with exciting jobs.

"Oh, and what would that be, then?" he asked.

"The strangest thing is that shortly prior to the accident they rammed the Storebælt toll barrier and then did all they could to avoid being caught up with by police."

Carl stared again at the road in front of him. This was a turnup. Fucking hell.

"Can you e-mail me the report so I can run through it on the computer here in the car?"

"Now? Let me check with my superior first."

And then he hung up.

Five minutes later, they were reading through the police report on the two women's driving. It was anything but the usual. Caught by speed cameras no fewer than four times, twice with each driver, and all on the same day. Toll barrier rammed on the Storebælt Bridge. Dangerous driving on the E20. Pursued by several patrol cars on the same stretch. After which, it seemed they had driven along Route 150 without lights, before ending up crashing on an isolated road leading through woodland.

"Why would they drive from Viborg to Sjælland, back to Fyn, and then over to Sjælland again, and all hell for leather like that? Any ideas, Assad?"

"I don't know, Carl. Right now, I am looking at this."

He pointed to the list of speed cameras the two women had been clocked by. Locations as widespread as the E45 south of Vejle, the E20 midway between Odense and Nyborg, and then again on the E20 south of Slagelse.

Assad moved his finger down a line in the report.

Carl saw the location he was indicating. It seemed the women had also run into a speed enforcement trial in some village or other. Carl had never heard of the place. Ferslev, it was called, and they had been clocked doing eighty-five in a fifty zone. When all their violations were added to the fact that they had shared the driving, the two of them had both done more than enough to lose their licenses that day.

Carl plotted Ferslev into the GPS and studied the map. Just outside Skibby. About halfway between Roskilde and Frederikssund.

Assad put his finger on the screen and moved it slowly upward toward Nordskoven. The same place Yrsa thought there might be a boathouse.

A fucking turnup, indeed.

"Call Yrsa," Carl said, shifting the car into gear. "Tell her to get all the information she can on these two women. Give her their civil registration numbers and make sure she gets a move on. And get her to call us back as soon as she knows which hospital they've been admitted to and what condition they're in. This has got me going, this has."

He heard the sound of Assad's voice, but he was immersed in his own thoughts, imagining the two women's frenzied dash across the country.

Probably just a pair of junkies, his common sense tried to whisper in his ear. Junkies, or at least drug couriers. Something like that, and stoned out of their minds most likely. He nodded to himself. That would be it. Why else would they have been driving like that? And who said there had to be another vehicle involved? It could just as easily have been some terrified innocent, torpedoed by mindless lunatics with their veins full of junk. Some poor soul, scared shitless, who'd just wanted to get the fuck away and back home.

"OK," he heard Assad say as he finished his call.

"Did you get hold of her?" he asked. "Did she understand what to do?" He tried to gauge Assad's expression.

"Hey, Assad. What did Yrsa say?"

"Yrsa?" Assad looked up. "I don't know, Carl. The person I spoke to was Rose."

40

He was not happy. Not happy at all.

Almost two days and nights had passed since the accident, and according to the radio one of the injured women was now making progress. The other one was still in critical condition, but the report didn't specify who was pulling through and who wasn't.

Whichever way around it was, he couldn't put off his counterstrike any longer.

The day before, he had gathered information on a new potential family and had then considered driving to Isabel's house in Viborg to perform a break-in in which her computer would be stolen. But what good would it do if she had already passed on what she knew to her brother?

And then there was the issue of how much Rachel knew. Had Isabel told her everything?

Of course she had.

He had to get rid of the women. He knew that now.

He turned his gaze to the sky. Always this eternal struggle between him and God. Ever since he was a boy.

Why couldn't He leave him in peace?

He collected his thoughts, switched on the computer, and found the number of the Trauma Center of the Rigshospital. He got through to an imperious secretary who gave him little to go on.

Both women had been moved to Intensive Care, that much she knew.

He sat for a moment staring at his notepad.

Intensive Care Unit: ITA 4131.
Phone 35 45 41 31.

Three tiny pieces of information, vital to him, fatal to others. It was as simple as that, no matter who might be watching him from on high.

He Googled the number of the department and found its homepage almost at the top of his search.

It was a tidy site. As clean and clinical as the Rigshospital itself. One click on *Practical Information,* another on *Information for Families.pdf,* and a brochure appeared on his screen containing everything he needed to know.

He scrolled through the document.

There was a shift change between three thirty and four P.M. That was when he would strike. When they were most unawares.

This unbelievably helpful brochure also told him that the presence of relatives and loved ones could be a source of great comfort and support to the patient. So from now on he was a relative. He would buy flowers. Flowers were always a comfort. And he would be sure to wear the right expression, so everyone would know how deeply affected he was.

He read on, and it got better. Relatives and close friends of any patient admitted to the unit were welcome at anytime.

Close friends, and at anytime!

He thought for a moment. It would be best if he pretended to be a close friend. That would be harder to check. A close friend and confidant of Rachel. Someone from her congregation. He would put on a friendly, innocuous mid-Jutland accent to justify him staying so long. Just as long as he needed. After all, he had come a long way.

All this and more he gleaned from the Intensive Care Unit's presentation. He found out where he could make tea and coffee and learned that doctors were available for consultation during the daytime. There were photos showing the layout of the rooms and how they were equipped and precise information about IV apparatus and monitoring equipment.

He studied the photos of the monitors and knew he had to make sure he killed quickly and vanished immediately. The very instant a patient expired in a unit like this, every piece of equipment in the room would go haywire. Staff in the observation center would be alerted as soon as it happened. They would be there in no time, initiating the resuscitation attempt within seconds. These people were professionals, as indeed they should be.

So not only did he need to kill quickly, he also had to kill in such a way as to eliminate the possibility of resuscitation and, most important, to raise no suspicion that the cause of death was anything but natural.

He spent half an hour in front of the mirror. Drawing lines on his brow, fixing a new hairpiece, changing the appearance of his eyes.

When he had finished, he considered the results with satisfaction. Here was a man stricken with grief. A man in late middle age, with glasses, graying hair, and pallid skin. A far cry from the real him.

He opened his medicine cabinet, pulled out a drawer, and took out four small, plastic packages. Ordinary syringes of the kind anyone could purchase without prescription in any pharmacy. Ordinary needles like the ones thousands of drug addicts jabbed into their veins every day with society's full blessing.

It was all he needed.

A syringe filled with air, a needle inserted into a vein. Death would come quickly. And he would be able to move from one room to the next and do away with them both before the alarms went off.

It was a matter of timing.

He was looking for Intensive Care, department 4131. There were directional signs and a lift straight to the door, so it seemed. The department number indicated entrance, floor, and section. At least, that's what it said in the hospital's official directory information.

Entrance 4, Floor 13, Section 1. But apparently the lift only went as far as Floor 7.

He looked at his watch. The shift change was approaching, so there was no time to waste.

He slipped past a pair of the walking wounded and found the information desk at the main entrance. The man behind the glass appeared to have come down in the world, but he was both efficient and friendly.

"No, that would be Entrance 41, Floor 3, Section 1. Take the lift from Entrance 3 over there."

He pointed, then wrote it down in pen on a photocopied location map that he shoved through the hatch for good measure. *Patient admitted to Department . . . ,* it said, followed by the correct combination of numbers.

Perfect directions to the crime scene. Thanks for the help.

He stepped out of the lift on the third floor and followed the signs that took him straight to the unit. Double doors with white curtains led inside. If he hadn't known better, he might have thought it was a funeral parlor.

He smiled. In a way, it was.

If the level of activity inside matched that in the corridor, where not a soul was to be seen and empty shopping carts lined the wall, it would suit him well.

He pulled the cord to open the doors.

The unit seemed at first glance to be bigger than it actually was. He had not anticipated much going on, imagining instead deep concentration and quiet industry. But it wasn't like that at all. Not at the moment, anyway.

Perhaps he hadn't chosen his time quite as well as he had thought.

He passed two small seating areas for visitors and headed straight for reception. A colorful arch that would make anyone stop.

The secretary nodded to say she would be with him in a second.

He glanced around.

Doctors and nurses milled about. Some were in with their patients; others sat at computer screens in small anterooms outside each patient room. Others strode purposefully up and down the corridor.

Maybe it was on account of the shift change, he thought to himself.

"Is this a bad time?" he asked the secretary in a broad Jutland accent.

She glanced at her watch and then looked up at him with a friendly expression. "Perhaps not the best. Who would you be looking for?"

Concern appeared in his face, exactly as he had practiced at home. "I'm a friend of Rachel Krogh," he said.

She tipped her head inquiringly. "Rachel? We've no Rachel here. Do you mean Lisa Krogh?" She looked down at her screen. "Lisa Karin Krogh, it says here."

What the hell had he been thinking? Rachel was the name she used in her congregation, not her real name. He knew that.

"Oh, I'm sorry. Lisa, of course. We belong to the same congregation, you see. We use biblical names there. Lisa's is Rachel."

The secretary's expression changed, though almost imperceptibly. Didn't she believe him, or was it merely an aversion to things religious? Was she going to ask for some ID?

"I know Isabel Jønsson too," he added, before she got ideas. "The three of us are friends. They were brought in together, as far as I gather from your colleagues downstairs at the Trauma Center. Would that be correct?"

She nodded. A rather clenched smile, but a smile nonetheless.

"That's correct, yes. You'll find them both in there." She pointed to a room and told him the number.

The same room. It couldn't be better.

"You'll have to wait, though, I'm afraid. Isabel Jønsson's being transferred to another unit. A doctor and some of the nurses are getting her ready. And she's got another visitor waiting at the moment, so could I ask you not to go in until he leaves? We prefer if there's only one lot in at a time." She indicated the seating area closest to the exit. "He's sitting along there. Perhaps you know each other."

Disconcerting information.

He turned quickly to look. True enough, a man was sitting on his own with his arms folded. A man in a police uniform. Isabel's brother. There could be little doubt: the same high cheekbones, the same-shaped face, the same nose. This wasn't good at all.

He looked at the secretary with a hopeful expression. "Has Isabel been making progress?"

"As far as I know, yes. We don't normally move people on to other departments unless they're improving."

As far as she knew. She knew perfectly well, of course she did. What she didn't know was when the move would happen, but apparently it was imminent.

Most inconvenient. And her brother here to boot.

"May I go in to Rachel? Is she awake? Lisa, I mean."

She shook her head. "I'm afraid Ms. Krogh is still very much unconscious."

He bent forward slightly. "But Isabel would be conscious?" he asked quietly.

"I'm not actually sure, to be honest. Try asking the nurse over there." She pointed toward a blond, rather weary-looking woman on her way along the corridor with some medical records under her arm. The secretary turned to a new visitor who had now appeared at the counter. His audience was over.

"Excuse me." He stopped the nurse in her tracks, his arm aloft. *Mette Frigaard-Rasmussen*, her badge read. "I don't suppose you could tell me if Isabel Jønsson is conscious? Would it be possible to see her?"

Maybe she wasn't her patient. Maybe it wasn't her shift. Maybe it wasn't her day. Or maybe she was just too exhausted to do anything else but peer at him through the narrow slits of her eyes and reply through equally narrow lips.

"Isabel Jønsson? Erm . . ." She stared into space for a moment. "Yes, she's conscious, but heavily sedated. Her jaw's fractured, so she can't actually speak. She's not communicating at all at the moment, but it'll come."

She mustered all her strength to raise a smile. He thanked her and let her get on with the rest of what was obviously a demanding day.

Isabel wasn't communicating. Good news at last. Now he had to take advantage.

He pressed his lips together resolutely, slipped away from the waiting area, and proceeded farther along the corridor. Soon he would need to get away fast. His preference was for the lifts outside, as if nothing untoward had happened. But if other alternatives existed, he needed to know what they were.

He passed several rooms in which lives hung in the balance and doctors and nurses worked calmly and diligently. In the observation center, a group of people in white coats sat staring at computer screens, talking softly among themselves. Everything under control.

An auxiliary walked past him and seemed to wonder for a moment what he might be doing there. But they exchanged smiles, and the man continued along the corridor.

There were colors on the walls. Bright, intense paintings. Stained glass. Emanating life. Death was unwelcome here.

He rounded a red-painted corner and discovered a second corridor running parallel to the one from which he had come, row upon row of what seemed to be small rooms for staff on its left side. Nameplates outside the doors indicated who occupied them. He looked to the right, expecting to end up at reception again if he continued in that direction. But the route seemed to have been blocked off. However, there was a lift. Another possible escape hatch.

He noticed a white coat hanging by the open door of a room full of linen and various boxes of equipment stacked on shelves. Probably both it and the linen had been left for the laundry.

He slipped inside, grabbed the coat, and put it over his arm, waiting a moment before heading back toward reception.

On the way, he nodded to the same auxiliary as before, then patted his jacket pocket to make sure the syringes were there.

Of course they were.

He sat down on a blue sofa in the first and smaller of the two seating areas. The policeman in the other area appeared not to notice him. Five minutes later, the officer stood up and went to the reception desk. Two doctors and a couple of auxiliaries had just left the room in which his sister lay. New faces were beginning to appear among the staff, distributing themselves into their respective places.

The shift change was in full swing.

The policeman sent an inquiring look in the direction of the secretary. She nodded back. It would be all right now. Isabel Jønsson's brother could go in.

He followed the man with his eyes and saw him disappear into the room. Before long, a porter would come to move the man's sister. Not the best circumstances for what he needed to do.

If Isabel was well enough to be moved, he would have to kill her first. There might not be time for the second job.

And time was of the essence. He would have to get the brother out of there as soon as possible, no matter the risk. The prospect of approaching the man didn't appeal to him at all. Perhaps Isabel had told him everything. That's what she had said. Perhaps the brother knew too much. He would at least have to cover his face in the man's presence.

He waited until the secretary began to gather her things together and vacate her chair for her replacement.

He put on the coat.

Now was the time.

At first, he failed to recognize the two women. But in the corner sat the policeman, talking to his sister, holding her hand.

So the woman nearest the door in that snarl of masks and tubes and IV equipment was Rachel.

Behind her was a high-tech wall of machines and monitors emitting flashes of light and beeping sounds. Her face was almost entirely covered, her body likewise, the blanket not quite hiding the suggestion of severe injury and irreparable damage.

He looked across at Isabel and her brother. "What happened, Isabel?" the brother had just asked.

Then he squeezed between the wall and Rachel's bed and leaned forward.

"I'm sorry, but we shall have to send you out again, Mr. Jønsson," he said, bending over Rachel and drawing open her eyelids as though to examine the dilation of her pupils. She was certainly unconscious.

"Isabel's going to be transferred now," he went on. "Perhaps you might like to visit the cafeteria in the meantime. We'll be sure to let you know where Isabel's been moved to when you come back. Say, in about half an hour?"

He heard the man get to his feet with a few short, parting words to his sister. A man used to obeying orders.

He gave the policeman a nod, his face turned aside as the man left the room. Then he stood for a moment, considering the woman lying in front of him. It seemed unlikely she would ever pose him any threat.

And at that very moment, Rachel opened her eyes and stared at him as though fully conscious. Stared at him with her empty gaze, and yet so intensely that he found it hard to wrest himself away. Then her eyes closed once more. He stood motionless to see whether it would happen again. It didn't. Probably it was just some kind of reflex. He listened to the beeping of her monitors. Her heart rate had definitely increased during the minute that had passed since he entered the room.

Then he turned to Isabel, whose chest now rose and sank at diminishing intervals. She knew he was there. She had recognized his voice, but what good would it do her? Her jaw was immobilized and her eyes bandaged. She lay hooked up to IV apparatus and monitoring equipment, though with no tubes in her mouth, no respirator. Soon she would be able to speak. Her life was no longer in danger.

Ironic, to say the least, he thought to himself, that all these positive life signs were to be the death of her. He stepped toward her, his eyes already seeking out a suitable vein in her arm.

He took the first syringe from his pocket. Tore the packaging from the needle and joined the two parts together. Then he drew out the plunger, filling the syringe with air.

"You should have contented yourself with what you got from me, Isabel," he said, noting that her breathing and heart rate now increased again.

Not good, he thought, going around her bed, pushing the support pillow away from her arm. Her reactions would be registered in the observation center.

"Relax, Isabel," he said. "I won't harm you. I've come to say the children will be safe. I'll look after them. When you're better, I'll send you a message saying where they are. Believe me, it was about money, that's all. I'm no killer. That's what I came to tell you."

He saw that her breathing remained heavy, but her heart rate slowed. Good.

Then he looked up at Rachel's monitors. The beeps were coming thick and fast now. All of a sudden, her heart seemed to have gone berserk.

Hurry, he told himself.

He took a tight grip on Isabel's arm, found a pulsating vein, and jabbed in the needle. It slid in as easy as could be.

Isabel didn't flinch. Most likely she was so doped up he could have stuck it right through her arm without any noticeable reaction.

He tried to depress the plunger of the syringe, but it wouldn't budge. He must have missed the vein.

He withdrew the needle and jabbed again. This time, Isabel gave a start. Now she knew what he was doing, that he meant her harm. Her heart rate shot up once more. He pressed down on the plunger, and again it refused to move. Fuck. He would have to find a new vein.

And then the door opened.

"What's going on here?" a nurse cried, her eyes darting from Rachel's monitors to this unfamiliar man in a white coat, with a needle pointed at Isabel's arm.

He dropped the syringe into his pocket and was in motion before the woman realized what was happening. The blow to her throat was delivered sharply and with great force, causing her to fall to the floor in front of the open door.

"Attend to her. She's collapsed. Overexertion, by the looks of it," he barked at the nurse who came running from the observation center to check the danger signals from the two women's monitors. Within seconds, the whole unit was an anthill. People in white swarmed forth, gathering at the door of the room as he stole away toward the lifts.

It was a disaster. Twice now the seconds had ticked in Isabel's favor. Ten seconds more and he would have hit a good vein and pumped it full of air. Ten seconds. Ten fucking seconds. All it took to fuck everything up.

Behind him came the sound of hectic cries as the doors shut in his wake. Outside in the lift area, an emaciated man with dark blotches under his eyes sat waiting for some message from the Department of Plastic Surgery. The man nodded in acknowledgment at the sight of his smock. Such was the effect of a white coat in a hospital.

He pushed the lift button, glancing around to locate the fire stairs as the doors opened. He nodded to other white coats and a couple of sad-faced visitors as he stepped inside, making straight for the rear wall so no one would notice his missing name tag.

On the ground floor, he almost bumped into Isabel's brother outside the lift. Apparently, this was as far as he had got.

The two men with whom he was speaking looked suspiciously like colleagues. Maybe not the little Arab, but the Dane at least. They looked concerned.

He knew how they felt. Fuck.

Outside in the open air, he looked up and saw an air ambulance approaching the roof of the main building. Next delivery of problems to the Trauma Center.

Keep them coming, he thought to himself. The more emergencies they had to deal with, the fewer resources would be left to attend to the two women whose presence there he had precipitated.

He removed his coat only when he reached the shadow of the trees in the parking area where he'd left his car.

He tossed the hairpiece onto the backseat.

41

He and Assad had scarcely descended into the basement before Carl registered the changes that had occurred. They were not for the better. Cardboard boxes and all sorts of junk lay scattered everywhere. Steel shelving units were stacked up against the wall, and the clattering that echoed through the depths indicated that whatever was going on certainly wasn't finished.

"Oh, Christ!" he exclaimed, staring down their corridor. Where the fuck was the door that was supposed to partition off the asbestos? Where was the wall they just had put up? Was it those gypsum boards leaned up against their case system and their blowup of the message in the bottle?

"What's going on?" he hollered, as Rose poked her head around the door of her office. Thank God. At least *she* was recognizable. Jet-black hair, white powdery stuff all over her face, and layers of eye shadow. Looking daggers, the way they knew her best. Good old Rose.

"They're emptying the basement. The wall was in the way," she said uninterestedly.

It was Assad who remembered to welcome her back.

"So lovely to see you, Rose. You look . . ." He stood for a second, as if searching for the right word. Then he beamed. "You look so lovely as yourself."

Perhaps not the wording Carl would have chosen.

"Thanks for the flowers," she said, raising her painted eyebrows slightly in what was probably a display of emotion.

Carl smiled briefly. "No problem. We've missed you. Not that we weren't happy with Yrsa, mind," he added quickly. "But still."

He pointed along the corridor. "This wall business means we'll have Health and Safety on our backs again," he said. "What the hell's going on, anyway? Emptying the basement, what's that all about?"

"It's all got to go, they say. Apart from us, the archive, stolen-goods storage, the mail department, and the Burial Club. It's all to do with the police reform. Two steps forward, then back to square one."

They were going to have so much room they'd never be able to find each other.

Carl turned to face Rose. "What have you got for us? Who are the two women from the accident, and what are their conditions?"

She gave a shrug. "Oh, that. I haven't got around to that yet. There was all Yrsa's stuff to sort out first. Did you want it in a hurry, like?"

From the corner of his eye, Carl glimpsed Assad's hand shoot into the air in an averting gesture. It meant: *Careful, or she'll go off in a huff again.* Carl counted to ten under his breath.

Stupid bloody woman! Had she really not done what she'd been asked? Is this what it was going to be like again?

"I do beg your pardon, Rose," he said, gathering all his cool. "In future, we shall endeavor to make our needs more abundantly clear. Now, would you be so kind as to find the information we need right away? It's rather important, you see, so *in a hurry* would indeed be just the ticket."

He nodded faintly in the direction of Assad, who responded with a thumbs-up.

Rose tossed her head, seemingly at a loss for what to say.

So this was how she had to be tackled.

"By the way, you've got an appointment with the psychologist in three minutes, in case it had slipped your mind," she said, glancing at her watch. "I'd get my skates on if I were you."

"What for?"

She handed him a slip of paper with an address on it. "If you run, you might just make it. Mona Ibsen said to tell you she was proud you're going through with it."

That did it. There was no shying away now.

Anker Heegaards Gade was only two streets from Police HQ, but still far enough away for Carl to feel like someone had stuffed a vacuum pump into his gob with the sole intention of collapsing his lungs. If this was Mona's idea of doing him a favor, he might have to have a word with her.

"Glad you could make it," said Kris the psychologist. "Was it hard to find?"

What was he supposed to say? It was two streets away. Aliens Division. He must have been there a thousand times.

But what was this shrink doing there?

"Only joking, Carl. I'm in no doubt there's little you wouldn't be capable of finding. And now you're probably wondering what I'm doing here, in this building. Actually, a lot of work here in the Aliens Division requires the services of a psychologist. But you realize that, obviously."

The bloke was giving him the creeps. What was he, a mind reader?

"I've got half an hour, max," said Carl. "We've got a job on."

He didn't even need to lie about it.

"I see." Kris made a note in his records. "Next time, I'd like you to make sure you can be here for the full session, OK?"

He produced a folder bulging with documents that must have taken two hours at least to get photocopied.

"Do you know what this is? Have you been informed?"

Carl shook his head, but he could probably hazard a guess.

"You've an inkling, at least. I can see that. These are your records. Basic data and all documents pertaining to the incident in which you and your colleagues were shot in that allotment house in Amager. I ought at this point to tell you that I am also in possession of certain information which I am unfortunately not at liberty to divulge in full."

"You what?"

"Reports from both Hardy Henningsen and Anker Høyer, with whom you were working on the case in question. Reports that seem to indicate that your knowledge of the case was rather more extensive than theirs."

"Not to my mind, it wasn't. Why would they say that? We were together on that job from day one."

"This is one of the things we might shed a bit more light on during the course of our sessions. My feeling is there's something that's got you in a jam here, something you've either suppressed completely or don't want to let out into the open."

Carl shook his head. What the fuck was this? Was he being accused of something?

"I can assure you there's no jam, as you put it," he said, his cheeks fiery with annoyance. "It was a normal case like any other. Apart from the fact that we got shot. What are you getting at?"

"Do you know why you continue to react so strongly to the shooting, such a long time after the event, Carl?"

"Yes, I do. And you'd fucking react the same way, too, if you'd been a millimeter from getting blasted to pieces while two of your best mates weren't quite so lucky."

"So you consider Hardy and Anker to have been your friends, is that right?"

"Mates, yeah. Good colleagues."

"There's a difference."

"Maybe. I don't know if *you* have a quadriplegic living in *your* front room, but I have. Doesn't that qualify me as his friend?"

"You misunderstand me. I'm in no doubt that you're a very decent guy in many ways. You've probably felt rather guilty about Hardy Henningsen, so I quite understand you'd want to make a special effort in his case. But are you sure your working relationship was as good as you make it out to be?"

"Yes, I am." This Kris bloke was irritating as fuck.

"Anker Høyer's autopsy revealed traces of cocaine in his blood. Were you aware of that?"

Carl sank back in what purported to be an armchair. No, he most certainly was not aware of it at all.

"Do you use cocaine, Carl?"

Somehow, the man's clear blue eyes, previously candidly assessing, were beginning to seem hostile. He had flirted brazenly with him in Mona's presence. That gay twinkle, lips pursed and smiling at the same time. And now here he was giving Carl the third degree.

"Cocaine? No, I don't. I hate all that shit."

Kris the psychologist raised his hands in a mock defensive gesture. "OK, let's take this somewhere else. Did you have anything to do with Hardy's wife before she and Hardy married?"

"Are we going to talk about her again?" He glared at the guy, who just sat there impassive as a statue.

"I knew her," he said after a moment. "She was a friend of a girlfriend of mine. That's how she and Hardy met."

"And there was no sexual relationship of any kind?"

Carl snorted. The man had his nose in everywhere. But how all this was supposed to get rid of the pain in his chest, he had no idea.

"You hesitate. Was there?"

"What kind of counseling is this, anyway? When do you get the thumbscrews out? The answer to your question is no. Petting, that's all."

"Petting? What would that cover?"

"Oh, for fuck's sake, Kris. You may be gay, but surely you can at least *imagine* mutual bodily exploration of a heterosexual nature?"

"So you got—"

"Listen, I'm not giving details, OK? We snogged and had a good grope, but there was no shagging. Satisfied?"

Kris noted it down.

Then his blue eyes returned to Carl. "To get back to the case. Let's call it the nail-gun case, shall we? Hardy Henningsen's reports suggest that you may have been in contact with those who were later responsible for the shooting. Is that right?"

"No, it fucking well isn't! He must have got the wrong idea."

"OK." He sent Carl the kind of look intended to encourage confidentiality. "The thing is, Carl, if you go to bed with an itchy arse, your fingers are likely to stink when you get up in the morning."

Oh, for fuck's sake. Not him as well?

"Are you cured, then?" Rose asked when he got back to their corridor. He smiled, perhaps rather too ingratiatingly.

"Very funny, Rose. Next time I'm there, I'll put you down for a course in etiquette."

"Like that, is it?" She was digging her heels in already. "I hope you're not expecting me to be friendly *and* PC all at once."

Friendly? Jesus Christ!

"What have you got on those two women, Rose?"

She gave names, addresses, and ages. Middle-aged, both of them. No known associations with criminal elements. Regular citizens.

"I haven't got around to Intensive Care yet. I'll get on to them in a minute."

"Who owned the vehicle they crashed? I think I forgot to ask."

"Haven't you read the accident report? The owner was Isabel Jønsson, but the other woman, Lisa Karin Krogh, was the one driving."

"Yeah, I know that. Are they Church of Denmark?"

"All over the place, these questions, aren't they?"

"I need to know. Are they?"

She gave a shrug.

"Find out for me, Rose. And if they're not, I want you to find out what denomination they otherwise might subscribe to."

"What am I, a journalist?"

He was just about to hit the roof but found himself interrupted by a sudden commotion of yells and cries from somewhere in the vicinity of the mail department.

"What's going on?" Assad exclaimed.

"How should I know?" Carl snarled back. All he could see was a man standing at the other end of the corridor with the sidepiece from a steel shelving unit raised above his head, and then one of the uniformed boys leaping from the adjoining corridor to send him flying. The sidepiece came down hard in the process, and the officer fell back in a heap.

At the same moment, the man caught sight of the assembled three members of Department Q, and without hesitation he began to charge toward them wielding the piece of steel. Rose retreated, but Assad stayed put next to Carl.

"Maybe we should let the lads upstairs take care of this, Assad? Get the duty officer down?" Carl suggested, over the man's unintelligible shouts.

But Assad didn't answer. He braced himself, legs bent at the knee, upper body leaning forward with his arms out like a wrestler. Their prospective assailant, however, was unperturbed, a fact he would very soon come to regret. At the instant he raised his improvised weapon above his head to strike, Assad sprang into the air and grabbed it with both hands. The effect was astonishing.

The man's arms buckled at the elbow, and Assad brought down the steel against his shoulder with such force that the crunch of breaking bone was clearly audible.

Presumably for form's sake, Assad completed his counterstrike by delivering a firm kick to the attacker's muscle-bound abdomen. It was not a pretty sight, and the sounds that escaped from the desperate man were of the kind a person would hope never to hear again. Carl had never seen anyone so berserk neutralized so swiftly.

While the man on the floor writhed in pain from his fractured collarbone and Assad's pinpoint strike to his guts, uniformed officers came running.

Only then did Carl notice the handcuffs dangling from the wrist of the man's right hand.

"We'd just brought him in from Yard 4 on his way to the Magistrates' Court," one of the uniformed guys said, snapping shut the handcuffs on the man's other wrist. "God knows how he managed to get the cuffs off, but the next thing we know he's away through the cargo hatch and on his way down to the mail department."

"He wouldn't have got far," a second officer said. Carl knew him. An excellent marksman.

It was pats on the back from all around for Assad. What did they care if he had put their charge in the hospital?

"Who is he, anyway?" Carl asked.

"Seems he might be the guy who bumped off three Serbian debt collectors in the space of the last two weeks."

And now Carl saw the ring grown into the flesh of the man's little finger.

Carl's eye caught Assad's. He didn't seem surprised in the slightest.

"I saw that," said a voice behind Carl's back as the officers dragged the groaning Serb back where he had come from.

Carl swiveled. It was Valde, one of the retired officers who presided over the Burial Club. Deputy chairman, as far as Carl recalled.

"What the hell are you doing here on a Wednesday, Valde? I thought you lot only met up on Tuesdays?"

Valde chortled and stroked his beard. "Well, we were all out for Jannik's birthday yesterday. His seventieth, so you can imagine. No going soft on tradition there, I'll tell you."

He turned to Assad. "Bloody hell, mate. I wouldn't mind seeing that again. Where did you pick up tricks like that?"

Assad gave a shrug. "Action and reaction. That's all."

Valde nodded. "Come into the parlor. You deserve a Gammel Dansk."

"Gammel Dansk?" Assad was mystified.

"Assad doesn't drink alcohol, Valde," Carl explained. "He's a Muslim. I'll have his."

They were all there. Mostly former traffic police, but Jannik the maintenance supervisor, too, and one of the commissioner's old chauffeurs.

Sandwiches, cigarettes, black coffee, and Gammel Dansk. Pensioners were on a cushy number at Police HQ.

"You bearing up all right, Carl?" one of them asked. A bloke he'd sometimes had dealings with in the Gladsaxe Police District.

Carl nodded.

"Dreadful business what happened to Hardy and Anker. Very nasty case indeed. Did you ever get to the bottom of it?"

"Can't say we did." He turned his gaze to the window above the row of tables. "You lot don't know you're born, having daylight in here. We could do with some ourselves."

The Burial Club all frowned at once.

"What's up?" he asked.

"All the rooms down here have got windows in them," one of them said.

"Not where we are they haven't."

Jannik, the maintenance supervisor, got to his feet. "I've been here thirty-seven years, and I know every nook and cranny in this old place. Would you be kind enough to show me this room of yours. I've to be getting on soon."

So much for his Gammel Dansk.

"There you go," Carl said a minute later. He gestured at the wall to which his flatscreen was affixed. "Where's this window of yours, then?"

Jannik peered. "What do you call that?" He pointed straight at the wall.

"Erm, a wall?"

"It's plasterboard, Carl. Plasterboard. My lot put it up when this place was turned into a stockroom. There were shelving units all over. Here, and further along where that cute little secretary of yours is. Same shelves the Support Unit later used to store all those helmets and visors. Same shelves that are cluttering up the bloody place now." He laughed. "Couldn't work it out, eh, Carl? Do you want me to knock a hole through so you can see out, or can you do it yourself?"

He could hardly credit it. "What about the other side?" He gestured toward Assad's cubbyhole.

"That place? That's never been an office, Carl. It's a broom cupboard. There's no window in there."

"OK. I reckon Rose and I can do without, too, in that case. Maybe later, once they've finished clearing this place out and I find Assad another office."

Jannik shook his head and chuckled.

"Hell of a bloody mess they're making down here," he said as they stood for a moment in the corridor. "What's that there in aid of?" He pointed to what was left of the plasterboard partition, the remains of which were now lined up along the wall from Assad's case overviews and on past Rose's office.

"We put up a dividing wall because of those pipes there. There's asbestos falling from them, apparently. Health and Safety kicked up a fuss."

"What, *them*?" The maintenance supervisor jerked a finger at the ceiling as he turned to go back to his Gammel Dansk. "You can pull all them down if you want. The heating pipes run through the crawl space now. Those ones on the ceiling have got no use anymore."

His laugh echoed through most of the basement.

Carl had hardly stopped swearing when Rose appeared. Maybe she'd been doing her job for once.

"They're both alive, Carl. Lisa Karin Krogh is still critical, but the other one's going to pull through. They're pretty sure of that now."

He nodded. In that case, they'd better get out there and have a word with her.

"As for their religious affiliations, Isabel Jønsson is regular Church of Denmark, and Lisa Krogh belongs to something called the Mother Church. I spoke to their neighbor in Frederiks. It seems to be a weird sect that keeps itself to itself. The neighbor woman reckoned Lisa Krogh's husband had been dragged into it by his wife. The husband calls himself Joshua, and she goes by the name of Rachel."

Carl took a deep breath.

"But that's not all," she went on, shaking her head. "Local plod in Slagelse found a duffel bag in the undergrowth at the scene of the accident. Slung out of the vehicle when it crashed, so it seems. And what do you think's in it? Only a million kroner in used notes, that's all."

"Now I have heard it all," Carl heard Assad say just behind him. "Almighty Allah!"

Almighty Allah, indeed. Carl's words exactly.

Rose cocked her head. "And to top it all, I've just found out that Lisa Karin Krogh's husband dropped dead on the train between Slagelse and Sorø on Monday evening. About the same time his wife crashed the car. Heart attack, the autopsy says."

"Fucking hell," Carl exclaimed with a mounting sense of foreboding. He almost felt a shiver run down his spine.

"I'll just stop in and see how Hardy's doing before we go up to Intensive Care," said Carl. He took the STOP paddle they used to pull in traffic offenders and put it on the dashboard where it could be seen through the windscreen. It was a good way of placating meter attendants in cases of dodgy parking.

"You stay outside, OK? There's a couple of things I need to ask him."

Carl found Hardy in a room with a view. Big windows filled with sky, ragged clouds like pieces in a jigsaw puzzle someone had dropped on the floor.

Hardy said he was doing fine. His lungs were on the mend and the tests almost done. "But they don't believe me when I say I can twitch my wrist," he said.

Carl let it pass. What good would it do, to crush his hopes?

"I had a session with a shrink today, Hardy. Not Mona, some twerp called Kris. He told me you'd put some things down about me in a report. A report I've never seen. Does that ring a bell?"

"All I wrote was that you knew the case better than me and Anker."

"Why would you feel the need to say that?"

"Because you did. You knew Georg Madsen, the old guy we found murdered."

"No I didn't, Hardy. I'd never seen him before in my life."

"Come off it, you used him as a witness in another case. I don't recall the details, but I remember you did."

"You're remembering wrong, Hardy." Carl shook his head. "Anyway, it makes no difference now. I'm here on other business. Just thought I'd pop in and see how you were doing. Assad says to say hello. He's here, too."

Hardy raised his eyebrows. "Before you go, Carl, there's something I want you to promise me."

"Anything at all, mate. Just say the word."

Hardy swallowed a couple of times before revealing what was on his mind. "Let me come back to your place again. If I can't, I'll die."

Carl looked him in the eye. If anyone could prompt his own expiry by willpower alone, it was Hardy.

"No problem, Hardy," he replied softly.

Vigga could stay put with that Gherkin bloke of hers from Turbanistan.

They stood waiting for the lift at Entrance 3 when the doors opened and one of Carl's old instructors from the police academy stepped out.

"Karsten!" Carl exclaimed, extending a hand in greeting. He received a smile in return when the man eventually recognized him.

"Carl Mørck," he said after a pause. "Older now, I see."

Carl smiled. Karsten Jønsson. Another promising career that had ended up in the traffic department. Another policeman who had moved sideways so as not to let the system grind him down.

They stood for a moment, exchanging reminiscences and a few words about how being on the force was so much harder now than it used to be, and then they shook hands to say good-bye.

But somehow shaking Karsten Jønsson's hand gave Carl an odd feeling, before his brain registered why. An unsettling, indefinable something that brought his system to a standstill. First this feeling, then the realization that he was missing something.

It came to him at once. Of course! It was too much of a coincidence.

The man seemed dejected, Carl reflected. He had stepped out of the lift that went up to Intensive Care. His name was Jønsson. That was it.

"Tell me, Karsten, are you here because of Isabel Jønsson?" he asked.

The man nodded. "She's my younger sister. How would you be involved?" He shook his head, unable to see the connection. "Aren't you Department A?"

"Not anymore. But listen, there's no need to worry. I've got a couple of questions I need to ask her, that's all."

"You'll have a job. Her jaw's immobilized, and she's heavily sedated. I've just been with her, and she didn't say a word. They sent me out again. Seems she's being transferred to another department. They told me to wait in the cafeteria for half an hour."

"OK. I think we'll go up anyway before they move her. Nice running into you, Karsten."

Another lift pinged its arrival, and a man in a white coat stepped out.

He glanced at them with a somber look.

They stepped in and pressed the button.

Carl had seen the unit countless times before. People unfortunate enough to get in the way of lunatics with weapons often ended up here. Last stop but one for the victims of violent crime.

The medical staff who worked here were top-notch. Of all places on earth, this was where he would probably want to come if things really went wrong.

He and Assad went through the doors and into a hive of activity. It looked like they'd walked in on an emergency. Not the best of times to appear, he could see that.

He showed his ID at the desk and presented Assad as well. "We're here to ask Isabel Jønsson a few questions. I'm afraid it's quite urgent."

"And I'm afraid that won't be possible at the moment. Lisa Karin Krogh, who's in the same room as Isabel Jønsson, just passed away a few minutes ago, and Isabel has taken a turn for the worse. Besides that, one of our nurses has just been attacked. There was a man here. He may have tried to kill them, we don't know yet. Everything's chaos. The nurse is unconscious."

42

They had been sitting in the waiting area for half an hour while the Intensive Care Unit was in turmoil.

Carl got to his feet and went up to the desk. They couldn't wait any longer.

"You wouldn't have any information on Lisa Karin Krogh, would you? The woman who died just now?" he inquired, producing his badge again for the secretary. "I need a phone number for her home address."

A moment later he stood with a note in his hand.

He took his mobile out of his pocket and went back to Assad, who sat tapping his feet as though they were a pair of drumsticks.

"Stay here and hold the fort," he said. "I'll be out by the lifts. Give us a shout when they say we can go in, OK?"

Then he called Rose. "I need some info relating to this number. Names, civil registration numbers of everyone belonging to the address, OK? And Rose, I want you to do it right away, are you with me?"

She huffed a bit but said she would see what she could come up with.

He pushed the button for the lift and went down to the ground floor.

He must have passed the cafeteria fifty times over the years without ever stopping. All that fattening *smørrebrød* at overinflated prices. This time was no different. He was hungry, certainly, but he had a different agenda.

"Karsten Jønsson!" he called out, before catching sight of the fair-haired man craning his neck to see who wanted him.

Carl asked him to come along, and as they walked he explained what had happened upstairs after Jønsson was made to go down and wait.

Concern swept across the man's face.

"Just a sec," said Carl as they reached the third floor and his mobile chimed. "You just go in, Karsten. Come and get me if you need to."

He kneeled down by the wall, wedged the mobile against his ear, and placed his notepad on the floor in front of him. "OK, Rose, what have you got for me?"

She stated the address, and then seven names and their respective civil registration numbers. Father, mother, and five children: Josef, eighteen years old, Samuel, sixteen, Miriam, fourteen, Magdalena, twelve, and Sarah, ten. He wrote it all down.

Was there anything more he needed to know?

He shook his head and snapped the phone shut without having answered her properly.

The information was alarming, indeed.

Five children, now orphaned, two of them almost certainly in grave danger. Same pattern as before. The kidnapper had struck a family strongly affiliated to a religious group and with more children than average. The only difference now was there would be little chance of him sparing one of the kidnapped children as was his usual MO. What reason would he have?

Carl felt himself on the brink of a life and death situation. All his instincts were now on alert. Further killings were imminent. He needed to prevent them, and an entire family's demise. There was no time to waste, but what was he to do? Apart from the dead woman's children and the medical secretary with whom the killer had spoken, now on her way home with her mobile switched off, the only person who could help was in a room beyond these double doors. Unable to see or speak and in a critical state of shock.

The killer had been here today. A nurse had seen him, but she was still unconscious. It was a truly hopeless situation.

He consulted his notes and dialed the number of the house in Frederiks. At moments like this, his job was unbearable.

"Josef speaking," said a voice. Carl glanced at his notepad. The eldest child. Thank God for small mercies.

"Hello, Josef. You're speaking to Detective Inspector Carl Mørck, Department Q of the Copenhagen Police. I'm calling because—"

The receiver was put down gently at the other end.

Carl stood for a moment and considered his error. He shouldn't have presented himself like that. The police had doubtless been there already and informed the children of their father's death. Josef and his siblings would be in shock. What was he thinking?

He stared at the floor. How could he get the boy talking ASAP?

Then he called Rose.

"Grab your handbag, Rose," he said. "Then grab a taxi and get over here to the Rigshospital as fast as you can."

"Very regrettable indeed," said the consultant. "Until the day before yesterday, we had a police officer posted to the unit around the clock. We've had victims in here from the gang war. If he'd been here today, this probably wouldn't have happened. Unfortunately, one might say, our two gangsters were transferred elsewhere on Monday evening."

Carl listened attentively. The doctor's face was kind. No airs and graces there.

"Of course, we fully understand that the police need to establish this intruder's identity as quickly as possible, and naturally we shall do whatever we can to assist. But I'm afraid the condition of the nurse who was attacked remains such that as a doctor I'm compelled to say that concern for her health must take precedence. There may be a cervical fracture here, and certainly at the moment she's in a state of shock. So you won't be able to see her until sometime tomorrow morning at the earliest, I'm afraid. In the meantime, we'll do all we can to get in touch with the secretary who saw the assailant earlier on. She lives in Ishøj, I believe, so she might well be home in about twenty minutes or so, providing she doesn't stop off on the way."

"We've already got a man waiting at her address so as not to waste time. But what about Isabel Jønsson?" Carl glanced inquiringly at her brother and received a nod in return. It was OK by him for Carl to do the asking.

"Yes, well. Understandably, she's very distraught. Respiration and heart rate are both still rather unstable, but our view is that she may benefit from seeing her brother. We'll be finished examining her in five or ten minutes, so he'll be able to look in on her then."

Carl heard a commotion by the entrance doors. Rose's bag trying to bring the curtains in with it.

"Right, thanks," Carl said, then gestured for Assad and Rose to follow him outside.

"What do you need me for?" asked Rose once they were gathered in the corridor. All her body language said the last place in the world she wanted to be was standing by some lifts outside an intensive care unit. Maybe she had a problem with hospitals.

"I've got a difficult job for you," said Carl.

"You what?" she replied, ready to dig her heels in.

"I want you to call a young lad and make him understand that he must help us right away or else a couple of his siblings are going to end up dead. That's what it looks like, anyway. His name's Josef and he's eighteen years old. His father died yesterday, and his mother is here in Intensive Care. I'm assuming he's already been told that by the police in Viborg. What he doesn't know is that his mother died in that room in there only a short time ago. It would be unethical to give him that message over the phone, but it may be necessary. It's up to you, Rose. We need him to answer our questions. That's the bottom line."

Rose seemed paralyzed, on the verge of protest, her words somehow stuck in the empty space between apprehension and necessity. She could tell by looking at Carl how urgent it was.

"But why me? Why not Assad, or you?"

He explained to her that the boy had hung up on him. "We need a neutral voice. A gentle woman's voice, like yours."

Had he referred to Rose's voice that way at any other time, he would never have been able to keep a straight face. But right now there was nothing, absolutely nothing, to laugh about. It was imperative that she do as instructed.

He told her what he needed to know, then he and Assad retreated to give her space.

It was the first time he had seen Rose nervous. Maybe Yrsa would have been better. Somehow, the toughest ones were always the softies inside.

They watched from a distance as she spoke, raising her hand slightly as though to prevent the boy from putting the phone down on her. More than once she pressed her lips together and turned her eyes to the ceiling, as though trying not to break down and cry. It was an unsettling sight to behold. A life was collapsing at the other end of the phone. What Rose had told the boy meant that his own life and that of his siblings would never be the same again. Carl understood only too well what she had to contend with.

And then she was listening, deep in concentration, drying her eyes at the same time. Breathing deeper now. Putting forward her questions, one by one. Allowing the boy time to answer. Then, after a few minutes, she waved Carl over.

She covered the receiver with her hand. "He won't talk to you, only to me. He's very, very upset. But he'll answer your questions."

"You've done very well, Rose, both of you. Have you asked him the things we agreed on?"

"Yes."

"Have we got a description and a name?"

"Yes."

"Anything that might lead us directly to our man?"

She shook her head.

Carl put his hand to his brow. "In that case, I don't think I've anything more to ask him right now. Give him your number and tell him to call if he remembers anything that might be significant."

She nodded, and Carl withdrew.

"Nothing to go on," he said, leaning back against the wall with a sigh. "This is serious, Assad."

"We shall find him," Assad replied reassuringly. But most likely he was quite as apprehensive as Carl. Afraid they wouldn't make it in time to save the children.

"Just give me a minute," said Rose, when she had finished the call.

She gazed emptily into space, as though it were the first time she had seen the world's dark underbelly, and now she never wanted to again.

She stood for quite some time, immersed in her own thoughts as tears welled in her eyes. Carl found himself willing his watch to tick slower.

She swallowed a couple of times. "OK, I'm ready," she said eventually. "The kidnapper has Josef's brother and sister. Samuel and Magdalena. They were abducted on Saturday, and their mother and father were trying to get a ransom together. Isabel Jønsson wanted to help them, though Josef wasn't quite sure how she came into the picture. She only appeared on Monday. That was all he knew. His parents didn't tell him much."

"What about the kidnapper?"

"Josef described the man just like he is on the police sketch. Forty-plus, perhaps a little taller than average. Nothing characteristic about the way he walks or anything like that. Josef reckons he dyes his hair and eyebrows and that he probably knows all sorts of stuff about theological issues." She stared into space again. "If I ever get my hands on that animal, I'll . . ." The sentence tapered off. Her face said it all.

Who was with the children now, Carl wanted to know.

"Someone from their church."

"How did Josef take his mother's death?"

She waved a hand in front of her face. She didn't want to talk about it. Not yet, anyway.

"And he said the man couldn't sing," she went on, her black-painted lips quivering. "He'd heard him sing at their prayer meetings, and he was no good at it. He drove a van. Not a diesel, I asked about that. At least, it didn't sound like a diesel engine, is what he said. A light-blue van, nondescript. He didn't know the registration or what make it was. He's not into cars."

"Was that the lot?"

"The man calls himself Lars Sørensen, but Josef remembered calling him by name once to get his attention and it was like there was no reaction at first, so he reckons his proper name is something else."

Carl wrote it down on his pad.

"What about that scar?"

"He hadn't noticed any." She pressed her lips together. "So it can't be that visible."

"Anything else?"

She shook her head. Her eyes told how sad she was.

"Thanks, Rose. See you tomorrow. You can go home now."

Rose nodded but stayed put. She probably needed more time to get herself together.

He turned to Assad. "Only our patient in there can help us now, Assad."

They stepped quietly into the room. Karsten Jønsson was speaking softly to his sister. A nurse busied herself with something at Isabel's wrist. The beeping from the panel above her bed indicated her heart rate was normal and that she had now calmed down.

Carl's gaze fell on the bed next to Isabel's. A white sheet with a shape underneath. Not a loving mother of five, a woman who had died in terrible grief. Just a shape beneath a sheet. A split second in a hurtling car, and here she lay. Everything gone.

"May we step closer?" he asked Karsten Jønsson.

The man nodded. "Isabel wants to talk, but we're having difficulty understanding what she's trying to say. A pointing board's no use at the moment, so the nurse is trying to loosen the bandages around the fingers of her right hand. Isabel has fractures in both forearms and several fingers, so she might not be able to hold a pencil at all."

Carl looked over the figure lying in front of him in the bed. Her chin was the same as her brother's, but otherwise there was no way to tell what this battered person might look like.

"Hello, Isabel. I'm Detective Inspector Carl Mørck, Department Q, Copenhagen Police. Do you understand what I'm saying?"

"Mmmmm," came the response, and the nurse nodded.

"Let me just explain to you briefly why I'm here, Isabel." He told her about the message in the bottle and about the other kidnappings, and that he now knew that this was a case of the same kind. Everyone in the room noted how the monitors showed her reaction to what he was saying.

"I'm sorry you have to listen to all this, Isabel. I know you're not feeling too good as it is, but I'm afraid there's no getting around it. Am I right in believing that you and Lisa Krogh are involved in a case like the one with the message in the bottle I just told you about?"

She nodded faintly and made sounds she needed to repeat more than once before her brother straightened his back and looked up. "I think she's saying the woman's name is Rachel."

"That's right," said Carl. "She took another name for use in her community. We're aware of that."

Isabel responded with a slight nod.

"Am I right in thinking that on Monday you and Rachel were involved in an attempt to save Rachel's two children, Samuel and Magdalena, and that the car crash you were involved in occurred during this attempt?"

Isabel's lips quivered. Then another faint nod.

"We're going to put a pencil in your hand now, Isabel. Your brother's right here if you need help." The nurse encouraged her to grasp the pencil, but Isabel's fingers would not obey.

The nurse glanced up at Carl and shook her head.

"This isn't going to work," said her brother.

"Let me try," said Assad from the rear of the room and stepped forward.

"My father was struck by aphasia when I was ten years old. There was a clot, and all his words were gone. I was the only one who could understand him after that, until the day he died."

Carl frowned. So the man Assad had been talking to on Skype the other morning hadn't been his father.

The nurse gave up her chair to Assad.

"Yes, I'm sorry, Isabel. My name is Assad and I am from Syria. I am Carl Mørck's assistant, and now we shall speak together. Carl will speak and I will listen to your mouth, OK?"

A tiny nod of her head.

"What kind of car was it that ran you off the road?" Carl asked. "Did you see the make or the color? Was it old or new?"

Assad put his ear to Isabel's mouth. His eyes were wide and lively as he listened to each and every breath that passed over her lips.

"A Mercedes. Dark. Rather old," he repeated.

"Do you remember the registration number, Isabel?" Carl asked.

If she could, there was hope.

"Dirty number plates. She could hardly see in the dark," Assad said after a while. "The last three digits may have been 433, though Isabel is not certain they were threes. They could have been eights, or both."

Carl ran it through in his mind. 433, 438, 483, 488. Only four combinations. That narrowed things down.

"You got that, Karsten?" he said. "Older Mercedes, dark in color, registration ending 433, 438, 483, or 488. That'd be your department."

Karsten Jønsson nodded. "Well, we can find out pretty quickly how many Mercedes there are on the roads with those final digits, but we still haven't got a color. And Mercedes is a fairly common make, so there could be quite a few with that combination."

He was right. Finding the cars was one thing, checking out their owners was quite another. It would take a lot more time than they had.

"Is there anything else you can tell us that might help, Isabel? A name, perhaps?"

She nodded again. Now it took longer for her to speak, and getting her words out required obvious effort. More than once, they heard Assad encourage her to repeat what she said.

Then came the names. Three in all: Mads Christian Fog, Lars Sørensen, Mikkel Laust. Added to the fourth, Freddy Brink, which they knew from the Poul Holt case, and the fifth, Birger Sloth, from the Madsen case, that made a total of eleven first and last names. Not promising.

"My guess is none of these is his real name," Carl said. "Most likely we can rule them out."

Meanwhile, Assad was still listening to Isabel's exertions.

"She says one of the names is on his driver's license. And she knows where he has been hiding out," he said all of a sudden.

Carl straightened up. "You mean she's got an address?" he asked.

"Yes, and one thing more," Assad replied, after another moment of deep concentration. "He had a light-blue van. She has the number in her head."

A minute later, they had the registration written down.

"I'll get cracking," said Karsten Jønsson, already halfway through the door.

"Isabel says the man has an address in a village in Hornsherred," Assad went on. He turned once more to Isabel. "I cannot quite understand what you are saying the place is called, Isabel. Does the name end on 'løv'? Something else then? 'Slev,' is that what you are saying?"

Isabel gave an answering nod.

The name of the place ended in "slev." Assad was unable to decipher the first part.

"We'll take a break until Karsten gets back. Is that OK?" Carl asked the nurse.

She nodded. A break would be more than welcome.

"I thought Isabel was going to be moved?" Carl added.

The nurse nodded again. "Given the circumstances, I think it's best to wait a few hours."

There was a knock on the door, and a woman entered. "Telephone call for a Carl Mørck. Is he here?"

Carl stuck his finger in the air and was handed a wireless phone.

"Yeah?" he said.

"Hello, my name's Bettina Bjelke. I understand you've been trying to get hold of me. I'm the secretary from Intensive Care who was on duty earlier."

Carl waved Assad over so that he could listen in.

"We need a description of a man who came to visit Isabel Jønsson just before your shift ended," he explained. "Not the policeman but the other man. Can you describe him to us?"

Assad's eyes narrowed as he listened. When the call was over, he and Carl exchanged glances, shaking their heads.

The description of the person who had attacked Isabel Jønsson fitted perfectly with the man who had stepped out of the lift on the ground floor when they had been talking to Karsten Jønsson.

Mid-fifties, grayish hair, sallow complexion, glasses, rather stooping. A far cry from the image of a tall, athletic, thick-haired man in his forties that Josef had provided them with.

"This man was in disguise," Assad concluded.

Carl nodded. They had failed to recognize him despite having stared at the police artist's likeness of him at least a hundred times. Despite the broad face. Despite the eyebrows that almost met above the nose.

"Goodness gracious," said Assad at his side.

Carl's words exactly. Goodness fucking gracious. They had seen him. They could have touched him, apprehended him. They could have saved the lives of two children. Just by reaching out and grabbing hold of him.

"I think Isabel wants to tell you something," said the nurse. "And then I think we need to have that break. Isabel is exhausted." She indicated the monitors, which were showing a lot less activity than before.

Assad returned to the bed and placed his ear to Isabel's lips for what seemed like a minute, perhaps two.

"Yes," he said eventually and nodded. "Yes, I will tell him, Isabel."

He turned to face Carl.

"Some clothes belonging to the kidnapper were on the backseat of the car they crashed. Clothes with his hair on them. What do you reckon now, Carl?"

He said nothing. It sounded good in the long run, but not much use to them at the moment.

"And she says the kidnapper has a small bowling ball with a number one on his key ring together with his car keys."

Carl thrust out his lower lip. The bowling ball! So he still had it. After more than thirteen years, it was still on his key ring. Was it special to him in some way?

"I've got the address." Karsten Jønsson came in with a notepad in his hand. "Place called Ferslev, north of Roskilde." He handed the address to Carl. "Owner registered as Mads Christian Fog, one of the names Isabel gave us."

Carl stood up immediately. "Let's get going," he said, waving Assad into action.

"I don't think you need to hurry," said Karsten Jønsson hesitantly. "Emergency services were called out to the premises on Monday evening. According to the fire service in Skibby, the place burned to the ground."

Burned to the ground! The bastard was ahead of them.

Carl exhaled sharply. "Any idea if this place is by the fjord?"

Jønsson pulled an iPhone out of his pocket and typed the address into the map function. A moment passed, and then he shook his head. He handed the phone to Carl and indicated the spot. Clearly, the boathouse was somewhere else. Ferslev was several kilometers from any body of water.

But if it wasn't there, then where was it?

"We should get over there anyway, Assad. Someone in the local area must know something about him."

He turned back to Karsten Jønsson.

"Did you happen to notice a man who stepped out of the lift just as we got in, after we ran into each other on the ground floor earlier on? Gray hair and glasses. He was the one who attacked your sister."

Jønsson looked shocked. "Jesus Christ. No, I didn't. Are you sure?"

"Didn't you say they kicked you out because Isabel was going to be moved? He was probably the one who spoke to you. Did you happen to get a good look at him?"

Jønsson shook his head and seemed genuinely distressed. "No, I'm sorry. He was bent over the other woman. I had no idea. He had a white coat on."

They stared in unison at the figure beneath the sheet on the adjoining bed. This was dreadful, indeed.

"Well, thanks anyway, Karsten," Carl said, extending his hand. "I only wish we could have run into each other under more pleasant circumstances. But it's a good thing you were here."

They shook hands.

A thought flashed through Carl's mind. "Hey, Assad and Isabel. One more question. Apparently, our man has a visible scar. You wouldn't know where, would you?"

He looked at the nurse at Isabel's bedside. She shook her head. Isabel Jønsson was already asleep. His question would have to wait.

"We must do three things now, Carl," said Assad as they left the room. "We must drive around and check out all the places Yrsa picked out for us. Perhaps also think about what Klaes Thomasen said, don't you think? And also the bowling issue. We must take our drawing to places where people go bowling. And we must make inquiries with the locals at the place where the house burned down."

Carl nodded. He had just spotted Rose still leaning against the wall by the lifts. That was as far as she had got.

"Are you all right, Rose?" he asked as they approached.

She gave a shrug. "Having to tell him about his mother was hard," she said in a quiet voice. Judging by the black streaks down her cheeks, she had been having a good cry.

"Oh, Rose. There, there," said Assad. He put his arm around her gently, and they stood like that for a while until Rose withdrew, wiped her nose on her sleeve, and looked up at Carl.

"We're going to get this bastard, all right? I'm not going home. Just tell me what I can do, and I'll frigging well make sure he won't do it again." Her eyes were ablaze now.

Rose was back.

After instructing Rose to pinpoint bowling centers in Nordsjælland and fax them the artist's likeness along with the various names the killer might be using, Carl went back to the car with Assad and entered Ferslev into the GPS.

It was already late afternoon, time most people would be going home. But he and Assad weren't most people.

At least not today.

They reached the scene of the fire just as the sun was giving up. Half an hour more and it would be dark.

The blaze had been fierce. Not only was the house completely razed, with only the outer walls remaining upright, the same was true of the barn and everything else within a range of thirty to forty meters from the house. The trees reached toward the darkening sky like charred totem poles, and the neighbor's winter cereals in the adjoining field were scorched.

No wonder fire services had been called in from Lejre, Roskilde, Skibby, and Frederikssund. It could have turned into a disaster.

They walked around the house a couple of times, and the wreck of the van jutting out of the living room prompted Assad to say it all reminded him of the Middle East.

Carl had never seen the like.

"We're not going to find anything here, Assad. He's covered his tracks. Let's go over to the neighbors' and hear what they have to say about this Mads Christian Fog."

His mobile rang. It was Rose.

"Do you want to hear what I've got?" she asked.

He didn't get a chance to answer.

"Ballerup, Tårnby, Glostrup, Gladsaxe, Nordvest, Rødovre, Hillerød, Valby, Axeltorv, and the DGI leisure center in central Copenhagen, Bryggen in Amager, Stenløse Shopping Center, Holbæk, Tåstrup, Frederikssund, Roskilde, Helsingør, and Allerød, where you live. Bowling centers located in the area you said to check. I've sent faxes out to all of them, and in a minute I'll start calling them on the phone. I'll get back to you later. Oh, and don't worry, I won't be taking no for an answer."

Poor bastards.

The neighbors on the farm a few hundred meters away from what remained of the cottage invited them in. They were in the middle of dinner. An indulgence of potatoes and pork with all the trimmings, mostly their own produce, Carl assumed. Big, hearty people, with big, hearty smiles. Clearly, they had made a nice life for themselves.

"Mads Christian? To be honest, I've not seen the old bugger for years. He did have some woman on the go in Sweden, so I reckon that's where he'll be," said the man of the house. He looked like he'd been born wearing a lumberjack shirt.

"We do see that van of his sometimes, that blue thing," the wife interjected. "And the Mercedes. He earned his money in Greenland, so he can afford it. Tax-free, I imagine." She smiled.

Tax-free was something she obviously knew all about.

Carl leaned across the solid wooden table, planting both elbows on its surface. If he and Assad didn't find somewhere to eat soon, they would be driven by the irresistible aroma of roast pork to confiscate it in the name of the law.

"Old bugger, you say. Are we talking about the same man?" he asked, almost drooling. "Mads Christian Fog, yeah? According to our information he'd be forty-five at the most."

The man and his wife laughed.

"Maybe that'd be a nephew or something," said the man. "But you people can get all that sorted in a jiffy at the computer, can't you?" He nodded at his own insight. "Maybe he lends the place out to someone. We've wondered a few times, haven't we, Mette?"

The wife nodded. "It was the van coming, you see, and then the Mercedes leaving shortly after. Then there'd be no sign of life for a long time, until the Mercedes would turn up again and the van would drive away."

She shook her head. "Mads Christian's too old for that sort of carry-on. I say that every time."

"The man we're thinking of looks like this," said Assad, producing the drawing from his pocket.

The couple stared at the likeness without a hint of recognition.

"That isn't Mads Christian. He must be knocking on for eighty now," she said. "And looks like something fished out of a slurry tank. This man's well groomed. Noble-looking, almost."

"OK. What about the fire, then? Did you see it?" Carl went on.

They smiled. It was an odd reaction.

"They could see it as far away as Orø or Nykøbing Sjælland, I shouldn't wonder," said the man.

"I see. Did you notice anyone drive up to or away from the cottage that evening?"

They shook their heads. "I'm afraid not," said the man with a smile. "We'd gone to bed. We country folk get up early in the mornings, you know. Not like you lot in Copenhagen, sleeping in until six o'clock."

"We need to stop off at a petrol station," said Carl once they were back at the car. "I'm starving, aren't you?"

Assad shrugged. "I've got my nibbles."

He thrust a hand into his pocket and produced a couple of garish packets of something clearly Middle Eastern. From the decoration on the paper, it seemed they contained mainly dates and figs. "Would you like one?" he asked.

Carl sighed with satisfaction as he got into the car and began munching. Fucking all right, they were, Assad's nibbles.

"What do you think happened to the man who lived there?" Assad gestured toward the scene of the blaze. "Nothing good, if you ask me."

Carl nodded and swallowed. "That place needs sifting through with a fine-toothed comb," he replied. "If the SOCOs do their job properly, I reckon they'll find what's left of an octogenarian, assuming he hadn't already shuffled off the coil."

Assad put his feet up on the dashboard. "My feelings exactly," he said, albeit looking slightly perplexed. "What now, Carl?" he went on.

"Don't know, really. We need to get hold of Klaes Thomasen and ask him if he's managed to have a word with the sailing clubs and that forest officer at Nordskoven. Then maybe we could call Karsten Jønsson and get him to check if any Mercedes fitting the description got caught in any of the speed traps around here. Like Rachel and Isabel were."

Assad nodded. "Perhaps they will find the Mercedes from the license plate number. Perhaps we will be lucky, even if Isabel Jønsson wasn't certain."

Carl started the car. He doubted things would be that easy.

And then his mobile chimed. Couldn't it have rung thirty seconds earlier, he thought to himself with a sigh, thrusting the gearshift into neutral.

It was Rose, and she was excited.

"I called all the bowling centers, and no one knows the man in the drawing."

"Shit," said Carl.

"What is the matter?" Assad wanted to know, returning his feet to the floor.

"But that's not all, Carl," Rose went on. "Like we reckoned, there was no one answering to any of the names we've got, apart from Lars Sørensen. There were a couple of Lars Sørensens."

"It figures."

"But then I spoke to this bloke in Roskilde. Very keen to help, he was. He was new to bowling, but he handed me on to one of the other players who happened to be there having a drink. They've got a game on tonight, apparently. Anyway, he reckoned there were several players he knew who looked like the man in the drawing. But there was one thing in particular he noticed."

"And what was that, Rose?" Why did she always have to drag things out?

"Mads Christian Fog, Lars Sørensen, Mikkel Laust, Freddy Brink, and Birger Sloth. He almost fell about laughing when I told him the names."

"How do you mean?"

"Well, he didn't know anyone with the exact names. But on the team he's playing with tonight, they've got a Lars, a Mikkel, and a Birger. He was the Lars. And what's more, there'd been a Freddy, too, a few years ago, who used to bowl with them at another center, but he got too old. No Mads Christian, mind, but still a bit of a coincidence, don't you think?"

Carl put the uneaten half of something figgy on the dashboard. He was all ears now. It was by no means unusual for a perpetrator to be inspired by the names of those around him. Names in reverse order. A "K" becoming a "C." First and last names mixed together. The psychologists could most likely account for the underlying mechanism, but Carl called it lack of imagination.

"And then I asked him if he knew anyone who had a bowling ball with the number one on it on their key ring, and he cracked up laughing again. They all have them on their team, he said. Seems they've been playing together for years, in various places."

Carl sat staring at the beam of the car's headlights. First the coincidence of the names, now the bowling ball.

He turned his gaze to the GPS. How far were they from Roskilde? Thirty-five kilometers?

"Hey, are you still there, Carl? Do you think there might be anything in it? Like I said, Mads Christian wasn't among the names he mentioned."

"No, he wasn't, Rose. But that name's from a different place entirely, and we know where now. And yes, I do think there might be something in it. Of course there is. Fucking hell, Rose, we're on to something here. What's the address of that bowling center?"

She sifted through some papers in the background. Carl gestured toward the GPS, so Assad would be ready to enter the address.

"Right," he said, as she read it out. "Well done, Rose. I'll call you back later."

He turned to Assad.

"Københavnsvej 51, Roskilde," he said and thrust his foot down immediately on the accelerator. "For fuck's sake, Assad, get it on the GPS!"

43

Use your brains, he kept telling himself. Do the right thing. Nothing hasty you might regret.

He drove the car slowly up the road. Returned the nods of his neighbors, then turned into the driveway with the weight of disaster bearing down on his shoulders.

He was out in the open, where keen-eyed birds of prey could watch all his movements from a distance. What had happened at the hospital could hardly have gone more wrong.

He glanced at the child's swing dangling loosely on its ropes. Less than three weeks had passed since he put it up in the birch tree. His image of a lazy summer at play with their little boy had been snatched away. He picked a small, red plastic shovel out of the sandpit and felt welling grief threatening to overpower him. It was a feeling unknown to him since boyhood.

He sat down on the bench in the garden for a moment and closed his eyes. Only months before, he would have been inhaling the scent of roses and a woman's nearness.

He could still sense the quiet joy of the child's arms around his neck, the gentle breath against his cheek.

Stop it, he told himself, and shook his head. It was all in the past now. Like everything else.

His parents were to blame for his life having turned out like it had. His parents and his stepfather. But he had hit back on many occasions since then. How often had he struck against men and women like them? What was he supposed to regret?

Any struggle would claim its victims. He would have to live with that.

He tossed the toy shovel onto the lawn and stood up. There were new women out there. He would find Benjamin a good mother. If he realized all his assets now, he could make a good life for the two of them somewhere in the world, until the time came for him to carry on his mission and bring in money again.

But right now, there were realities to deal with.

Isabel was alive and recovering. Her brother was in the police and had been at the hospital when he had come to eliminate his risk. That was the greatest threat. He knew these people. They would make it their personal goal to find him. But they would not succeed. He would make sure of it.

The nurse he knocked out would remember him. From now on, every time she encountered a stranger with an unfathomable gaze, she would recoil. The shock of the blow he had delivered to her throat would remain deep inside her. Her confidence in others would be shattered. He would be the last person on earth she would be likely to forget. The secretary, too, would remember him. Nevertheless, he was not afraid of these two women.

When it came down to it, they had no idea what he looked like.

He stood in front of the mirror, considering his reflection while he removed his makeup.

He would be all right. More than most, he was familiar with people's ability to observe. A sufficiently furrowed face and people would notice nothing else. And a stiff gaze behind a pair of glasses was always enough for a person not to be recognized without them.

A conspicuous wart, however, would be seen and noted, though oddly enough its absence after being removed would go unseen.

Some things served to disguise, others did not. Yet one thing was certain: the best disguise was one that made a person look ordinary, ordinary being unremarkable. And the unremarkable was his area of expertise. Putting wrinkles in the right places, applying shadow to the face and around the eyes, arranging the hair in a different way, manipulating the eyebrows, allowing complexion and hair condition to indicate age and state of health. He used all these things to achieve the perfect result.

Today, he had been the average man in the street. They would recall his age, his accent, and the glasses. But they would be in doubt as to whether his lips were narrow or full, his cheekbones vague or distinct. He knew this, and it made him feel safe. Naturally, they would not forget what had happened, and certain of his features would remain salient, but they would not recognize him the way he really looked.

Let them pursue their investigations. They knew nothing. Ferslev and the van were gone, and he would be, too, before long. Exit the average man, from this average residential street in Roskilde. A man in a comfortable detached home, one of a million others in this small country.

In a few days, when Isabel was able to talk, they would know what he had been up to all these years, but would still have no idea of his identity. That was something known only to him, and that was the way he wanted it to remain. But there would be mention in the media. A lot, even. Warnings would go out for potential victims to be aware, and for that reason alone he would have to suspend his activities for some time. He would live modestly on his savings and find himself new bases from which to operate.

He looked around his tidy home. Although his wife had looked after the place and they had spent a fair amount of money on repairs and improvements, the financial crisis meant it was a bad time for selling property. Still, it would have to go.

Experience told him that if a person was compelled to disappear, burning selected bridges would always be insufficient. There could be no half-measures: new car, new bank, new name, new address, new circles. As long as there was a good explanation, so friends and neighbors understood why you were going, things would work out. A new job abroad, good money, pleasant climate. Anyone could understand that. No one would bat an eyelid.

In other words: no sudden, irrational behavior.

He stood by the open door in front of the mountain of packing cases and said his wife's name out loud a couple of times. When there was no sign of life after a minute or so, he turned and left.

It suited him well. Doing away with a pet of which the family had been fond was something few people cared to do, and that was the way he felt about her.

Now it was yesterday's news. And all for the best.

Tonight, after bowling, he would put the body in the car and drive up to Vibegården and get it all over and done with. His wife and the two children up there had to go.

And once the bodies had dissolved and the tank had been rinsed and cleaned in a couple of weeks, everything would be ready.

His mother-in-law would be devastated. The farewell note from her daughter would say that their poor relationship had been a significant factor in their decision to emigrate, and that she would be in touch once the wounds had healed.

And when, as was inevitable, her mother eventually began to wonder, perhaps even express suspicion, he would travel home and force her to write her own suicide note. It would not be the first time he had given a person a lethal dose of sedative.

But to begin with, he would have the packing cases destroyed, get the car mended and sold, and put the house up for sale. He would sit down at the computer and find a comfortable place in the Philippines, collect Benjamin, assure his sister that he would still be sending her money, and then he would set off through Europe to Romania in some nondescript vehicle he could abandon in a street somewhere, secure in the knowledge that within hours it would be stripped to the chassis.

The plane tickets made out in their new assumed names would reveal nothing about their true identities. No one would take notice of a little boy and his father traveling from Bucharest to Manila. Only in the opposite direction, perhaps, would the pair be remarked upon.

A fourteen-hour flight to the future.

He went downstairs into the hall and found his Ebonite bowling bag. In it were the accoutrements of his sporting success. He had triumphed so often over the years, and if there was one thing he was going to miss about this life, it was bowling.

Truth be told, he was not overly fond of his teammates. Two of them, at least, were morons he would prefer to see the back of. All were simple men, of simple ideas and simple lives. Average, by name and by nature. Yet to his mind it didn't matter who they were, so long as their usual score was the right side of two hundred and fifty. The sound of the ten pins scattering was the sound of success. On that count, all six on the team were as one.

That was the beauty of it.

The team went out to win. It was the reason they could count on him being there whenever there was something at stake. That, and his very useful friend: Pope.

"All right?" he said as he approached the bar. "Sitting here, are we?" As if they would sit anywhere else.

High-fives all around.

"What are we drinking?" he asked. The usual entry into team togetherness.

Like the rest of them, he stuck to mineral water prior to a game. Their opponents generally did not, which was their mistake.

They sat for a few minutes, kicking around the pros and cons of the team they were up against, conversation drifting on to how certain they felt about winning the district championships on the coming Ascension Day.

And then he told them.

"I'm afraid you're going to have to find a replacement for me before then." He spread his arms out apologetically. "Sorry, guys."

They fell silent, gawping at him with accusations of treachery blazing in their eyes. For a while there was silence. Svend, always with gum in his mouth before a match, upped his chewing rate. He and Birger looked decidedly pissed off. He had expected as much.

Lars broke the silence. "Sorry to hear it, René. What happened? Trouble with the wife? Typical!"

It was an interpretation that won support.

"Nah." He allowed himself to chuckle. "It's not the wife. It's work. I've been offered an executive position with a new company spearheading solar technology in Tripoli. But don't worry, I'll be back in five years, once the contract runs out. I reckon you'll be needing me for the Old Boys team by then."

No one laughed, but then he could hardly blame them. What he had done was sacrilege. The worst thing anyone could do to a team before an important match. A distracted mind could only ever put a wrong spin on the ball.

He apologized for his poor timing, knowing it was all he could do.

He was already on his way out. Just like he wanted.

He knew exactly how they felt. Bowling was their escape. For them, an international top job would never loom on the horizon. Now that he had driven in the wedge, they would be feeling like mice in a trap. He had felt like that, too, once. But that was a long time ago.

Now he was the cat.

44

She had seen the light of morning percolate down through the packing cases three times and felt certain that she would see it no more.

She had cried a few times, until she was no longer able. Until she hadn't the strength even for that.

When she tried to open her mouth, her lips would not part. Her tongue stuck to the roof of her mouth. A day perhaps had passed since there had been spit enough in her mouth to allow her to swallow.

Now the thought of death seemed liberating. To sleep forever, with no more pain. To end this desolation.

"Let he who stands before death, he who knows that the end is nigh and who sees the moment at which it all must cease, let him speak of life," she recalled her husband once having sneeringly quoted his father as saying.

Her husband! That man, who had never been alive in the slightest, how dare he heap scorn on such a sentiment? In a moment, she might even be dead herself. Certainly that was how she felt. But at least she could say she had lived.

Hadn't she?

She tried to recall when, but everything merged into one. Years became weeks; partial recollections ricocheted in time and place, mingling together in all sorts of impossible patterns.

My mind will die first, I know that now, she thought.

She was no longer aware of her own breathing. It was so faint that she could not feel the air passing through her nostrils. The fingers of her free hand tingled. The fingers that yesterday had scratched a hole in the packing case above her and encountered something made of metal. For a while, she had tried to figure out what it was, but couldn't.

Now her fingers tingled again. It felt like they were being pulled by strings directly attached to God. Tinglings, and the occasional flutter, like butterfly wings.

Do you want me, God? she asked. *Is this the first touch, before you take me to heaven?*

She smiled inside. She had never been this close to God before, this close to anyone. And she felt neither afraid nor alone. All she felt was exhaustion. The weight of the boxes on top of her no longer existed. Only this exhaustion.

Then suddenly she felt a pain in her chest. A stabbing sensation, so astonishing it made her open her eyes wide in the dark. *The day is gone, my last day,* flashed through her mind.

She heard herself groan and felt the muscles of her chest contract around her heart. Her fingers opened in spasms of cramp. Her face tightened.

Oh, it hurts. Please, God, let me die now, she prayed, over and over, until these portents of death at once ceased with a stab of pain almost more unbearable than the first.

In the seconds that followed, she was certain her heart had stopped. She waited for the darkness to come and take her away once and for all. And then her lips parted in a desperate attempt to snatch one final breath. A slight gasp that lodged itself in the tiny place inside her where her will to live stubbornly remained.

She felt a vein pulsate at her temple. Another in her lower leg. Her body was still too strong to succumb. God's ordeal for her was not yet over.

Fear of what might now be in store made her pray. A brief prayer that she might escape the pain and that death would come soon.

She heard her husband open the door and say her name. But she was no longer able to form or utter a response. And what good would it do?

She felt her index and middle fingers twitch reflexively. Felt them strike the box above, her nails against the metal object she had encountered before. Metal, cold and unreal, until a spasm of cramp caused all her fingers to splay, and she sensed that protruding from the smooth surface of this object was something in the shape of a little V.

She tried to think rationally. Tried to separate things, so the nerve impulses from her colon that had ceased to function, from cells that screamed for water, and from skin that was no longer sensitive would not disrupt the image she now struggled to comprehend. The image of something metal with a raised V on its surface.

Her thoughts dissolved. Again, this void that threatened to consume her brain. This emptiness that returned to her at increasingly short intervals.

And then the pictures came rushing into her mind. Images of smooth objects, the menu button of her mobile, the face of her watch, the mirror in her dressing table, leaped forth and danced before her. Everything smooth that she had ever registered in her life jostled to find a place in her mind, a place where it would be recognized. And then, there it was. An object she had never used but which men had often produced from their pockets with pride when she had still been a child. A status symbol from an age long gone, to which her husband, too, had yielded. There it lay, the Ronson lighter with its little V, tossed into a packing case, perhaps so that she alone might find use for it. So that it might provoke her thoughts, or make for a final solution in what was left of her meager life.

If I could extract it and light it, everything would quickly find an end, she thought. And everything he owns would disappear with me.

Again, she smiled inside. The thought was so oddly life-giving. In burning everything, she would at least be making her own mark, planting a thorn in his life, which he would never, ever be able to remove. He would lose everything for which his crimes had been committed.

Retribution.

She held her breath and began again to scratch away at the cardboard, realizing at once how tough the material was. How unreasonably resilient.

Scratching away tiny pieces at a time. Like a wasp consuming the surface of the table in the garden. She imagined paper dust descending through the air in front of her face. Tiny particles that together might make a hole, if only her fingers were strong enough. A hole through which the Ronson lighter might fall into her hand.

Eventually, when she had labored enough to dislodge the lighter only a few millimeters, her strength ebbed away.

She closed her eyes and pictured Benjamin for a moment. Bigger than he was now, talking, and nimble on his feet. A gorgeous little boy running to greet her. A fine leather ball in his hands and his eyes full of mischief. How she would have loved to have been there. For his first proper sentence. His first day at school. The first time he looked into her eyes and said she was the best mummy in all the world.

The emotion she felt may have been no more apparent than a slight moisture in the corner of her eye, but it was there. Emotion at the thought of Benjamin. Her little boy, who would now have to live without her.

Benjamin, who would have to live with . . . him.

NO! everything inside her screamed. But what was the use?

And yet the thought kept coming back, more and more insistent. *He* would be with Benjamin, and this thought would be the last thing on her mind when her heart finally succumbed.

She extended her fingers again. The nail of her middle digit found a shred, and she began to scrape, scratching with this one finger, until its nail broke. Her only tool denied her. And then she drifted into sleep, tormented by her realization.

The cries from outside came at the same time as the mobile again chimed in her back pocket. It sounded weaker now. Soon the battery would be spent. She knew the signs.

The voice belonged to Kenneth. Perhaps her husband was still in the house. Perhaps he would open the door. Perhaps Kenneth would know something was wrong. Perhaps . . .

Her fingers moved slightly. It was the only response she could muster.

But the front door did not open. The sounds of arguing never came. All she perceived was her mobile ringing, its tone becoming fainter. And then the lighter suddenly dislodged and came to rest against her thumb.

The slightest wrong movement and it would be lost to the darkness that surrounded her.

She tried to disregard Kenneth's cries, to ignore the fact that the vibrations of the phone in her pocket were now growing weaker. And then, with the slightest twitch of a finger, the lighter lay in her hand.

Once she felt certain she had a proper hold, she twisted her wrist as far as she could. Perhaps only a centimeter, but enough to give her hope. Her ring finger and little finger were lifeless and numb, and yet she believed in her endeavor.

She pressed as hard as she could and heard the faint escape of gas as the valve opened. So very faint.

How could she ever press hard enough to make a spark?

She tried to channel all that remained of her strength into the extremity of her thumb. Into this last display of will to show the world how she had lived her final hours, and where she had died.

She pressed again. All the life inside her went into this one action. And like a shooting star in the night sky, the spark burst out in front of her in the darkness, igniting the gas and making everything bright.

She twisted her wrist the one free centimeter back toward the cardboard and allowed the flame to lick the sides of the packing case. Then she let go and watched the sliver of blue turn yellow and widen, wandering slowly upward and leaving behind it a blackened fan of soot for each centimeter's advance. What for a moment had been aflame was then extinguished incrementally, like a trail of gunpowder leading nowhere.

After a moment, the weak flame reached the top of the box and died. Only a deep red glow remained. And then it, too, was gone.

She heard him call and knew it was over.

No more strength.

She closed her eyes and imagined Kenneth outside in front of the house. The brothers and sisters they could have given to Benjamin. A beautiful life.

She sniffed in the smell of smoke, and new images darted in her mind. Camps by the lake. Bonfires of Midsummer Eves in the company of older boys. The aromas of a farmers' market in Vitrolles, the one time she and her brother had spent a camping holiday with their parents.

The smell of smoke seemed stronger now.

She opened her eyes to a yellow light dancing with blue above her.

And the next moment everything was in flames.

Burning.

She had heard that almost everyone who died in fires died from smoke inhalation, and that if a person wanted to save themselves they should crawl along the floor, underneath the smoke.

She wanted to die from smoke inhalation. It sounded like a merciful, painless death.

But the smoke was rising and she was unable to stand. The flames would consume her before the smoke. She would burn to death.

And then came the fear.

The final, definitive dread.

45

"There, Carl!" Assad indicated a smooth-rendered, sienna-colored building facing out on to Københavnsvej in the process of being done up.

WE'RE OPEN—SORRY ABOUT THE MESS! a banner read over the door. It didn't look like an entrance.

"Turn down here toward the shopping center, and then to the right. We must go around the building site there," instructed Assad, pointing in the direction of a dark, empty area amid new buildings.

They pulled onto a dimly lit car park next to the bowling alley and found a space. Carl got out and walked around. No fewer than three dark Mercedes were parked here, though none looked as if it had just been involved in an accident.

Carl wondered how long it might take to get a car repaired. Longer than this, surely? His thoughts darted to his service pistol, lying inside the gun locker at Police HQ. He probably ought to have brought it with him, but how could he have known when they left this morning? It had been a long and eventful day.

He looked up at the building.

Apart from a sign composed of a pair of enormous bowling pins, nothing at the rear of the pretentious building even remotely suggested the place might be a bowling alley.

The same was true when they went inside and found themselves in a stairwell filled with steel lockers. It was a bit like left luggage at a railway station. Otherwise, the walls were bare. An empty space with a couple of doors and no indication of where they might lead. Stairs going down, done out in the national colors of Sweden. The place was utterly devoid of life.

"Let's go downstairs into the basement," Assad suggested.

THANK YOU FOR YOUR CUSTOM—HOPE TO SEE YOU AGAIN AT ROSKILDE BOWLING CENTER—SPORT, FUN, AND EXCITEMENT! read a sign on the other side of the door.

Carl wondered if the last phrase was supposed to refer to bowling. To his mind, bowling was neither a sport nor fun nor exciting. It was more lukewarm beer, saggy arses, and indigestible food.

They went straight through to reception, where a man was on the phone amid a jumble of rules and regulations, bags of sweets, and reminders to display your parking permit.

Carl glanced around the place. The bar was packed. Bowling bags and duffel bags dumped all over. People gathered in animated clusters around the twenty-odd lanes. Men and women in shapeless trousers and a variety of polo shirts with club logos on them. It looked like a typical match night.

"We need to speak to a Lars Brande. Do you know him?" Carl asked when the man behind the counter had finished on the phone.

He gestured toward a group at the bar. "That's him over there, with the glasses on his head. Just shout for Bumble, you'll see."

"Bumble?"

"Yeah, that's what we call him."

They went over, noting inquisitive eyes weighing up their conspicuous clothes and footwear, wondering what they wanted.

"Lars Brande? Or do you prefer Bumble?" Carl asked, extending a hand. "My name's Carl Mørck, Copenhagen Police, Department Q. Mind if we have a word?"

Lars Brande smiled and shook hands. "Oh, right, I'd almost forgotten. One of our teammates just dropped a bombshell. Says he's leaving us, just as we've got the district championships coming up. Bit distracted. Sorry about that."

He gave the man next to him a thump on the back. Most likely the one who was letting them down.

"Are these your teammates?" Carl asked with a nod in the direction of the others.

"Roskilde's finest," Brande replied, thumbs aloft.

Carl gave Assad a look: *Stay here and keep a sharp eye on them, so no one does a runner.* That was the last thing they needed.

Lars Brande was a tall, sinewy man with a slender frame. His features distinguished him as a man whose work involved long hours sitting indoors, a watchmaker, perhaps, or maybe a dentist. But his skin was weathered and his hands broad and tanned. All in all, it was a rather confusing impression.

They went over to the rear wall and watched the bowling for a moment before Carl commenced.

"You spoke to my assistant, Rose Knudsen. I understand you identified a coincidence of names and that you found it quite amusing. The bowling ball on the key ring, too. I want you to know that this isn't just some routine matter we're dealing with. We're investigating a very serious case of the greatest urgency, and everything you say may be taken down in evidence."

Brande looked out of sorts. The glasses perched on top of his head seemed almost to sag into his hair.

"Am I under suspicion? What's this about?" The man was clearly ill at ease with the situation. It felt odd, especially as Carl had in no way considered him a suspect. Why would he have been so accommodating with Rose if he had something to hide? No, it didn't make sense.

"Under suspicion? Not at all. I'd just like to ask you some questions, if that's OK?"

Brande glanced at his watch. "Well, it's rather a bad time, to be honest. We're on in twenty minutes, so normally we'd be getting ourselves together now. Can't it wait until later? Not that I'm not curious, mind."

"No can do, I'm afraid. Can we go over to the officials' desk a minute?"

Brande looked puzzled but nodded all the same.

The tournament officials seemed just as bewildered, but when Carl produced his badge, they were immediately compliant.

Carl and Brande returned to the far wall, passing a number of tables as the message came over the speakers.

"Due to unforeseen circumstances, the order of play has now been revised," one of the officials explained and proceeded to outline the changes.

Carl glanced toward the bar, where five pairs of eyes now stared in their direction. Five faces wearing baffled expressions, and behind them Assad, his gaze fixed on the backs of their necks with the keenness of a hyena.

One of these men was the man they were looking for. Carl was certain of it. As long as they remained here, the children would be safe. Provided they were still alive.

"How well do you know your teammates, exactly? I understand you're the captain?"

Brande nodded and answered without returning Carl's gaze. "We've been together since the center opened. Before that, we played in Rødovre, but this is more convenient. There were a couple more of us back then, but those of us who live in the Roskilde area decided to carry on here instead. So, yeah, I know them pretty well. Especially Beehive, the guy with the gold watch over there. He's my brother, Jonas."

Carl thought Lars Brande seemed nervous. Was he hiding something?

"Beehive and Bumble. Odd names," said Carl. Perhaps a polite distraction would ease the tension. Right now, it was imperative that the man opened up as quickly as possible.

Brande gave what looked like a wry smile.

"Maybe. But Jonas and I are beekeepers, so it's not that strange really," he explained. "We've all got nicknames on the team. You know how it is."

Carl nodded, even though he didn't. "I notice you're all rather tall. You're not *all* related, are you?"

If they were, they would cover each other's backs, come what may.

Brande smiled again. "No, only Jonas and me. But you're right, we *are* above average height, all of us. Long arms make for a better swing, you see." He laughed. "No, it's pure coincidence, that's all. Never really thought about it until now."

"I'm going to ask for your civil registration numbers in a minute, the whole team. But before I do, would you happen to know if any of you has been in trouble with the police?"

Brande seemed genuinely astonished. Perhaps the gravity of the matter was only now dawning on him.

He took a deep breath. "We don't know each other well enough to say," he said. It was clearly not entirely true.

"Do any of you drive a Mercedes?"

He shook his head. "Not Jonas or me. I've no idea what the other lads have got, you'll have to ask them yourself."

Was he covering up for someone?

"Surely you know what cars they drive? Don't you go off to tournaments together?"

He nodded. "Yes, but we always meet up here first. Some of us keep our gear in the lockers upstairs, and Jonas and I have got an old VW camper with room for the six of us. It's cheaper, going together."

His answers were plausible and seemed natural enough, even if the man was beginning to look like a poor excuse for himself.

"Who are the other team members, exactly? Can you point them out to me?" Carl said, then thought better of it. "No, hang on a minute. First tell me where you got those bowling-ball key rings of yours. Are they common? The sort of thing you can buy in any bowling alley?"

Brande shook his head. "Not these ones. The number one is because we're good." He smiled wryly again. "Normally there's nothing on them, or just a number indicating the ball size you use. Never a number one, because they don't make them that small. No, one of the lads brought these home from Thailand." He produced his own from his pocket. Small, dark, and worn. Nothing special to look at, not even with the number engraved on it.

"The lads here and a couple more from the old team are the only ones who've got them," he went on. "I think he came home with ten, if my memory serves me right."

"And who would that be?"

"Svend. Bloke in the blue blazer. Sitting over there chewing gum, looks like a gentlemen's outfitter. I believe he actually was once."

Carl eyeballed him. Like the rest of the team, he was keeping a close eye on proceedings, wondering what the police might want with their captain.

"OK. So you're on the same team. Does that mean you practice together and stuff?" Carl asked. He made a mental note that it would be good to know if any of them made a habit of not being able to turn out.

"Jonas and I do, and one or two others might join us once in a while. Mostly for laughs, though. We used to more in the old days, not so often now." He smiled again. "A couple of us might get in a bit of practice before a match, but apart from that, we don't really train at all. Maybe we should, but what the hell. If you're notching up over two hundred and fifty almost every game, there's hardly room for improvement, is there?"

"Would any of you have a visible scar?"

Brande gave a shrug. They would have to check each of them individually afterward.

"Is it OK to sit down, do you think?" Carl gestured toward the eating area, where tables were lined up with white tablecloths on them.

"I don't see why not."

"Right, I'll sit down there, then. Would you ask your brother to come over?"

Jonas Brande was plainly confused. What was this all about? Why was it so important they had to change the order of play?

Carl didn't answer. "Where were you this afternoon between three fifteen and three forty-five? Can you account for your whereabouts?"

Carl considered him. Masculine. Forty-fiveish. Was this the man he had seen outside the lifts at the hospital today? The man in the drawing?

Jonas Brande leaned forward slightly. "Between three fifteen and three forty-five? I couldn't really say, to be honest."

"I see. Nice watch you've got there, Jonas. You don't look at it much, then?"

The man laughed unexpectedly. "Well, I do actually. I just don't wear it when I'm at work. It's worth about thirty-five thousand, this. I inherited it from our father."

"So you were at work between three fifteen and three forty-five? Is that what you're saying?"

"Yeah, I'm pretty certain I would have been."

"So how come you couldn't say?"

"What I meant was I couldn't say whether I was in the workshop, outside repairing beehives, or over in the barn putting a new cog in the extractor."

He wasn't the brighter of the two brothers. Or was he?

"Do you sell a lot on the side?"

This was a turn he had not been expecting. So obviously they did. Not that it bothered Carl. That was another department altogether. All he wanted was to get a picture of who exactly he had in front of him.

"Have you got a criminal record, Jonas? And I can check as easy as that." He snapped his fingers in the air. Or tried to.

Jonas Brande shook his head.

"What about the other blokes on the team?"

"Why are you asking?"

"I'd like an answer."

He withdrew slightly. "I think maybe Johnny Go, Throttle, and Pope."

Carl leaned his head back. Fucking stupid names. "And who might they be, when they're at home?"

Jonas Brande narrowed his eyes as he looked over at the men by the bar. "Birger Nielsen, the bald bloke, he plays the piano in a bar. That's why we call him Johnny Go. Throttle's the bloke next to him. Mikkel, his proper name is. He's a motorcycle mechanic in the city. I don't think either of them ever did anything serious. In Birger's case I think it was just some little racket selling booze without the revenue stamps. Mikkel got done for dealing stolen cars. A good many years ago now, though. Why do you want to know?"

"What about the third guy you mentioned? Pope, is that right? That would be Svend, the bloke in the blue blazer?"

"Yeah. Catholic, he is. Hence the nickname. Don't know much about him apart from that. He was up to something in Thailand, I think."

"And who's the one remaining? The guy sitting talking to your brother. Is he the one who's leaving the team?"

"Yeah, that's René. He's our best player, so it's a bit of a blow. René Henriksen, like the footballer, the central defender who used to play for Denmark. That's why we call him Three."

"Because that was Henriksen's shirt number?"

"It was at some point, anyway."

"Have you got any ID on you, Jonas? Something with your civil registration number on it?"

He reached obediently into his pocket and produced a driver's license.

Carl wrote down the number.

"By the way, do any of you drive a Mercedes?"

Jonas Brande shrugged. "I wouldn't know. You see, we usually meet up . . ."

Carl didn't have time to hear the same story twice.

"Thanks, Jonas. Can I ask you to send René over, please?"

Their eyes were fixed on each other from the moment he stood up in the bar to the moment he sat down in front of Carl.

On the face of it, an agreeable sort. Not that one should ever be taken in, but decently dressed, well groomed, and with a firm, affable gaze.

"René Henriksen," the man said by way of introduction, tugging at the creases of his trousers as he sat down. "I understand from Lars Brande that you've got some kind of investigation on the go. Not that he said anything. I'm surmising, that's all. Has it got something to do with Svend?"

Carl considered the man closely. Perhaps rather too narrow in the face, though maybe it was just the chubby cheeks of youth falling away as the years advanced. High temples, hair recently trimmed. But a hairpiece would cover all that. There was something about his eyes that gave Carl a funny feeling. Those fine wrinkles weren't just smile lines.

"Svend? You mean Pope, I suppose?" Carl smiled, though it was the last thing he felt like doing.

The man raised his eyebrows.

"Why would you think this has to do with Svend, I wonder?" Carl said.

The man's expression changed. No longer keen and on his guard, now almost the opposite. A shameful, caught-in-the-act kind of look, like being found out to be ignorant instead of clever.

"Oh," he said. "My mistake. It was wrong of me to mention Svend like that. Can we start again?"

"OK. You're leaving the team, I understand. Planning on moving?" Carl asked.

Again, that same look, as if the man suddenly felt naked.

"Yes, as a matter of fact. I've been offered a job in Libya, in charge of a project. Huge solar panels in the desert, generating power through one central unit. It's quite revolutionary. Perhaps you've heard of it?"

"Sounds interesting. What's the company called?"

"Ah, that's the dull part." He smiled. "For the time being, it's nothing but the company's registration number. The people behind it haven't been able to agree yet whether the name should be in Arabic or English, but I can tell you that the company presently goes under the name 773 PB 55."

Carl nodded. "How many on the team here drive a Mercedes, besides you?"

"Who says I've got a Mercedes?" The man shook his head. "As far as I know, Svend's the only one with a Merc. Usually, though, he comes here on foot. He hasn't that far to go."

"How would you know Svend drives a Mercedes? Jonas and Lars gave me the impression you drive to the tournaments together in their camper."

"And so we do. But Svend and I see each other privately. Have done for some years now. Or used to, at least. I haven't been around to his place for some time, though, obviously. But before that, we used to see quite a bit of each other. He's still driving the same car, I know that for sure. A disability pension doesn't go far."

"What's 'obviously' supposed to mean?"

"Well, his trips to Thailand, you know? Isn't that what this is about?"

This had all the hallmarks of a diversionary maneuver. "What trips? I'm not from the Drug Squad, if that's what you think."

Now the man looked like he was at a total loss. Was he play-acting?

"Drugs? No, that wasn't what I was thinking," he said. "Listen, I don't want to land him in it. It's probably just me getting the wrong idea, that's all."

"Maybe you ought to elaborate on these suspicions of yours? Unless you prefer to be taken in for questioning at Police HQ?"

The man cocked his head. "No, thanks, anything but. What I mean is, Svend let it slip once that these trips of his to Thailand were all about organizing local women to accompany infants to Germany. Babies selected for adoption by approved childless couples. He takes care of all the paperwork and reckons he's doing people a favor. The thing is, I don't think he's that bothered about where the kids are coming from, if you understand what I'm getting at?" He shook his head. "He's a great tenpin bowler, so I've no qualms about being on the team with him, but since I found out what he was up to with those children I've not been over to his place once."

Carl looked across at the man in the blue blazer. Could it be a smokescreen to cover up for something else? Stick to the truth but not too closely was the code of most criminals. Maybe he didn't go to Thailand at all. Maybe he was the kidnapper and needed an alibi for his bowling mates while carrying out his despicable trade.

"Does anyone on the team sing particularly well, or badly?"

The man cracked up laughing. "I'm afraid we don't sing that much."

"What about yourself?"

"Oh, I'm a good singer. I was a verger once, at the church in Fløng. In the choir, too. Do you want to hear me?"

"No, thanks. What about Svend, is he a singer?"

He shook his head. "No idea. Is that why you're here?"

Carl forced a crooked smile. "Does any one of you have a visible scar?"

The man gave a shrug. Carl couldn't eliminate him yet. He sensed it. Definitely not.

"Have you got any ID on you? Something with your civil registration number on it?"

The man said nothing but reached into a pocket and produced a thin wallet of the kind meant only for credit cards and the like. Lars Bjørn at Police HQ had one, too. Maybe it was a status symbol of some sort. What would he know?

Carl wrote down the man's details, noting his age. Forty-four years old, which fitted their assumptions.

"What was the number of your new company again?"

"It's 773 PB 55. Why?"

If Carl himself had made up such a ridiculous name on the spur of the moment, he would have forgotten it again two minutes later. So the man was probably telling the truth.

Carl shrugged.

"One more thing. What were you doing between three and four o'clock this afternoon?"

The man pondered.

"Let me see. Between three and four. Getting my hair cut at a place on Allehelgensgade. I've got an important meeting tomorrow, so I need to look presentable."

The man smoothed a hand over his temple to demonstrate. It certainly looked like it had just been cut. But they would have to check as soon as they were done here.

"Mr. Henriksen, I'd like you to take a seat at the white table over there in the corner, if you don't mind. I may need to speak to you again."

The man nodded and said he would be only too pleased to help.

Nearly everyone said that when the police came around.

Carl signaled to Assad to send over the man in the blue blazer. There was no time to waste.

Svend looked like anything but a man on a disability pension. His shoulders amply filled his jacket without him having to resort to eighties-style shoulder pads. His features were pronounced, the muscles of his jaw clenching visibly as he chewed on his gum. A broad-faced man with thick eyebrows that almost came together above the nose. Hair worn short in a buzz cut. A stooping kind of gait. This was a man who most certainly possessed more resources than might immediately be apparent.

He smelled pleasantly of nothing in particular. His gaze was somewhat vague, with dark rings under his eyes that made them look closer together than they actually were.

Definitely a profile worthy of further investigation.

He gave René Henriksen a nod as he sat down.

In a way, it was all very cordial.

46

He wasn't very old the first time he realized he could control his emotions to the extent that they could not be observed.

His life at home in the pastor's residence accelerated the process. Living not in the light of God but in His shadow, emotions would often be misinterpreted. Joy was perceived as shallowness, vexation as antipathy and defiance. And each time he was misunderstood, he would be punished. For that reason, he kept his feelings to himself. It was the safest way.

It had since proved useful to him, when injustice dragged him down or disappointment struck.

So no one knew what was inside him.

And today, this was what saved him.

The sudden appearance of these two policemen had been a bombshell. But he had absorbed the shock and shown nothing.

He recognized them the moment they walked in. The two men he had seen talking to Isabel's brother outside the lifts at the Rigshospital that afternoon as he had made his escape. An odd pair like them would always stick out a mile.

The question was whether they had recognized him.

He thought not. If they had, their questioning would have been more incisive. The detective he had spoken to would have looked at him in a completely different way.

He considered his options. There were two escape routes, if things came to a head. Round the back into the maintenance room, through the rear door, and then up the fire escape past that stupid chair with no legs that someone had placed there to make it clear there was no exit. Or he could take the direct route past the other policeman, the assistant. The toilets were over between the reception and the exit, so going that way would not initially arouse suspicion.

But the dark one would see him as soon as he went past the door to the gents. He would have to leave his car behind. As always, he had parked at a distance, in the parking structure over by the RO's Torv shopping center. But if he went for the car, he wouldn't have time to get out. They would cut him off and he would be trapped.

No, the second option wasn't on. Leaving the car meant he would have to run for it. And while he knew the town well enough to be familiar with the shortcuts, he had no way of knowing if he was fast enough.

His best bet would be to divert their attention in some way. If he was to get away and remain in control of the situation, which was absolutely imperative, he would have to employ more radical means.

One thing was certain: he needed to put some distance between himself and these two policemen, who had been able to trace him this far. How the hell they had done so, he had no idea.

He was undoubtedly under suspicion. Why else would they be asking about the Mercedes, his singing, the name of the company he had invented? He was lucky he had remembered the number.

He had produced a false driver's license, in the name he had been using for years in the club. Seemingly, they had accepted it at face value, so he wasn't completely exposed yet.

The problem was, they quite literally had him cornered. Things he had just lied about could be easily checked, and soon he would run out of identities and bolt-holes in which to hide out. But his most immediate concern was that for the moment he was boxed in, with no way out without being seen.

He glanced across at Pope, who sat opposite the detective, chewing frenziedly on his gum and looking sheepish.

This man was the consummate sacrificial lamb. He had used him on several occasions as his role model. A man like Pope was the quintessence of nondescript. Of what to look like if you didn't want to be noticed. Ordinary, like himself. In fact, they resembled each other a lot in many ways. Same-shaped face, same height, stature, and weight. Affable-looking, both of them. Credible in appearance, even rather dull. Men who bothered to take care of their looks without ever going over the top. It was from Pope he had got the whole idea of making himself up so his eyes looked too close together and his eyebrows appeared to be joined. And a dab of powder on his cheeks made them look just as broad as Pope's.

They were features he had borrowed more than once.

But there was another thing about Pope, which he now intended to use against him.

Svend went to Thailand several times a year, and it wasn't to enjoy the scenery.

The detective sent Pope to sit at the table next to his own. His face was as white as chalk, and if his expression was anything to go by, he had been dealt a body blow of some considerable force.

Now it was Birger's turn, and then there would be only one left. There was no time to waste; the interviews would soon be over.

He went and sat down next to Pope. If the policeman had tried to stop him, he would have sat down anyway. He would have kicked up a fuss about police-state methods. It would have come to an argument, and he would have casually walked away and out of the door with the message that they could contact him at home if they wanted anything more from him. He had given up his civil registration number, so it wouldn't be hard to find his address if they needed to question him again.

This, too, was an escape route. They couldn't just arrest him with nothing to go on. And it seemed obvious to him that concrete evidence was the one thing they lacked. Even if a lot had changed in this country of theirs, the police still didn't go around arresting people unless they were on solid ground, and Isabel had most certainly not yet been able to provide them with any substantial reason to charge him.

That time would come, inevitably so. But not yet.

He had seen the condition Isabel was in.

No, they had no proof of anything. No corpse, no knowledge of his boathouse. Soon, the fjord would swallow up his crimes.

Ultimately, it was just a question of keeping his distance for a couple of weeks and then eliminating all traces.

Pope glared at him angrily. His fists were clenched, the muscles of his neck were taut, his breathing quick and heavy. All the right reactions, so very useful in the current situation. If this was done right, it would all be over in minutes.

"What did you tell him, you bastard?" Pope hissed as he sat down at the table.

"Nothing they didn't know already, Svend," he replied softly. "I can assure you, he seems to know everything. You've got a record from before, remember?"

He sensed the man's breathing become more agitated.

"It's your own fault, Svend. Pedophiles just aren't popular these days," he said, louder this time.

"I'm no pedophile. Is that what you told him?" Pope's voice had risen a tone.

"He knows it all. They've traced you. They know you've got child porn stored on your computer."

Pope's knuckles were white.

"I don't believe it. They can't." His words were controlled but louder than Pope would have liked. He glanced around.

It seemed to be working. The detective was looking their way, keeping an eye on them, just as he had anticipated. He was cunning. Most likely he had put them next to each other just to see what would happen. They were both under suspicion. That much was obvious.

He turned his head toward the bar and discovered that the dark-skinned assistant was just out of sight. So he was hidden from that angle.

"They know you don't actually download that stuff from the Internet, Svend. But they do know you get it from your mates on a flash drive," he said casually.

"That's not true!"

"But that's what he told me, Svend."

"Why's he asking you lot, if it's all about me? Are you sure it's me they're after?" For a moment, he forgot to chew his gum. His jaw stood still.

"He's probably questioned all sorts of people you know, Svend. Now he's doing it here in public, to see how you react."

Pope began to tremble. "I've got nothing to hide. It's not like nobody else is doing the same. That's how it is in Thailand. I'm not harming any of those kids. I just like to be with them, that's all. There's nothing sexual. Not when I'm with them."

"Well, *I* know that, Svend. You told me that. The thing is, our detective here reckons you're trafficking these kids. Says it's all on your computer. Trafficking and exchanging kiddie porn. Didn't he mention that to you?" He frowned. "Would there be any truth in that, Svend? You're always so busy on those trips. You've said so yourself."

"He thinks I'm *trafficking*?" Svend realized his voice was too loud and glanced around again before continuing in a quieter tone. "Is that why he asked if I was good at filling in forms and the like? And how I could afford to travel so much on a disability pension? That's something *you* put in his head, René. You know perfectly well I'm not on a disability pension. But that's what he said you'd told him. I had to put him straight. My money's from the business I sold off, you *know* that."

"Don't look, but he's looking our way now. If I were you, Svend, I'd get up nice and easy and head for the door. I doubt they'll stop you."

He reached into his pocket and unfolded the knife, keeping it discreetly in his hand.

"Once you get home, destroy everything. Anything that might compromise you, all right? Word of advice from a friend, that's all. Names, contacts, old plane tickets, the lot. Are you with me? Go home and do it now. Just get up and go. Do it now, otherwise they're going to put you away, Svend. You know what they do to people like you in prison, don't you?"

The man they called Pope glared at him, his eyes widening for a moment before becoming calm. Then he pushed back his chair and stood up. He had got the message.

He got up, too, reaching out as though to shake hands. He curled his fingers around the knife, palm facing down, the blade turned inward toward himself.

Pope considered him cautiously for a moment, then smiled. All his reservations seemed to vanish at once. He was a pitiful individual, with desires he was unable to control. A religious man who struggled against shame and who bore the disapprobation of the Catholic Church upon his shoulders. And here was his friend, standing in front of him with his hand outstretched. He meant him well.

He made his move at the instant Pope reached out to shake his hand, pressing the shaft of the knife into the man's palm, prompting Pope to take hold of the weapon in a reflex. And then he jerked the bewildered man's hand toward him in a sudden lurch that caught him just above the hip, a flesh wound, but clean. Not much pain, but it would bleed and look serious enough.

"Hey, what are you doing? Look out, he's got a knife!" he cried and pulled Pope's hand toward him again. The two wounds were perfect. He was already bleeding through his polo shirt.

He saw the policeman leap to his feet, his chair falling backward. Everyone at their end of the room turned toward them.

He shoved Pope away from him. The man staggered sideways, staring at the blood on his hands. He was in shock. It had all happened so fast. He was clueless.

"Run, you fucking murderer," he hissed, clutching at his side.

And then Pope turned on his heel in panic, knocking over a couple of tables as he fled toward the lanes.

He clearly knew the place like the back of his hand. He was heading for the maintenance room and the rear exit.

"Look out, he's got a knife!" he shouted again, and saw everyone step aside as the man came running.

He watched as Pope leaped across lane 19, the little dark guy from the police setting off in pursuit like a predator after its prey. It was an uneven match.

And then he stepped forward and picked up a bowling ball from the rack.

As the detective's assistant caught up with him at the end of the lane, Pope began to slash at the air in front of him like a madman. Something inside him had snapped. But the policeman dived at his legs, and the two of them went headlong into the gutter between the last two lanes.

The detective was already halfway toward them, but the bowling ball the team's best player sent hurtling down the far lane was faster.

There was an audible crack as it struck Pope in the temple. Like an unopened bag of potato chips crushed underfoot.

The knife slipped out of Pope's hand onto the floor.

All eyes moved from the inert figure to the man they all seemed instinctively to know had delivered the strike. A couple of them, at least, also knew why he now sank to his knees, clutching his side.

It was all so perfectly executed.

The detective seemed genuinely shaken when he eventually came over to where he had flopped down on a chair.

"This is serious," he said. "Svend won't survive, as far as I can see. His skull's smashed. If I were you, I'd say a prayer and hope the paramedics do a good job."

He looked toward the far lane where ambulance crew were clustered around the injured Pope. Say a prayer, the policeman had said. But that was the last thing he was going to do.

A paramedic emptied Svend's pockets and handed the contents to the detective's Arab assistant. These two were thorough. They would call for assistance now and start going through the information. Checking civil registration numbers, his own as well as Pope's. Scrutinizing alibis. Calling up a hair salon he had never visited. Before long, he would be under renewed suspicion. The time in between was all he had.

The detective at his side stood frowning, his thoughts already churning. And then he looked him straight in the face.

"The man you might just have killed has kidnapped two children. It's possible he's already murdered them. But if they're still alive, they're going to die of thirst and hunger if we don't get to them first. In a moment, we're going to go over and search his house. Maybe you can help us in that respect. Would you have any idea whether he owns a cabin, a weekend retreat, or anything similar in a remote location? A place with a boathouse?"

He managed to disguise his astonishment. How did they know there was a boathouse? How the *hell* could they possibly know?

"Sorry," he said, his voice controlled. He looked over at the figure on the floor. "I'd like to help, but I've no idea."

The detective shook his head. "Circumstances notwithstanding, there'll be charges against you for this. Just so you know."

He nodded deliberately. Why protest against something so obvious? He wanted to seem cooperative. Maybe they would ease up a bit.

The assistant came over, shaking his head.

"Perhaps you are stupid?" he said incredulously, looking him straight in the eye. "This situation was under control. Why did you throw that bowling ball? Do you realize what you have done?"

He raised his bloodied hands by way of explanation. "The man had lost his mind," he said. "I thought he was going to stab you."

He clutched at his side again and winced, so they could see how much pain he was in.

And then he sent the assistant an injured, angry look.

"You ought to be grateful I've such a good aim," he said.

The two policemen conferred for a moment.

"Local police will be here in a minute. They'll take your statement," the detective said. "We'll make sure someone has a look at those wounds of yours. There's already another ambulance on its way. Just stay calm, it'll help check the bleeding. It doesn't look that bad, if you ask me."

He nodded and withdrew a couple of steps.

Time for the next move.

An announcement came over the PA system. Tournament canceled, due to unforeseen circumstances.

He glanced across at his teammates, who stared emptily into space, almost oblivious to police instructions to stay put.

They had their work cut out now, the police. Things had got out of hand. Most likely they would be tied up with reports all night.

He stood up and walked calmly along the far wall toward the paramedics at the end of lane 20.

Nodding briefly as though in acknowledgment of their efforts, he ducked down and picked up the knife, glancing back and slipping through the narrow passage that led into the maintenance room in one inconspicuous, seamless movement.

Less than twenty seconds later he was up the fire escape and outside in the parking area, hurrying away toward the parking structure by RO's Torv.

He swung the Mercedes out onto Københavnsvej, just as the blue lights of the ambulance came into view farther down the road.

Three sets of lights and he was gone.

47

What had happened was disastrous. A catastrophe, no less.

He had put the two men together, and it had gone terribly wrong.

Carl shook his head in despair. Fucking hell. He had been too eager, too determined. But how could he have known things would go so badly? All he had wanted to do was put the wind up them and see what happened.

Both of them fitted the bill, but which was their man? That was the issue. Both bore at least some resemblance to the police artist's likeness, and he wanted to see how they would react under duress. He was expert at spotting those burdened by guilt. So he had thought, anyway.

And now it had all gone pear-shaped. The only person who could tell him where the children were was being carried on a stretcher out to a waiting ambulance with his life in the balance, and it was Carl's fault entirely. The situation was even graver than before.

"Look at this, Carl."

He turned to Assad, who had Pope's wallet in his hand. He didn't look happy.

"Yeah, what is it, Assad? No address?"

"Actually, there is. But that's not it. There's something else, and it is not good, Carl. Look!"

He handed him a checkout receipt from a Kvickly supermarket. "Look at the time on it, Carl."

Carl stared at it for a moment and felt sweat begin to trickle down his neck.

Assad was right. Something else that wasn't good.

A checkout receipt from Kvickly in Roskilde. It was a modest amount, for a lottery ticket, a newspaper, and a packet of Stimorol. Bought that same day at three twenty-five P.M. Only minutes after Isabel Jønsson was attacked at the Rigshospital in Copenhagen. More than thirty kilometers away.

If this receipt belonged to Pope, then he wasn't their man. And why shouldn't it belong to him, being in his wallet?

"Shit," Carl groaned.

"The paramedics found half a packet of Stimorol chewing gum in his pocket," Assad said, gazing around the room with a gloomy look on his face.

And then his expression changed. Like a light going on. "Where is René Henriksen?" he burst out.

Carl scanned the premises. Where the fuck was he?

"There!" Assad yelled, pointing in the direction of the narrow passage that led out into the room where the pin machines were serviced and maintained.

Carl saw it straightaway. A streak on the wall, hardly a few centimeters long. But it was blood.

"Bastard," he snarled and took off across the lanes.

"Be careful, Carl," Assad shouted behind him. "The knife is gone, too. I think he took it with him."

Please let him be here. It was his only thought as he entered a room a couple of meters wide, filled with machinery, tools, and junk. But the place was too quiet. Much too quiet.

He darted past ventilation pipes, ladders, and a work surface cluttered with spray cans and ring binders. And then he was at the back door.

He wrenched it open with dread and peered out into a dark void with a fire escape leading away.

Their man was gone.

Assad returned after ten minutes. Sweating and empty-handed.

"I found blood over by the parking structure," he said.

Carl exhaled slowly. He had been on tenterhooks and had just received word back from the duty officer at Police HQ.

"No, sorry. Name and civil registration number don't match," the officer had told him.

No match! It meant that René Henriksen didn't exist. And yet this was the man they were looking for.

"OK, thanks, Assad," he said wearily. "I've called in the dog team. They should be here any minute. At least they've something to go on, even if it's our only hope."

He filled Assad in on the situation. They had no data on the man calling himself René Henriksen. What they did have was a serial killer on the loose.

"I want you to get hold of the chief superintendent here in Roskilde. His name's Damgaard," Carl said after a moment. "I'll call Marcus Jacobsen."

He was not unused to disturbing his boss at home. Jacobsen was available at that number around the clock. That was the standing agreement.

"Violence never rests in the city, so why should I?" he always said.

Nevertheless, Marcus sounded anything but pleased to be dragged away from his domestic bliss when he heard why Carl was calling.

"For God's sake, Carl. Roskilde's not my jurisdiction, you know that. Get on to Damgaard instead."

"I know that, Marcus, and Assad's trying to find his number as we speak, but the moron who fucked up is one of yours."

"Well, I never thought I'd hear that kind of admission coming from Carl Mørck, I must say." He sounded almost pleased.

Carl dismissed the thought. "There'll be journalists crawling all over this place any minute now," he said. "What am I supposed to do?"

"Put Damgaard in the picture, then pull yourself together. You've let your perp get away, now it's up to you to catch the son of a bitch. Bring in local plod. Good night, Carl, and good hunting. We'll follow up in the morning."

Carl felt a pain in his chest. He and Assad were on their own. With fuck all to go on.

"Here is Chief Superintendent Damgaard's private number," said Assad. All Carl had to do now was press the right keys on his mobile.

He listened to the phone ringing at the other end, feeling the pain in his chest again. No, for Chrissake. Not now!

"Damgaard here. I'm not available right now. Please leave a message," said the voicemail.

Carl snapped the phone shut angrily. Wasn't a chief super supposed to be available 24/7?

He gave a sigh. They would have to make do with the local lot once they turned up. Maybe one of them might even know how to stop the tabloid circus before it got started. They'd have to, before every journalist on Sjælland got there. Two of the local vultures were already taking pictures at the back entrance. Jesus Christ! Rumor ran even faster than events themselves in this multimedia age. A hundred pairs of eyes had witnessed the incident and a hundred mobile phones had been on hand to preserve it for posterity. No wonder the scavengers were already on the scene.

He nodded to the two local detectives who had been let through by uniformed police posted at reception.

"Carl Mørck." He flashed them his ID. Both seemed to recognize the name but said nothing. He put them in the picture. It wasn't easy.

"So we're looking for a man who can disguise himself beyond recognition. We don't know his name. And the only thing we've got to go on, basically, is that he drives a Mercedes. Not much, is it?" one of the detectives recapped. "Let's get some prints off that bottle of mineral water he was drinking. Maybe that might give us something. What about your statement? Do you want us to take it now?"

Carl gave his colleague a pat on the shoulder. "My statement can wait. You know how to find me, so start with the staff here. I'll have a word with his bowling mates."

They let him get on, albeit reluctantly. He was right.

Carl nodded to Lars Brande, who was looking pretty shaken. Two men gone at once. A stabbing, and most likely a death. His team was in tatters. People he thought he knew had let him down unforgivably.

He was gutted, no doubt about it. His brother and the pianist, too, for that matter. Silent, moping faces, all three of them.

"We need to establish René Henriksen's true identity, so think hard. Is there anything you know that might help us? Anything at all. Has he got kids? If so, what are their names? Is he married? Where has he worked? Where does he do his shopping? What bakery does he use when it's his turn to get the pastries in? Think!"

Three of the bowling team didn't react at all. The fourth, the mechanic they called Throttle, shifted uneasily on his bar stool. He didn't seem quite as affected as the others.

"Actually, I have wondered once or twice how come he never talked about his work," he said after a moment. "I mean, the rest of us do all the time."

"And?"

"Well, he always seemed to be so much better off than the rest of us financially, so he must have a pretty decent job. Always got more rounds in after tournaments than we did. So, yeah, I reckon he's well-heeled in comparison. Take that bag there, for example."

He jerked his thumb in the direction of the floor behind an adjacent bar stool.

Carl stepped backward at once and found himself staring at an odd-looking sports bag composed of different compartments joined together by zips.

"That's an Ebonite Fastbreak," said the mechanic. "Do you want to know what one of them costs? Thirteen hundred, at least. You should see mine. Not to mention the balls he uses . . ."

Carl wasn't listening anymore. This was just too incredible for words. Why hadn't they thought of this before? Here was the guy's bag, for Chrissake.

He shoved the bar stool away and pulled the bag toward him. It was like a little suitcase on wheels, the various compartments seemingly able to combine in different ways.

"You sure this is his?"

The mechanic nodded, surprised that his information should create such interest.

Carl waved his Roskilde colleagues over. "Gloves, quick!" he barked.

One of them delved into his pockets and produced a pair of latex examination gloves.

Carl felt sweat begin to drip from his brow and onto the blue sports bag as he opened it. It was like entering some long-forgotten burial chamber.

The first thing he saw was a large, multicolored bowling ball. Smooth and shiny, consummately modern. Then a pair of shoes, a tin of talcum powder, and a small bottle of Japanese peppermint oil.

He held the bottle up in front of the bowling team. "What would he use this for?"

The mechanic stared. "It was just something he did. A drop in each nostril just before a game. Probably reckoned it helped his breathing. For concentration, maybe. You can try it yourself. Wouldn't recommend it, though. Horrible stuff."

Carl unzipped the other compartments. Another bowling ball in one, the next empty. And that was it.

"Can I see, too?" Assad asked as Carl straightened up and stepped back. "What about these front compartments? Have you checked them?"

"I was just going to," Carl replied, his thoughts already elsewhere.

"You wouldn't know where he bought this bag, I suppose?" he asked no one in particular.

"Off the Internet," said three voices all at once.

The bloody Internet.

"What about the shoes and the other stuff?" he asked, as Assad pulled a pen from his pocket and proceeded to poke it into the finger holes of one of the bowling balls.

"We get all our gear off the Internet. It's cheaper," said the mechanic.

"Didn't you ever talk about more private things? About your childhoods and growing up? How you got into bowling? The first time you scored over two hundred?"

Come on, you oiks. You're holding back on me, you must be.

"Actually, no. Apart from work, the only thing we ever talked about was the game," the mechanic continued. "And when it was over, we talked about how we'd got on."

"Here, Carl," Assad said suddenly.

Carl stared at the piece of paper in his assistant's hand. It was compressed tightly into a ball.

"I found it at the bottom of the thumbhole," Assad explained.

Carl stared at him, at a loss. The bottom of the thumbhole, was that what he said?

"That's right, yeah," Lars Brande said. "René always lined his thumbholes. His thumbs were rather short. He had this idea that he had to have contact with the bottom. Said it gave him a better feeling of the ball when he put the spin on it."

Brande's brother Jonas chipped in: "Everything always had to be just right with him. Lot of rituals. The peppermint oil, the thumbholes, the color of the ball. He couldn't ever play with a red ball, for instance. Said it took away his focus."

"Yeah," the pianist added. It was the first time he had opened his mouth. "And he used to stand like three or four seconds on one leg before making his run-up. We should never have called him Three. Stork would have been better. We've often joked about it."

They all broke into laughter, then stopped just as abruptly.

"This one is from the other ball," said Assad, handing Carl another wad of paper the same as the first. "I was very careful when extracting it."

Carl smoothed out the two paper pellets on the counter.

And then he looked up at Assad in disbelief. What the hell would he do without him?

"These are receipts, Carl. Receipts from an ATM."

Carl nodded. Some bank staff would be putting in overtime now.

A checkout receipt from Kvickly and two withdrawal receipts from Danske Bank. Three small, utterly unremarkable slips of paper.

They were back in business.

48

His breathing was calm. It was how he kept the body's automatic defense mechanisms at bay. If he allowed adrenaline into his veins, his heart would accelerate, and that was the last thing he wanted since he was already bleeding profusely from his hip.

He took stock.

The important thing was that he had got away. He had no idea how they had come so close, but he would analyze that later. Right now, the long and short of it was that there was nothing in his rearview mirror to indicate that he was being followed.

The question was what the police's next move would be.

There were thousands of Mercs like the one he drove. Many had been taxis; they were all over the place. But if police blocked the roads leading in and out of Roskilde, stopping any one of them would be a simple matter, indeed.

He had to proceed as quickly as possible. Get back home, bundle his wife's body into the boot along with the most incriminating of his packing cases. Lock the place up, and then get off to the cottage by the fjord.

He would make it his base for the coming weeks.

And if he found it necessary to venture out, he would just have to disguise himself. He had always protested when the team had had their photographs taken with trophies they'd won, and mostly he had succeeded in avoiding it. But they would find photos of him if they were determined enough. No doubt about it.

A couple of weeks on his own at Vibegården was in every respect a good idea. Get the bodies dissolved in the tank. Then get out.

He would have to give up the house in Roskilde, and Benjamin would have to remain with his sister. When the time came, he would collect him again. Two or three years in the police archives and the case would be covered in dust.

He had thought ahead and had already stashed some necessities at Vibegården for just such an eventuality as this. New identity papers and a reasonable amount of money. Not enough for a life of luxury but sufficient to live simply in some out-of-the-way place and then gradually get things started again. The idea of a couple of years' peace actually appealed to him.

He glanced into the rearview mirror and began to laugh.

They'd asked if he could sing.

"Of course I can, of course I ca-aa-an!" he sang out, chuckling to himself at the thought of the prayer meetings at the Mother Church in Frederiks. Everyone would surely remember how out of tune he sang there. That was the whole idea. So they thought they knew him, but they didn't.

The fact of the matter was he had a good voice.

But there was one thing he would have to do: find a plastic surgeon who could remove the scar behind his right ear, the gash from the nail when they caught him spying on his stepsister. How the hell did they find out about his scar? Had he been careless with his disguise at some point? He'd always made sure he covered it up ever since that strange boy he killed had asked him how it got there. What was his name again? It had got to the stage now where he could hardly tell them apart.

He let it go and thought instead of what had happened at the bowling center.

If they reckoned they were going to find his prints on that bottle of mineral water, they were mistaken. He had wiped it clean with a serviette while they were questioning Lars Brande. They wouldn't find anything on the tables or chairs, either. He had been much too careful for that.

He smiled to himself. Yes, he had been meticulous.

And then he remembered the bowling bag. Two bowling balls with his fingerprints all over them, and in the thumbholes two receipts that could lead them to his address in Roskilde.

He took a deep breath and tried to concentrate on staying calm so as not to worsen the bleeding.

Nonsense, he thought to himself. They won't find those receipts. Not to begin with, at least.

No, he had all the time in the world. Maybe they would trace him back to his house in Roskilde in a day or two. But all he needed was half an hour.

He turned down his road and immediately saw the young man on the lawn in front of the house. Standing there, calling Mia's name.

Another obstacle.

Remove him from the equation. Do it now.

He would park the car a little farther away.

He reached for the blood-covered knife in the glove compartment, then drove slowly past the house, turning his head away as he passed. Her suitor sounded like a randy tomcat, wailing pathetically like that. Did she really prefer that adolescent to him?

And then he noticed the elderly couple across the road peeping through their curtains. How come old people always had to be so nosy?

He speeded up.

There was nothing he could do. Not with witnesses.

They would just have to find the body in the house. What difference would it make? The police already suspected him of serious crimes. He wasn't sure which, but serious enough.

Maybe after a while they would find a packing case full of prospectuses from estate agents concerning weekend retreats for sale, but what good would it do them? They were in the dark. No documents existed to indicate which of them he had decided to buy.

He had no immediate cause for concern. The deeds to Vibegården were at the house itself, in the box with the money and the passports. There was nothing to worry about.

If only he could staunch this bleeding soon and didn't get stopped on the way, everything would be all right.

He found the first-aid box and stripped to the waist.

The stab wounds were deeper than he had anticipated. The second of them, especially. He had felt sure he'd jerked Pope's hand toward him with just the right degree of force, but somehow he had expected him to offer more resistance.

That was why he was bleeding so much. He would have to take the time to remove the traces from the front seat of the Mercedes before he got rid of it.

He found the syringe and the anesthetic and sterilized the wounds. And then he injected himself.

He sat for a moment and looked around the living room. He really hoped they weren't going to find Vibegården. This was the place where he felt most at home. Away from the world, away from its deceit and all its faithlessness.

Next he prepared the needle and suture. Within a minute, he was able to jab the needle into the flesh around his wounds without feeling a thing.

Another couple of scars for the plastic surgeon, he thought to himself, and laughed.

When he had finished, he inspected his work and laughed once again. It was hardly an expert job, but the bleeding had stopped.

He applied a compress with sticking plaster, then lay down on the sofa. When he was ready, he would go down to the boathouse and kill the children. The sooner he did it, the sooner he could be rid of the bodies. And before long he would be away again.

Ten minutes. Then he would go to the outbuilding and get the hammer.

49

Twenty minutes went by before they knew who had made the cash withdrawal and where he lived. The name was Claus Larsen, and it would take them less than five minutes to get to his house.

"What are you thinking, Carl?" Assad asked as Carl negotiated the roundabout on Kong Valdemars Vej.

"I'm thinking it's a good thing we've got backup on our tail and that they remembered to bring their service pistols."

"You think that will be necessary, then?"

He nodded.

They turned into the road. Even from a distance they could see a man, faintly illuminated by streetlamps, yelling up at a window.

It wasn't the man they were looking for. He was younger, slimmer, and utterly desperate.

"Hurry! Help me! The house is on fire!" he screamed as they ran toward him.

Carl glanced back as his colleagues screeched to a halt in the car behind, already calling for assistance. The elderly couple standing in their dressing gowns across the way had most likely done the same.

"Is there anyone in the house?" Carl barked.

"Yes, I think so. There's something definitely not right about this house." The man was completely out of breath. "I've been stopping by the last few days, but no one answers the door, and when I call my girlfriend's mobile, I hear it ringing upstairs, but she never takes the call." He pointed up at the window in the roof, then put his hands to his head in despair.

"And why is it on *fire* now?" he cried.

Carl looked up at the flames that were now clearly visible in the upstairs window just above the front door.

"Have you seen a man enter the house within the last half hour or so?" he asked.

The man shook his head. He could hardly stand still. "I'm going to break the door down," he shouted, frantic now. "OK?"

Carl glanced at his colleagues. They nodded.

He seemed strong and in good shape and plainly knew what he was doing as he took a short run-up, sprang feetfirst at the door, and delivered a sharp, forceful kick against the lock with his heel. Only to give out a painful groan followed by a stream of invective as he fell heavily to the ground, the door still totally intact.

"The lock's too strong!" He turned in panic toward the patrol car behind him. "Help me, for God's sake!" he yelled. "I think Mia's in there!"

And then came an earsplitting crash. Carl spun toward the sound in time to see the hunched figure of Assad enter the house through the shattered front window.

Carl went after him, the young man on his heels. Assad had made a good job of it. Double glazing and window frame lay shattered on the floor, along with the spare wheel he had hurled through the pane.

They climbed inside.

"This way!" the man shouted, almost dragging Assad and Carl along with him into the hallway.

There wasn't that much smoke on the stairs, but there was plenty once they reached the first floor. It was already impossible to see a hand in front of your face.

Carl pulled his shirt up to cover his mouth and told the others to do the same. Assad was already coughing behind him.

"Go back, Assad!" Carl barked. But Assad wasn't listening.

From outside came the sound of approaching fire engines, but it was of no comfort to the young man as he felt his way along the wall.

"I think she's in here. She says she always keeps her mobile with her," he spluttered in the thick smoke.

"Listen, tell me if you can hear it." He must have dialed a number on his phone, because a couple of seconds later they heard a faint ringing close by.

The man staggered forward, fumbling to find the door. And then they heard what sounded like a window on the other side of the wall exploding in the blaze.

One of the local colleagues from Roskilde made it up the stairs, spluttering violently. "I've got an extinguisher here, just a small one," he stammered out. "Where's the fire?"

The answer to his question immediately became apparent as the young man flung open the door of the room and flames leaped out at them. There was a loud hiss from the fire extinguisher. Its effect was minimal but enough for them to be able to see inside.

The sight that met them was not encouraging. The blaze had got a good hold on the ceiling and a mountain of cardboard boxes stacked inside.

"Mia!" the man yelled in anguish. "Mia, are you in there?"

And at that same moment a jet of water burst through the shattered roof window from outside, turning the air to steam.

Carl threw himself to the floor and felt a searing pain in his arm and shoulder as he instinctively covered his face.

They heard shouts from below, and then came the foam.

It was all over in seconds.

"Get all the windows open," the officer from Roskilde coughed. Carl jumped to his feet and felt his way to a door, the other officer doing likewise.

As the smoke was sucked out of the upper level, the scene of the blaze was revealed. The young man stood in the doorway, on a sopping wet floor, feverishly heaving packing cases out onto the landing. Several were still aglow, but nothing could stop him.

And then Carl saw the lifeless body on the landing.

It was Assad.

"Out of the way!" he yelled, shoving one of the officers aside.

He vaulted down a couple of stairs and grabbed hold of Assad's legs, dragging his body toward him and hauling him over his shoulder.

"Help him," he snarled at a pair of rescuers as he came out onto the lawn. They responded quickly with an oxygen mask.

For God's sake, help him, was the only thought in his mind, even as cries went up from upstairs.

He didn't see the young woman when they brought her down. He noticed her only when they laid her on a stretcher next to Assad. She looked like her body was caught in a seizure, as though rigor mortis had already set in.

Then they brought out the young man. He was covered in soot, and much of his hair had been singed away, but his face seemed untouched.

He was crying.

Carl turned from Assad and went over to him. He looked like he might collapse any minute.

"You did all you could," were the only words of comfort Carl could muster.

And then the young man began to sob and laugh all at once.

"She's alive," he stuttered and sank down to his knees. "I felt a pulse. Her heart's beating."

Behind them, Assad began to cough.

"What's going on?" he shouted, arms suddenly flailing.

"Lie still," a rescuer told him. "You're suffering from smoke inhalation. It might be serious."

"This is not smoke poisoning. I fell on the stairs and hit my head. I could not see the arse of an elephant in there."

Ten minutes passed before the woman opened her eyes. The oxygen and the IV therapy administered by the paramedic worked wonders.

In the meantime, the firemen were damping down the remains of the blaze, and Assad, Carl, and the local police from Roskilde had already gone through the house, finding no immediate signs of documents relating to any René Henriksen or Claus Larsen. And nothing about any property close to water.

The only thing they found were the deeds to the house they were in, and they were in the name of another person altogether.

Benjamin Larsen.

They checked to see if any Mercedes might be registered at the address. Negative again.

The guy had so many exit strategies it was beyond belief.

In the front room was a pair of framed wedding photos, the bride all smiles, bouquet in hand, her groom at once stylish and expressionless. So the woman on the stretcher was his wife. Their names were on the door: Mia and Claus Larsen.

Poor Mia.

"It was a good thing you were here, otherwise all this could have been much worse," he told the young man, who had climbed into the ambulance and was now holding Mia's hand. "What's your relationship to this woman? And who are you?" Carl asked.

He said his name was Kenneth. That was all. Everything else would have to wait.

"You'll need to move over a bit, Kenneth. I need to ask Mrs. Larsen some questions of the utmost urgency." He glanced inquiringly at the paramedic, who flashed a pair of fingers in the air by way of response.

Two minutes. That was all he could have.

Carl took a deep breath. This might be their last chance.

"Mia," he began, "I'm a policeman. You're in safe hands now, so there's no need to be frightened. We're looking for your husband. Is he the one who did this?"

She nodded silently.

"We need to know if your husband owns a property, or has access to one, in close proximity to water. A weekend retreat, perhaps. Would that ring a bell?"

She pressed her lips together. "Maybe," she said faintly.

"Where, Mia?" he asked, trying his best to control his voice.

"I don't know. The boxes." She nodded slightly in the direction of the house.

This was going to be impossible.

Carl turned to the Roskilde guys and told them what to look for. A property with a boathouse somewhere along the fjord. If they found a prospectus or anything like it in the packing cases Kenneth had heaved out onto the landing, they were to get hold of him without delay. For the moment, they could forget about the boxes left behind in the room. They had almost certainly been destroyed.

"Do you know your husband by any name other than Claus Larsen, Mia?" he asked.

She shook her head.

And then she lifted her arm very slowly. The exertion of it made her tremble. She put her hand gently to Carl's cheek.

"Please find Benjamin. Please." And with that, her hand fell back and she closed her eyes in exhaustion.

Carl gave the young man an inquiring look.

"Benjamin's their son," he said. "Mia's only child. He's just eighteen months old."

Carl sighed and gave the woman's arm a cautious squeeze.

What suffering her husband had caused in the world. And who would stop him now?

He straightened up and allowed a quick check of his singed arm and shoulder. It would hurt like hell for the next couple of days, the paramedic said.

Too bad.

"Are you OK, Assad?" he asked. The firemen were already rolling up their hoses as the ambulance drove off down the road.

His assistant rolled his eyes. Apart from a bit of a headache and soot all over him, he was fine.

"He's got away, Assad."

Assad nodded.

"What can we do now?"

Carl gave a shrug. "It may be dark, but I think we need to get out to the fjord and check the places Yrsa put a ring around."

"Do we have the photos with us?"

Carl nodded and retrieved a plastic folder from the backseat. Fifteen aerial photos. Rings all over them.

"Why do you think Klaes Thomasen never called us back?" Assad pondered as they got into the car. "He said he would speak to the forest man."

"The forest officer. Yeah, he did. Maybe he couldn't get hold of him."

"Do you want me to call Klaes and ask, Carl?"

Carl nodded and handed Assad his mobile.

It took a while for Thomasen to answer. When he did, Assad's frown plainly indicated something was wrong. He snapped the phone shut and turned to Carl with a troubled look on his face.

"Klaes Thomasen was surprised. He said he told Yrsa yesterday that the forest officer from Nordskoven had confirmed there was once a boathouse at the end of the track leading to the gamekeeper's cottage." He paused for a second, as though puzzled by the word, then continued. "He told Yrsa to pass the message on. I think that was when you gave her the flowers, Carl. She must have forgotten."

Forgotten? Was that what he said? How the hell could she have forgotten? This was crucial information. Was the woman completely brainless, or what?

He stopped his inner rantings. They wouldn't help.

"Where is this boathouse, Assad?"

Assad drew the map up to the dashboard and pointed. The property had been encircled twice. Vibegården. On Dyrnæsvej, Nordskoven. The same place Yrsa had picked out for them. It was almost too much to bear.

But how could they have known she had hit the bull's-eye? And how could they have anticipated that the situation would now be so very urgent? That a new kidnapping was in progress?

He shook his head. But a new kidnapping *was* in progress, and the outcome didn't bear thinking about.

Everything indicated that two children were now in the same situation Poul and Tryggve Holt had found themselves in thirteen years before. Two children in the most acute danger. At this very moment.

50

Reaching Jægerspris, they turned right at a red pavilion that read *SCULPTURES AND PAINTINGS*, and before long they were in the woods.

They carried on along asphalt made wet by rain until a sign appeared reading *MOTOR VEHICLES PROHIBITED*. An address down the track here would be perfect for anyone not wishing to be disturbed.

They drove slowly on. The GPS told them there was still a fair way to go down to the house, but their headlights lit up the way ahead. If they came to a clearing, they would have to turn them off and carry on in the dark. In a few weeks, there would be leaves on the trees, but for the time being, nature afforded rather less in the way of cover.

"We're coming now to a track called Badevej, Carl. You must turn off the headlights. Once we are past, the woods open out."

Carl gestured toward the glove compartment, and Assad took out the torch.

Then he killed the lights.

They continued on in the beam from the torch. It was just enough to show them where they were going.

They became aware of marshland down to the fjord. Cattle, too, at rest in the grass. And then a little substation on their left-hand side. They heard its faint hum as they passed.

"Was that what they heard, do you think?" Assad wondered.

Carl shook his head. No, it was too faint. Gone already.

"There, Carl." Assad pointed to a dark outline. A second later, they saw it was a windbreak extending from the track down to the water's edge. Vibegården lay just beyond.

They pulled in to the side, got out, and stood for a moment, taking stock.

"What are you thinking, Carl?" Assad asked.

"I'm thinking about what we're going to find. And about that service pistol I left in the locker back at HQ."

Beyond the windbreak was a paddock, and behind that another cluster of trees extending down to the fjord. Not a big property, by any means. But the location could hardly have been better. Here were the makings of a happy life. Or the perfectly concealed crime.

"Look!" Assad pointed. Carl saw what it was immediately. The shape of a small structure close to the shore. An outbuilding of some sort.

"And there," Assad exclaimed, gesturing toward the trees.

A dim light.

They pressed through the branches of the windbreak and found themselves looking at a redbrick cottage. Timeworn and rather neglected. Light was coming from two windows facing the track.

"He is inside the house, don't you think?" Assad whispered.

Carl said nothing. How should he know?

"The track leads up to the house on the other side, I think. Maybe we should see if there is a Mercedes there?" Assad whispered again.

Carl shook his head. "There is. Believe me."

And then they heard the sound. A deep-toned drone coming from the bottom of the garden. Like a motorboat returning home across a calm lake. A gentle, resonant hum in the near distance.

Carl's eyes narrowed as he listened. They had been right all along. There *was* a sound. "It's coming from the outbuilding over there. Can you see it, Assad?"

Assad grunted an affirmative.

"The boathouse must be down in that thicket beyond. Wouldn't you say, Carl? That would be the fjord there," Assad surmised.

"Maybe. I'm just worried he might be in there. And about what he might be doing," Carl replied.

The quiet of the cottage and the disconcerting drone from the outbuilding sent a shiver down his spine.

"We'll have to go down there, Assad."

His assistant nodded and handed Carl the torch, now switched off. "Take this for a weapon, Carl. I trust more in my hands."

They squeezed through bushes that tore at Carl's injured arm. If his shirt and jacket hadn't been damp and the drizzle so refreshingly cool, the pain might have brought him to a standstill.

As they neared the outbuilding, the humming sound became more audible. Monotonous, deep, and insistent. Like a well-oiled engine ticking over.

A sliver of light escaped from under the door. Something was going on in there.

Carl pointed to the entrance and tightened his grip on the heavy torch. If Assad flung open the door, he would rush in ready to deliver a blow. They could take it from there.

They stood staring at each other for a moment before Carl gave the sign. Assad gripped the door handle. In a split second it was open, and Carl hurled himself inside.

He scanned the room and lowered the torch. The place was empty. Empty, apart from a stool, a few odd tools left lying on a workbench, a large oil tank, some hoses, and the generator humming on the concrete floor, a throwback to an age when things were built to last forever.

"What is that smell, Carl?" Assad whispered.

Carl recognized the pungent odor instantly. It had been a while since he had last come across it, back in the days when the trend was for antique pine furniture, which had to be stripped down. The acrid, clammy stench that pinched the nostrils. The smell of caustic soda, the smell of lye.

He turned to the oil tank. Horrifying images flashed through his mind. He pulled the stool over, stepping onto it with trepidation before lifting the lid from the tank. He raised the torch, and it occurred to him that he was now one flick of a switch away from the shock of his life. Then he turned on the beam and shone the light into the depths.

But he saw nothing. Only water and a long heating element loosely fixed to the inside wall.

He had no difficulty imagining what the setup might be for.

He turned off the beam, stepped down, and looked at Assad.

"I'm guessing now, but I think the children might still be in the boathouse," he said. "They might even be alive."

They left the outbuilding again with extreme caution and stood for a moment in silence as their eyes adjusted once more to the dark. In just three months, it would be as light as day at this time of the evening. But right now, all they could see were indistinct outlines in the space between them and the fjord. Could there really be a boathouse down there, in that low vegetation?

He signaled to Assad to follow on behind. They crept forward, squashing fat slugs beneath their feet. Assad clearly didn't care for it.

Then they reached the thicket. Carl bent forward and pulled aside a branch. And there, right in front of his eyes, was a door, perhaps half a meter aboveground. He reached out and touched the thick planks in which the door was mounted. They were smooth and damp.

There was a smell of tar. It must have been used to seal the cracks. The same tar Poul Holt had used to seal the bottle containing his last message.

Water sloshed gently in front of their feet. So they had been right: the structure was built out into the fjord, almost certainly on stilts. This was the boathouse they had been looking for.

They had found it.

Carl turned the handle, but the door wouldn't open. He felt around in the dark and found a bolt fixed with a split pin. He lifted the pin cautiously and allowed it to drop on its chain. If the door was bolted from the outside, then the bastard obviously couldn't be in there.

He pulled the door open slowly and heard the faint, faint sound of someone catching their breath.

A stench of stagnant water, rotting weed, urine, and excrement greeted his nostrils.

"Is anyone here?" he whispered.

A moment passed, and then came a muffled groan.

He switched on the torch. The sight that met him was gut-wrenching.

Two figures huddled two meters apart in their own filth. Wet clothes, greasy hair. Two bundles of life that had given up all hope.

The boy stared at him with wide, frightened eyes. He was sitting hunched under the roof, his hands tied behind his back, and chained. His mouth was covered by heavy-duty tape that pulsed perceptibly as he breathed. Everything about him was like a scream for help. Carl turned the beam and saw the girl hanging limply in her chains, head flopped to one side as though she were sleeping. But she was awake. Her eyes were open and reacted to the bright light with a series of bewildered blinks. She hadn't the strength to lift her head.

"We're here to help you," Carl said, pulling himself up onto the floor and crawling inside on all fours. "Just stay quiet. You're going to be all right now."

He found his mobile and dialed a number. A moment later, he had the Frederikssund police on the line.

He explained himself and asked for immediate assistance before snapping the phone shut.

The boy's shoulders dropped. The phone call made him relax.

Assad crawled in and removed the tape from the girl's mouth, then loosened the strap by which her hands were bound. Carl began to help the boy. He was cooperative, though he remained silent even when his gag was removed, shifting his weight so that Carl could reach the buckle of the strap behind his back.

They pulled the children away from the wall and tugged at the chains around their waists, finding them linked to another that was bolted firmly to the thick wooden planks of the wall behind them.

"He put the extra chains around us yesterday and locked them together. Before that, there was only the chain in the wall going through the strap. He's got the keys," the boy explained hoarsely.

Carl looked at Assad.

"There was a crowbar in the outbuilding. Can you go and get it, Assad?"

"Crowbar?"

"For Chrissake! A crowbar, yes!"

Carl could see from Assad's expression that he knew perfectly well what a crowbar was. He just didn't fancy wading through all those slugs again.

"You take the torch. I'll fetch it myself."

Carl squeezed back out through the door. They should have taken that crowbar to begin with. It was a useful weapon, too.

He squelched his way cautiously through the slippery mush of slugs alive and dead and noticed a dim light in one of the windows of the house facing out to the fjord. It hadn't been there before.

He stood quite still for a moment and listened.

Nothing.

He carried on toward the outbuilding and warily opened the door.

The crowbar was right in front of him on the workbench, underneath a hammer and a monkey wrench. He lifted the hammer and shoved the monkey wrench aside, only to jump in fright as it tipped over the edge and fell to the floor with a clatter.

He froze, listening.

Then he picked up the crowbar and crept away.

The faces he saw on his return looked relieved. As though every movement he and Assad had made since opening the door of the boathouse had been a miracle in itself. No wonder.

They carefully broke the chains away from the wall.

The boy immediately crawled into the middle. The girl stayed put, groaning.

"What's the matter with her?" Carl asked. "Maybe she needs some water?"

"Water, yes. She's in a bad way. We've been here a long time."

"You take the girl, Assad," Carl whispered. "Keep tight hold of the chains so they don't make a noise. I'll help Samuel."

He felt the boy stiffen and turn his head toward him, staring as though Carl all of a sudden had lifted the lid on a demon inside his soul.

"You know my name," he said warily.

"I'm a policeman. I know a lot about you and your family, Samuel."

The boy withdrew slightly. "How come? Have you spoken to our parents?"

Carl took a deep breath. "No. No, I haven't."

Samuel drew back his arms and clenched his fists. "There's something wrong," he said. "You're not a policeman at all."

"Yes, I am, Samuel. Would you like to see my badge?"

"How did you know where we were? How could you possibly know?"

"We've been trying to find your kidnapper for quite some time now, Samuel. Come on, we need to hurry," Carl insisted, as Assad drew the girl through the door opening.

"If you're with the police, then why do we need to hurry?" A look of horror appeared on his face. Clearly, he was beside himself. Was he in shock?

"We had to break your chains loose from the wall, Samuel. Isn't that proof enough? We haven't got a key."

"Is it to do with our parents? Haven't they paid up? Has something happened to them?" He began to shake his head frantically. "Where are our parents?" he demanded, raising his voice.

"Shhh," said Carl, urgently now.

There was a thud outside. Assad stumbling on the slippery path? "You OK, Assad?" Carl whispered. No reply. He turned to Samuel again. "Come on, Samuel. We have to get out of here."

The boy stared at him distrustfully. "You weren't talking to anyone on the phone just before, were you? You're taking us outside to kill us, aren't you? Isn't that what you're doing?"

Carl shook his head. "Listen, Samuel. I'm going to go outside now. Once I'm out, you can look through the door and see that everything's all right." And then he crawled out backward into the fresh night air.

There was a sudden sound. A sharp, heavy blow against his neck.

Everything went black.

51

Maybe it was a noise outside or pain from his wounds. Whatever it was, he woke up with a start and glanced around the room in bewilderment.

Then he remembered what had happened and looked at the time. Almost an hour and a half had passed since he'd lain down.

Drowsy, he pulled himself upright on the sofa and turned onto his side to see if he had been bleeding.

He nodded to himself, satisfied with his work. The wounds seemed to be dry and healing. Not bad for a first attempt.

He got up and stretched his limbs. There were cartons of juice and canned food in the kitchen. A glass of pomegranate juice and a piece of crispbread with tuna would give him sustenance after losing all that blood. A quick bite, and after that he would go down to the boathouse.

He switched on the light in the kitchen and peered outside into the darkness for a moment before drawing down the blind. No need to advertise his presence if anyone should be out there. Safety first.

Then suddenly he paused and frowned. What was that? A noise of some kind. He stood motionless for a moment. All quiet now.

A startled pheasant, perhaps? But what would startle a pheasant in the dark?

He pulled back the blind and stared intently in the direction he thought the sound had come from, standing stock-still.

And then he saw it. A shape in the dark. A figure moving.

Whoever it was, was at the outbuilding, and then gone.

He darted back from the window.

Now his heart was beating faster than he cared for.

He pulled open the drawer in front of him and picked out a fileting knife. With the right positioning, the intruder would never survive the thrust of such a long, thin blade.

Then he put on his trousers and crept outside into the night in his bare feet.

He heard the sounds from the boathouse clearly now. As though someone was pulling the place apart inside. Grating against the timber.

He stood for a second and listened. Now he knew what it was. They were at the chains. Someone was jimmying the bolts that fixed the chains to the wall.

But who?

If it was the police, then he would be up against weapons better than his own. But he knew the terrain. He knew how to turn the darkness to his advantage.

He slipped past the outbuilding and saw right away that more light was escaping from the door than was supposed to.

The door was ajar now, but he knew he had closed it behind him after he had been down to check the temperature in the tank. He was certain.

Maybe they were more than one. Maybe someone was in there now.

He drew back against the wall and considered what to do. He knew this place like the back of his hand. If anyone was inside, he could knife them before they realized what was going on. One lunge at the soft spot beneath the breastbone. He could take out more than a couple like that in only seconds, and he would not hesitate to do so. It was either them or him.

He entered swiftly with the knife extended in front of him and scanned the empty room.

Someone had been there. The stool was in the wrong place, and his tools had been messed with. The monkey wrench was on the floor. That was the noise he had heard.

He picked up the hammer from the workbench. It felt better in his hands than the knife. More familiar.

He moved stealthily down the path toward the water, the slugs slimy between his toes. Bastard things. He would exterminate them as soon as he got the time.

He leaned forward, craning his neck to see, and made out a faint light in the crack of the boathouse door. He heard hushed voices from inside. He listened hard, but he was unable to make out who they belonged to or what they were saying. But what difference did it make?

Whoever was inside had only one way out. All he had to do was steal forward and bolt the door, and they would be locked in, with no way to escape before he fetched the jerrican from the car and set the place alight.

The blaze would be seen from a long way off, but what option did he have?

He would set fire to the boathouse, gather together his documents and money, and head for the border as quickly as possible. It was the only way. A man who couldn't adjust his plans deserved to perish.

He tucked the fileting knife into his belt and moved cautiously toward the door. But at that very moment, it opened and a pair of legs came into view.

He darted aside. Now he would have to deal with the problem more directly.

He watched the figure as its feet made contact with the ground, the rest of the body still stretched into the boathouse.

"Where are our parents?" he heard the boy say loudly all of a sudden, his question answered immediately by urgent hushing.

And then he saw the dark-skinned policeman draw the girl out through the door and into his arms, stepping backward toward him in the process. The same little Arab from the bowling center. The one who'd rugby tackled Pope. What was he doing here?

How had they found him?

He turned the hammer in the air and brought the flat side down hard against the nape of the man's neck. He fell without a sound, the girl on top of him. She looked up with empty eyes, long since reconciled to her fate, and then closed them. One forceful blow away from death. But it would have to wait. She was no threat to him now anyway.

He looked up, preparing himself for the second policeman to come out.

Legs appeared in the door opening again. He heard the man assuring the boy that everything would be all right.

And then he struck.

The policeman slid to the ground.

He let go of the hammer and stared at the two unconscious men, listening for a moment to the wind rushing in the trees, the rain against the paving stones on the path. The boy was alerted now, his movements inside the boathouse audibly agitated. But otherwise there was no sound.

He picked up the girl in his arms and heaved her back into the boathouse in one seamless movement, slammed the door shut, and fastened the bolt with the split pin.

He straightened up and glanced around. Apart from the boy's protests, all was still quiet. No sirens. No sounds that didn't belong. At least, not yet.

He took a deep breath. What might he expect now? Were more police on their way, or were these two working off their own bat, trying to impress their superiors? He needed to know.

If they were on their own, he could carry on with his plan. But if they weren't, he would need to make a getaway. Whatever the circumstances, he would have to get rid of all four of them as soon as he knew one way or the other.

He was back at the outbuilding in leaps and bounds and snatched up the baling twine that hung behind the door.

He had tied people up before. It didn't take long.

There was a commotion from inside the boathouse as he secured the unconscious men's hands behind their backs. It was the boy, yelling now at the top of his lungs, demanding to be let out. Screaming that his parents would never pay if he and his sister didn't come home.

He was a fighter. He'd give him that.

And then the lad began to kick at the door.

He checked the bolt. It had been years since he had fixed it to the door, but the timber was still good. It would hold.

He dragged the two men away from the boathouse, so the light from the outbuilding would illuminate their faces. Then he pulled the larger of the pair half upright until he sat bent double on the path.

He got down on his knees in front of him and slapped him hard and repeatedly in the face. "Hey, wake up!" he commanded.

Eventually, the detective came around. His eyes rolled in his head. He blinked a couple of times and tried to focus.

They stared at each other. The roles were reversed now. He was no longer the suspect questioned at a table in a bowling alley, having to account for his whereabouts.

"Bastard piece of shit," the officer mumbled. "We'll get you. Backup's on its way. We've got your prints."

He stared into the detective's eyes. The man was clearly still stunned. His pupils reacted too slowly when he leaned aside and let the light from the outbuilding fall suddenly on his face. Maybe that was why he was so surprisingly calm. Or was it because the man simply didn't believe he was capable of killing them?

"Backup. Nice try," he replied. "But let them come, by all means. You can see all the way to Frederikssund across the fjord from here," he said. "We'll see the blue lights as soon as they hit Crown Prince Frederik's Bridge. Plenty of time to do the necessary before they get here."

"They'll come from the south. From Roskilde. You'll see fuck all, you bastard," said the policeman. "Let us go. Give yourself up. You'll be out in fifteen years. If you kill us, you're a dead man, I promise. Shot by police, or else you'll rot away serving a life sentence. Same difference. Police killers don't survive in this system."

He smiled. "You're talking like someone had hit you on the head. And you're lying. And if you don't answer my questions, you're going to be in that tank over there in the outbuilding in . . ." he glanced at his watch ". . . let's say twenty minutes from now. You and the kids, and your mate there. And do you know what?"

He thrust his face into the policeman's. "I'll be long gone."

The banging from the boathouse intensified. It was more forceful now, and more metallic. Instinctively, he glanced toward the spot where he had dropped the hammer.

His instinct was right. It was gone. The girl must have picked it up without him noticing before he carried her inside. Shit. She hadn't been as far gone as he'd thought, the sneaky little bitch.

He drew the knife slowly from his belt. There was no alternative now.

52

Strangely, Carl wasn't frightened. Not because he doubted that the man in front of him was insane enough to kill him without a moment's hesitation, but because everything around him seemed so very peaceful. Clouds drifting across the sky, blotting out the moon. The gentle lapping of the fjord. The smell of the earth. Even the hum of the generator behind him felt calming. It was odd.

Maybe it was all still down to the blow he had been dealt. At any rate, his head was throbbing, shifting all focus from the pain in his arm and shoulder.

Then came the banging from the boathouse again. Louder than before.

He looked at the man. He had taken a knife from his belt.

"You want to know how we traced you, am I right?" Carl said, sensing some feeling return to his hands that were tied behind his back. He glanced up into the drizzling rain. It was the wet, making the twine expand. He needed to gain time.

The man's eyes were cold as stone. Then came a slight twitch of the lip.

He was right. If there was one thing the bastard wanted to know, it was how they had found him.

"There was a boy once, a boy called Poul. Poul Holt, do you remember him?" he asked, soaking the twine in the wet grass behind him. "He was a bit special, was Poul." His hands were working now, twisting and straining indiscernibly.

He allowed his words to hang in the air and nodded reflectively. There was no hurry. Regardless of whether the twine held or not, the longer he kept the killer's attention, the longer they would remain alive. He smiled to himself. It was interrogation in reverse. How ironic.

"What about him?" the man demanded to know.

Carl laughed. The intervals between hammering from the boathouse were longer now, but the blows sounded more precise.

"Long time ago now, isn't it? Do you remember? That girl in there wasn't even born then. Or maybe you never think about your victims? No, of course you don't."

At that, the man's expression changed, and a shiver ran down Carl's spine.

In one swift movement, the man sprang to his feet and pressed the knife to Assad's throat. "You answer me now. No more bullshit, or your friend here will be choking on his own blood. Are you with me?"

Carl nodded, his hands working. The guy meant what he said, no doubt about it.

And now he turned toward the boathouse. "I'm going to make you suffer before you die, if you keep that up, Samuel. Believe me!" he yelled.

The banging stopped for a second. Carl could hear the girl sobbing inside. And then Samuel continued.

"Poul managed to send a message in a bottle. You should have chosen a better place to shut people away than a boathouse over water," Carl said.

The man frowned. A message in a bottle?

Now the twine began to give. "It turned up in a fishing net off the coast of Scotland some years ago. And eventually it ended up on my desk," he went on, his wrists working purposefully and without pause.

"Too bad for you," said the man, though clearly his curiosity had yet to be satisfied.

It wasn't hard to read his thoughts. How could a message in a bottle possibly harm him? None of the children he had held captive in the boathouse over the years had any way of knowing where they were. How could a message in a bottle change that?

Carl detected a movement in Assad's leg.

Stay put, Assad. Sleep on. There's nothing you can do anyway. The only thing that could help them now was if he could loosen the twine around his wrists sufficiently for him to get his hands free. And even then there was no telling what would happen. The man was strong and unscrupulous and brandishing a very nasty-looking knife. The blow to Carl's head had undoubtedly slowed his reactions. All in all, there was little hope. If only he *had* called Roskilde for backup, so their aid would come from the south, they might have had a chance. But the Frederikssund police could hardly avoid heralding their own arrival. The bastard was right about that. As soon as they hit the bridge, the sky would light up blue. That would be in a couple of minutes at the most. And then it would all be over. He realized that now. The twine was still too tight.

"Get out of here, Claus Larsen, or whatever your name is. Get away while you still have the chance," Carl spat, as the blows Samuel was delivering to the door suddenly took on a deeper resonance.

"You're right about one thing, at least. My name's not Claus Larsen," the man said, still straddling Assad's lifeless body. "And you've no idea as to my true identity. What's more, my guess is that you and your mate are all on your own tonight. So why would I want to run away? What makes you think there's anything at all for me to be afraid of?"

"Get going, whatever your name is. It's not too late. Disappear and find yourself another life. We'll be looking for you, but maybe you can repent in the meantime. Are you capable of that?"

The twine gave unexpectedly.

He stared into the man's eyes and saw the reflection of blue. Police cars crossing the bridge. The end had come.

Carl straightened his back and drew his legs up beneath him. The man looked up, seeing the blue lights burst forth into the sky, mirrored in the fjord. He raised the knife into the air above the defenseless Assad. And at that moment Carl launched himself forward, headlong into the man's leg. The kidnapper staggered and fell, still with the knife in his hand, then clutched at his hip and gave his assailant a look Carl was sure would be the last thing he ever saw.

And then his hands were free.

He scrambled to his feet and put up his guard. Empty hands against the man's knife. What good would it do? He sensed how dazed he still was. Unable to run, however much he wanted to. However much the monkey wrench on the floor of the outbuilding beckoned, he was unable to coordinate his limbs and run. Everything around him seemed to contract and expand at once.

He staggered a couple of steps backward as the man got to his feet with the knife pointed toward him. His heart pounded, his head throbbed. Mona's gorgeous eyes flashed before him.

He planted his feet to keep himself steady. The paving stones were slippery, and once again he felt the mush of slugs on the soles of his shoes.

The flashing blue reflections from the bridge were no longer visible. They would be here in five minutes. If he could just hold his ground a little longer, he might be able to save the children's lives.

He looked up at the branches of the trees hanging over the path. Could he reach them and perhaps pull himself up? He took another step backward.

But now the man rushed forward with the blade aimed at Carl's chest, his eyes flaming with rage.

What sent him flying was a small foot, shoe size barely 40.

Assad stuck out his short leg, striking the man's ankle just enough to knock him off balance. At first, it looked like he would manage to stay upright, but then his bare feet went from under him in the gastropods' slime. There was a sickening smack as his cheek hit the paving. Carl stepped forward immediately and kicked him as hard as he could in the stomach until he let go of the knife.

Carl picked it up, then hauled the man to his feet. He stared into his eyes and pressed the blade against his jugular. Behind them, Assad struggled to raise himself onto his elbow, only to vomit and fall back. A stream of Arabic expletives issued from his mouth along with the bile of his stomach. If the sound of his invective was anything to go by, he was going to be all right.

"Do it," said the man. "I'm tired of your ugly face."

And abruptly he thrust his head forward in a desperate suicide bid. Carl saw it coming and jerked the knife away from him. The blade nicked the man's throat. The wound was superficial.

"I thought as much," the man sneered, blood now running down his neck. "You can't, can you? You haven't got the guts."

He was wrong. One more move like that and Carl knew he would let the man run himself through on the blade. Assad would be his bleary witness that the man had effected his own death. So let him just try. Save the courts the bother.

At that moment, the noise from the boathouse ceased.

Carl glanced over the man's shoulder and saw the door fly open.

And then the bastard in front of him was in his face again.

"You never said how you found me. Still, it'll come out at the trial," he said. "How long did you reckon I'd get? Fifteen years, was it? It'll be a doddle." He threw his head back and began to laugh. Any second now and he could make a renewed thrust toward the knife. His decision.

Carl tightened his grip on the shaft, fully aware of how horrific an experience it would be.

Then came a sound like the breaking of an egg. A short, rather unremarkable sound. The man sank to his knees and slumped silently onto his side. Carl looked up at Samuel, standing before him with the hammer in his hand, eyes red with tears. He had smashed open the lock from the inside using the hammer. Where the hell had he got it from?

Carl looked down. He dropped the knife from his hand and bent over the man, who lay twitching on the ground. He was still breathing, but the life would be gone from him in minutes.

What he had witnessed was an execution. Premeditated murder. The man had already been restrained. The boy had almost certainly realized that.

"Drop the hammer, Samuel," he said and glanced toward Assad. "It was self-defense. We agree on that, don't we, Assad?"

Assad cocked his head and thrust out his lower lip.

His reply came in spurts as he threw up. "We are always in agreement, Carl. Are we not?"

Carl considered the crumpled figure lying in the slime on the path in front of him. The kidnapper's mouth was agape, his eyes wide open.

"Fuck you," the man breathed.

"Fuck you, too," said Carl.

The sound of sirens came through the woods.

"They say confession makes for an easier death," Carl said quietly. "How many have you killed?"

The man winked. "Many."

"How many?"

"Many."

And then he seemed to succumb. His head lolled to the side, exposing the terrible injury to the back of his skull. That, and the long line of a ruddy scar behind his ear.

A gurgling sound came from his mouth.

"Where's Benjamin?" Carl demanded, urgently now.

The man's eyes closed slowly. "He's with Eva."

"Who's Eva?"

He winked again, a strained movement. "My ugly sister."

"What's your name? I need a surname. Who are you?"

The man smiled, then uttered his final words:

"I'm Chaplin."

EPILOGUE

Carl was knackered. He dumped a folder on top of a pile in the corner.

Case closed. Solved and done.

Since Assad had sent the Serbian gorilla flying down the basement corridor, a lot of water had run under that particular bridge. Marcus Jacobsen's people had taken care of the three most recent arsons, but the one from Rødovre in 1995 had been kicked back downstairs to Department Q. The continuing gang conflict was taking up too many resources for the third floor to be arsed with it.

Arrests had been made in Serbia and Denmark. Now all they needed were a couple of confessions. Carl reckoned they'd have a long wait. The Serbs they'd apprehended would rather molder in a Danish prison for fifteen years than get on the wrong side of those they had been working for.

The rest was up to the regional prosecutor.

He stretched and decided to grab a few minutes' shut-eye in the flicker of the flatscreen. The drone of the news channel. Something about government ministers not being able to get on a bike without falling off again and breaking their bones.

Then the phone rang. Fucking contraption.

"We've got visitors, Carl," said Marcus at the other end. "Could you come upstairs, all three of you?"

It was the middle of July, and it had been raining for ten days solid. The sun had gone into hibernation. What reason on earth could there possibly be to go upstairs? The third floor was just as dark as the basement.

He climbed the stairs without managing so much as a word to Rose and Assad. These god-awful holidays. Jesper was home all day and his girlfriend with him. Morten was away on a cycling trip with some bloke called Preben, and they seemed to be in no hurry to get back. In the meantime, they had a nurse looking after Hardy, and Vigga was traipsing around India in the company of a man who kept two meters of hair stashed in his turban.

And he was stuck here while Mona and her kids were off tanning in Greece. If only Assad and Rose had got their arses away somewhere, too, he could have spent the whole day with his feet up on the desk watching the Tour de France in peace.

Holidays were the pits. Especially when they weren't his.

He glanced in the direction of Lis's empty chair as they arrived on the third floor. Maybe she was away in that camper van again with her horny husband. Perhaps Ms. Sørensen ought to give that a try. A couple of weeks shagging in the back of a camper would surely put some life into even a mummified specimen like her.

He gave the old heron a restrained wave and was given the finger in return. Very sophisticated. Miserable cow.

He opened the door of Marcus Jacobsen's office and found himself face-to-face with a woman he failed to recognize.

"Carl," said Marcus from behind his desk. "Mia Larsen is here with her husband to thank the three of you in person."

Only then did Carl notice the man standing slightly apart. He knew his face instantly. The man from outside the burning house in Roskilde. Kenneth, the one who rescued Mia from the blaze. He looked again at the woman standing so sheepishly in front of him. Was this really the same person?

Rose and Assad extended their hands in greeting. Carl hesitantly followed suit.

"I do apologize," said the young woman. "I know how busy you must be, but I wanted to thank you personally for saving my life."

They stood for a moment and stared at each other. Carl was at a loss for words.

"I would not wish to say it was nothing, if I may say so," said Assad.

"Me neither," Rose added.

The others laughed.

"How are you getting on now? OK?" Carl asked.

Mia took a deep breath and bit her lip for a moment. "I'd like to know how the two children are doing. Samuel and Magdalena, wasn't that what they were called?"

Carl raised his eyebrows. "To be honest, there's no real way of knowing. The two oldest, the boys, moved away from home. I think Samuel's doing OK. As for Magdalena and her two sisters, the congregation took care of them, so I heard. Maybe it's for the best, who knows. Losing both parents like that must be almost unbearable."

Mia nodded. "I understand. My former husband caused a lot of suffering. If there's anything I can do for the girl, I'd very much like to." She tried to smile, only for more words to come instead. "Losing your parents is a terrible thing, of course. But for a mother to lose her child is unbearable, too."

Marcus Jacobsen placed his hand on her arm. "We're still working on that, Mia. The police are doing everything they can with the information you've given us. It'll pay off, I'm certain of it. No one can keep a child hidden away in this country forever, believe me."

Her head dropped as the word "forever" sank in. Carl would have put it differently.

The young man at Mia's side now spoke. "We want you to know how grateful we are," he said, his gaze fixed on Carl and Assad. "The uncertainty is tearing Mia apart, but that's another matter."

This poor couple. Why not just say it like it was? Four months had passed, and the boy still hadn't been found. The proper resources hadn't been allocated in the various systems, and now it was probably too late.

"We haven't much to go on," said Carl tentatively. "Your former husband's sister is called Eva, that much we think we know. But what about her surname? His, too, for that matter? It could be anything at all. We're not even sure of his first name. In fact, we know precious little about your former husband or his past. All we know is that his and Eva's father was a pastor somewhere. Eva wouldn't be that uncommon a name for a clergyman's daughter. We know she's about forty years old, but apart from that, nothing. We've got Benjamin's picture on display at every police station in the country, and my colleagues have informed the social authorities to be on the lookout. That's where we are right now."

She nodded, trying not to be disheartened by what Carl was saying.

Kenneth held a bunch of roses up in front of him and explained that Mia spent every day trawling the Internet and everywhere else for church newsletters or newspaper articles that might contain a picture of her former husband's father. It had become a full-time activity, and if she ever found anything they would be the first to know.

And then he thrust the flowers toward Carl with their thanks.

After they had gone, Carl stood for a moment with the bouquet in his hand and a funny taste in his mouth. Forty bloodred roses, at least. He wished they were for someone else.

He shook his head. No way was he going to have them on his desk. But he wasn't about to give them to Rose and Yrsa, either. There was no telling what the consequences might be.

Instead, he dumped the bouquet on the counter in front of Ms. Sørensen as they went by. "Thank you so much for holding the fort, Ms. Sørensen," was all he said, leaving her in a flurry of confusion and inarticulate protest.

The three of them exchanged glances as they went down the stairs.

"Yeah, I know what you're thinking," he said, nodding.

They needed to put out a bulletin to all relevant authorities to be on the lookout for a child of Benjamin's age and description suddenly popping up somewhere unexpectedly. The same bulletin, in fact, that had already been put out once. Only this time with the additional instruction to the leading officials of these authorities to take care of the matter personally.

That would at least ensure the search was made a priority and delegated to the appropriate persons in a hurry.

In the last two weeks, Benjamin had learned at least fifty new words, and Eva could hardly keep up.

It was only to be expected. They chatted so much together, the two of them, for Eva loved the little boy more dearly than anything in the world. They were a family now, and her husband felt the same way.

"What time are they coming?" he asked for the tenth time that day. He had been busy for hours. Hoovering, baking bread, getting Benjamin ready. It all had to be perfect.

She smiled. How their lives had changed since the boy had come to them.

"They're here now. I can hear the car. Give Benjamin to me, Villy."

She felt the boy's soft cheek against her own.

"Some people are coming to tell us if we can keep you, Benjamin," she whispered in his ear. "I think we can. Do you want to stay with us, my darling? Do you want to stay with Eva and Villy?"

He pressed himself against her chest. "Eva," he said, and chuckled.

She sensed him pointing toward the entrance, from where the sound of voices now came. "Someone here," he said.

Eva cuddled him, then adjusted her clothes. Villy had told her to keep her eyes closed so as not to unnerve them. She took a deep breath, said a prayer, and gave the boy a little squeeze.

"Everything will be all right," she whispered.

The voices were friendly. She recognized them. These were the people whose job it was to assess the case. They had been there before.

They came over to greet her. Their hands were kind and warm. They said hello to Benjamin, then sat down a little way off.

"Well, Eva. We've reviewed matters, and obviously you and Villy are not the most typical of applicants. Having said that, however, we can tell you right away that we've decided to disregard your visual handicap. There are a number of precedents where blind people have been approved as adoptive parents, and as far as functionality and your basic approach to this goes, we certainly don't consider your impairment to be any significant obstacle."

She felt something release inside her. No significant obstacle. Her prayers had been answered.

"We're very impressed by how much income you've been able to put aside. That demonstrates to us that you can manage your finances better than most. Moreover, we've given you a big plus for losing so much weight in such a short time, Eva. Twenty-five kilos in three months, Villy tells us. That's amazing. Well done, indeed. You look fantastic."

Now she felt warmth spreading through her body. Her skin tingled. Even Benjamin felt it.

"Eva's nice," the boy exclaimed. She felt him wave at the two women. Villy said he looked so irresistibly cute when he did that. God bless him.

"You've a lovely home here. A secure and caring home for a child to grow up in."

"And of course, Villy's new job counts on the positive side, too," the other woman added. A huskier, more mature voice. "You don't think it'll be a problem for you, him not being home as much during the day?"

Eva smiled. "You mean, will I be able to cope with Benjamin on my own? Well, I've been blind since I was a young girl. But I don't think there are many sighted people who can see as well as me."

"How do you mean?" said the deeper of the two voices.

"Isn't it all about sensing the needs of others? I know Benjamin's needs even before they arise. I can tell what people are feeling by their voices. For example, you're very happy at the moment. I sense a profound smile, deep in your heart. Has something happened in your life just recently to make you this happy?"

The two women chuckled. "Well, now you mention it, I became a grandmother only this morning."

Eva offered her congratulations, then answered a lot of questions of a practical nature. She was in no doubt now that despite her handicap and their relatively advanced ages their application would be approved and sent on for further assessment. It was what they had been hoping for. Now they had got this far, their chances would be considerable.

"At the moment, we're talking about approval as foster parents. Until we know what's happened to your brother, that's as far as we can go under the circumstances. But I think with that proviso we can consider this to be the first step toward formal adoption."

"When was it you said you last heard from your brother?" the first woman asked. It was perhaps the fifth time during their two interviews that she had asked the same question.

"We've not heard from him since March, when he left Benjamin with us. As we've explained, our fear is that Benjamin's mother passed away due to illness. My brother told us she was seriously ill." Eva made the sign of the cross. "He had a very brooding nature, my brother. If Benjamin's mother is dead, then I'm afraid he might well have chosen to go with her."

"We haven't been able to establish the identity of Benjamin's mother. The civil registration number on the birth certificate you gave us is illegible. Has the document been in contact with water or something?"

She gave a shrug.

"It certainly looks like it. It was like that when he gave it to us," said her husband from the corner of the room.

"It seems Benjamin's parents were just living together. There's no record of your brother ever having been married, at least not if we've got the right civil registration number. In fact, your brother seems to be a man of considerable mystery. We can see he applied to join the commando forces, but after that it's as if all information about him stops."

"Yes," she said and nodded. "Like I said, he had a very brooding nature. He never let us in on anything."

"And yet he left Benjamin in your care."

"Yes."

"Benjamin and Eva," said the little boy and climbed down onto the floor.

She heard him totter across the carpet.

"My car," he said. "My car big. Good car."

"He's obviously thriving," said the deeper voice. "Very advanced for his age."

"Yes, he takes after his grandfather there. He was a very clever man."

"Yes, you've told us about your background, Eva. Your father was a pastor not far from here, wasn't he? A highly respected man, I understand."

"Eva's father was a magnificent human being," Villy said in the background. Eva smiled. He always said that, though he had never met him.

"My teddy," said Benjamin. "Good teddy. Teddy got blue ribbon."

They all chuckled.

"Our father gave us a good Christian upbringing," Eva went on. "Villy and I would like to bring Benjamin up in the same spirit, if the authorities allow us to keep him. My father's approach to life will be our guideline."

She could sense how this pleased them. There was warmth in their silence.

"You'll need to go through a preparatory course over two weekends, before the Adoption Council comes in and makes its assessment. Obviously, that can go either way, but on the big issues my feeling is you're in better shape than the majority, so . . ."

But now she sensed that something was wrong, as though all warmth had suddenly been sucked out of the room. Even Benjamin had stopped what he was doing.

"Look," he said. "Light. Blue."

"I think it's the police outside," said Villy. "I wonder if there's been an accident."

The thought that it might be something to do with her brother flashed through her mind. Then she heard the voices in the entrance, her husband's protests, his anger.

She heard footsteps enter the living room, the two women rising from their seats and stepping back.

"Is that him, Mia?" a man's voice asked. An unfamiliar voice.

Then whispers. She couldn't make out what they were saying. It sounded like the man was explaining something to the two women with whom she had been speaking.

Her husband raised his voice in the entrance. Why didn't he come in?

Then she heard a younger woman crying. Across the room to begin with, then closer.

"In God's name, will someone tell me what's going on?" she begged.

She sensed Benjamin approach. He took her hand and she felt his knee on her lap. She picked him up.

"Eva Bremer, we're from the Odense Police. We're here with Benjamin's mother. She wants to take Benjamin home."

She held her breath. Prayed to God for them all to go away. Prayed that He might let her wake from this nightmare.

They came toward her, and now she heard the woman speak to the boy.

"Hi, Benjamin," she said in a trembling voice. A voice that wasn't supposed to be there. A voice Eva wanted to go away. "It's Mummy. Do you remember Mummy?"

"Mummy," said Benjamin. He seemed anxious and clung to Eva.

"Mummy," he said again, and hugged her tighter. "No."

The room fell silent. For a moment, Eva heard only the boy's breathing. The breathing of a child she loved more dearly than her own life.

And then the breathing of another. As heavy and as frightened as Benjamin's own. She listened and felt her hands begin to shake as she clutched the boy to her chest.

She heard the breathing of another person, and then she heard her own.

Three people, all breathing heavily. In shock, and in fear of the moment that was to follow.

She held the child tightly in her arms. Held her breath so as not to weep. Held him so tightly they were almost as one.

And then she relaxed. She took his little hand and held it in her own. For a moment, she fought back her tears. Then she reached out her hand with the little boy's inside it and heard her voice as if from afar.

"Mia. Was that your name?"

She heard the trembling reply: "Yes."

"Come here, Mia. Come over here, so we can feel who you are."

ACKNOWLEDGMENTS

A warm thanks to Hanne Adler-Olsen for daily inspiration, encouragement, and clever, insightful contributions. Thanks also to Elsebeth Wæhrens, Freddy Milton, Eddie Kiran, Hanne Petersen, Micha Schmalstieg, and Karlo Andersen for indispensable and painstaking comments, and to Anne C. Andersen for her keen eye and boundless energy. Thanks to Henrik Gregersen, Lokalavisen/Frederikssund. Thanks to Gitte and Peter Q. Rannes and the Danish Center for Writers and Translators at Hald Hovedgaard, as well as Steve Schein, for their generous hospitality at times of need. Thanks to Bo Thisted Simonsen, deputy director of the Department of Forensic Medicine, University of Copenhagen. Thanks to Police Superintendent Leif Christensen for generously sharing his experience and for corrections concerning police matters and procedure. Thanks to Maintenance Supervisor Jan Andersen and Chief Inspector Knud V. Nielsen of the Burial Club of the Copenhagen Police for their warmth and hospitality.

Thanks to all you fantastic readers who have visited my website, www.jussiadlerolsen.com, and voiced your encouragement at jussi@dbmail.dk.